Captured Pearl

Rachel Gies

© Copyright 2004 Fairburn Publishing Corporation

First Edition

All rights reserved. Reproduction in whole or part of any portion in any form without permission of the publisher is prohibited.

P.O. Box 1164
St. Charles, IL 60175
www.capturedpearl.com

ISBN: 0-9709960-1-2

Library of Congress: 2004107653

Printed in the United States of America

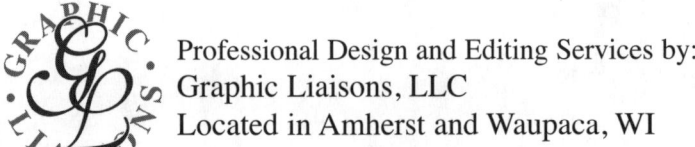

Professional Design and Editing Services by:
Graphic Liaisons, LLC
Located in Amherst and Waupaca, WI

Detailing and Research by:

He moved on to her silken limbs. Her arms delighted him; her dainty elegant fingers would thrill him when they caressed his form. He moved to the front of the tub to extract one silken leg running the bar of soap up and down its length. Her toes were perfect. Dainty feet were attached to long legs that Garrett imagined clinging to him. The thought brought heat to his male member with a rush of blood. Would she let him continue? Silently he slid the bar of soap upward across her rib cage to the base of her throat and then down to her exciting collarbone. Garrett found the desire to nibble upon it irresistible and he bent to follow the thought in his mind.

"If you're born to be a dime,
you'll never be a quarter."

Acknowledgments

I would like to extend my thank yous to the following people, without their involvement in this project the final book would not have been possible.

To Graphic Liaisons for the editing, proofing, graphic, and cover design. Camin Potts and Marcia Lorenzen have been an important part of both of my book projects, their personal involvement has been a great help to me.

The imaginative detailing and research of vj bardship allowed my characters and their story to come to life.

Denny Farrell, "Chicago's Very Own International Radio Host", has been involved in the narration of the story on CD and has advised me on the whole CD process.

Thanks to Dea Hamelton for technical support and Ben Swaab for the development of my logo.

My sincere gratitude to all of you!

—Rachel Gies

Chapter One

She awoke on a road under a canopy of thick, foreboding, tall trees. The moonlight made an eerie, ominous appearance. The stillness of the forest added to her chill. She sensed something was terribly wrong. Was this a dream? How did she get here? Where was she? Who was she?

A gentle breeze brought the chill of the night to her skin. The girl could hear the tiny night creatures as they crept around her. She wrapped her arms around herself feeling the coolness of her skin. Everything was too real, too chilling, to be a dream.

She trembled and pressed her hands to her temples as she shakily stood. Her head hurt unbearably. The coldness of the dirt on her feet made her shiver. The nightdress she was wearing gave her no comfort. There were no slippers on her feet, no robe to ward off the chill. Why couldn't she remember? Had she wandered off from some place in the middle of the night? She must try to think!

Did she hear something? She stood very still listening intently. Yes! A sound was coming from the distance. She didn't know why she should feel frightened, but she did. Should she hide or should she seek help? The pounding of her head made it difficult to make sense of her thoughts. The sounds were closer now! She heard the cadence of hoofbeats coming through the dark. Maybe help was on the way—or could it be the danger she had fled from coming to seek her out? Her heart began to beat frantically and like a frightened young doe she ran for the cover of the forest.

Too late! With no way to avoid the object in his path the rider closed his legs on his mount, lifting the reins, thus causing the steed to rear. Hopefully, he could avoid hitting whatever was in the road.

The rider steadied himself for the collision. Sable's impact with the obstruction jarred both horse and rider, causing Garrett to bring both his strength and horsemanship into play in the hope of avoiding a spill for them both. Regaining control, Garrett halted the frightened stallion and cursed at whatever had blocked his path. He dismounted to examine Sable for injuries as a second rider came to a halt beside him.

"Captain, you all right?" asked the older rider. He was a man of height with a lanky frame that bespoke of harder and leaner times. His face was lined with the wear of the open sea and when he dismounted there was a definite sway to his step.

"Yes, but Sable is shaken. We collided with something and I'm afraid he might have injured himself," answered the younger man. Even as the older rider was tall, this man towered over him. In the year 1588, he was a stately man at six foot. But the grace and power in his every move belied the great length of his frame. He was more muscular than the first man, but with a leanness that had left many a Lady swooning. His jet-black hair reflected the moonlight peering through the clouds. The piercing blue eyes could turn cold as a stormy sea when he was angered, or become the dazzling sapphire blue of the stone that rested in the hilt of his sword. He was a hard man made harder by the sea—but to his friends, a loyal companion. He took his wealth for granted, but did not believe that it gave him the right to supremacy over other men. Deeds and loyalty were of great value to him.

"Quite a homecoming, eh? I thought all our dangers were left behind us once we made land."

Garrett took a closer look at his mount. The stallion looked to be fine. As he turned to his companion they spotted an object lying in the road. The moonlight did not provide enough light for them to make out what it was.

"My God," the second rider exclaimed, "it's a woman!" He walked closer to get a better look at the figure lying face down in

Chapter One

the road. A sense of dread washed over him.

"Who is it Miles?" the Captain asked.

"I don't know, Sir. She doesn't look familiar to me."

Miles carefully turned the woman over to get a better look at her face. Blood and dirt covered her. Suddenly her eyes opened and two startled green eyes looked up at the two men crouching over her. A painful groan escaped from her lips before her eyes fluttered shut again.

"Captain, she's hurt bad," Miles said to his companion. "What shall we do with her?"

Garrett puzzled over this new predicament in his already complicated life. They couldn't just leave the girl in the road. However, there were already too many secrets in his life for him to welcome this one. Heaven knew he didn't need a vengeful father, or a jealous husband, knocking on his door in search of this battered girl.

"Well, we've scared the hell out of her for sure, and we can't just leave her here in the road. We'll have to bring her with us. Mame can tend her till we can locate her family."

Miles, one of the Captain's oldest friends, agreed. He wondered at the Captain's interest. It wasn't like the Captain to show much interest in the ladies lately. There were too many secrets, which Miles shared, for the Captain's attention to be turned from his course.

Garrett had been commissioned by Queen Elizabeth to sail, intercepting the Spanish Armada, and doing as much damage as possible to the enemy fleet. In this year of 1588 the English were an upcoming power trying to wrestle control of the high seas from the Spanish. This was no small job. A dangerous and risky business that must be kept secret if the Captain was to continue his success. Miles had been present from the start of his commission from the Queen. They had spent many months together traveling both on land and on sea in the Queen's service. Bess rewarded her commissioned Captains richly, but her whim could easily change.

Captured Pearl

Garrett walked a fine line running her special missions. Less than a handful of men knew of his secret. Miles felt privileged to be one of those few.

Sir Jason Riley, one of the Captain's close associates, was another of the privileged few. Riley, himself, worked for the Queen. He was in charge of a bevy of spies who traveled the kingdom and Europe reporting developments to the Crown and their Masters. He was Garrett's contact to the Queen and the two often met to discuss new missions and problems. Some might suspect but would never speak of it. The Captain was a deadly adversary and Elizabeth's wrath was vengeful.

Garrett held the girl in his arms as he and Miles traveled to his manor. Her long blonde hair fell across his arms as it revealed her face. Garrett wondered what she would look like when she was cleaned up. Her silky hair reminded him of Chinese silk, and as this thought tickled his senses, he felt a shiver of pleasure course through his body. Her body felt soft and sweet in his arms. Determinedly Garrett pulled his thoughts away from the girl.

"I've no time for this nonsense!" he thought to himself. Bess was a harsh taskmaster and her jealousy of her Captains was well known. Indiscretions without her approval could land a man in the tower.

Shortly they came within sight of the Estate. The lights were on as the Captain was expected. As Sable ambled up toward the house Mame came running out the front door.

"Master Garrett, it's so good to have you home!" Her joy was like an overflowing river washing over Garrett. He smiled at Mame, basking in the genuine fondness his housekeeper felt for him. His true love had always been the sea, however Mame's welcomes home brought a warmth to his soul that the sea could not.

Mame's grandmotherly look was enhanced by her neat, gray hair and twinkling eyes. Her short stature was bolstered by her expanded waist. Her large lap and warm hugs had often chased away the hurts of the two small Jamison sons—as had her buttered

Chapter One

tarts. A squeeze and a sweet had mended many boyhood bumps and scrapes. Even after the loss of Lord and Lady Jamison her twinkling blue eyes and ease of showing affection had helped to close the gaping wound.

"Master Garrett, what have you got there? My Lord, what has happened to this poor child?" In the darkest of night, Mame hadn't noticed the figure draped across Garrett's lap until he moved to get a better hold of her in order to hand her down to Miles. Mame began to fuss and ply Garrett with questions as he lowered the unconscious girl from Sable's back into the open arms of Miles.

"I ran her over in the road just down from the Estate. The girl jumped right out in front of poor Sable. You'll need to tend to her and get her cleaned up so we can take a good look at her. Maybe someone will recognize her face so we can get her back to her family."

"Oh my, bring the poor creature in and let Mame take care of her!"

With Mame hovering over them, Miles handed the girl over to Garrett so he could take her into the house while Miles summoned the stable boy to care for the horses.

Inside, Mame led the way to one of the guest rooms where Garrett gently deposited the still form on the bed. By Mame's candlelight they could see how filthy the girl was, head to toe.

"Go on now Master Garrett. You have business of your own to attend to. I'll care for the girl. I'll get her washed up. A hot bath and clean clothes will do her a world of good. She looks to be the same size as your mother. Would you agree to it that she should wear one of your mother's old gowns? Oh the poor dear! What happened to you? Where have you been . . . and how long? If she is to awake with some answers, or a name, well . . . , as soon as I know anything, I'll bring you word."

He hardly got a word in to agree, what with Mame babbling like a mother hen, but with that small assurance Garrett left, heading toward his study where Miles waited to discuss their latest venture.

Chapter Two

The Jamison Estate was located on the seacoast not far from Plymouth, England. The location was ideal for Garrett Jamison's secret services for the Queen. The Estate lay close enough to Plymouth for correspondence to easily arrive, while the secluded bay allowed for the unseen arrival and departure of Garrett's vessel, the *Green-Eyed Lady*. In fact, this was such an ideal location that earlier in the year of 1588 he had seen the Spanish Armada come into view when they had attacked England in the spring. Garrett was in the Queen's service by that time and had seen his share of the fighting.

Garrett had been sailing with Sir Francis Drake during the fighting. Drake had taken Garrett on as his second-in-command knowing that Bess had been favorably impressed with the young Captain, intending to give him a commission. She had seen promise in Garrett and, as usual, the Queen was proven right. Drake had found Garrett to have a quick mind and an unusual grasp for tactics. The bond that developed during that time had remained strong even after Garrett's commission and he often sought Drake's advice and opinion before setting out for the Queen. Drake had become a true friend and formidable teacher. Though Garrett was a very private man, he and Drake had become very close, sharing many things no one else knew—or if they knew, never talked about.

The Estate was magnificent. It was incredibly large and always well cared for. The house had been in the family for several generations. Garrett had become the Master of the Jamison Estate in 1576 when his parents had been lost to an outbreak of typhoid fever. Garrett had also become the guardian for his brother at this time. When Shane had come of age in the early days of March 1578, Garrett had begun looking for some other interest to occupy his mind. The Spanish Armada had caught his attention, and as his father's oldest son, he had long sailed and then commanded the trading vessels of the Jamison family. With his family's fleet, wealth, and a ready command of the sea Garrett had caught the Queen's attention. His courtly manners and good looks had clinched her attention in his direction. That he was open to her advances to join her service had pleased her greatly and insured his family's favor in Queen Elizabeth's court.

This wasn't the first time the Jamison family had been in service to the Crown of England. Garrett's Great-Grandfather had served as an advisor to the English monarch of his time, securing the lands and fortune of the Jamison family. But a Monarch's favor could be a whimsical thing. Refusing service could set a family at odds with the Crown causing unforeseen tragedy and financial difficulties. Garrett had seen others fall and history was written on the misfortune of those who had thwarted the Crown of England. He had no intention of bringing such misfortune down upon his family name. That he enjoyed the adventure and danger of being one of service to the Queen was an added extra that allowed him to enjoy his service with a daring and battle readiness not seen in many who sailed with him.

Garrett had his family's good looks. Being a tall man and powerfully built, he towered above even the most regal of the Queen's court. Garrett had piercing blue eyes that could either melt a woman's heart or put the fear of God in a grown man. He had all the social graces but was one who preferred to spend his time commanding his ship. Garrett was not one to spend his time searching out women, although, if the need arose, there were plenty that would come at his beck and call. It rarely happened, but when pushed, his good judgment could be overridden by his temper.

Miles was waiting in the study when Garrett entered. Garrett poured them both a brandy and motioned for Miles to be seated.

Chapter Two

"The Queen should be well pleased with your latest mission," offered Miles.

"Yes, she should. Have you ever noticed how with the more people possess the more they want?" queried Garrett. Bess was becoming more and more demanding of her Captains while at the same time the Spanish were becoming more wary. A dangerous combination to be sure.

"We'll need to be delivering our booty to the storehouse soon. The girl certainly complicates matters. I don't feel comfortable leaving Mame alone here with her. I find it rather odd that she has appeared just when we have returned from this latest foray."

"You daren't wait long, Captain. You know how that will look to the Queen."

"Yes, Elizabeth has never been known for her patience. However, I believe we could delay a day or two as we try to unravel this latest mystery. You might as well head home Miles. I'll see you midday tomorrow and then, hopefully, we can question the girl."

"Yes Sir, Captain. Till morning." With that Miles departed leaving Garrett to his thoughts.

Mame found him deep in thought as she knocked on the study door before entering.

"Master Garrett, the young lady is sleeping peacefully right now. She has been badly bruised, although, I don't believe that it's from her run in with you."

"What are you saying, Mame?"

"The young lady's been beaten, Sir, and her clothes, Sir. You really should look at them."

Garrett followed Mame up the stairway to the girl's room where he examined the young lady's things. Her nightgown was of a fine quality, but tattered. It was hardly more than a rag. Was she running from an enraged father or husband? Or was this all a ruse to take him in? It wouldn't be the first time that his enemies had tried to dupe him, although this was a new tactic not used before. Hell! He didn't have time to worry about this. The way his life had been going lately this was going to be an entanglement that would consume more time and effort than he was willing to put forth. If something didn't surface by tomorrow he would leave her in the capable hands of Miles and Mame while he continued with his ventures. She would be well cared for while he was gone.

Miles arrived at midday for his meeting with Garrett and was directed to Garrett's study. Garrett was reading his correspondence, but put it aside as Miles entered.
"Miles, I find that I am going to have to leave this afternoon for a meeting with Sir Riley. I'm leaving you in charge of the girl. Mame will tend to her but I want you to keep an eye on her, too. I don't trust this timing—see what you can find out while I'm gone."
"Aye, Captain. You needn't worry. I'll see to things here."
Garrett made preparations to leave for his meeting with Sir Riley, one of his contacts for the Queen. Together they had accomplished many missions for Queen Elizabeth over the last few months. Riley had worked as an agent for his country for many years and although he was getting up in years the thrill of sailing always lured him back. He would soon retire, but working with Garrett Jamison had reassured him that he was leaving his duties in good hands. The one person missing on these missions was Sir Frances Drake. On many occasions Garrett had found himself wishing for Drake's input, but the older man was not very well and only sailed occasionally. Riley and Garrett visited him whenever they were in London, keeping him informed on the latest developments in the Queen's Navy. The Old Sea Dog always had such wisdom to add to their stories that Garrett always left feeling re-energized from his sage advice and wonderful hospitality.

Garrett informed Mame of his imminent departure while Miles left to see to Sable's saddling.
"I should be back tomorrow afternoon all things permitting. I'm leaving the girl to you Mame. Do what you need to keep her comfortable but I don't want her wandering around the Estate.

Chapter Two

Don't let her go off on her own, either. There's no telling what she might be involved in."

Mame was slightly irritated with Garrett's cold demeanor. Goodness, anyone could see the poor child was an innocent! She loved Garrett as if he was her own son but sometimes she thought he could be cold and uncaring. That Scottish strumpet, Cara, had changed him! However, when all was said and done Garrett was still her employer so Mame kept her thoughts to herself.

Mame had long ago lost her own child to consumption. The poor thing was only seven years old. Mame and her husband, Andrew, had grieved for months. Andrew was so devastated by the child's death that he never recovered. He lost his will to live and while some said it was an accident others were convinced that his death was of his own choice. Mame would never, could never, believe that her beloved Andrew purposely took his own life.

Andrew had gone down into the mine as he did every day. The miners, who had escaped the fatal shaft cave-in, had said Andrew hadn't even tried to get out when the shaft began to collapse. He had just sat there staring off into the distance. They had called to him as they ran past, but he motioned for them to go. Had he been in shock, or had he decided to join his beloved child in the afterlife? Mame would never know. Since that day she had given all her love to the two Jamison boys.

Garrett was the oldest and had seemed so self-assured until his parents had died in 1576. Then he had been consumed with self-doubt. He had been aboard ship on family business when they had died. He was filled with the guilt of a survivor, so sure that things would have been different if he had just been home to help them. His brother, Shane, had been spared as he was off in Paris studying at the time. Shane had the same Jamison features as Garrett but there the comparison ended. Garrett was darkly broody and self-contained while Shane, with his lighter blue eyes and complexion, always had a contagious smile. He was always immaculately dressed. Shane's carefree outlook on life had charmed many a Lady out of her skirts. With his good looks and easy wit, the ladies were fascinated with him. Shane Jamison was considered quite a handsome catch.

With Garrett off on this latest trip, Mame made her way upstairs to check on the young Miss. As she opened the door, Mame heard a soft moan. She entered to see the girl had opened her eyes and was looking at Mame with a puzzled expression on her face. "Where am I?"

Mame with a relieved smile replied, "Miss, you're on the Jamison Estate. How do you feel? Do you remember what happened to you?"

"I don't remember," the girl responded. "I just hurt."

Mame told the girl how she had gotten there and how Master Jamison had carried her to the house. "Do you remember your name, child?"

The girl was quiet for a moment. She sat up in confusion and shook her head. "I don't know," she whispered as tears welled up in her eyes.

Mame looked at the girl's brilliant green eyes. She had never seen eyes so vivid or a girl that looked so much like an angel. Her blonde hair seemed to shimmer in the afternoon light, framing an angelic face. Her pale complexion was a perfect frame for those eyes, which drew your attention to her pert nose and pale rose lips.

"Well, we need some kind of name for you until you can remember yours. Let's call you Angel, for one was certainly looking out for you last night."

Angel agreed after one look at Mame's expectant face. The housekeeper seemed so kind and caring. It would be a shame to disappoint her over so small a matter. With Mame's help Angel was dressed in a gown that had been one of Garrett's mother's. Then Mame led her down to the dining room where she fetched her some tea and toast. Mame kept up a running dialogue about the Estate and its staff hoping to give Angel a sense of calm. Miles was introduced to Angel when he stopped by to check on her before going about other business. He would busy himself close by the house to keep an eye on her but, it was obvious that

Chapter Two

his presence made her nervous. Interesting that. Was it because a man had given her those bruises or was it because she had something to hide? The Captain may have had the right idea about her after all.

Garrett's ride into Plymouth to collaborate with Sir Riley was uneventful. Unfortunately, Garrett found this mystery lady occupying far too many of his thoughts. Usually women did not manage to arouse his interest since the disastrous affair with Cara. What was it about his green-eyed houseguest that was so intriguing? She was easy on a man's eye, but many of the women at court could say the same. Was the mystery that surrounded her what had snagged his thoughts? Or was it the feel of her silken hair across his arms? Was this the enemy's plan—to confuse his thoughts and to tangle his judgment? Well, if so they would not find Garrett Jamison such easy game!

He arrived at the inn specified by Riley's correspondence to find the man seated at an out-of-the-way table where he had a view of the door. Garrett moved to join him motioning for the innkeeper to bring him a tankard of ale.

"Things went well, I assume," Riley stated.

"As planned," Garrett replied, "at least until I reached the Estate."

Riley lifted an eyebrow in question, always a sign that Garrett had peaked his interest.

"Ran into a woman on the road near my Estate last night—literally," Garrett responded.

"Well that makes for an interesting tale."

Garrett continued his tale relating his suspicions of the girl's involvement with their enemies to Riley. "I didn't have time to question her if I was to meet you tonight. Miles is keeping an eye on her until I get back."

"It wouldn't be the first time the Spanish included a woman in their tactics. Although, I'm not sure you can just assume that the girl isn't innocent. Her description doesn't match with any of the señoritas in the minister's employ. However, I'll keep my ears open and see if I can pick up any information for you. Perhaps my contacts at the docks have heard some news."

"I'd appreciated it, Riley. A man can't be too careful these days," Garrett replied.

"You know, it might just be some scheming Father trying to capitalize on all that Jamison wealth," Riley responded with a laugh. Both men smiled and turned their conversation to the Queen's business.

"I'll inform the storehouse to expect you within a few days and since I'm returning to court I'll let the Queen know of your planned arrival. We'll cover your delay by telling her that there was business at the Estate that needed attention. She won't want your cover questioned so everyone should be satisfied. Solve your mystery woman's story quickly Jamison."

Riley's warning was well understood by Garrett. He appreciated his friend covering for him, just as he knew that staying in Bess's good graces was critical to his well being. It wouldn't do to test her patience unduly. Due to the lateness of the hour Riley and Garrett took a room at the inn. Both would start out early the next morning.

Chapter Three

When Garrett returned home the next afternoon he found Mame in the kitchen altering a gown for Angel. "How's the girl, Mame?"

"You mean Angel? She is feeling better, Sir. How was your trip? Would you care for some refreshment after your journey?" Mame queried.

Garrett found himself taken back by the girl's name. It certainly fit his green-eyed lady. "So she remembered her name. Did she tell you anything else?"

"Oh, she hasn't remembered anything, Sir. I just call her that. Can't be calling her 'the girl' can we?" Mame replied with a sparkle in her eye. She had seen that look of wonder in Garrett's eye before he had closed himself off. The man was more interested than he wanted anyone to know.

"I suppose that I'd better see what I can find out then. Where is Angel?"

"I can fetch her for you, Sir. Would you be wanting to converse with her in the dining room or the study?"

"In the study, Mame."

Minutes later Mame returned with the girl following close behind. As Angel entered she found herself facing the most handsome man she had ever seen. She felt very self-conscious wearing one of his mother's altered gowns. Angel recognized the flash of anger in his glance wondering what she had done already to make him angry. Mame excused herself from the room leaving the two of them alone. Garrett used the time to size up the girl then turned his piercing, blue eyes on his possible adversary.

"Who are you? Where did you come from?"

The girl was startled by the coolness in his voice. "I don't know, Sir. The last thing I remember, I was just standing in the road when I was struck down. I can't remember anything else."

"How did you get on the road?"

Angel thought for a moment and lowered her head. "I don't know." Her eyes began to tear while her head began to throb once more. What was wrong with her and why was Lord Jamison being so cruel? The cutting edge of his questions left her little doubt that he didn't believe her.

"Might I sit down, Sir?" her voice trembled as she asked.

Garrett motioned her to a chair opposite his desk feeling somewhat like a heel as he noticed the pain etched across her brow. She had become quite pale and he wondered if she was going to faint right there. He rang for Mame who instantly appeared in the doorway. She took one look at Angel then turned her disapproving glance on the Master.

"Can't you see that she is tired and frightened, Sir? She needs to rest if she is ever to regain her strength and memories!"

Garrett looked at Mame who always seemed to know best about these things, and then looked back at the girl. "All right, Mame, you handle it."

"Yes, Sir," Mame replied, with a twinkle in her eyes. She felt sorry for Angel and knew that she needed time to rest. Mame looked at Garrett and then to Angel. "Come along Angel. Let's put you to bed. I'll bring you up some nice hot tea and in no time you'll be feeling better."

Garrett looked at the girl admitting to himself that she did, indeed, look like an angel. An angel who didn't have much to say. As Mame escorted Angel out of the study Garrett mumbled a, "Rest well."

Mame looked at Angel and nodding toward her employer said," He really isn't a bad person. He is just very busy and has a lot on his mind right now."

Angel gave a tired little smile and thanked Mame for her concern. Unlike Lord Jamison, she had instantly liked Mame. It was obvious the housekeeper returned her feelings. After settling Angel into the cozy bedchamber Mame left to bring the tea.

Chapter Three

When Angel had finished the light meal Mame picked up the tray saying, "Now, Miss, if you need anything at all call for me."

"Thank you, Mame. I shall."

"Sleep well, Miss."

Left alone Angel tried to recall the events leading up to her stay at the Jamison Estate. Her head hurt with her concentration leaving her feeling weak and confused all over again. Maybe if she could get some sleep her memory would return by morning.

Downstairs in the study, Garrett poured himself a brandy while he waited for Miles to make his appearance. When he arrived, Garrett motioned to the squat bottle and watched as Miles sloshed a small portion in his glass.

"Did you find any answers, Miles?" Garrett questioned.

"No, Sir, the girl stayed close to Mame while you were away. I did notice that she seems pretty nervous around any man that appears in her sight."

Garrett heaved a weary sigh. More unanswered questions to complicate his life. Just once couldn't the fates smile on him, making things easy? "I'll have to be leaving within the next couple of days to deliver the ship's goods. I don't relish taking Angel along but I don't feel comfortable leaving her here with Mame if she's bent on causing mischief."

"Did Sir Riley offer any advice?" Miles asked.

"Not really. He did remind me that sometimes things could be just as they seem to be and not to write her off just yet. He'll send out his ferrets to gather information." Garrett found his thoughts turning to the young woman upstairs and he wished that he could keep her out of his mind.

"Miles, where do you think she came from? Any thoughts on who she might be? This is all pretty coincidental, her having no memory, and showing up just when we've returned from this mission, and now Sir Riley informs me that there is more treachery about the countryside requiring us to soon set sail once again.

"I wonder," Garrett continued, "if she could be a spy for Duprell? She does have a slight French accent. Perhaps she is pretending she doesn't know who she is."

Captured Pearl

Miles frowned at this and said, "Do you think so? She looks so innocent to be involved with that scoundrel."

Miles had been told of the history between the Captain and Duprell by one of the Estate owners who lived nearby. The two men had been at odds since Miles had taken service with the Jamison family. There was bad blood between them and had been for years. Duprell had often tried to destroy the Jamison name and financially ruin them—from poisoning the Hereford cattle at the Estate to running down the ships of the Jamison shipping line—nothing was beneath the man.

"That's just it. What could be more perfect? It would be just like him to use a beautiful, innocent, young woman to do his dirty work," Garrett replied.

Donovan Duprell was a swarthy complexioned man with a bulky body that had not yet gone to fat. His dark, straight hair was worn too long to enhance his looks, but it was one of his vanities. Silky and thick, it enamored many a Lady. His dark eyes were constantly narrowed in suspicion reminding many of a narrowed-eyed weasel—vicious when cornered, sneaky, and given to robbing others. He wasn't as handsome as a court dandy, but nevertheless, his dark, dangerous look drew many a gold-seeking woman to his side. He gave the impression of a wealthy Captain, but actually, his family estate had been restored through his blackmailing plots and his pirating forays.

During his grandfather Duprell's time the ancient lines of the family and its contacts had continued to garner a substantial wealth for the family. But driven by a gambling addiction, his father had lost nearly everything. Donovan's hatred for the straits his father had put him in had driven him to commit the ultimate sins. His father's mysterious death and the ensuing blackmail had helped restore the family house. But Donovan had only begun. His self-assured belief that he was entitled to every bit of wealth he could obtain had driven him to betray Queen, country, and every friend the family had managed to retain. Unfortunately, his rash spending habits greedily consumed the wealth of his endeav-

Chapter Three

ors almost as fast as he could rake them in. Lately, it was becoming more evident that he needed another source of income. He claimed to the world that his wealth came from his family's importing of exotic items from the East. No one had been able to prove it yet, but he was a scavenger who pilfered ships that were left unseaworthy by previous battles. He killed, maimed, or smuggled anything that was left. An ending to the conflict between England and Spain was not in his best interests—and Donovan Duprell always looked out for his best interests!

Some thought of him as a pirate, but he was a "small fish" in a "large sea" when compared to a real pirate. He was unprincipled, and a coward—he was indefensible and had no loyalties to anyone but himself.

He and Garrett had several run-ins throughout the years. None were without strengthening their resolve to destroy each other. Of course, Duprell was unaware that Garrett worked for the Queen.

The irony of Duprell and Garrett's relationship was that once they had been loyal friends. Both had attended the elite school, Eaton, as boys where their friendship had blossomed. Being from old money, their families often had come into contact with each other at the social functions of the court.

By banding together from the outset at Eaton, Duprell and Garrett had avoided many of the taunts and teasing inflicted upon the new arrivals. Garrett's readiness to stand up for his convictions and Duprell's willingness to fight had earned them the respect of the older bullies. Garrett's father was convinced that an education was necessary and Garrett agreed. Garrett had maintained decent scores throughout his years at Eaton. He and Duprell had not only studied together they had joined the same clubs. All the young men had pulled pranks on and with each other; but sometimes they went a little too far. Duprell once pulled an especially dirty trick on Garrett. He had intercepted a letter to Garrett's parents that contained his scores and Duprell had changed them. Garrett's parents were enraged. It had taken Garrett several letters and notes from his teachers to straighten out the mess and convince his parents to leave him in school.

Captured Pearl

Garrett could only respond in kind. He and Duprell rode into the countryside one fine spring day to spend the day with some school friends, riding, hunting, and drinking. It was an incredibly hot day for England, and Garrett suggested that they stop for a dip in the stream. They undressed and jumped in. Duprell dove under the water and when he came up Garrett and all the boys from school were on the shore laughing. They had taken his clothes forcing him to walk the three miles back to school naked. Duprell had fumed at the embarrassment allowing it to fester into a poison whose target was Garrett. His chance at revenge came later that fall when Garrett began keeping company with the miller's daughter, Chantelle.

She was soft-spoken and sweet. Her strawberry-blonde hair, clear blue eyes, and contagious laugh had captured Garrett's heart.

Duprell was throwing a party at the school's hunting lodge. Everyone was invited. Whether they liked Duprell or not, everyone was going. The drink and rowdy behavior was just what the boys were after that fall evening. Because Chantelle's parents trusted Garrett they allowed him to escort her about the village without a chaperone. Garrett and Chantelle had been walking when Duprell approached them. By this time Garrett and Duprell's friendship was beginning to erode. Garrett was reluctant to attend the gathering, as was Chantelle, but with Duprell's badgering they decided to attend.

Things began to go from bad to worse as the young men at the party consumed more drink. Their language became more vulgar, their actions more daring and careless. While Garrett's back was turned several of the young men spirited Chantelle off, whose protests were not heard above the raucous noise.

As Garrett's eyes frantically searched for his sweetheart he noticed Duprell returning from a side room.

"Have you seen Chantelle?" questioned Garrett.

"Can't you keep track of your Lady, Garrett? If that's the best you can do maybe you don't deserve to have her," responded Duprell with a snide laugh.

Garrett felt sick as he realized that Duprell was concealing

Chapter Three

Chantelle's location from him. It had been a mistake to come, he knew that now. He could only hope that it wasn't too late. As his concern grew Garrett noticed more men leaving the room where Duprell had been. When he made his way over to investigate he was stricken by what he saw. The scene would haunt his memory for the rest of his life.

Chantelle was bound to the bed with a neck stock. Her hands stretched high to meet the bedposts while her legs had been bound to leave them spread wide in open invitation to the invasion of the men in the room. Her mouth had been stuffed with a torn piece of handkerchief to stop her screaming. Her blouse lay in tattered strips on the floor while the rest of her clothing was scattered about the room. Garrett thought he was going to be sick at the sight of one of his classmates viciously thrusting into her. Chantelle was past the point of caring—lying dreadfully still and quiet.

Garrett had never felt such raw rage and hatred! With a bellow of rage he yanked the man from between Chantelle's thighs throwing him across the room and into the wall. The rest took one look at Garrett's face and fled before they received the same fate. Garrett rushed to her side, gently untying her bound hands and feet. As he gathered her into his arms his heart plummeted at the vacant look in her eyes. He removed the gag but no sound came from her frozen lips. Quickly he covered her with his waistcoat before carrying her out of the room. The main room fell silent as he entered, except for Duprell. His laughter rang in Garrett's head.

"Someday, somehow Duprell, you'll pay for this," Garrett's low response was all the more deadly for its low tone.

Later the authorities at school bemoaned the fate of the miller's daughter, but she was just a commoner. Garrett was enraged anew at their callous dismissal. With his father's powerful backing and the Jamison name brought to bear with all off its weight and power, Garrett had the satisfaction of seeing Duprell expelled from school in dishonor. Duprell was humiliated . . . and so the feud began. Duprell's fetish toward the cruel and deviant had driven a wedge in their friendship, which had only widened with time. Now they sought to destroy each other at every opportunity.

Chapter Four

Cara sat in the magnificent parlor in Duprell's home admiring the beautiful emerald ring adorning her finger. Duprell had given it to her just days before he had left on business. She, of course, knew his business. Cara made it a point to unravel Duprell's secrets. She couldn't care less how he made his money as long as he had plenty to ease her life. Cara had grown up with the hand-to-mouth existence of a Scottish coal miner's family. At an early age she had decided that any price, any price at all, was worth the comfort of food on the table, a roof over her head, and the pretties that came from a contented, rich man. That Duprell was cruel and often sadistic in his treatment of her only kept her wits sharpened to ferret out his secrets. He would not dispose of her as easily as his last amour! Her exotic, highland looks had always kept the men enthralled. Golden eyes and high cheekbones surrounded by thick, black, wavy hair were complimented by her round, voluptuous curves. Every head turned when she entered a room—following the swaying tease of her hips.

Cara had chosen her gown with care today noticing that the men about the Estate were busily readying things for Duprell's arrival. His ship must have come in late last night. As soon as his plunder was unloaded he would return. The sultry, green gown Cara wore complimented her looks leaving her no doubt that Duprell's attention would focus on her. She thought she'd had him wrapped around her finger but lately his attention had begun to wander. Even with his cruel deprived demands Cara had no wish to be cast out to fend for herself before she had lined up another protector.

She would give anything to have a second chance with Garrett. Those wishful thoughts were unlikely to come to fruit since their falling out several years ago. Duprell could be a horrible man yet Cara was willing to put up with anything for the money that saw to her comfort. She would never go back to the menial existence of a laborer's daughter!

Cara wanted Garrett more than anything else—even Duprell's money. Garrett's wealth rivaled Duprell's and while Cara had him it had been wonderful! His thoughtfulness and caring had touched Cara's heart as nothing since. They had met through one of Garrett's friends. Cara had thought to make herself a fine match with Garrett's neighbor, Lord Ashley's eldest son. But one look at Garrett's handsome features combined with the wealth of the Jamison name had convinced Cara to move to greener pastures. The party had been a wonderful interlude of dancing and small talk. She had turned all her charm Garrett's way. No man could resist her talent for innocence. For a while they had been happy until Garrett's responsibilities to his family name reared its ugly head. He cared deeply for her yet would not marry her. The Jamison name would only be given to one of equal blood—one the Queen approved of. She had tried everything! She had consoled him after his parents' death; she had even managed to entice him into her bed leading him to believe that he had been her first. Nothing had worked. He began to lose interest in everything after his parents' death. Her mama told her to give him time—time to heal. But Cara needed to know that Garrett still cared for her. She had thought by playing up to Duprell she would arouse Garrett's jealousy bringing him running back to her side. The plan had backfired when Garrett had spotted the two of them together in the village. Suddenly the relationship was over. Garrett wanted nothing more to do with her. Cara had known there was bad blood between the two men but in her worst nightmares she had never expected this. Duprell was suddenly her lifeline to staying comfortable and pampered.

The door flew open. Duprell stomped in followed by the two men who always accompanied him. The enormous house filled with its wealthy furnishings had been obtained with ill-gotten wealth. Duprell might be a coward, however, he wasn't stupid. He

Chapter Four

took great measures to protect himself from bodily harm. Cara sauntered over to Duprell seductively and put her arms around him.

He pushed her aside, "I need a drink."

"Yes, my love," Cara replied pretending concern. Lately she had grown to hate Duprell. He treated her like dirt, she who could have had any man she chose! She poured the port into a crystal glass taking it to him. He downed it with one toss of his wrist. Cara poured him another, which was gone equally as fast.

"You must have had a rough trip, my Darling," she said in her sweet, seductive voice.

His growled reply of, "Yes," warned Cara to stay out of his way tonight. "The trip was not as fruitful as I had predicted. I'll have to sail again shortly." Her eyes grew wide with pretended concern.

"There hasn't been any sign of Cassandra has there?"

"None, Darling."

"Damn! Where is that bitch?" Cara could see his temper rising as she hastily groped for a reason to leave. She hated him most when he took her in these black moods. He would be cruel and calculating. Duprell grabbed her arm bruising her tender skin forcing her mouth to his. His slimy tongue demanded entrance to her mouth. To refuse would encourage him to beat her. Cara submitted to his stabbing tongue tasting the port upon his breath. She rubbed her breasts against him as if she desired him immensely. Duprell's other hand forced its way down the front of her gown squeezing and pinching her tender flesh. Lately, he had delighted in the bruises he bestowed upon her. Cara's only hope was to encourage him to finish as quickly as possible.

Finishing with her mouth, his lips traveled down her neck licking, then biting. His discolored teeth nipped and scraped as their travel lowered to her shoulders.

Cara managed to free her hands. She quickly loosened his breeches; his hands freed her breasts for his animalistic feeding. With his member freed, Cara began to stroke and fondle him, feeling him harden in her hand. Her skirts were quickly rucked up about her waist as he forced himself into her soft, womanly parts. He began to thrust rapidly gripping her waist to allow him harder and deeper penetration. Cara bit her lip to contain the moans of pain that gathered behind her pearly teeth. It seemed like forever before she felt his warm seed shiver into her body. As fast as that it was over. Duprell unceremoniously dumped her on the floor while he stood to straighten his clothes. Cara kept her head down as she put herself to rights, so he wouldn't see the red-hot hate in her eyes. He was an animal! Duprell had no concern for anyone but himself. His rough treatment only brought home the tenderness with which Garrett had loved her.

Chapter Five

Back at the Estate Angel was tossing and turning. She hadn't slept well and with a groan she sat up in bed. It was dark in the room, which added to her disorientation. At first she didn't know where she was—then it slowly came back. She was at the beautiful Jamison Estate. It was a warm evening in August. The perspiration stuck to her body leaving her feeling sticky. Angel didn't want to wake anyone but perhaps someone was still awake whom she could ask for a cool wet towel to ease her discomfort.

Angel opened the door softly looking out into the large hallway. She picked up the candle she had lit on her bed stand and went downstairs. The house was incredibly silent. Throughout the hallway and down the staircase the walls were adorned with family portraits in gilded frames. The rugs under her bare feet were thick and soft. It was such a big house, in fact, much bigger than she was accustomed to. Where had that thought come from?

The study door swung open as she reached the bottom of the staircase. Angel could see the silhouette of a man and her heart began to beat frantically.

"What do you think you're doing, sleuthing about in the middle of the night?" Angel heard his booming voice echo through the house.

She looked up at him stammering, "It was very hot. I couldn't sleep and I was looking for some moist towels to cool myself."

"Is that so?" queried Garrett. By now he had lit several candles. He took in the tiny figure standing before him. "Do you always wander about other people's homes after they have gone to bed?"

Angel looked at Lord Jamison. His cold blue eyes had a chilling look about them—quickly she dropped her gaze to the rug-covered floor.

Captured Pearl

"No . . . , well, I don't think so," she stammered.

"God, she was good!" Garrett thought to himself. He found himself wanting to believe her. It would be too easy to throw his cautions to the wind, yet too much rode on his judgment of this girl. No, there was no way he was going to be able to leave her here when he sailed. Mame was too taken in by her, and if she did work for the Spanish, or Duprell, there was no one else he could trust to watch her. She was going to have to go with him.

He didn't know what he was going to do with her on board the ship or how he would explain her to his men. Sailors were well known for their superstitions. Bringing a woman on board would likely have them ready to throw him overboard. However, that was the way it had to be. He was their Captain, and they would follow his orders.

But how to get the girl to agree without dragging her forcibly along? Then he recalled Miles' comment on the fact that men seemed to make her nervous. Yes, he was sure it would work!

"I'll be sailing within the next couple of days, Angel. I think it would be best if you accompany me on my trip."

Her head popped up so she could look him in the eyes. Her eyes were wide with astonishment and a hint of fear.

"Whatever are you talking about? Why would I want to go with you? I don't even know you! Can't I stay here with Mame?"

"I really don't think it would be wise. If, in fact, you were fleeing from something and they tracked you here, Mame and everyone else would be endangered if you were here. You'll really be much safer on board with my men and me."

"Mame can help you chose some of my mother's clothing. There are plenty of dresses upstairs. Choose what you want. Mame can have them altered to fit you before we leave. Pack enough for three days."

"Where are you taking me?"

"Please, Angel, just do as you are told."

She backed up and ran upstairs, bumping into Mame.

"What is going on here?" asked Mame.

Angel was in tears. What Lord Jamison had said made sense,

Chapter Five

yet to leave the one person she trusted was devastating.

"Lord Jamison is taking me with him when he leaves."

Mame's heart cried out for this young woman, she could barely be of "coming-out" age yet look at the turmoil her young life was in already. But Mame knew that once Lord Jamison said something, he meant it. She, herself, got by with quite a lot, but she never dared to tell the Master how to do his business.

"I am sorry child," said Mame, "I can't help you even if I wanted to, which I do. I'm sure he is only doing what he feels is best. Lord Jamison is a good man."

"I think that is a matter of opinion," replied Angel.

"Why don't you go back to bed, Miss. In the morning things will look better. Then I'll help you ready yourself for the trip."

The next morning Mame helped Angel choose several gowns and accessories for the trip. Lady Jamison had been a lovely, petite woman who had kept her figure throughout the years. Mame didn't have much work altering the gowns for Angel.

When the time came to depart Mame took the girl's hands and said, "God go with you Miss. Everything will be all right. I know it will." Then she put her arm around Angel and walked her downstairs. Garrett was waiting impatiently at the front entrance. He looked up to see Angel as she came down the stairs with Mame. She was beautiful! The name Angel certainly fit her. She was going to be quite a distraction on the journey. He'd have to remember to keep his mind on business.

They left the house and went to the stable where Rudy had readied his Master's horse. Garrett put Angel up on Sable's back before gracefully mounting behind her. Garrett thanked the boy as they departed.

They rode silently for several minutes when Garrett stopped his horse and dismounted. He held out his hand to help Angel down. She lifted her chin and said, "I can help myself, thank you."

Garrett had to give her credit. She had spunk. He sent Sable back to the stable with a slap on his rump knowing full well that Sable would go straight back to the waiting Rudy. The stallion knew the routine as well as any man.

Captured Pearl

Angel was frightened; she didn't know this man who was leading her away. "Where, may I ask, are you taking me?" she questioned as he walked beside Garrett.

"No," replied Garrett, "you may not ask."

"But why? What gives you the right?" Her temper was beginning to rise at his highhandedness. Couldn't he see that with his long stride she had to run to keep up? Angel was so frustrated tears stung her eyes, but she fought them back. Did he intentionally mean to be cruel? Mame thought him to be a good man; however Angel was having trouble believing the housekeeper's words.

"Could you slow down?" Angel breathlessly threw the words at him.

Garrett glanced down to see her heightened color and heaving breasts and realized that her slight stature could not keep pace with his lengthy frame. His mother would have his head for behaving in such an ungentlemanly manner. He slowed his pace relaxing his grip on her arm. After all where could she go that he couldn't find her?

"You gave me the right when you accepted my protection and while you accompany me on this journey, you will do as I say for your own safety. Now do not ask me any more questions. Until you tell me who you are, or where you came from, I will just have to take you with me. I have something important to do and I can't take the chance that you are a spy," said Garrett.

"A spy? Where did you get that idea? I am no spy!"

"You know you aren't a spy, but you don't know your name?"

She had no answer. Angel didn't know how, but she knew she could not be a spy.

As they neared the shore she spotted a sailing ship at anchor in the bay, and a small skiff was waiting nearby to take them to the ship.

It was a huge vessel with nine sails and cannons both fore and aft. It was a fighting ship and it was armed for war. Who was this statuesque man she was accompanying? Even with her limited memory Angel knew this was no common trading vessel. Only the Queen's naval fleet or an unscrupulous scavenger could com-

Chapter Five

mand such a ship. Even with her fear and dislike of the man he couldn't possibly be the later! He was too mannerly, too courtly, too caring, and . . . too handsome! There was just no way that this man with his classical Greek features and beautiful dark black hair could be evil! Or could he?

"Who are you?" Angel asked with an awed tone.

"You should know, and if you don't I'm sure in time someone will inform you."

"What are you talking about?"

"You damn well know what I'm talking about!" Garrett was hoping this would trick her into revealing some information about herself—and if she turned out to be as innocent as she looked—well, he'd deal with that situation later. Angel just looked at him in puzzlement. "Until you are ready to confide in me I will discuss this no further. And, by the way, for the duration of this voyage you shall be my wife."

"Your wife! Whatever gave you that idea?"

"Let's get one thing straight, Angel. This is my ship and if you want to remain safe while you are on board you will play along. Sailors are a superstitious lot. They don't like women on board, bad luck you know. They also tend to think one for all, if you get my meaning."

She did. Angel swallowed her anger, allowing that she did want to stay safe. But could she play the actress? They would soon see.

Angel saw a dozen men of all ages and sizes gathered at the bow awaiting the arrival of their Captain. They grinned at her as she walked by, but the scowl on their Captain's face soon turned their grins into frowns. They all stared as she walked by scaring her to death! Angel could feel the dislike and hatred as if it were a blanket wrapping around her. Her lungs felt tight. It became hard to breathe and she thought she might faint. Garrett called the men to attention.

"I would like to introduce you to my new wife, Lady Jamison. She will be sailing with us on this trip. I expect you to show her the respect due a Captain's wife." With that Garrett

Captured Pearl

called over Jim Peters, his second-in-command, and introduced him to Angel.

"Mr. Peters, my wife, Angel."

"If you need anything send for Mr. Peters if I'm not available."

"Mr. Peters, I trust you to see to my wife's well being on this voyage, and now you can show her to my cabin."

"Angel, you, of course, will stay there unless under my escort. Is that understood?"

Angel thought to protest, but one look at Garrett's hooded, stormy, blue gaze changed her mind. Perhaps this discussion was best left until they could talk in private. She nodded her understanding, following as Peters took her below.

It was a spacious cabin and the walls were paneled with a rich, dark mahogany. How fitting! It reeked of male. Yet it was rich in a subtle way, just like Jamison. It had wall hangings and a thick carpet on the floor. A heavy oak desk and two massive chairs occupied one wall. The desk was neat and the drawers were locked. There was a bunk against one wall across from the desk. This was very much a man's room. A man that was powerful and used to commanding.

Garrett materialized behind Mr. Peters, dismissing him with a nod.

"We'll have to share, you know."

"You must be out of your mind! There must be a cot that you can use!"

"Of course there is, however, you must admit that wouldn't fit with the picture of a newly married couple. If the men get superstitious well . . ."

Garrett let the statement trail off unfinished. "Let her make of it what she will," he thought to himself.

Angel glanced at his massive frame finding that her throat didn't want to work. She tried swallowing again. From some unknown place deep inside a terrible horror began to crawl up out of her belly to encompass her whole being. Her vision narrowed to a pinpoint of light. As if from a great distance she heard someone calling her name, but her ears were ringing with every breath

Chapter Five

she tried to take. Suddenly there were hands on her. Male hands! Frantically she began to struggle! No, not again! She won't let it happen again. Angel clawed at the hands holding her, kicking with her feet, and swinging her head back and forth.

Garrett steadied his grip on her arms surprised by the vacant look in her green eyes. Finally, as he realized he was only increasing her terror he gathered her into his arms and gently pulled her into his chest, soothing her with soft words and a gentle caress against her hair. Slowly, she calmed. Her breathing slowed and then steadied. Finally as reality was regained she became limp in his arms. What had happened to this green-eyed mystery lady in his arms?

Garrett gently deposited her on his bunk, then crouched down on the floor next to her.

"Angel, we'll figure something out. Don't worry about it. I want you to promise me that you won't leave this room without me. Mr. Peters will keep an eye on you for your own safety. My men are loyal—most of them. I have some new men and you can't always trust everyone, especially with an attractive woman. So stay here. I will see that you have all that you need. I'll send one of the men down with some water for you to wash with and some food."

"Are you holding me as your prisoner?"

"Until I know who you are and what happened to you I don't think we have much choice."

"But I'm telling you the truth. I truly don't remember!"

He looked at her face. A beautiful face that could make a man act foolishly. But he was no fool and he wasn't taking any chances.

He could almost believe her, but he thought better of it. "Have a good day," he said to Angel as the door closed behind him.

Angel heard the key turn and then it became apparent that she really was a prisoner. She walked over to the bunk, sat down on the soft, feathery mattress, and began to cry. She felt lost and lonely. Who she was, or where she came from, were mysteries.

Captured Pearl

She wanted to hate the Captain, yet Mame's words ran through her head along with the kindness he had just shown her. She was sure that she had done nothing to deserve this treatment. Yet, what if Garrett was right? Was she a spy sent here to ensnare him? Angel turned the thought over in her mind yet another time. No, it just didn't feel right. That wasn't her. She had to believe in herself or no one else would! Did she have a family that was looking for her and worrying about her? Why couldn't she remember even her name?

Garrett was thinking the very same thing. Why would a beautiful young woman, hardly more than a girl, be out in the night dressed only in her nightclothes? Her reaction in the cabin spoke of terror—possibly abuse. Garrett was so busy thinking about the girl below that he didn't hear his name being called.

"Captain," reported Mr. Peters, "we are underway."

Garrett turned away from the view of the sea. He had been staring out at his mistress, the sea, lost in thought. This was not like him. He always knew every move his crew and ship made. He wished now that he had not brought the girl on board. He had enough to worry about.

Before long a knock at the door and a turn of the key announced Mr. Peters with a pitcher of water. He quietly entered the cabin, setting the pitcher on the oak table.

"You'll find towels in that trunk at the foot of the bunk, Madam. Your trunk arrived before we set sail. I'll have one of the men bring it down directly. It will be a while before Cook has anything hot in the galley. I could bring you some biscuits until then."

"Thank you, Mr. Peters, but I will be fine," Angel replied softly.

The Captain was right to keep his Lady safely locked up for right now, Peters thought to himself. Why, if he was a younger man, he might try to catch her eye. What a bonnie lady the Captain had found for himself! She was of obvious good breeding. A man could tell from her carriage and looks. Polite, too. Most ladies he

Chapter Five

knew would not bother to thank a man for doing his duty. She was like the Captain that way. With a small nod and flip of his finger the Captain could make you feel like you'd just been knighted by the Queen herself! His men would sail through the gates of Hades for him.

"Well then, Madam, I'll be back to check on you later," and with that Peters turned to go.

"Mr. Peters?" questioned Angel.

"Yes, Madam?"

"Do the men like Captain Jamison?"

The question puzzled Peters. "Like him Madam? Those that have sailed with the Captain respect him, Madam. He has brought us through some rough times over the years. Most of us have come back in one piece. And the Captain, Madam, he appreciates his men's loyalty. Anything else Madam?"

"No, thank you Mr. Peters." As Peters left, Angel turned his answer over in her mind. It wasn't exactly what she had wanted to hear, but perhaps it gave more insight into Lord Jamison than the wiry Irish sailor had intended. It was clear that Peters respected his Captain. The comment about coming back in one piece puzzled her. Did Jamison go to battle often? He wasn't in the Queen's Navy or his men would wear the uniform of the realm, as would their Captain. What was going on?

Angel aimlessly wandered the cabin studying the items on the desk, in the shelves, and she even went through the trunk at the foot of the bunk. On the desk were items that would be of use to any Sea Captain: quill and ink; an intricate, expensive-looking compass; and a sextant. The drawers of the desk stood locked against her curiosity. The bookshelf held seafaring journals from a Captain Drake, maps of the seas, and several of the prominent books of the period. One was Homer's *Iliad* written in Greek. To her surprise Angel was able to cipher through bits and pieces of the epic poem. This was a surprising development! Most women of her day didn't read, let alone read Greek. Another piece of her puzzle to collect and cherish. Just who was she? Faintly she heard the shouts of the men on deck as the ship moved out of the bay into the open sea. Already she could pick out Lord Jamison's deep throaty bark above the others.

    Back above deck Peters reported to the Captain then resumed his duties aboard ship. There'd be no slipshoddiness aboard the Captain's ship on his watch! This vessel sailed with military precision. The men knew that and respected the officers for it. The attention to detail that was expected and enforced kept them alive and their ship in top-notch condition. Captain Jamison expected no less and paid well for a job well done.

    The Captain and Peters had been sailing together for several years now. They had met at a tavern on the docks of Plymouth. It had been a balmy night in August when Peters had stopped in for a few pints. He had gotten in on a card game and was doing quite well. His opponent, on the other hand, was not. To top things off the other man was not a gracious loser and drew a knife. Captain Jamison ordinarily would have left the two to themselves, as this was not an uncommon sight to see a dispute settled in this manner in a dockside tavern, but another man also drew a knife and suddenly the squabble was lopsided. Thinking to even the odds, Garrett had drawn his own knife and walked toward the brawl unnoticed. As he reached the second man Garrett had given him the option of stowing his knife and letting the first two settle their disagreement. However, the second man had been drinking for several hours and was determined to earn some of his chum's coins back. He drunkenly lunged at Garrett who immediately had his knife at the man's throat, overpowering him. Garrett escorted the drunk outside with a hard kick in his posterior. When Jim had offered to buy his ally a pint, Garrett had accepted remarking how he never could stand an unfair fight. They had been inseparable ever since. Garrett was on the lookout for a replacement for Miles, who had just informed Garrett he would not be returning to the sea with him and Jim had accepted Garrett's offer of second-in-command.

    Peters also doubted that the Captain was actually married to the girl. It just wasn't like the Captain to go off and marry with no

Chapter Five

warning. Captain Jamison thought things through. Even though the Captain was a tight-lipped man, he often discussed his plans and problems with Miles or himself. No, this just didn't seem to fit the Captain at all. The Captain must be protecting the girl from something or someone, but who in their right mind would follow the *Green-Eyed Lady* to sea? Her Captain and crew were well known on the seas for their daring and bulldoggedness. You crossed her path at your own peril. He had never questioned Garrett about his decisions once made and he wouldn't start now. This was unlike Garrett but it would make for an interesting voyage. He hoped that having the girl on board wouldn't stir up the men.

"Captain, Sir, you really shouldn't keep the girl locked in the cabin."

"And why shouldn't I? I can't have her running all over the place disrupting my men. We have too much to do and I can't be worried about some sailor stopping in to take a look."

"Whatever you think, Sir."

Garrett knew Jim was displeased with his actions by the very formal tone he used. Jim was always overly polite when he was disgusted with Garrett. Over the last few years Garrett had heard that tone enough to know the thinking behind it. Garrett ignored him, turned, and went about his business.

Garrett reviewed his orders in his mind. First he'd need to stop in Portsmouth to rendezvous with his contact before joining the other Captains off the coast of Spain for their next attack. As long as they were in the port city he might as well order some things for Angel that could be picked up on their return.

From the corner of his eye he kept an eye on the new hands as they went about their duties. The sails had been tacked to perfection. Jim was helping to stow some of the rigging. It was a fine day for sailing! A crisp wind was at their back moving them smoothly over the water. As they made the open sea Garrett spotted several gulls winging over the sails. It was a sight that never failed to give him joy. The sea was his home. Her spirit called to his.

Chapter Six

Angel had been pacing the length of the cabin floor—she felt like a caged animal. He certainly wouldn't keep her locked in here all day would he? Her eyes were drawn again to the Greek manuscript on the Captain's bookshelf. Angel felt powerless to resist its magical pull on her. Once more she traversed the space between herself and the manuscript to run her finger along the spine of the leather covered volume.

The misty fog that encompassed her memories shifted slowly to part the curtain showing her the picture of a dark-haired man bending over a small, blonde, girl child. His finger led hers across the strange characters of the script as his musical voice uttered the surreal language of the ancient Greeks. Angel felt no fear at the memory. A welcome warmth flooded her heart as she watched the man and child utter the words together. Their book had been covered in red leather with gold scripted letters on its binding and cover. The volume was ancient, even the child could see that, and she handled it reverently. Angel became lost in the vision as it revealed its entirety to her.

Garrett found himself wondering about Angel and how she was faring below in his cabin. Perhaps he should check on her. It wasn't uncommon for people to become seasick on their first voyage to the open sea. He walked down the stairs and unlocked the door.

What little light streamed through the portholes only served to enhance the uncommon beauty of the woman in his cabin. She was lovely in the altered gown that had belonged to his mother. Ironically, Lady Jamison had worn this same gown on many of her voyages with his father. Garrett was struck again by how beautiful

Captured Pearl

Angel was. How could he possibly have thought she was as spy? He was chastising himself until he looked into her face. An angel's face consumed in deep thought. She was spellbound by whatever she was looking at. He softly entered the cabin and silently positioned himself to look where her gaze was focused. She held his copy of Homer's *Iliad* in her hands. Her lips silently moved as she read the ancient words of the Greek epic. What woman could read—let alone read Greek? All of Garrett's suspicions raced to the forefront of his thinking. A spy would read Greek. What better words to use for secret communications between master and servant!

Without warning Garrett reached over her shoulder to reclaim the book. At his brush against her shoulder Angel was jolted out of her fog. She instinctively jumped dropping the volume with a loud thump onto the floor. They both bent over to pick it up finding themselves eye to eye. Startled green eyes met suspicious, stormy, blue ones. Angel moved to rise just as Garrett reached for her arm. Steely fingers locked about her wrist. His hold was unbreakable even though at this time it did no harm.

"What are you doing?" growled Garrett.

"I didn't mean any harm," stammered Angel. "I was bored. I didn't hurt the book—I was careful."

"Where did you learn to read Greek? And who taught you to read?"

Angel could not force a sound from her lips. He looked too angry, so foreboding! What did he plan to do to her?

Garrett rose bringing Angel with him. When no answer was forthcoming he gently shook her as he repeated his questions. Her eyes darting frantically about the cabin only increased Garrett's ire. Again he shook her increasing his grip upon her.

"Angel, answer me. Be honest at least. We may still be able to get you out of this mess!"

Angel could only stare at him numbly wondering what he was talking about. "I don't know! I DON'T KNOW! Stop shaking me, you're making my head hurt!"

Garrett calmed himself taking a deep breath before contin-

Chapter Six

uing. "Angel, not just anyone can read. You know that—and for a woman to read Greek! You have to admit anyone would wonder!"

"I don't know! It's like a dream. This man holding my hand as we read together. I can't remember him! Why can't I remember him?"

Garrett wanted to distrust her, after all his commission from the Queen demanded diligence, mistrust, and following his instincts, but the wounded look on her face was reminiscent of the look she had had earlier. What memories lay hidden behind the startled green eyes? Garrett would approach his contact about this puzzle as well. Garrett didn't like surprises and he meant to ensure that Angel gave him none. Meanwhile he would play the concerned benefactor. Perhaps if she was lying this approach would release more information than the tirade of temper and mistrust.

"Let it go, Angel, memories can't be forced. They will come in time. In the meanwhile why don't I take you up on deck for some air? The sea is beautiful today, much nicer than this cabin."

Angel wasn't sure about this change, one minute he was scaring her to death and the next he was concerned about her welfare. What was Lord Jamison doing? She didn't want to trust him, yet something in him called to her whispering to trust him, to lean on him.

"Yes that would be nice," she replied. With that Garrett escorted her to the deck. The sun was warm on her shoulders adding to the heat being radiated by Jamison's body. Angel found herself growing warm—too warm. She cast side glances at Jamison wondering if he felt the heat as intensely as she did, but he seemed unaffected by the warming power of the sun.

"See the gulls, Angel? They follow the ships to sea. They're always looking for handouts. It's considered a favorable sign for sailing to have them escort your ship."

She watched as the gulls dipped and swayed with the ship's dance over the brilliant blue sea. Angel glanced at Garrett bemused at the look of pleasure on his face. This man has many facets to his nature. Mame's parting comment ran through Angel's mind, "He has too many things on his mind."

Captured Pearl

A day up the coast *The Green-Eyed Lady* docked at Portsmouth. Garrett watched from the wheel as the hands heaved to, gently bringing her alongside the dock. After they were tied up and the Queen's cargo had been transferred to wagons that would deliver it to the storehouse, Garrett proceeded below deck to gather Angel.

He found her watching the goings on from the porthole, standing on tiptoe to watch the business of dockside. He rapped on the door before entering allowing her to gather herself before facing him.

"Ready to go?" he questioned.

"Where are we going?"

"I thought the first stop might be Mrs. Lewis the dressmaker. I imagine you'd like something besides hand-me-downs to wear. My mother always thought Mrs. Lewis was better than anyone in London. We'll order you some gowns of your own along with anything you might be needing."

"Lord Jamison, you can't do that! I mean, I'd love to have a gown, but you can't be buying me things! How would it look, how will I repay you? I don't even know if I can repay you!"

"Angel, I have more than enough wealth to purchase you some frocks. Why don't you let me worry about priority? After all we are married." Garrett chuckled at the astonished look on her face.

She was speechless. Really, the nerve of the man! And with those thoughts tumbling through her mind Garrett had her down the gangplank, in the carriage, and on their way to Mrs. Lewis' shop.

The dressmaker was located in one of the better parts of Portsmouth. The block boasted a baker, a shoemaker, an inn, and a jeweler so that the well-dressed lady or gentleman might procure all they might need within the confines of the neighborhood. Garrett introduced Angel to Mrs. Lewis. Then, while Angel fingered the rich materials, he took Mrs. Lewis aside.

"Mrs. Lewis, I'd like the Lady to have everything she needs.

Chapter Six

Don't let her sway you, and make sure to include a ball gown. Perhaps in that rosy-pink satin I see there on the trunk."

Mrs. Lewis knew the fabric to which Garrett was referring. Not usually a color for a married woman, however, the gentleman was right. With the Lady's blonde hair and green eyes the dusty pink would flatter both the wearer and the escort. Oh to be young again! The Jamison men had always known how to dress their women. What a godsend—that the Lord had finally found a Lady to settle down with. Her business had been affected by the untimely demise of his Lordship's parents, and his refusal to marry. Now if she could just capture the Lady's favor the future would be set.

"Of course, I will see to your Lady's needs Lord Jamison! Is there something in particular that you request for your wife?"

"I'm afraid that I'm much like my father in this regard Mrs. Lewis. I have little taste for the brash new styles. Although, Lady Jamison will need a few on the chance that I present her at court. Stay away from the gaudy colors and please do not overburden her with pearls and gems in the gowns. Like my father, I prefer the richness of the cloth and the elegance of the cut to flatter my lady. The green velvet there would be spectacular on her, as would the azure blue silk. Other than that let's see what Mrs. Jamison picks."

For the second time that morning Mrs. Lewis found herself appreciating Lord Jamison's taste. The man was flawless in his choice of both color and women. Even at her age, with two grown children of her own, the man's charm and demeanor hypnotized Mrs. Lewis. His manners, his graceful way of carriage, and his speech made him a man that was not easily forgotten. Just like his father! He had such a presence about him—it was a certainty that he would be called to court. She must do her utmost to represent herself well. The new Lady Jamison would be the perfect foil for her creations!

Mrs. Lewis whisked herself off to gather her sketches for the Lady's perusal. As she passed through the back room she called for her apprentice, Jane, to assist her and she sent Libby off to the baker for refreshments for the Lady. If Garrett Jamison was anything like his father, and she'd be twice a fool if she was wrong, the man would reward her well for her efforts toward his Lady.

Oh those Jamison men, they knew how to take care of their own. But they were also a knife in the side to their enemies. She still recalled the altercation between the past Lord and his notorious gambling neighbor that had taken place outside the jeweler's shop several years ago to this day. Some sly comment concerning Lady Jamison had been overheard by Lord Jamison and he was at the other man's throat with a knife. Ah, to be defended by such a man!

Garrett watched with amusement as Mrs. Lewis scurried about her shop gathering the materials of her trade. Angel was seated next to a table where Mrs. Lewis' sketches were displayed and she was being plied with opinion and comments about the fabrics and styles. He found himself enjoying the look of pleasure that adorned her face. She acted as if she had never had such an experience before. She wasn't greedy, as most women would have been. Rather she was selective, often looking in his direction for approval; hesitant to order something until his silent nod would sweep Mrs. Lewis on to another selection.

God, he hadn't realized how long and detailed a woman's dress fitting could be! Would the hour never arrive for Peters to come allowing him to escape this tedium? It seemed like ages instead of hours since they had first arrived. How had his father ever tolerated this nightmare? Finally, when Garrett thought he'd never be allowed to escape, Peters walked through the door.

"Sorry to interrupt, Captain. But there has been a problem with the cargo that will need your attention immediately!" Just as arranged Peters brought the necessary excuse for Garrett to leave for his rendezvous with his contact from the Queen.

A look of disappointment swept across Angel's face before it could be stopped.

"Peters, I'd have you stay with my Lady while I take care of this. If she finishes before I return you know where we're staying the night. Escort her there and see that she is comfortable and entertained until I return."

"Yes Sir, Captain."

Chapter Six

Garrett made his way to The Ferret's Roost, a seedy tavern dockside, where a man could go unnoticed and his business was his own. Captain Smith would have reserved the back room for the Captains' meeting. The tavern was used often for clandestine meetings, not only for the Queen's men but for Riley's ferrets as well.

Garrett had a job to do. He was with the English in their continuing fight against the Spanish and the Queen depended on him. Elizabeth Tudor was a powerful woman and she demanded undying loyalty from all those in her service. She had only one desire and that was to destroy the Spanish. To that end Garrett and the other Captains in her service would plot and plan for their next foray against the Armada. Several of the other men had already arrived. Garrett joined a small group that was pouring over the latest information containing the statistics of the Spanish Armada fleet size and the ships that were deployed in the general area.

Garrett was surprised to see Sir Francis Drake there with his friend John Davis. If these two legends were in on this foray something major must be in the planning. Smith called the meeting to order then turned to Drake, "Sir Drake, if you would continue, I believe you have the information most informative to our group."

"Well, Gentlemen, it seems that the Spanish have decided to try to take England again—and in our home waters. Captain Davis has come into some vital information that will allow us to perhaps, once and for all, give the Queen what she so earnestly desires. The Spanish are gathering off the coast of France intending to leave within the next ten days for England.

"Captain Howard already sails his fleet to meet us at Brighton. From there we sail to intercept the Spanish near Calais, France, where they wait for their reinforcements from the Netherlands. Gentleman, if the two Spanish fleets combine I need not tell you of the consequences! We sail for Brighton the day after tomorrow for perhaps the greatest battle of our careers!"

Men cheered at the thought of finally defeating their age-old enemy! Plans were quickly finalized and the occupants scattered to ready their men and ships for the upcoming battle. Garrett sent word by way of one of Riley's trusted men, that his crew should gather and ready the ship. Then he set off to Josh Birmingham's townhouse to see if he could arrange for Angel to stay out of harm's way, as well as under strict watch, in the case all his common sense was leaving him regarding the girl.

The Birminghams had long been family friends. Josh had been in service to the Queen as well until a fatal battle had taken his right hand and forearm. Duty to Queen was replaced by duty to family. Because of his service, Josh could be trusted with Garrett's latest mission as well as his suspicions concerning Angel. The arrangements were made with Josh's promise to come and collect her early the next morning so that Garrett would be free to handle his ship's affairs.

Chapter Seven

After many arduous arguments on Angel's part and exasperated sighs on Mrs. Lewis' part the selection and fitting for Angel's wardrobe was finally concluded to everyone's satisfaction. Mr. Peters' statue-like presence along with the pained expression upon his face, caused many a smile to come to both women's faces. It was obvious to both females that the man would rather have lost his right arm in battle than endure the anguish of a woman ordering her wardrobe.

"I'll have these two frocks delivered to you later this day, Madam. Then you'll be needing to come back in three or four days for the final fittings for your gowns. Be sure to remind Lord Jamison of the date if you wish to have them done within a fortnight."

"I shall take your words to heart, Mrs. Lewis. Thank you so much for your advice and concern." With that Mr. Peters escorted Angel out of the shop and down the street.

"The Captain wasn't sure when he'd be back, Madam. Would you like refreshments or would you prefer to go straight to the lodgings that he has procured?"

"Would it be possible to have tea and biscuits at the lodgings, Mr. Peters?" Angel queried. Although the day was far from over the flurry of activity at the dressmaker's had worn her out. A nice rest and tea sounded lovely.

"Of course, Madam. I'll arrange it once we have you checked in."

Two blocks up from Mrs. Lewis' was a quaint old inn. Although it had seen better days it was obvious the owner took great care to keep it up to the standards required by the upper class of the town. The innkeeper met them at the door and escorted

Captured Pearl

Angel and Mr. Peters to a lovely second story loft. The room was adequate in size with a homey appeal. Angel felt immediately at home.

"I'll see to your refreshments, my Lady. Should you need anything else I am just across the hall." With that Peters quietly withdrew softly closing the door behind him.

Angel quietly wandered about the room softly fingering the embroidered pieces upon the bedside tables. Someone had lovingly crafted these beautiful adornments. Why did she feel such sadness at this thought? Had there been such a lack in her previous life that even now her heart could weep with sadness? What kind of man would clothe a stranger he knew nothing about? Someone, it was obvious, he didn't trust. What kind of upbringing allowed one to show kindness in the face of such mystery? She had indeed been fortunate to fall into Lord Jamison's hands. At every turn he had shown understanding and a gentle caring. If he had questions who could blame him? She had questions, too, and to be perfectly honest Angel couldn't blame him for his lack of patience at times. Wouldn't if be wonderful to be able to ease his mind, and her own, with some small bit of information. But no matter how hard she tried nothing would part the black curtain of her memory.

A soft knocking on her door interrupted her musing. Angel reached the door opening it a crack to see a stout-looking woman bearing a tray with tea and biscuits.

"Your order, Madam, I'm Mrs. Scott the innkeeper's wife. Come now and let me in before your tea starts to cool," she stated as she swept her boisterous presence into the room. Mrs. Scott poured the tea quickly adding cream without asking Angel's preference, as if she assumed that all Ladies drank their tea with cream. Angel found herself smiling at the thought of Mrs. Scott adding cream to Lord Jamison's tea. She'd bet the Lord would grit his teeth, politely tell her thank you, and drink it without showing a grimace. The thought brought a smile to her face.

"If you need anything at all Madam you just let that man of yours know. I'll be just downstairs if you need me." And with that

Chapter Seven

she left the room as boisterously as she had entered.

Angel found her appetite taking over as she sipped the tea and quickly finished two biscuits. After another cup of tea she began to feel a bit drowsy. A nap seemed to be in order. The big, beautiful bed was inviting; the sunlight streaming through the window was warm. Why fight it? Angel found herself curling up in the middle of the big bed nestled under the quilt before she had time to think.

When Garrett entered the room shortly before dusk this was the scene he encountered. The slight maid nestling in his bed brought a start to his heart. Fierce protective instincts rose up from his soul. He found himself wishing to protect her for all time. With a quick shake of his head he tried to clear his mind of such thoughts. There was no way he could afford to be letting down his guard at this point in his life.

Quietly he moved toward the bed, and mindful of how she had awoke the last time he had found her thus, he began calling her name softly.

Angel was having the most pleasant dream. A beautiful man had come to rescue her from the dreadful harsh man controlling the house she lived in. As she found herself awaking the gentle voice continued to call her name bringing her softly back to the waking world.

Her shy smile and gentle, "Good day, Sir," took him completely by surprise.

"Good evening to yourself, my Lady. How was your day?"

"Tiring but very pleasant, Lord. I don't think I've ever been to a fitting quite like that before. In fact, I don't think I've ever been to town before."

"What makes you say that, Angel?"

"Just a feeling, Lord Jamison. Everything seems so new as if it's happening for the first time. When we came to the inn, I felt so sad. As if I'd never had beautiful things around me before. As if my life had been filled with ugliness and cruelty. Does that sound as strange to you as it does to me?"

"Not really, Angel. But for right now let's go downstairs and

Captured Pearl

have our evening repast. I'm famished and we need to talk."

"All right, Lord Jamison. If you'll just give me a moment."

"Certainly, Madam. I believe it would be in order for you to refer to me as Garrett—at least in private. I find that this formality begins to grow old. What do you think?"

Angel rolled the thought about and then nodded her agreement. She liked the sound of Garrett as it echoed in her mind. Shortly they made their way downstairs to dine. As the meal progressed Garrett plied her with questions about her time with Mrs. Lewis. Eventually the questions in her eyes could be put off no longer.

"Angel, there has been some problems with my cargo and I find that I need to sail tomorrow to put things to right with the consignor. I know this is very sudden and I don't expect you to accompany me. A dear family friend, Josh Birmingham, has agreed to host you at his family estate until I return. Please do not argue with me on this turn of events Angel, I simply cannot tolerate another setback today." The last was not said in anger, or angrily, and as Angel took a closer look at the man's face she could see the concern and preoccupation upon his brow. She nodded her acceptance of his decision hoping that she would not regret placing her trust in this man.

"Josh sailed with me before he lost part of his right arm in a sailing accident. I trust him as I do my brother, Angel. You will be safe with him. His sisters and parents live at the estate also so there will be plenty of company for you there until I return. Josh will be arriving at mid-morning to collect you and if my business should take longer than expected he'll see to it that you keep your appointment with Mrs. Lewis."

"All right, Garrett. I'll trust your judgment on this, even though I'm not comfortable with this solution." Garrett could read the unspoken statement in her eyes to please not break the fragile trust she was putting in him.

The next morning after Josh came to collect Angel, Garrett made his way quickly to the *Green-Eyed Lady*. Peters was there as well as the crew, awaiting his orders. Quickly, the ship was freed

Chapter Seven

from its moorings to make her way out into the open sea. Although the sun was shining the wind was brisk and cold as if it knew a secret that it wished to keep to itself. The crew was quick and smart, as Garrett steered their way clear, to open the sails of the swift vessel sending her bounding out into the sea. They would be in Brighton before the setting of the sun leaving them plenty of time to rendezvous with the other Captains for their venture against the Spanish.

One of Riley's ferrets had returned from Lisbon, Spain, with word of the Armada's movements. It seemed the Spanish were bent on taking England in order to tighten their hold on the Netherlands. The spy had brought back valuable information on the ships and commanders that were, even now, anchoring off the French coast. Phillip of Spain had made a vital error in placing Parma in command of his fleet. The man had no sailing experience, and against the likes of Howard and Drake the English were sure to win! Howard had sent 18 powerful galleons, armed with 32 pieces of brass ordinance each, ahead. The English waited at Brighton for the signal to send the 191 vessels to sail for the French port of Calais.

They launched at night. The ships were anchored far enough out to sea that the inhabitants of Brighton could not see them. Silently, the vessels received their orders and began grouping together for their run across the channel. The English fleet was made up of smaller, fleeter ships, which made them more maneuverable close to shore. They were led by the *The Ark*, the English Admiral's warship that carried 55 guns along her decks. Garrett's lighter ship carried her usual 23 guns, but even though her armament was lighter that the regular navy, *The Green-Eyed Lady*, had the reputation as one of the fastest vessels on the sea.

The plan was to sail silently in after the forward group had silenced the sentries. Lord Howard had ordered fire ships to be led in by Sir Palmer from Dover. They would strike terror and mayhem into the Spanish sailors as the Armada burst into flame.

As they neared the shore of Calais, France, a small group

manned the dinghies and rowed for the looming silhouette of the Spanish Fleet. Every sailor feared a fire aboard ship. There was no escape from the sea when your ship was consumed in flames. The fire ships had been prepared with explosives and consumable materials. Their guns had been removed and placed among the other vessels in the fleet.

Garrett watched in fascination and horror as the fire ships set sail. There was a light south-southeast wind to help the ships into Calais. The best the English could hope for was that the Spanish ships packed so tightly into the port would catch flame and sink. Garrett doubted even a man as inexperienced as Sidonia would be so stupid as to have no backup plan—and he was right. The crew watched as the flames of the fire ships closed on the Armada. Garrett and Peters could hear the shouts of the Spanish across the water as they watched the crews cut their cables to flee from the flames encroaching ever closer to the huge Spanish ships. The Hellburners began to explode with a dismal effect. While the wind had been in the English favor the Spanish had managed to creep far enough away that not even one vessel had caught fire! The good news was that the Armada had been in such a panic to evade the Hellburners that several had collided with each other, helping the English in their rout.

Hand-to-hand fighting would come next. Garrett called out orders to the crew and Peters, gathering his men and vessel for the turmoil to come. The English vessels would now have the advantage! Garrett's *Lady*, with her swiftness and 23 guns coming to bear would dart about among the Armada firing her cannon as she swept by. His gunners were ready and the cannon were loaded. All that lay waiting was the signal from the *Ark* to engage. The thrill of battle hummed through Garrett's veins warming his blood and giving him coolness of head, to go with nerves of steel. His men swore that even in the darkness of the night you could see the sparks of battle sweep from his eyes to consume his enemies. His fearlessness in battle, as well as his coolheadedness, fortified his crew into an unbeatable opponent.

The signal light came from the *Ark*. Garrett bellowed the

Chapter Seven

order to raise the topsail and strike the sprit. The crew sprang into action as their ship caught the wind moving smoothly and rapidly through the water. Garrett's foresight in installing his cannon at a higher water level allowed his gunners to fire at longer distances and at greater accuracy than most other ships of his time.

As the *Lady's* guns began to bellow the crew raised a rousing shout of exhilaration. No one, not even the Admiral's galleon, had the range and accuracy of the *Lady's* cannon. With Roberts setting his sights on the Spanish invaders and the Captain at the wheel the ship and crew were a deadly weapon. The Captain's jet-black hair streamed in the breeze just as the sails filled with the friendly wind. His legs set to take the roll of his mistress Garrett rode as easily as if on a cloud of retribution sent from God above. His crew gripped their swords and pikes to dissuade the Spanish from catching their grappling hooks upon the *Lady's* fore and aft castles. Mr. Peters' shrill whistle alerted the crew to trouble on the broadside of the ship, but before he was finished Garrett had lashed the wheel, swinging himself to the trouble spot with a loose sail line to dispatch the grappling hook before a man could board the English vessel. Tanner had run to man the wheel in Garrett's absence ensuring that no Spanish minion might commandeer the ship leading her into troubled waters. The young sailor had proved Garrett's trust in his abilities this night ensuring him a place on the *Lady* for as long as he cared to sail with her.

As the *Lady's* crew finished their first run through the jumbled mess of Spanish galleons Tanner swung her about and neatly cleared her out of the path of the vessel following her line of attack. Garrett was back to relieve the young man in time to set the next line of attack before some other could beat him to the task. Roberts had the guns reloaded and his sights upon the first in the next line before Garrett had straightened their path. Roberts shouted his orders covering his ears as his precious guns barked their deadly song of destruction upon the enemy. Tanner had resumed his station on the lee side watching for any Spanish attempt to slow their progress or board the *Lady*.

Sidonia attempted to lead his fleet out of Calais to reform.

Captured Pearl

The jumble of heavy Spanish ships made the going slow and Garrett, ever vigilant, spotted the ploy attempted by the Spanish commander. Garrett's well-aimed throwing knife shivered by Mr. Roberts' ear drawing the man's snarley eyes to find the chap who had come so close! Garrett met his eyes directing the man's gaze to the lead galleon trying to escape.

Roberts briskly reloaded his favorite ordinance and brought it to bear on Sidonia's ship. With a loud roar the cannon let fly shearing one of the riggings from the ship to effectively slow her further, and then they were out of range. Slowly, the winds began to change allowing the Spanish to fill their sails in another attempt to escape from the English.

The *Lady* was finishing her second line run pummeling the riggings and castles of the foe when the light began to break in the east. The red glow of the morning sun was matched by the fading glow of the Hellbreakers as their fires slowly died and the ships began to sink. As the wind continued to shift the lumberous Spanish vessels moved out of Calais toward the open sea in search of deeper waters and respite from the English vengeance. Peters quickly took stock of the crew and ship and was relieved to be able to report to his Captain that there were no serious injures to either. They had been most fortunate this night. The Captain had the devil's own luck when it came to battle. He was most often the giver of destruction and not the receiver.

Drake and Howard were determined to squash the Spanish once and for all. Garrett was in hearty agreement. The collection of English vessels pursued the Spanish Armada as it sailed for open sea. Four of the galleons grouped together to try to stall the English pursuits. Garrett wisely left it to the heavier English vessels to engage these vessels in close combat. As the English opened fire the wind favored them again lending her breath to their sails in pursuit. The Spanish galleons were outgunned by the English who did severe damage to the galleons, sinking three of the great vessels before the rest could escape.

Garrett fumed at the delay. The *Lady* was not equipped for this kind of battle. He knew that but it chafed at him to have to

Chapter Seven

wait behind in an observer's position until he could sail free to catch the other ships. Finally the way was clear! Garrett and the other Captains loosed their sails. The lighter ships leapt into the sea as if they, too, were anxious to engage the foreign vessels that had dared to enter their home waters. For the next nine hours Garrett and the other Captains tacked back and forth in line against the Spanish inflicting considerable damage until a heavy wind and rain blew in forcing them to desist in their efforts.

When the storm had passed the English found that the Spanish had managed to make their way farther out to sea. Howard and Drake vehemently argued to pursue, but Garrett and the other Captains pointed out that they were short on ammunition. They would sail back to Brighton to re-supply before deciding on the next course of action. Howard fumed but Garrett pointedly replied that the Captains of private vessels were commissioned to harass and harry. Since they were not in the naval command Howard could not command them to comply with his demands. Only the Queen had that power. With that Garrett turned his ship toward home and Angel.

Even with the battle ensuing about him, Garrett had not been able to completely dismiss her from his thoughts. As he mulled this over in his mind he thought he saw a faint ghostly outline of a ship off to his right, but when he turned to really examine the spot it was gone. Probably just another of Howard's vessels continuing the chase.

Although the *Lady* had not been damaged badly she had taken a beating during the last run and after Garrett had decided to sail for Brighton they had run afoul of some broken mast from a sunken ship. Only through a lot of luck had they managed to sail free of the debris from the battle floating in the channel. Garrett hoped he wouldn't have to face any unfriendly ships on their return.

Jim Peters stood by the helm where he noticed lights off the port side. He grabbed his spyglass and yelled, "Captain there is a ship coming this way!"

Captured Pearl

"One of ours Mr. Peters?"

"No, Sir. A strange vessel."

Garrett went forward to take a look for himself. He peered through the spyglass locating the strange ship. In the darkness there was no way to tell if it was friend or foe. Garrett knew his ship was in no shape for another battle at that point in time, nor could they outrun the vessel, after the rudder damage due to the wreckage that had caught them unaware.

Garrett never ran from anything, and this would be no different. He could be leading them into real trouble with their repairs still to be put underway. He knew his crew would fight to the death if need be, but they were not at their best after a full day of battling the Spanish Armada, either. The night was dark and beginning to cloud—perhaps Lady Luck would smile upon them this night. He gave the order that there was to be no noise and they waited as they quietly floated by hoping the ship would pass without spotting them. Was this, then, the ghostly image he had caught a glance of earlier? One of the injured coughed and the other ship came alive! As his men came alive preparing to protect their ship, Garrett still had one last trick up his sleeve. With a soundless rush he ran up the black flag of a pirate vessel.

The flag flying, Jim and Garrett looked about them at the men and each other. There was nothing left to do but wait and pray.

Duprell had been thanking his lucky stars that his informant from France had been so timely with his information. Following along behind the battle was going to net him some badly-needed revenue. He usually commandeered ships that had been disabled either by previous confrontations or bad weather. Tonight both had come into play.

The Spanish vessel cut down by the English had not been far below the surface when Duprell arrived. His cutthroat crew had rapidly divested the ship of anything they could manage to find of value before moving on to the next. Many of the Spanish fleet had run aground. They were busily trying to contend with their

Chapter Seven

wounded and dead by the time Duprell had arrived. His crew had quickly dispatched them at their weakest. They stole anything of value that was left on board the ships and their crews, killing the survivors without remorse. Duprell himself was a coward, leaving his men to do his dirty business. He was well known for his cruelty and depravity leading others, as wretched as he, into more evil deeds with each passing day.

Sometime after midnight they spotted another ship. Duprell could not believe his luck — another disabled vessel trying to make its way to home port. It mattered little to him if it was Spanish or English. Both were fair game. As he neared the ship preparing to dispatch its crew, Duprell spotted the Jolly Roger flying defiantly in the wind. A pirate ship! This was one fight Duprell did not want! Pirates were the masters of the seas. Their crews even more bloodthirsty than his own. They would have no easy victory here. This had been a moderately profitable trip thus far. If he could just get his goods to his contact in Hastings he could sail on following the skirmishes between the two opposing Armadas and make this a very profitable run, indeed. He hastily searched his brain for a plausible story to avoid the inevitable fight.

As the two ships neared each other he called out in an oily voice, "I am a friend — not an enemy, let me pass. We carry laborers from China and wish no harm to anyone."

Garrett could not believe his good luck! Exactly what he wanted! But no self-respecting pirate would allow a ship by with those mere words of intent.

In a gravelly voice he countered, "Announce your contact. Be he friend — you may pass by!"

Duprell was in a quandary. To announce his contact could have far-reaching repercussions, on the other hand, not to do so could sink his vessel. Even in the faint light he could see that this ship was rigged for battle. She was outfitted with heavy cannon. The chance was too great.

"Monsieur Monay of Burgundy!"

Garrett was taken back in surprise. This Monay was one the Queen's agents had been after for years. Always he was too slippery to catch. Now when they had the very Captain that might lead him to the man, he could do nothing about it! What a fine mess this was! Oh well, another chance would come along—eventually.

"Peters remember that ship for further identification. If we come across her again I want to know it!"

"Aye, aye, Captain."

"Safe passage be yours upon your journey," Garrett called out in his gravelly tone. Then as he silently fumed he watched the other vessel sail past, heading north. His vessel and crew continued south toward Plymouth and needed repairs.

Chapter Eight

As the carriage traversed the last streets of town, Josh surveyed with intent interest the young woman seated across from him. She was pretty and not at all like Garrett's previous ladies. They had all known the rules to the game they played with the Lord Jamison. After escorting his sisters to court and various entertainments, Josh could not believe that Angel was either an experienced spy, or woman. She radiated innocence and youth, not the texture or feel of experience or deception. What had Garrett gotten himself into this time? If he didn't watch himself the Queen would be calling him to task because sooner or later word would get around that there was a Lady Jamison. The Queen did not take lightly a momentous move such as this by a favorite without her expressed permission even if it was just for the Lady's protection. Quietly, Josh continued to assess the Lady across from him on the ride to his family Estate. Since his father's bout with health trouble he had been running the Estate. Even when his father had recovered enough to pick up the reins of the family business he had left Josh in charge. Frankly, Josh thought his father enjoyed the leisure of being able to do as he pleased for most of the day, especially when this left Josh to the escort duties at court. His father had never enjoyed the politics and scheming of staying in the Queen's favor. But Josh thrived on the thrill of the game.

Angel watched the countryside with obvious enjoyment. The colors of late summer were rich, thrilling her heart with the hues and shadows of rich greens from the trees enhanced with the vibrant yellows and purples of the flowers growing along the lane. Lord Birmingham had been pleasant and entertaining. Angel appreciated the fact that the man across from her was

Captured Pearl

comfortable with silence allowing her to gaze freely at the country passing by.

A shiver of fear lanced down her spine, its cause unknown. Where had that come from? She felt comfortable with this stranger it wasn't from him. Had there been something her memory recalled in the scenes passing by that had made her heart go cold? What could it have been?

Angel gazed intently at the countryside again, but the feeling was gone only leaving her with a slight feeling of unease. She glanced at Lord Birmingham to find him watching her intently. For all his youth, he looked much younger than Lord Jamison; the man's eyes were intent and watchful leaving a feeling that he was older than his years. His lack of the right arm only added to the watchful feeling the man emanated. She found herself thinking that this man could be a loyal friend or a deadly enemy.

"Do you mind if I ask you something, Lord Birmingham?"

Josh gave a slight smile and replied, "We'll never know if you don't."

"How do you know Lord Jamison?"

Josh's look became serious, "I once sailed with Garrett. Our families have the commonality of shipping. My father thought it would be best if I learned from an expert before allowing me to head out on my own. Garrett was already known for his sailing prowess even then. We found that we had much in common, which only helped us to become loyal friends. I lost my arm when pirates attacked us on one of our ventures into the sea off Spain. If it hadn't been for Garrett's quick reflexes I'd have lost more than my arm. He's a dangerous man, Lady. Be careful not to cross him. After Garrett brought me home he took his crew searching for the man that took my arm. When they finally met up there wasn't a man left standing on the vessel by the time Garrett was through. He doesn't take his responsibilities lightly, Lady. He protects his own at any cost and his retribution is lethal.

"Look, we've reached the lane leading to the Estate. I've

Chapter Eight

always loved the fact that lilacs line this lane. They emit such a fragrant smell in the spring. This time of the year their foliage is so lovely. What do you think, Lady Jamison?"

"Yes, they are nice. Won't your family be wondering about me?"

"My family would walk through fire for Garrett, Lady Jamison. My father has his only son because of him."

"Then you have an exceptional family, Lord Birmingham."

"I don't believe so, Lady. Most families that I know would feel the same way."

Angel's silence was disheartening. The heavy silence emanating from her soul spoke volumes for the kind of family life this young Lady had experienced. Even without her memory, her past was easily read if one really looked. To Josh's experienced eye many facets of the woman were an open book. After the subterfuges of the court and its skilled players Josh's eyes could read volumes in the stature and slight nuances of the looks and postures of any person he might encounter. This was one reason Garrett had requested his help. Very little escaped Josh's keen eyes. As masterful as Garrett was at nautical tactics and strategies, Josh's expertise put Garrett in the position of student at the subtle nuances of court politics where the ability to read a man's thoughts could avert a war or throw a country into a battle.

The road curved gently around a hill and once traversed the Birmingham Estate became visible. Josh heard Angel's slight gasp as the house loomed into her sight. It was as impressive as the Jamison Estate with formal gardens sprawling out from each side. Sheep grazed on the grass flowing out from the front gate adding to the peaceful, yet impressive, first impression.

"It tends to take your breath away, doesn't it?"

"It's so beautiful!" Angel answered breathlessly. Never had she felt such an overwhelming sense of ethereal beauty. The vision of a dark and foreboding house crept into her thoughts. A place of loneliness and fear. Had she lived in such an awful place? Was that why this lovely vision seemed unreal?

Josh watched the shadow cross her brow making a mental note to pursue it further at another time. There was a plausible wrongness about the Lady he would investigate later. If Angel was to be believed . . . the interlude at the Birmingham residence might stir distant thoughts to the surface.

The horses came to a stop in front of the wide marble steps. The footman was there to open the carriage door as Josh descended and then turned to help Angel down.

"Welcome to my home, Lady Jamison."

"Thank you, Sir."

"Well, son, let's take a look at Garrett's Lady. My Lady, let me introduce myself. Lord Birmingham, the elder. But I will be extremely hurt if you address me as anything other than Phillip," the older man finished with a bow. Angel was immediately enchanted with him. His courtly manners and ready smile made her feel immediately at ease. It was easy to see where Josh had gotten his charm.

"Thank you, my Lord. I'm sorry, Phillip. Thank you so much for allowing me to stay at your home while Garrett finishes his business." Angel did not notice the knowing look that passed between the two Birmingham men.

"Please, come inside and meet the rest of the family. My wife and daughters have arranged for refreshments. You know Garrett has been considered quite a catch for many years. Everyone is eager to meet the Lady that finally captured his heart."

Angel managed a pained smile at his remark. It felt almost evil to deceive these lovely people with the fabricated lie that allowed her entrance into their home. She hoped that this would not harm the friendship Garrett had with this family. To have such friends must be a wonderful feeling. She wouldn't know — where had that come from?

They made their way to the dining room where four equally lovely ladies waited. The first was obviously Lord Phillip's

Chapter Eight

wife. Her dark hair was upswept adding to her stately demeanor, but there was a warm smile upon her face and a warm welcome escaped from her lips.

"May I introduce my wife, Lady Patience, my daughters Beth, Caroline, and Jolene." Each Lady stepped forward as they were introduced to Angel.

"Here, my dear, please be seated and have some tea. We're so pleased to have you with us," Lady Patience stated.

"We'll keep you so busy you won't have time to miss Garrett," chimed in Jolene, the youngest of the Ladies. "And we've put you in the east room. It will be just perfect for you! The morning sun makes the rose flowers in the green wallpaper on the walls come alive. And you can smell the flowers from the east garden at mid-day."

The buzz of conversation continued as tea was served. The lovely dessert tray was passed around the table and before long Angel was lost in the complicated menagerie of five different conversations. She found herself adding bits and pieces to the topics without even being aware of the fact. However, Josh was most intent on following her conversation. To his puzzlement he found that Angel seemed to have only the most cursory knowledge of court and the present goings-on of a country that had been at war for several years. Her grace and manners showed breeding, however her lack of knowledge showed isolation. An interesting dilemma for him to puzzle out before Garrett returned.

"Girls, why don't you show Lady Jamison to her rooms. She may wish to refresh herself before you completely overwhelm her," Patience stated laughingly.

"Please, Lady, call me Angel. I find that I am not weary at all. You are all so wonderful!" Tears began to fill Angel's eyes and she politely turned her face away that the family not see how much their welcome had meant to her. Warm arms embraced her as Phillip gave her a light hug and then laughingly said, "My family can be quite overwhelming at times but I wouldn't trade them for all the wealth in the Orient."

Captured Pearl

The days passed quickly for Angel as she became embedded in the routine and high energy of the Birmingham family. There were long walks in the flower gardens, music and laughter, but most of all there was the quiet bonding with Lord Phillip. Angel found herself drawn to him and he, in turn, was happy for her company. They found they had a common love of the ancient, old books in his study. The dusty tomes intrigued Angel as almost nothing else. Here she felt she belonged, as if she had come home.

This morning she and Phillip were puzzling over an old Greek variation of Spartan history.

"I find myself confounded by this passage Angel. Every translation I try leads me down a road of nonsense. Obviously, I translated it wrong again!"

Angel leaned over his shoulder as the quiet of the study permeated into her bones. This scene was familiar to her. The elder man with the ancient book, the girl looking on in interest, except in her mind the man's hair was black not gray, and the carpet was red not blue. The tome she remembered had a cracked leather binding that had been dyed red, instead of the well-oiled plain leather one that Phillip held in his hand. She almost held her breath as the image unwove within her mind. Distinctly in her mind she heard the same words, but this time in French not English. Then, she had stood on a high stool to peer over the man's shoulders and he had called her *mon bel enfant de fille* (my lovely girl child). She had loved this man as a child! Angel clung to the memory with all her might. She must not lose this piece to her puzzle!

"Angel, dear, are you all right?" questioned Phillip as he turned to look at her face. She was pale and breathing rapidly. For a moment he feared she might faint.

"Yes," she answered softly, "I remember doing this as a child with another man. Perhaps my father? He called me *mon bel enfant de fille* (my lovely girl child).

"Here child, sit down before you fall down," replied

Chapter Eight

Phillip. "What else do you remember?"

Angel related what she could remember to the elder Lord. Phillip found himself drawn into the mystery of the young woman as he recognized the ancient book from her description. The copies of the old tome were rare and costly. There were only four beside his own that he knew of, one belonged to the ruling family of Venice, one to an ancient family in Rome, and the other was housed in the University in Paris. He'd bet his best racer that the one she referred to was in Paris! Paris, the center of subterfuge and knowledge, bribery and theft. Which had the man in her memory belonged to?

As much as he had come to love her, this could not be kept from his son. Josh would be able to ferret out the answers. Hopefully the answer would be the right one for all involved!

"Well, that's good that you have remembered something. Give it time Angel; things will come back to you."

"But what if it's not good, Lord Phillip? What if I bring trouble down upon your family? You all have been so kind, I couldn't bear to bring you misfortune!"

"Not to worry Angel. This family has weathered trouble before and will again. It's the nature of life. But forewarned is prepared. Josh will need to know about this. His quick mind will turn us an answer soon, to be sure.

"But first let's see about some refreshments shall we? Translating the past always makes me famished, how about you?"

Angel nodded her agreement before leaving to bring up a tray. Phillip rang for the footman instructing him to locate the young master and send him to the library with all haste. Josh arrived before Angel had returned allowing Phillip to impart his perception of the event before Angel's return. When she arrived Josh gently led the conversation back to the event in question softly prying information from her memories that Angel hadn't realized she had.

"So you see the first thing we need to ascertain is which volume is the red cracked-covered one from Angel's memory.

Captured Pearl

After that I'll delve into who would have had access to the volume. Are we agreed Father . . . Angel?"

Phillip glanced at the girl's pale face waiting for her consent. Angel's nod was slight although it was easily read. She wanted answers, too.

"Yes, Josh let's proceed—but use your utmost discretion. Let's not rile anyone up unnecessarily."

Josh's smile was infectious. "I thought you left court to get away from the intrigue."

"Intrigue and family are two different things. Angel is family! And we take care of our own!"

The next morning word came from Mrs. Lewis stating Angel should return for her fittings. The family decided to venture into town that same day, escorting Angel. The girls were excited to see the new gowns, and Josh would make arrangements to garner information about the old books. Phillip remarked that they might as well all go and make it a family outing. The carriages were summoned while the family members prepared for the drive into town.

Angel found herself laughing at the silliness of the two youngest Birmingham Ladies. Their imitations of the Lords and Ladies at the latest ball were extremely entertaining. Both their mother and father admonished them for their comic mimicry of the nobles and Josh looked extremely pained. But it was in innocent fun. In public the Ladies were perfect in ideal manners and gentry.

Mrs. Lewis welcomed them into her shop where the Birmingham women oohed and aahed over the gowns ordered for Angel. The rosy-pink ball gown was so splendid that Angel's eyes began to tear. Mrs. Lewis smiled at her response to her great work of art, quickly dispelling the awkward moment with another fabulous creation. Jane appeared with the pins and tape to finish the changes while Mrs. Lewis whisked Angel off to the back room. As soon as one gown had been accessed Angel was fitted with another, and all the while Mrs. Lewis kept up a run-

Chapter Eight

ning commentary. Before long her conversation turned to the Jamison family.

"Oh, I remember Lord Jamison's beautiful Mother. The past Lord would bring her here for all her gowns. And there were many—for even then the Queen favored the family! Why it just seems like yesterday when the old Lord Jamison and that old Lord Duprell had their altercation at the jewelry store. I never did like that Duprell. What a wastrel that man was! Married into one of the best families around and then proceeded to squander every cent they had at the gaming tables. You know they fought over your Lord's mother? And then when Lord Jamison outbid Duprell for that beautiful emerald necklace to present to the Queen, things just went from bad to worse!"

The chatter continued but Angel no longer heard her. Her mind was reeling and her stomach felt quite upset. Resolutely, she locked her knees determined not to faint in front of Mrs. Lewis. Heaven knew what the woman would make of that!

When she no longer felt as if her legs were going to betray her, Angel ran the story back through her mind. Each time it was the name Duprell that caused her heart to flutter and miss a beat. She became convinced that somehow she was linked to that evil name. Should she tell Lord Phillip and his family? No! They would hate her, she was sure, if she were part of that sordid family. Their loyalty to Garrett was clearly demonstrated time and time again. If Duprell had caused trouble for Garrett's family there would be no leniency. And, my God, if she was in some way accompanied with Duprell . . . hadn't Josh warned her, he protects his own at any cost and his retribution is lethal?

Angel focused on the present again as the girls came runnning up to her with concerned looks with Mrs. Lewis following closely behind with another gown.

"Angel? Angel did you hear me? Are you alright? My God, you look like you've seen a ghost!"

"Dear, sit down. I will fetch you some tea." Mrs. Lewis rushed out of the room to get her tea.

Captured Pearl

"Perhaps I have . . . ," she said quietly, . . . "seen a ghost." But she left it at that.

Chapter Nine

At Brighton Garrett and Peters saw to the repair of *The Green-Eyed Lady* and the revival of the crew. As he walked about the deck seeing to the repairs Garrett thought Bess would be pleased and he smiled thinking of the Queen. Of course, she would argue about the money for his ship's repairs and the crew's wages. She would probably reprimand him for not taking more booty. She always expected her Captains to bring her valuables—especially gold and jewels. Well, thought Garrett, she'd have to settle for a little of his charm this time around.

As he stood with feet planted on the deck, he found himself thinking of Angel. His first thought was of how she was faring. There was also the information he hoped Josh would glean from her. Almost desperately he found himself hoping that she would be just what she seemed. Had the waif gotten her hooks into him already? He actually found the idea stimulating. What a surprise that was!

What to do about Angel? Garrett thought. An idea finally came to him—a perfect way to find out who she really is and where she came from. What if he escorted her about taking her to some of the prominent places? Someone was bound to recognize her. We will find out who she is then, once and for all, and that will be the end of it. His heart took a small lurch at the thought of never seeing her again.

Garrett filled Miles in on his plan and Miles agreed that it might shed some light on the mystery of Angel's background. Then Miles dropped the other boot.

"You'd better go see the Queen before you start this, Captain. You know what she'll be like if she thinks this is for real before hearing from you. There will be hell to pay and then some!"

Uncharacteristically, Garrett had completely let that side of his service slip his mind! God, Bess angry with him would be a disaster! The woman knew no bounds when her anger was surfacing. Yes, he'd have to visit her very shortly to explain the situation and maintain her good graces. Maybe he should take Angel along to meet the Queen.

Repairs were quickly finished leaving the crew of the *Lady* to sail for Plymouth and a well-needed rest. Once there he'd dismiss the crew for some land time while he collected Angel. It would be grand to visit with the Birmingham family! It had been a long time since his last visit.

The way was short between Brighton and Plymouth, seeming even more so because of the brisk wind that filled the sails of the fast vessel. Garrett leaned into the wind at the wheel as if his stature could lend even more speed to the ship. The crew caught his enthusiasm hopping to in a brisk manner eagerly looking forward to their land time. They would all return at his call—they always did. Garrett and his crew were more than just Captain and crew. They were part of the same army manning a vessel at sea. The crew looked after the ship as Garrett looked after his crew and had molded them into a fighting force unequaled in the British seas. Garrett paid well, both in booty and respect, and his men returned the favor.

Perhaps he'd send Jim on to the Jamison Estate with the *Lady*. Jim was getting tired of all the travels and he longed to take it easy for a while. Garrett had work for Jim at the Estate while they were on land and he often managed the property for Garrett when he was gone. It was Jim who had traveled to Wales to view the new cattle developed by Lord Hereford. They were finally going to have their first crop of calves from his breeding stock and Jim hoped to head the team of herdsman Garrett had employed to handle the future herd. But he owed his life to Garrett and would never ask to leave. Garrett turned the thought over in his mind again. Perhaps it was time Jim remained landside. The new man, Tanner, had proved himself able and capable on this trip. With the right guidance he might make a reliable and fast-thinking first mate. He'd consult Jim about his thoughts on the matter before deciding. Jim had definitely earned his heart's desire of breeding cattle and staying landside. To

Chapter Nine

Garrett's advantage, there would always be someone at the Estate that he could trust to make cool decisions that were best for the Jamison family.

He had thought he would send a gift on to the Queen with Sir Riley, however, now that he had discussed matters with Jim, Garrett decide to arrange for an audience and deliver it himself. The gift must be something that would delight her as well as keep him in her graces. Jim was right on the fact that she would be infuriated about this pretend marriage.

Bess dearly loved jewels. The emeralds his father had given her were still a great favorite. Garrett had found the largest emerald he had ever seen on board one of the Spanish vessels from the last foray. He had the jeweler set it in a gold mount and then had it surrounded by yellow diamonds. The effect was stunning! The brilliant green of the emerald was perfectly reflected by the pale yellow of the diamonds. Perhaps the diamonds were not as valuable as white ones, but they were harder to find and Bess would appreciate his efforts—he hoped.

As they entered Plymouth port Garrett was pleased to see how well the repairs to the *Lady* had held up. He was going to need a new ship if he was to continue in this line of business for the Queen. He hated the thought of retiring the *Lady*. She had been his second home, and a worthy vessel, carrying the crew and himself in and out of battle valiantly. She had held together under fire bringing them all home safely, time and again. Garrett chuckled to himself. Now he was starting to sound as superstitious as the rest of the crew!

He would need to collect Angel from the Birmingham Estate and there was no doubt that Josh and his family would want him to stay a few days. He'd best send word to the Queen requesting the audience forthwith. They could wait for the reply at the Birmingham's. He'd send Jim on to the Jamison Estate where he could see to packing some proper clothing for him. By ship Jim could make the trip before the summons came from the Queen. Then he and Angel would sail for London.

While Garrett was occupied with the ship, Jim sent Tanner down to the local livery to obtain mounts for the Captain and Miles.

Captured Pearl

Though Jim was elated to be heading back to the Estate he could not help feeling that his place was with the Captain whether it be on land or sea. He'd had a bad feeling ever since they had reached port and he didn't like it. A sailor learned to take heed of the warnings sent by parts unknown. Many a time such feelings had saved his life. He'd warn Miles to watch the Captain's back extra carefully this time. Meanwhile, Jim would make sure the trouble wasn't coming from the Estate.

Garrett and Miles fastened their personal effects to the horses as last minute instructions were given to the men.

"Stick close to home men. I'll be needing the *Lady* shortly, but I promise you a longer stay in London with extra pay for the inconvenience." There was a hearty shout from the men before the *Lady* lifted her anchor setting sail for home. Garrett and Miles mounted setting off for the Birmingham Estate. It was just a short journey by horseback and they should arrive by noon.

Garrett found himself wondering how the rosy-pink ball gown would look on Angel. She'd be stunning he was sure. He shook his head thinking that he'd better be careful not to forget that this marriage was pretend and not real. Angel certainly had managed to capture his thoughts.

As they approached the lane leading to the Estate, Garrett urged his mount into a canter. Beside him, Miles did the same and Garrett caught the amused smile on Miles' face before he directed his eyes back to the road.

"Anxious to see the young Miss, are we Captain?"

There was no use denying it, Miles knew him too well so Garrett just smiled in return and soon they were involved in a horse race. Both men had the foresight to rein in their mounts as they rounded the curve of the road and spotted the Estate's sheep grazing along the path. The sheep dog quickly rounded up his charges ushering them out of the path of the horses hooves, then turned to give an indigent bark to these strangers upsetting his charges. Both Garrett and Miles laughed at the indigent set of the collie's tail as he headed off.

Garrett heard the welcoming bell as it rang the announcement

Chapter Nine

of company. Leftover from older times when it had warned of attack, the family now used it to welcome friends. By the time the men reached the marble stairway a stable boy had appeared to take their mounts and Josh was at the door to welcome the visitors.

"By God, Garrett did you ride that horse from London?" Josh joked as he took in the sweaty hides.

"Ah you know the Captain; if it ain't as fast as the *Lady* it's too slow!" Miles remarked. All three men laughed as they headed into the cool interior of the house.

Soon Garrett was mobbed by the Birmingham women. There were hugs from all and the incessant chatter of three young females all talking at one time. Even as he answered their questions his eyes sought out Angel.

She stood back from the crowd near Phillip and he read the wariness and welcome in her eyes. His smile dazzled her as he broke free to come to her.

"Are you well, Angel?"

"Quite, thank you. The Birminghams are a lovely family, Sir."

Josh walked over and clasped Garrett's shoulder, "Give it up man. The family all knows you're not married! I have filled them in on the details surrounding Angel, besides they will all keep the secret. However, I can't say as much for Mrs. Lewis. There are too many Ladies asking about the spectacular ball dress."

Garrett groaned.

"You've gotten yourself into it this time man!"

"I'm sorry, Sir," Angel spoke softly.

"Don't let it worry you Angel. I've been in worse messes," and with that Garrett gave her a smile.

"I've sent word to the Queen that I would request an audience with her. Best not to have her too angry with me for not asking her permission for the marriage. You'll need to come along Angel. She'll understand that I needed to do this once she sees you." I hope, he thought.

"Come, come, let's all go into the dining room for some refreshments. Enough of this gloomy talk!" insisted Lady Birmingham.

Captured Pearl

After they were seated and the tea was poured Garrett proceeded to pull small velvet boxes from his pocket. The Birmingham girls knew what was coming, but Angel was puzzled.

"Lady Patience, this one is for you. But you'll have to have your husband take care of the setting for you," stated Garrett. She opened the small box to discover a small, but perfect, pink pearl nestled inside. "I know thanks aren't necessary but thank you for opening your house to Angel," stated Garrett. The other boxes were passed around to the other women seated at the table. Beth's contained a small teardrop sapphire suspended from a gold chain. Caroline's was a fragile gold filigree necklace, while Jolene, the youngest, had a single strand of pearls. Nothing that was terribly expensive yet thought had been taken for each gift. Angel was finally the only one left to open her box. Hesitantly, she cracked open the gift and then began to cry. Garrett was horrified! Did she hate it that much?

"Oh, Garrett, they're so beautiful!" she sighed softly. "No one has ever given me such a gift!" The other women were just as spellbound as they viewed the single ruby pendent and ear bobs that were an exact match for the rosy-pink ball gown.

"Wherever did you find those?" questioned Josh. "No don't answer that! If you do they'll all be wanting me to take them there!" Everyone laughed and the uncomfortable moment passed quickly. Garrett caught Josh's eye with a puzzled look and Josh's nod in reply answered the unspoken question. Angel was remembering her past.

After a respectable time, Garrett and Josh along with Lord Phillip, adjourned to the library. With the door soundly closed behind them the Birmingham men began to fill Garrett in on their discoveries.

"So you see, Garrett," Josh explained; "until I get some correspondence on those books we're pretty much in still waters. Father truly believes it's the book from the French University that Angel remembers. That could cause complications, as you know. But I just can't find any evidence from the Lady herself to support the idea that she is up to no good. From her body language and her speech she has had an unhappy life to this point, but I would bet that she is

Chapter Nine

upper class, if not nobility itself. She obviously isn't a commoner and you just don't teach someone what she unconsciously knows without investing years of training."

"What do you suggest as the next plan of action, Josh?"

It was Lord Phillip who answered Garrett's question. "Once you get your summons from the Queen hightail it to Her Majesty's side. You will need her on your side, and if, as I think, Angel is innocent I feel that something or someone very bad will be on her trail. She will need the protection of the Crown and you as well, Garrett."

"What do you know Lord Phillip?" questioned Garrett.

"I'd really rather keep my suspicions to myself at this point, Garrett. Stop giving me that look Josh! If what I think endangers our family in any way, you know that I would not keep it from you. I'm not the man of intrigue in this house and if I'm wrong no harm will have been done. Call it an old man's foolishness if you need a reason."

There was no use arguing with Phillip when he spoke in this manner, so Josh and Garrett would have to be content to wait for the information to arrive from France.

Three days later the summons arrived from the Queen. Lord Jamison was to present himself with all possible speed to the Royal court. "Bugger, Bess has her skirts in a twirl this time," Garrett thought to himself! The *Lady* had returned the previous evening ready to answer her Captain's call. Garrett informed Miles and the Birmingham family of their immediate departure. Then he sought out Angel to give her the news. He found her in the gardens with Beth.

"Excuse me Ladies, but Angel and I need to talk privately, Beth." After Beth had departed, Garrett took Angel's small hand in his and led her to the bench next to the old oak tree.

"Angel, the summons has come from the Queen. It seems I am in some deep water with her and I want you to be prepared. The Queen can be cruel and vindictive, but she can also be one of the best allies you can have. I want you to be prepared for her when we arrive. Try to remain calm and answer her honestly. We need to leave on the night's tide in less than one hour. By making all haste to reach her, I hope she will realize that I would not deceive her intentionally. Can you be ready in that amount of time?"

Captured Pearl

The concern was not easily read on his face but Angel had learned much of this man in the three days they had spent together at the Birmingham's. His worry could be read in the posture of his body and the slight nuances of his speech.

"Of course, Garrett. If that is what you need to do I'll be sure of it."

He escorted her to the house to see to her packing while he saw to the readying of his personal effects. Jim had brought the emerald necklace with him on board the ship. There was nothing left but to gather Angel and say good-bye to the Birminghams.

Angel was waiting in the foyer along with Josh. "I'm coming with you Garrett. My contacts can just as well send their findings to the court as here. The Queen knows I'm not lightly taken in and I believe that you're going to need your friends."

"Josh, I can't allow it. If she truly is angry I'll not have her scorn coming down upon your family!"

"I hate to tell you this Garrett," Josh replied with a tight smile, "but you are way out of your league at court—unlike me. You can't stop me from returning to court so you may as well accept gracefully the help that is offered."

So with Miles and Josh leading the way, Garrett and Angel followed to the waiting carriage. Angel's trunks had been loaded and the footman waited with the door open—ready to assist them inside. The men settled themselves in as soon as Angel was comfortable. Phillip and Patience came forward to see them off.

"You take care of this Lady, gentlemen. I expect to see her again soon!" came Lord Phillip's gruff farewell as he pressed a small Greek coin into Angel's palm. "It has always brought me luck child—may it do the same for you."

The horses moved off carrying them away from the only safe haven Angel was sure she had ever known. She looked around her at the three men accompanying her. Miles was obviously the Captain's man, loyal and stout of heart under fire. Josh, who appeared to be the young country Lord, was actually the man of intrigue ferreting out the mysteries of the world; and Garrett, the man who had given her his protection even while distrusting her. Three fine gentlemen. No Lady could do better—and one was beginning to capture her heart.

Chapter Ten

Duprell was in his element. He had followed the Armada as it headed north to avoid the English ships. The heavy north winds blew the Armada about smashing some against the cliffs while others were buffeted by the heavy waves that had been stirred up. As experienced as the Spanish were these seas were not for inexperienced voyagers. Duprell had often sailed these waters as they were often battering ships against the cliffs providing him with treasure and booty.

The fates had been with Duprell on this voyage for the last ship they had scuttled had been carrying gifts from France for the King of Spain. In one small chest in the cabin of her Captain, Duprell had found the most impressive perfect black pearl he had ever seen! Its size alone was enough to command your attention. The luster and shape were just as impressive and Duprell knew exactly what he was going to do with it! For once in his life he would present the Queen with a gift that no one could match. His family honor and reputation would be restored, as it rightly should be! Duprell could just see it! The black pearl set in a gold backing surrounded by diamonds and the entire necklace would be strung with dozens of perfect creamy pearls descending in sizes to the clasp which would also be a diamond. He already had the rest of the gems in his possession. He knew the perfect jeweler to take care of the setting, too.

His crew would continue to ghost along behind the remaining ships of the Armada as they made for the coast of Spain. When the time was right and he could no longer garner any booty from the decimated vessels he would sail for home.

His body was hungry for a ripe female. His sexual prowess was always bolstered by a fruitful foray. Cara would be hard pressed to satisfy his desires upon his return. He knew that she had only come to him to spite Garrett, and that thought infuriated him! Garrett and the Jamison family had been a thorn in his family's side even before the fiasco at school. The Jamison's were to blame for his family's straits. But soon with the help of the necklace that would all change!

Duprell was thrilled by the fact that Garrett was unaware of the damage his crew did to the English and Spanish alike. Each time Duprell could pass on information to his French contact about the English he derived supreme satisfaction from the fact that he sat right under Garrett's nose, unobserved.

His body hardened at the thought of retribution against Garrett. Cara's voluminous body sprang into his mind. He would enjoy driving into her squirming body, thrusting harder and harder into her womanly parts. Damn, maybe they had better make for home shortly. He dare not sail into any nearby port to release his sexual tension. He knew himself too well. His particular form of entertainment tended to rile the local people and brought too much attention to bear on his crew. As much as his body now craved release Cara would be the instrument of that release. There was no one she could turn to when he became violent. She also knew better that to deny him his sport. Yes, they would need to head home very soon.

His thoughts turned to Cassandra. Where had that little bitch gotten herself off to? His plans for increasing his wealth through her had momentarily been thwarted by her disappearance. Lucas would not wait forever. Perhaps it had not been the best course of action to turn her over to Judah for persuasion. That was another thorn in his side given to him by Garrett! Who could have known that the little slut, Chantelle, would become pregnant after the night of sexual glory at the school hunting lodge? The Jamison family had paid for her keep at the hospital, but after discovering Garrett's visits the old Lord had put a stop to that. Just as well!

When the babe had been born with the Duprell family birthmark, Lady Duprell had thrown a major fit! Nothing would do but that the babe be brought to the Estate and raised. When it became

Chapter Ten

clear that the boy was not quite right Donovan's father had finally persuaded Lady Duprell to allow a servant to raise him. Judah had proven useful over the years. His cruelty had shown itself early on and Donovan had recognized the usefulness of keeping his son on the Estate. Oh, yes he had proven very useful.

The first task Donovan had set for him was the elimination of that bitch, Chantelle. It had brought him great satisfaction to know that her own son had carried out her demise. Good riddance. The daft woman was always babbling nonsense. Thank God, no one had ever given her ramblings any thought.

Women! They were weak of mind and good for nothing but rutting! Even his mother did not garner a place in his heart. Why she had continued her friendship with Lady Jamison even after the episode at school was beyond his comprehension! Her visits to the Jamison Estate for tea with the Lady had infuriated his father. He was sure that eventually she would let slip the fact that their son had fathered a son on the miller's daughter. Every night until Chantelle's death Donovan had waited for Garrett to appear at his door, calling him out to deal with his depravity.

Yes, that accident of his parents' death had been too timely and people were immediately suspicious. His father had owed large amounts of money to the wrong people. It had been fortunate that his mother had died in the carriage accident along with his father before he had been forced to get rid of her, as he had Chantelle, too.

Donovan had already made contacts in the underworld of London so it wasn't long before he had been able to ascertain who had been responsible for the accident killing his family. The men involved had made the mistake of judging him inexperienced because of his youth. His cohorts had quickly convinced them it was easier to pay him off than kill him. That was just the beginning of his blackmailing schemes. He had developed contacts throughout the country, and even in France. Some of his contacts had figured out that Duprell, while cruel and mentally capable of committing atrocious crimes and murders, was basically a coward and so had called him into their service. Thus far, his service to others had been in his own best interests. The information given to him by his superiors had allowed him to plunder and maim with some safety from capture. If he had to share the profits—well he was doing all right. Cassandra would bring him a tidy profit, and the necklace for the Queen would guarantee him a place in the realm.

The skies cleared later that evening after a week of heavy weather. Duprell skirted the dangerous shallows that might take a ship unaware and made a run for Plymouth. They should arrive on tomorrow's evening wind.

Cara nervously primped before her mirror as she waited for Duprell's arrival. One of Duprell's men had come delivering news of his eminent arrival. Cara was nervous and it showed. She must get herself under control before he arrived! She knew his tastes. He would be cruel and rough after being gone so long, and if he had managed to obtain the needed new wealth the night would be never ending. He had been stingy with his wealth lately. She needed more before she could leave him! Why was she unable to play her part these days? The sexual forays into the unknown with Duprell used to excite her, now they only bored her.

The dust from the wagons carrying his treasures was the first indication that Duprell had arrived. Cara waited until he was at the gate before descending to the foyer to meet him. She had refreshments waiting as well as his favorite drink. She wouldn't meet him at the door—he rather admired her aloofness and unwillingness to cater to his needs.

He entered with shouted orders to the men carrying a small exquisite chest to place it in the study. Immediately her curiosity was brought into play. "Get out," he growled to the men. Immediately they scattered like the rats they were. He grabbed her arm, pulling her along into the study with him. The chest was carefully placed on the side table before he pushed her back into the giant old mahogany desk. His hands were forceful as they roamed over her voluptuous breasts, squeezing and tugging her nipples into peaks. His breath was hot. The pace of his breathing

Chapter Ten

increased as he slathered her neck with his slimy tongue making his way down to her collar bone where he fastened his teeth into her as he ripped open the front of her gown with his pawing hands. His groping fingers inched and fondled as he bent her back over the desk leaving her open to his administrations. That he bothered with his own type of foreplay boded ill for the night to come. Cara already recognized the signs of a long and painful night by his advances to her now. His mouth soon followed his hands leaving painful bites along the way.

"Release me," he growled into her chest, and Cara's hands felt their way down his breeches to the lacings. He was hot and hard making the untying of the laces difficult. He ground himself against her mound as she finished with the laces. Quickly his hands wound themselves into her mass of hair clenching tightly as he forced her to her knees in front of his male member. She was roughly jerked forward and knowingly opened her mouth for his entrance. Her tongue slid up and down his member as her sharp little teeth grazed the head. Soon she had him panting. Roughly he jerked her head away as he pulled himself free of her. In the blink of an eye he had spun her around to lie face down on the desk as he rucked up her skirt. With no thought to her pleasure or pain he thrust into her hard and fast setting an unbearable pace.

He was hard and huge, larger than she could remember him being in previous encounters, and he used every bit of his strength to push into her. He was deeper than Cara could imagine a man ever getting. The pain began as he continued to thrust, grabbing her hips for a better hold. Cara began to squirm in an effort to find some relief from his assault but he was not to be denied. One hand encompassed the back of her neck to hold her still as he continued his intolerable pounding. Soft moans began to escape from her throat which only served to urge him on harder and more violently. He seemed to swell even larger as he bent over her back sinking his teeth into her shoulder, just as he released his seed into her body. He leaned heavily upon her back as he recovered his breath. But though he had released he was not sated and it began all over again.

Captured Pearl

He pulled her up from the desk then walked her over to the near wall where he pinned her tightly upright and began to pound into her again. This was even worse that the previous encounter. The angle was wrong for her to obtain any comfort from his vice-like grip and her naked breasts became irritated from the wooden panels covering the wall. Cara pulled her lip between her teeth biting into it in an effort to control the animal like moans that were trying to escape from her throat. He continued to pummel her, then with a mighty upward thrust had his second release as the scream of pain escaped from Cara's mouth.

Duprell allowed her slack body to slide down the wall to the floor as he stepped back to adjust his breeches. He enjoyed the glazed look in her eyes and her scream had only tightened his still hard erection. He left her there as he walked over to release the hidden panel in the wall in which he concealed the small chest. He sloshed himself a bit of port into a snifter as he regarded Cara's still limp form. She had only teased his sexual appetite to this point. She would be most satisfying as the night progressed. Her warm soft body was just what he needed and he was inspired by her screams of pain. Yes, it would be a delightful evening indeed.

Chapter Eleven

Angel had no idea what time it was when Garrett came down to the cabin. She only knew it was late when she heard the key in the lock. He was stumbling around and kicked his foot against the desk. He muttered an oath as he slammed down his weapons. He was tired and ready for a bath. The unforeseen added stress of the shadow ship trailing them, again, did not set well upon his shoulders. At first he had thought the evening shadows were deceiving him, but as several of the crew became uneasy with the glimpses of shadows on the waves behind them, Garrett worried they were being stalked. Pirate or the Spanish? Either way he had stayed on deck readying the men and himself for an encounter—which hadn't come. Again, there wasn't time to force the other Captain's hand, as he must appear before the Queen. It did seem that since meeting up with Angel his life had taken on many more complications.

Carefully, he made his way over to the desk and struck a match. With the lanterns lit at least he wasn't stumbling into anything. He saw that Angel was awake but at that moment there was a knock at the cabin door.

"Enter," Garrett barked. Two of the crew made their way into the cabin with a large tub and another brought in hot, steaming water. The sight of the tub brought Angel to her feet. What was he thinking? Here it was two o'clock in the morning and the man was taking a bath! Had he forgotten she was in the cabin with him?

"You're not actually going to take a bath here, are you?" questioned Angel sitting on the edge of the bed.

"Well, of course I am."

"Where will I go while you are taking your bath?"

"Angel, as far as my crew is concerned you are my wife. They will think it quite strange if you leave."

"But Miles and Josh know! I simply can't stay in here with you!"

"Angel, right now I'm too tired to do anything about the situation. There isn't anywhere else for you to go and you might as well get used to it. We'll be sharing the cabin until we reach London."

"But you can't bathe in front of me, it's not proper!"

"This is still my cabin. Besides you could probably use one yourself," said Garrett devilishly. He knew the comment would be upsetting to her. Women took pride in their appearance and it was a fair bet that she would, too.

"I beg your pardon?" she said haughtily, "there is nothing wrong with my grooming!"

As exhausted as he was from the day's events he was laughing. His spirit had returned some from the spirited banter with Angel. She really was quite easy to tease.

He started to remove his clothing.

Angel was appalled! She could not believe this was happening. She didn't know which way to look. She peered through half-closed eyes as he removed his shirt. The lantern light bounced off his broad shoulders to illuminate taunt muscles across his abdomen. She watched his strong arms as he tossed his shirt onto the chair. As he removed the rest of his clothing she looked away. Garrett stepped into the tub and slid down into the steamy water with a sigh of relief. He laid his head back with a long sigh of satisfaction allowing the hot water to ease the ache in his neck and relax the stiff muscles in his back. Heaven!

He knew she was watching him because the small hairs on the back of his neck refused to lie down. "Why don't you come scrub your husband's back, Angel?"

"What? Are you losing your mind?" she sputtered indignantly.

"Come on Angel, I won't bite. Besides I'm tired and I'm sore. This is one small service you can perform for me, if for nothing else out of gratitude, for all I've done for you."

Angel tugged her lip between her teeth as she considered his

Chapter Eleven

request. If she was honest with herself the prospect wasn't distasteful at all. His body was beautiful and she was warmed by his concern over her welfare. What would if feel like to run her soapy hands over his broad back? The idea was just too appealing and Angel found she had no control over her feet as they carried her ever closer to the tub. Slowly she picked up the sponge and soap gathering her nerve before soaping his back. At first she barely touched him. Then as she thought about everything that had been taken from her she began to scrub harder.

"Ouch! I would like to keep my skin, thank you very much!" As Garrett grabbed her wrists to halt her scrubbing he pulled harder than anticipated—pulling her into the tub with him—nightgown and all. Angel's startled yelp brought a laugh to his face.

"You!" she sputtered. "You are horrible!"

"Oh dear, I think I've made you angry." He had no idea why he was teasing her this way. All he knew was that it was great fun.

"Let go of me!" She was starting to panic.

"Very well," he said and let her go. She sank back into the water and came up sputtering. Garrett couldn't stop laughing.

"Now, it's my turn to scrub your back."

"No, you just stay away from me, Garrett!" It was the first time he had heard his given name from her lips. The sound greatly pleased him. He couldn't help but admire her spirit. She was beautiful with the water dancing on her lashes and her lovely blonde hair hanging across her face. His breath hitched as he took in the totality of her beauty. He'd have to be extra careful not to fall in love with her.

She was staring at him, embarrassed and humiliated. Here she was in a tub with a total stranger—her nightgown clinging to her body, leaving little to the imagination. As she stepped out of the tub and tried to pull the nightgown away the light from the lantern cast her in its translucent light. Garrett almost stopped breathing. Then he noticed her shaking. The cabin had chilled during his teasing interlude.

"Here," said Garrett getting out himself and handing her the large soft towel. Angel averted her eyes as she wrapped it about her cooled body. She could hear Garrett clothing himself in the robe that had been left by the desk chair. He knew that his teasing had been excessive and he felt sorry for his actions as they had caused her discomfort. "You are shivering, Angel, let me warm you."

Angel stood very still as Garrett approached refusing to look at him. Slowly he dried her body. He shielded her from his view with the towel as she disrobed, clothing herself in one of his shirts.

Not for the first time, Garrett felt fierce protectiveness well up into his heart for this girl. He remembered the feel of her soft curves when he'd helped her out of the tub, her soft skin, and the smell of her sweet breath. He would have liked to make love to her right there but he was an honorable man. Elizabeth crept into his mind. Why the Queen would have him flayed alive if he dishonored this girl and she turned out to be of social importance! Best to keep his urges under control! Would he ever know the truth about his Angel? Did it really matter?

"I'm sorry, Angel," he whispered in her ear. "The devil himself was in me tonight. It wasn't fair to use you for my entertainment. If you are truly that afraid of me I'll attempt to sleep in the chair at my desk." Garrett dearly hoped that wouldn't be so, for the chair would do nothing to relieve his tiredness.

"No, you need the bed, Sir. After all you are the Captain of the ship. Truly you must have your rest."

"As nice as that sounds, a true gentleman would never let a Lady sleep in a chair."

Angel puzzled over this dilemma. The looks flirting across her face were quite amusing to Garrett, but he knew better that to allow her to be aware of his amusement. After some small time had passed Garrett broached the subject again.

"How about we share the bunk? Let me finish, Angel. You can wrap yourself up in the blanket and I give my word to behave myself. That way we can both get some rest."

Considering the subject, Angel found to her discomfort that this idea did not alarm her. In fact it sounded very nice. With a nod of approval she turned to the bunk scooting to the far side nearest the wall. After she had settled herself comfortably, Garrett doused

Chapter Eleven

the lantern and lay down beside her. "God, I'll never sleep," was his last thought before drifting off into one of the most refreshing night's sleeps he'd ever had.

They entered London harbor early in the morning with a heavy fog overlaying the land. Garrett found the heaviness of the air was matched by a tangible weight he felt, as if something was trying to warn him of a foulness that was following him. He was still mystified by the mystery ship they had encountered during the battle off France. Then some ship had dogged their path as they made their run for London. Garrett was too skeptical to believe there was that much chance in the world. Was someone on to him? If there was dire trouble on his horizon it would be good to have friends along.

The crew began docking procedures after their ship had been identified by the harbor master and allowed in. Many of the vessels were familiar to his eye. Off to his right lay the *Ark;* in for repairs from the battle. Looked like she was getting a new mast and mainsail. Tough luck, there, Garrett thought to himself. The *Ark* would be out of commission for the better part of a fortnight. Her commander would not be happy.

Josh joined him on deck escorting Angel to the forward deck out of the way of the men, but where she could watch the goings-on. The *Green-Eyed Lady* gently rubbed her berth as the crew tied her off. Garrett sent Tanner to locate transportation for their journey to the castle. He returned shortly with a queer look upon his face.

"Captain, there is a carriage awaiting you, along with an escort from the Queen."

Josh and he exchanged troubled looks before Garrett ordered the luggage transferred to the carriage. "Miles, keep a sharp look about you. Obviously, I've made Her Majesty unhappy. Get off this ship, both you and Peters, in case we have need of you later. You know the procedure. Tanner?"

"Yes, Sir!"

"I'm leaving the *Lady* in your command. You're able and you have a quick mind, keep her safe."

Captured Pearl

"Captain," interrupted Peters. "let me stay, I'm too old to be of much help on land. The *Lady* and I are old friends, I'll see to her well being. Tanner will be of more use on land with Miles. If you're going to trust him with the ship he might as well learn the rest of the ins and outs of this game. No time to start but the present."

"Miles, what do you think?"

"He's quick and fast, plus he's good with that knife of his. He might come in handy. It works for me."

"Tanner, how are you off ship?"

"I'm your man, Captain. You gave me a chance when others wouldn't and you're more than fair. Unfortunately, I've always liked to scrap."

"All right then. Tanner goes with Miles, but stay out of trouble. There might be plenty of that later. Josh, Angel, follow me. Best not to keep Her Highness waiting."

They were met at the end of the walkway by six of the court guard. They were all business and Garrett knew better that to think he'd get any information out of them. They entered the carriage in silence and maintained it for the trip to court. Angel could feel the tangible worry from the men accompanying her. Josh looked particularly fierce. Garrett's face could have been carved from stone. Right after they passed through the gates Josh removed a handsome green velvet box from his coat and handed it to Garrett who quietly slipped it inside his jacket.

The carriage stopped just short of the steps leading up to the main entrance of the castle. Another set of guards waited for them there. They were led down the hall to the anteroom where they were bid to wait on Her Majesty's pleasure. The honor guards stood erect along each side of the large receiving room, their clothing reflected the royal colors. Garrett chose to stand, but Josh seated Angel and then himself. He quietly patted her hand in mute comfort. Much to their surprise their wait was not long. They reached the two wooden doors, which were immediately opened and they were allowed to enter the royal hall.

Garrett preceded Angel and Josh into the Audience Room. The Queen was truly magnificent in her robes of state. Her attire

Chapter Eleven

was appropriate for a Queen, very regal and stately, perhaps a little too colorful and ornate for Garrett's tastes. She almost seemed larger that life as they approached the throne of England. Her look was indomitable, but Garrett was relieved to see that she wore the emerald necklace his father had presented to her. Things were not so bad as all that if she was adorned with his family's gift. As he reached the base of her throne he bent a knee in homage to his ruler. He heard the soft swish of Angel's skirts as she and Josh followed suit.

Elizabeth waved away her ladies in waiting and dismissed everyone from the room. Not even her secretary of state, Lord Burghley her greatest confidant, was allowed to remain.

"Arise and explain to us these rumors we have been subjected to of your marriage!" Elizabeth's tone was harsh, but Garrett had encountered her temper before and seen it at its worst.

"Your Majesty, I have always been a loyal subject. Nothing has occurred to change that. I have not married without my sovereign's permission, but only used this as a means of protection for one that could not protect herself. May I present Angel, the young woman in question?"

With a nod of her head permission was given and Garrett motioned Angel forward. Angel sank into a deep curtsy before the Queen hoping no one would notice her shaking.

"Explain, thyself!"

Garrett took the initiative to unfold the story of his meeting with Angel. When he reached the part where she had become the Birmingham houseguest, Josh took over. Angel added the bits and pieces of her memories that had begun to surface, hoping the Queen would believe her.

Just when Angel thought they must carry on this story forever a gentleman appeared and walking over to the Queen remarked, "Come now Your Majesty, much of this you've heard before. Why not put the man out of his misery and tell him all is forgiven?" Sir Riley's engaging smile was bestowed on the Queen and she was unable to ignore him.

"Of course he is forgiven! We are extremely pleased to know

there are some gentlemen of the realm that still sport the chivalry of the Court. However, this rumor of marriage has greatly upset us!"

"My Queen, please accept this small token of my family's regard for its sovereign." With those words Garrett withdrew the green velvet box from his coat presenting it to the Queen. Sir Riley came forward to receive it, where upon he opened it for the Queen to view. The white satin backing of the box perfectly set off the green emerald and the attending yellow diamonds. The smile of appreciation that came to Elizabeth's face was enough for Garrett to know that he was out of the woods for now. Like a small child at Christmas she beckoned for Sir Riley to hand her the box so that she might more easily view the gem inside.

"My, my," she exclaimed hardly able to maintain her composure, "I'm not going to ask where you found this treasure."

"And I won't tell," laughed Garrett. He was more relaxed now and felt confident. He knew Bess. She could be very intimidating and was capable of making an encounter with her uncomfortable when she chose.

"Garrett, my boy," she said still clasping the necklace in her hands," it is my pleasure to accept your generous offering, but now on to business. As you guessed Riley has kept me informed of your strange guest. How do you plan to find the answers for this mystery?"

Josh stepped forward. "Your Highness, even now plans are in motion. Angel recognized a book in my father's library as being very similar to one she remembered from her childhood. I only wait for my contacts to return with information on the owners of said book. Hopefully that information will help us to pinpoint our young Miss's origins."

Garrett could tell from the look in Bess's eye that this would not be good enough. She thoughtfully stroked Garrett's necklace as she took an all encompassing look at Angel.

"Come here, child," she beckoned to Angel. Angel slowly made her way toward the Queen, as Elizabeth looked her up and down once more.

"It has not come to our ears of any young Lady of the realm

Chapter Eleven

to be missing. So whom might you be, hum?"

"I wish I knew, Your Majesty."

"You have the look of nobility, and your social graces are quite good, but we have never seen you before. Perhaps you have been hidden away for some reason?

"We have decided to help you. Lord Jamison has been ever faithful to our cause; therefore we shall do likewise. We have decided that you shall be present at the next royal gathering in ten day's time. We shall invite all the prominent families of the realm. Perhaps one will recognize you. Have no fear child," the Queen stated, "no harm shall come to you in our presence."

Garrett found himself highly displeased with the Queen's turn of affairs. What if some scoundrel showed up to claim Angel? How would they know if they had any relationship to her at all? She was a beautiful young woman, there was no telling what might happen to her!

"Your pardon, Majesty, but how will we know if the claim made is in Angel's best interests?"

The Queen gave Garrett a chilling look. "Lord Jamison, it pains our person that you should have such little faith in your Queen."

"Your pardon, Majesty, I do not fault your intentions. After serving as the girl's guardian for this time I find myself rather protective of her well being. No insult was intended."

"It is quite unlike the Jamison I have known to involve himself with the problems of any young Lady. Perhaps you should search your feelings for her before someone else claims her.

"We shall see to the assigning of rooms here at the palace for you and your party, Lord Jamison. The young Lady shall also need a wardrobe if she is to appear at court."

"Pardon, Your Majesty, Lord Jamison has already provided me with an exquisite wardrobe and a ball gown."

"Well, it seems you are full of surprises this day, Lord Jamison," the Queen replied with a twinkle in her eye.

Garrett didn't like that look. She was plotting. He knew it, and she knew that he knew it!

Captured Pearl

"One more item before we allow you to be on your way. Tomorrow at 10 in the morning we will have you all present back here. Since you are so concerned for our young Lady's welfare we see fit to pronounce you her guardian until her family can be found. We shall have the papers drawn up for tomorrow. Lord Birmingham, you will stand as witness before the crown since you have already a vested interest in the outcome." With that Elizabeth rose to take her departure.

The threesome bowed before her departure then turned to leave. Garrett would have preferred to take his usual room above the tavern where he usually stayed but that was not to be. Josh had permanent rooms in the castle as he spent the majority of his year with the court. As they walked toward Angel's apartments Josh queried, "What do you suppose she meant by the 'vested interest' part? She is definitely plotting Garrett."

"Well, you are the one that has the gift for intrigue and court politics. Figure it out man and fast!"

Angel couldn't help but giggle at the look on the two men's faces. The Queen had confounded both of them with one delft statement. What had she meant?

Garrett sent word to the ship to have their personal belongings brought over, and then sent a message to Miles and Tanner. If he was going to have to suffer the fools at court he might as well have company doing it! He informed the staff that two of his men would be joining him and to see that suitable rooms were made ready.

Taking a look around him, Garrett found himself impressed with Bess's choice for his accommodations. There were two rooms off the main audience room, the bedroom and a type of study that was filled with charts and journals. Why that clever old busybody! He'd bet his last coin that these were the rooms Sir Drake used when he was in town. Bess was trying to put him off guard and damn she was succeeding. He might as well get comfortable it would be awhile before the men arrived, or his luggage. He entered the study and began to examine the charts and journals

Chapter Eleven

that filled the bookcases against the wall.

Miles and Tanner received word from Garrett to return to the court and to seek him out. Tanner would have rushed off immediately (a show of his inexperience), but Miles waited for the code words ensuring the message was truly from the Captain.

"Your Captain's love has green eyes," the man offered.

Miles nodded. The message was true. Miles took a minute to remind Tanner of their mission explaining to him to never trust a message that didn't contain the special code words. They quickly finished their pints and then made off for court. Miles was anxious to arrive, as he had been hoping he might chance a visit with the lovely Lady Camilla. She happened to be one of the attending ladies for the Queen. She was a lovely widow woman of approximately his own age. Their chance visits were few and far between, but the spark that had drawn them together at first glance continued to burn just as brightly from absence. Somewhere in the distant future Miles knew his sailing days would have to end. Lady Camilla was what he had always hoped for in a woman. His only doubt lay in his social status; even widowed he doubted the Queen would allow a Lady to bond with a mere sailor man, even if he was Captain Jamison's right-hand man.

Miles continued to ponder as they made their way to court. He couldn't say he was a repulsive man—and he had all his teeth, along with most of his hair! A lot of Lords of his years could not say the same. He was tall for a man that had spent his life at sea. Perhaps she wanted a shorter man? Ah, he was what he was! The Captain had never had any reason to fault him and that should be enough of a recommendation to a Lady. He had managed to put aside a nicely sum over the years and the Captain had allowed those of seniority in his crew to invest in his family business insuring that those who retired after loyal service would never find themselves out on the streets. That Captain! What a man he was! Miles knew many sailors that once their sailing days were finished their Captains left them stranded portside with no hopes for the future.

When they arrived at court, Miles and Tanner were shown to

Garrett's chambers, which were right down the hall from the quarters the two men would share. Even after all the times he had been here, Miles was not comfortable in these surroundings. Tanner seemed to take it all in stride. He'd make a fine Captain's man when he got some age on him. Garrett answered their knock beckoning them inside.

"Did you find out anything down on the docks?" Garrett asked.

"No, Captain, weren't there long enough but to just get settled in. The boy and I will head back this evening to see what we can pick up," replied Miles.

"Leave early and get yourselves both measured for dress clothes. It seems the Queen will be having a party, which Angel and I must attend. I'd like to know who's at my back," he said with a grin.

Miles uttered a groan. The Captain knew how he hated these functions. If it weren't for the fact that it gave him a chance to see Camilla he'd throw a fuss about attending. Might be interesting to see how young Tanner handled all the court Ladies that would be fawning over his good looks and youth!

"Aye, aye, Captain. I'll see that the young man gets measured for some fancy clothes." Tanner had a pained look on his face now also and Miles began to feel some better. The boy might be excited by the prospect of a court party but like any man of worth he detested the necessity of a new wardrobe. "Get used to it boy. If you're going to be the Captain's man court is part of the job."

Garrett fetched his coin pouch and generously handed out coin to both men. "Miles give my calling card to the tailor and tell him to add your tailoring to my account. He should remember you from previous visits."

After further discussion of the upcoming nightly events Miles and Tanner were off. Garrett braced himself for a night of courtly manners and was comforted by the thought that Angel would be at his side.

Chapter Twelve

Duprell's ship had slunk into the harbor minutes behind the *Lady*. He had come to London to have the mounting of the black pearl accomplished after setting things in order at his Estate.

He was still seething after finding Cara opening the secret panel to cast her eyes upon the pearl. That little bitch was getting way too nosey! Imagine, thinking he would throw such a treasure away on her! All her mewing and fawning had not fooled him one bit. She only loved his money and when she found out there was little to be garnered from him she would become dangerous. That was why he had brought her along on this trip. His men could keep an eye on her when she wasn't entertaining him in his bed. At least Cara had enough wits about her to realize she was now treading on dangerous ground. After the night he had just given her she would be minding her place for a few days. Perhaps he could find himself a new paramour while he was here. His men had always followed the Welsh lass with their eyes. When he had no further use for her she might provide a tasty treat for them.

But he would have to do something about that old crone of a Mother first. That woman knew too many of his contacts after working in his household for so long. When Margaret and her man had first come to work for him, after being dismissed by Jamison, he had thought to use their knowledge to further his gains against the Jamison family. At first things had gone well, but gradually her man had proved too greedy for his own good and Duprell had had him eliminated. Margaret had no where else to turn and so had proven to be an excellent housekeeper while Cara was small. When Cara had run off the old woman had begged to stay in case her little girl would come back and not find her at the Duprell house. Again, Duprell had worked things to his advantage—then

Captured Pearl

Cara had turned up in Jamison's bed!

The only enterprising event of this whole trip had been finding out the ship he had been shadowing—the one that had almost had him at Calais—was none other than Jamison's vessel. What a piece of information for his contact! He could certainly damage Jamison's ability to travel anonymously by the time he was through here in London.

He exited the ship heading for the jeweler. There was no one else with the talent of Shingler's in all of London. Duprell had not used the man's services since he had sold the emerald necklace out from under his father. Only now, because there was no one else that could do justice to the black pearl, would he lower himself to go to the man.

Duprell rented a carriage rather than walk the distance to the jeweler's shop. On the ride he reveled in the glory of presenting his gift to the Queen. His fortunes would surely change after Elizabeth saw the pearl and diamond necklace. When he reached the shop of Shingler he dismissed the livery rather than expend coin on a carriage at rest.

A small bell rang announcing his presence to the shopkeeper. A young man, probably the craftsman's apprentice, came out to answer the summons.

"How may I be of assistance to you, Sir?"

Duprell knew the protocol. The young man would look the jewel over for its worthiness to have its setting prepared by the family, and, if qualifying, would then summon the old man to inspect it. Duprell removed the case from his coat and handed it over reverently to the young apprentice.

Even with his experience the young man was clearly impressed by the pearl and its accompanying stones.

"A moment please, Sir," and with that he disappeared behind the curtain, which separated the storefront from the work area. Shortly, the older Shingler, the man Duprell remembered from his youth, appeared. He opened the case, pulling out his glass to examine the stones before commenting.

"Very lovely, Sir. Quite unusual as I am sure you know. Your

Chapter Twelve

plans for these gems?"

"A gift for Her Majesty. I have an idea for the setting I would like."

"Proceed please."

Duprell, continuing, outlined the setting with the diamonds and the string of creamy pearls that would line the necklace and then the diamond clasp.

"You do realize that while the craftsmanship you desire is well within the talents of this family, the cost will not be nominal."

Duprell affirmed his willingness to expend the needed sum, whereupon the jeweler began to sketch out the design.

"Whose name might I put on this order?"

"Donovan Duprell."

Clear distaste appeared fleetingly on the man's face. "I am sorry to inform you, Sir, but due to previous problems with your family, payment will be required in advance."

Duprell's face grew red at the insult! How dare the man impugn his credit!

"You should feel lucky that I should allow you the privilege of working on these stones after that prank you pulled on my father. Selling the stones to a higher bidder after promising them to the Duprells!"

The jeweler puffed up like an angry alley cat before lowering his voice to state, "I will have you know, Sir, I held that necklace awaiting payment from your father for better than a month before looking to recompense my family for its cost. If your father had attended to his business there would have been no need for the altercation that resulted!"

Duprell was left speechless, momentarily. Of course, he had always suspected, but to have the man put it into words. The thought that others knew about the family straits rubbed him raw, like a badly-fitting shoe.

The guildsman was too much the businessman to want to lose this job. Money was secondary to the reputation of setting the black pearl. "Sir, perhaps we can come to an agreement amiable to both our families. I am willing to proceed with the required work if you would be willing to forward a small sum in good faith of the final payment to come."

Duprell continued to fume, this was the only man that could do justice to the gems. But he would have the last say.

"Do not bother to fret yourself man, I am more that capable of paying your sum in full!" With those words Duprell pulled out a small, but brilliantly-colored, ruby and spun it on the counter. "That should be enough payment for the work involved. Are we agreed?"

The jeweler held the small stone up to the light and peered at it intently. His tight smile told Duprell all that he needed to know. They agreed that Duprell would return in two day's time to approve the final design before the actual setting of the stones took place.

With family business finished, Duprell needed to catch up on other ventures. He made his way down to the docks and entered the Black Frog, the tavern where he regularly met his contact. The man may, or may not, be here tonight but his presence would get back to the man who would then arrange a meeting at his convenience. He ordered a pint and sat back to watch the local seedy patrons that came and went.

And what was he to do about Lucas? The man wouldn't wait forever for his bride. He would have to pressure his men to find some sign of her and do it quickly. He couldn't have Lucas taking back his land and property. This deal would put the family name back into social circles as well as make them solvent.

The night became late as Duprell continued to nourish his pint. He'd had his men deliver Cara to the family house earlier, but he felt no need to return to her side. He was losing interest in her.

Cara sat at the Duprell townhouse on the north side of London sipping a brandy in the drawing room. After tonight she knew that Duprell was losing interest in her. He would not be tossing her aside—she would see to that! She knew his secrets. Between her mother's scheming and her ability to cat around the house, they were in possession of many of Duprell's secrets. It

Chapter Twelve

would not be wise to cross the man, but she would not be cast aside without anything! She had had him right where she had wanted him until Cassandra had shown up! When she had shown up as an adolescent orphaned niece, Cara had never dreamed the girl would become such a threat. Duprell had become obsessed with the girl and much to Cara's surprise she had not seen that coming!

She needed Garrett back! She missed the way he had looked at her, and the way he had loved her. His family standing was not in question, as was Duprell's, nor was his family fortune in dire straits. There must be some way she could get him back! Perhaps the way back into his bed could be obtained by bringing him some of Duprell's secrets!

The more she turned that thought over in her mind the more positive she became that this was her answer! Garrett would surely be outraged by Duprell's two-sidedness. To bring the fiend before the Queen for justice would surely put Garrett in her debt. And her payment? Perhaps she could string it into the marriage she had wanted earlier. If she could, she would be set for life! To be Lady Jamison would be the perfect ending to her relationship with Duprell! Carefully, Cara set down her brandy and began twirling sensuously about the room, curtsying before the Queen and entertaining other Lords and Ladies. As she played out the scene in her mind, her scheme to regain Garrett began to take form. Her mother would be the perfect accomplice. Margaret would do anything for her daughter!

Duprell ordered himself a last pint. The hour was growing late with no sign of his contact appearing this evening. He'd savor this ale and then head to the house. A swarthy-looking man missing two front teeth served his tankard.

"Be ye interested in a game of chance, man?" asked the stranger.

Duprell perked up at the obscure reference. This might be his man.

"What did you have in mind, my friend?"

Captured Pearl

"What think ye of the game of shell?"

Duprell nodded his agreement. If he won the first three this was his man. The shells were placed face down on the table and then the man removed a pea from his pocket, placing it under one of the shells. Slowly at first and then ever quickening, he scuffled the shells about, finally lining them up in a row.

"Pick."

Duprell tapped the one in the middle, which was revealed to hold the elusive pea. Again the man scuffled the shells, casting them about at a frantic pace.

"Pick."

Again, Duprell tapped the one in the middle — again, revealing the pea.

The third time the man slowed the scuffle but used exaggerated care to make it seem as if the pea was moving ever closer to the middle position. However, this time Duprell tapped the left shell. When lifted — there sat the pea.

"What type of payment do you require?"

"Information," stated Duprell.

"Then return here two nights hence and watch for the man in the red cloak." The stranger rose and left the table skirting the many patrons making for the door. Duprell finished off his ale and then rose, leaving the tavern for the night.

Chapter Thirteen

Angel awoke stretching luxuriantly in the large, comfortable bed. She felt as if she were caught somewhere between a girl's most splendid fantasy and a nightmare. The room was wonderful, and the maid last night had been friendly and kind. But she found herself anxiously waiting for the monster to appear and turn this into a nightmare. A Lady Camilla had come to visit and partake in the evening meal with her. Lady Camilla had explained that she was a Lady-in-Waiting for the Queen but for Angel's visit Camilla would be available to guide her about the castle affairs and etiquette.

This morning Angel must appear before the Queen for some falderal about making Garrett her guardian. How could she do that? Maybe she didn't want a guardian, and who knew; what if she was too old for such a thing? Angel twirled this about in her mind until she almost made herself dizzy. She might as well get up and go about the process of getting dressed for this meeting.

What to wear? Always a woman's dilemma. The gowns Garrett had commissioned for her were lovely and expensive! Had he somehow known of things to come? Or was the man simply used to the finest money could buy? What to pick? Hum. The blue velvet was nice but perhaps a bit too warm for this day. What about the green silk? She was particularly taken with this gown. Maybe it was too rich for this event? Then her eyes fell on the amber-colored gown with the undershirt of creamy yellow. Striking in its simplicity, Garrett had chosen these colors stating that they brought out the highlights in her golden hair, and the amber flecks in her eyes. The thought of pleasing him warmed her soul, even though Angel wasn't sure about having him as her guardian. His smiles were rare. When genuinely given they could make her heart sing.

The appointment with the Queen wasn't until ten so there was time to break her fast. Angel pulled the rope by the bed summoning a maid. Quite strange to her way of thinking. She didn't think she had ever had servants before. One appeared shortly from the servants' entrance. Angel expressed her wishes for something light, as her stomach still wasn't sure that it was in favor of the day's activities. The girl helped her to dress before leaving to fetch her meal.

While she waited, Angel pulled back the curtain from the long, narrow window looking out onto the courtyard. It was already bustling with activity. Guards were moving about as well as servants scurrying to see to the demands of their Lords and Ladies. She preferred the view from her room at the Birmingham residence. There the gardens had soothed her soul and the peacefulness of the place had brought her a calm amidst all the turmoil in her life. This scene only made her more aware of the bustle and franticness of her life and the people about her. She turned her back on the scene before she became depressed.

A knock on the door diverted her attention. "Come in." Lady Camilla swept into the room followed by the maid with a meal for at least two!

"I encountered Rachael here on my way to greet you this morning and have invited myself to break fast with you. I do hope that you don't mind. I thought you might use the company before heading to your appointment."

Lady Camilla generously went through the protocol with Angel for the upcoming ceremony, informing her of what would take place and what she should do.

"Most importantly, dear, remain respectful no matter what. Queen Elizabeth believes she is seeing to your welfare, and Lord Jamison is a favorite of hers, so remember to be properly thankful to your sovereign.

"Now, do you play Ruff and Honours, dear? We really must do something to pass the time until you are summoned."

Angel did not, but this did not deter Lady Camilla. With

Chapter Thirteen

careful consideration for Angel's inexperience at the game, she laid out the rules as they began to play. Lady Camilla was fair company enlightening Angel about the Lords and Ladies that she would encounter during her stay at court and so the time passed quickly until there was a knock on the door.

Camilla answered the guardsman who had come to escort them to the receiving room, assuring Angel that she would stay by her side. After all, she was to witness for Angel—as Josh was witness to Lord Jamison.

After all the fuss and worry that had enveloped her Angel was a little put off by the quickness and simplicity of the occasion. Garrett promised to care for her, see to her welfare and well being, and to keep her safe from harm, while Angel promised to obey her guardian until the day either the Queen, or her marriage, released her from Garrett's care. "Sounded an awful lot like a marriage contract," Angel thought to herself. Then the Queen summoned refreshments for everyone and it was over. They were released from the Queen's presence to go their own ways while the sovereign got back to the business of running her kingdom.

The days dragged on—Angel thought, not that there wasn't always something going on, but she was edgy and nervous. It was like waiting for the monster to leap out from around the corner. She had the most awful feeling that if she stayed here, everything kind and good that she had come to know would disappear. Garrett was ever the gentleman, coming to visit her each day, and escorting her around the castle gardens to small receptions and teas, and once, to a formal dinner with the Queen. He informed her the Queen's formal party would take place in less than two weeks time and the Queen had sent out the call to most all the nobles of the land.

Josh had heard back from his contact in Greece; they could eliminate that book. This left Venice and France. Angel could tell that there was worry from the men that it would be the book in France that she remembered. Lady Camilla explaining that the French and the English weren't on much better terms than they were with the Spanish, and that Paris was a hot bed for intrigue and spies. This was why they were worried.

One night Garrett and Josh appeared at her door with Lady Camilla declaring they were taking her for an outing. There was a circus in Piccadilly that she simply must see. Lady Camilla expressed great interest in the outing but Angel noticed that once they arrived and were joined by Miles and Tanner most of Lady Camilla's time was spent eyeing up the older sailor. She began to think that Garrett and Josh had schemed to throw the two together, for it was obvious they cared for each other.

After several acts, Miles conceded that the Ladies were probably thirsty and offered to fetch mulled wine. Angel found herself smiling when Lady Camilla insisted on accompanying him as her tastes were quite refined and she would need to select her own favorite brew. Tanner, with a wink, included himself in the action stating they would need more hands if they were to bring something back for everyone. As the threesome disappeared into the crowd Garrett began to laugh. Soon both Angel and Josh joined in. Poor Miles! They had managed to arrange for him to meet his ladylove and then confound him at every turn!

Camilla, Miles, and Tanner made their way through the press of people until they found a wine vendor that met with their approval. Tanner offered to wait in line to place their order giving the two time to talk in private.

"Miles," Camilla looked at him with tear-filled eyes, "I thought I'd never see you again."

"But of course you would," Miles stated feeling wonderfully young again. "Why would you think I wouldn't come back?"

She looked at him shyly and took his rough callused hand in hers. "You and Lord Jamison lead a very dangerous life. Some day I am afraid the sea will take you from me. I've missed you so much. I haven't stopped thinking of you!"

Miles squeezed her soft, delicate hands. "I have missed you, too. Granted I have been busy on the Jamison Estate and tending to his Lordship's business, but when I knew we were sailing for London I felt ten years younger!"

They talked and held each other's hands until a shrill whis-

Chapter Thirteen

tle from Tanner brought Mile's attention to the fact that the young man was dexterously trying to carry six mulled wine goblets on his own. Camilla and Miles hurried to save Tanner from the fiasco of losing the wine he had so valiantly stood in line for, carefully readjusting until each member of the party carried two goblets.

The rest of the party was where they had left them—still enjoying the entertainment provided. The wine was a welcome relief as the air had begun to turn cool. Angel was delighted by the light, warm taste as it warmed her body. She found after finishing the drink she felt quite jolly, and her companions seemed very entertained by her behavior. After the show they wandered about the streets eyeing the vendors and occasionally the men would purchase a trinket for one of the women or themselves. Angel saw tears glistening from Lady Camilla's eyes when Miles purchased a silver brooch and then presented it to the Lady in question.

As the group made their way back to the castle, Miles and Camilla fell behind. They talked of their plans, and hopefully, their future. Miles would have to leave again to follow his Captain leaving the only woman that he had ever loved, promising to return for her. Camilla would have to contend with her family and the Queen when it became known that she loved a commoner and wished to marry a man below her station. Miles promised to approach the Captain for Garrett was a natural problem solver and had the ear of the Queen.

Chapter Fourteen

Duprell's return to the jeweler's shop found him in a much better frame of mind. He would be meeting with his contact tonight at the Black Frog to exchange information. The spicy tidbit of the identity of the *Allegro,* as the Spanish called Jamison's ship, was sure to reap him rewards. He strode jauntily along the street considering the turn of events since coming to London. Cara had even seemed to have a change of heart. Oh, he wasn't fooled that her affections had changed but perhaps she had learned to proceed with caution. Her waspish tongue seemed to have been curbed for the moment. Of course, he was suspicious, the woman had only her own best interests at heart, mayhap she had decided that he was in her best interest.

He entered Shingler's shop with a jingle of the small bell. The apprentice stuck his head through the curtain, then disappeared. Shortly the elder Shingler emerged, one hand carrying the design for the pearl. Duprell examined the design closely—looking for flaws in the design. Shingler wasn't considered a master of his craft by being shoddy. Duprell could find nothing to complain about. The man had captured perfectly the idea in his head.

"How long?"

"Two—three weeks."

"Too long! I need it within a fortnight."

"My Lord! Great works can not be rushed, why just molding the setting, fitting the stones, and cooling time will consume at least a week! Then to fasten them together . . ."

Duprell interrupted with a growl. "A fortnight!" and with those words he spun another small gem, this time a garnet, on the counter. "There will be another when the job is completed."

The jeweler looked at the gem and then Duprell and nodded

his acquiescence.

Now, to secure an audience with the Queen. Considering that his family had been in disfavor for some years the prospect was daunting. How to get in? Duprell turned these thoughts over as he hired a carriage to convey him to the gates of Elizabeth's court. There must be a way!

When he reached the courtyard he was met by an officer of the court who took his name, then glancing at a parchment retorted, "Your family name is on the list for the ceremony in ten days hence to celebrate the defeat of the Spanish Armada. The affair will begin with conversation and dinner proceeding to the celebratory dance and ceremonies. Here is your invitation. You have graciously saved me the time and trouble of finding a rider to take it to your country Estate. I will place your name on the Queen's list for interviews and you may approach her then."

Duprell couldn't believe his luck! The timing couldn't be more perfect. The pearl necklace would be done, his contacts satisfied, and his family back in the Queen's graces all within a fortnight! He supposed he could take Cara on his arm for decoration. No one could gainsay that the woman wasn't strikingly beautiful, and heaven knew where she had picked it up—but she could have pretty manners when the occasion suited her. He'd have to invest in a gown for her as well as new apparel for himself. Duprell hated the thought of parting with any coin but what must be, must be. He made his way to a respectable clothier where he approved the items for himself and the color scheme he wanted. The man recommended the dressier across the street for Cara. Duprell entered the shop of Mrs. Garner and immediately saw the cloth for Cara. The striking red and black velvet would match the color scheme he had picked for himself. Now, to get the woman to agree.

Mrs. Lewis had a long memory. She had come to London to visit her sister, Mrs. Garner, and to help with the massive orders coming in for the Queen's celebration. Her sharp eyes had not dimmed over time so she recognized Lord Duprell when he entered. Personally, she couldn't stand the man. But business was

Chapter Fourteen

business and the tales she would be able to tell if she did his work!

"May I help, your Lordship?" She knew how to stroke the feathers of the most reluctant cock.

"Perhaps. I am looking for a gown for a Lady in these colors, but it must be done within a fortnight. And it must be a magnificent ball gown."

"Attending the celebration at court are you? Well, that is a bit of a rush, but if you can have the Lady here, say in an hour's time I can start immediately." It was driving Mrs. Lewis to distraction to know who the Lady was!

"That will not pose a problem as the Lady is in town. I shall return with her within the hour."

Mrs. Lewis made a supreme effort not to rub her hands together in glee! Oh what stories she would have to regale her competitors with!

Funny, how the world turned. First the Fathers of the two Lords brought their wives here for their ball gowns now the sons followed the same pattern. She could still remember with vivid detail the gowns chosen by the Ladys' Duprell and Jamison. Even as the dresser's apprentice she had had a sharp eye for detail. Both she and her sister had helped fashion the former Ladies stunning creations. She hoped this Royal ball had a happier ending than the last.

She, of course, had married and moved to Plymouth while her sister, Mrs. Garner, had taken over this shop when her Mistress had retired.

Cara heard the slamming of the iron gate and wondered who was coming. She quickly closed the desk drawer to look out the window to see Duprell striding up the walk. Damn! How would she explain her being in his study? She quickly looked around. He would never believe she came in for a book. Duprell would assume she was snooping, and he'd be right. Her eye fell on the small unobtrusive box on the mantle. It looked like a matchbox but she knew it held a small amount of gems that could be used as collateral if the need arose. Perfect! She'd be toying with them

Captured Pearl

when he came in. This would be so like her that he'd never think that she had been digging for his most intimate secrets! Cara seated herself in the leather highback chair with the box and began to run her fingers through them before Duprell entered.

Immediately he became enraged that she would be fondling his gems! That woman had a nose for gems and jewelry. Cara merely smiled, "Very nice Donovan—and such an imaginative hiding place, too."

"Put them back Cara," he growled. "We haven't time for this. You have a fitting at Mrs. Garner's within the hour."

"What?!"

"You heard me. The Queen is throwing a celebration within a fortnight and I have been invited. I'm taking you to be fitted for a gown so you may decorate my arm that night. Do you not wish to attend?"

Of course, she wished to attend! Cara quickly dashed upstairs to fetch her cloak. As she descended the stairs she wondered how he had gotten the invitation. His family had been censored from court for years! Garrett would be sure to be there! She must move ahead quickly with her plans!

"You should send for my mother to keep the house and to help me to dress if we are going to stay that long, Darling."

Duprell grumped, but the woman was right. Margaret would be needed. He'd send the ship to pick her up. It would be much faster than travel by coach. Cara was deposited in the carriage where silence reigned until they approached the shop of Mrs. Lewis' sister.

"Exactly how magnificent am I going to be?" asked Cara.

"Price isn't an object. Please try to use some taste. Mrs. Garner and her sister already have the cloth. Remember you're going to see the Queen."

With that Duprell escorted her into the shop. Introductions were exchanged then Duprell left promising to return in two hours' time. Mrs. Lewis eyed up the sensuous woman in her shop and immediately took a dislike to her. Too bold, too loose, but very eye-catching. The red and black suited her. The colors of power

Chapter Fourteen

and treachery. The woman was definitely treacherous, and the seamstress would bet she wanted power.

"The Lord has requested these colors. Do you have a style in mind, Miss?"

Cara minded Duprell's parting comment and politely asked the seamstress for her opinion.

"Smart, too," Mrs. Lewis thought. "A dangerous combination." She quickly replied, "I'll get some sketches for you to look at. Then we can discuss what would look best on you."

Finally Cara settled on a style, very up to date with the bodice to alternate between the red and black with a stunning cream underskirt. Next came the decoration of the gown. Again, Cara asked for Mrs. Lewis' suggestions.

"How ornate do you wish to be?"

"I truly do like much more than is probably tasteful, Madam. Your help would be appreciated." Cara was not so out of touch that she didn't know that Duprell had commissioned one of the best.

"Something that will set off the colors and your complexion yet not overwhelm the gown's design. My suggestion would be to have a twisted silver braided chain to decorate the bodice as well as your belt. We could have the local jeweler make up ear bobs for you as well, as I see that your ears are pierced, Miss. I know it sounds plain, yet if you will let me once again guide you the results will be stunning."

For once Cara allowed someone else to chart her destiny and agreed with the dressmaker. Next came the measurements for the gown. By the time they had finished Duprell was walking through the door.

"Please return with the Lady in four days for a fitting, my Lord." The appointment was confirmed and the meeting was over. Cara was deposited back at the house while Duprell made his way to the meeting with his contact.

The Black Frog was unusually crowded for this early in the afternoon. When Duprell inquired the cause the tavern owner growled, "Ah, it's that celebration the Queen is throwing. Every rat has crawled out to see if they can skim the Lords and Ladies. Seeing as you've become a regular, remember to watch your purse. I've a fine stew this day."

Duprell ordered a bowl and a pint to wash it down. Then relaxed to wile away the time until his appointment. He was ready to take to the sea again for being on land for long truly bored him. Not enough action by far, and his own particular brand of entertainment was frowned upon by most of the general public. He supposed he would have to rein in his appetites if he were going to be at court. In a town as big as London there was probably a spot he could find that would cater to his needs when he finally eliminated Cara.

His contact should pay well for the information he had. Besides the fact that Duprell now had the identity of the Captain of the *Allegro*.

Another piece of information would be well received—there was one last-ditch effort under way to repeal the Protestant faith as that of the nation and he had the names of the leaders. Duprell, because of his French father being Catholic, was privy to such information. It had suited his purposes to allow the Catholics some access to his land allowing them to think that he sympathized with them. The French would delight in stirring up more trouble for England. Yes, this day was going to end on a very productive note indeed.

Josh groaned when he opened the door of his apartments to find his entire family standing at the threshold. Good Lord, he had been invaded! The girls were all atwitter with the prospect of the celebration. Not that they hadn't been to court before but surely he could see that this was different. Like chicks in the henhouse they continued to babble on. Where were Angel, and Garrett, and when could they go explore London?

Josh's mother had a twinkle in her eye obviously due to his discomfort and his father had a look that, well, Josh hadn't seen before. Almost like he was privy to news that he knew Josh wanted but didn't have.

Chapter Fourteen

"We've informed the household staff we have arrived for the festivities dear, and our apartments should be ready before long," Lady Patience stated. "Girls settle down this instant! You'll not be going to London town if you can't exhibit better manners than this!"

Immediately, his sisters conformed to their mother's wishes. Not that she would actually keep them from touring the town, but she might make them wait for days! They settled quietly about the room giving their brother a needed breather before the next storm. How his father kept his head with these females underfoot at home was beyond his comprehension.

"Let me see if I can answer your questions: Angel, I believe, is on the south court lawn with Lady Camilla playing lawn ball with several of the other Ladies, Garrett is visiting with some of the other Lords that have import business—and visit the town? Well, that will be up to Mother and Father to decide. Perhaps we can discuss it at dinner where Garrett and Angel are joining me."

The girls squealed in delight, then quickly quieted again. Patience smiled and his father nodded at his keen answer. Lord, save him from the intrigues of family life, court business was much simpler and easier to understand if you asked him!

Angel was having the best time! This lawn ball was invigorating and silly. But the Ladies were all good sports. The best part of this game was that it had allowed Miles and Camilla time together again. She was so glad she could be the reason they were together. It was perfect! Camilla was assigned by the Queen to be her guide at court, and Miles was assigned by Garrett to protect her. Well, do you suppose that Garrett was plotting on Miles' behalf as well?

It wouldn't surprise her at all! Garrett was keen on observing the behavior of others. He surely knew the two were in love. There had been several times during the last few days when it seemed that Miles and Camilla were thrown together. It would be a shame if things didn't work out for them.

Then a flurry of activity hit the lawn party as if an August snowstorm had descended upon them! The Birmingham Ladies had arrived! The three girls were all a bustle wanting to hear everything from Angel even though they had hardly been parted. Lady Patience chided her charges gently as the Ladies on the lawn seemed to be amused by the girls' activity, rather than annoyed. Soon the women on the lawn went back to their game and things resumed a somewhat normal routine.

Garrett had been watching from the window of Lord Birhym's apartments when the family had arrived. He smiled to himself enjoying the frantic gaiety of the Ladies. The Lords were taking a brief respite from their planning of the Queen's campaign against the Spanish to discuss other pressing matters of the sea. It seemed the scuttling of wounded ships had become a matter of some concern. If a ship ran into trouble there was little chance of her making it home as of late. Were there more of these pirates coming forth, or had the regulars become braver? A hard question to answer. Something would have to be done soon before the honest merchants refused to chance sailing the seas. Many ships of the merchant class where not rigged with cannon. The fleet could not chance becoming escort just yet while the Spanish might still be fortifying for another attack.

And what about Angel? Garrett had questioned those he knew at court—but to no avail. No one seemed to be familiar with her. The more people arriving at court with no leads as to her background only drove home the fact that maybe his first assumption had been correct. God, he hoped not! He was fast becoming too concerned with the Lady behind the mystery. His heart jumped at the thought that his green-eyed Lady might just turn out to be his adversary.

He hoped Josh would have some information soon about the book from Angel's memories. Both men were fervently praying it was the book from Venice she remembered, but realistically this was doubtful. With each passing day the outcome pointed toward France. Of course, there were other possibilities such as a Lord she knew (her father?) had actually owned the book, or someone in the family had taken her to see the book, and it could all point

Chapter Fourteen

to her innocence from intrigue. Garrett looked honestly into his interest in Angel and wondered if he would have been as intrigued if he had knowledge of her background and family. He enjoyed a good chase and the strategy of a mystery, could this be the only reason he found himself interested in her? Things would certainly be much easier if this were so, but again the lurch of his heart warned him that perhaps the Lady herself had shown him a safe port that he had not realized he hungered for.

Lord Birhym called the men back to the table to finalize a plan of action in case the Spanish were to be spotted plotting again. Then talk turned to the upcoming ceremony. Of course, Davis would not be there as he was still casting about the sea in search of the Armada. But most of the other Lords and court favorites would be attending. Fathers would be eyeing the available titled looking for matches for their unwed daughters. At least having Angel on his arm should save him from scheming fathers this time around. Then the thought leapt into his mind that he would be warding off young rakes from Angel! With the title of guardian of the Lady he was responsible for her safety and well being, and if anyone knew what young unattached nobles were capable of it was Garrett. My God, how did Lord Birmingham survive?

With the meeting dismissed, Garrett arrived at his rooms to find Josh and his father waiting for him. The look they both broadcast was not favorable.

"Well, what is it?" Garrett demanded in a growly tone.

"I'm sorry, Garrett, it's France." Garrett's heart dropped to the toes of his boots until Lord Phillip broke in.

"Come now, it's not that bad. The other information I obtained is somewhat heartening." Lord Phillip continued, "It seems that approximately ten years ago there was a Monsieur Gourdue who was translating the manuscript for the University in Paris. At the time he was employed by the University. There was an attempt during that time to steal the tome and the Monsieur was killed. I have sent enquires to France as to his family and his background. Obviously, Angel would have been too young at that time to be involved in something sinister.

Garrett had to agree. That would have made Angel what? At the youngest, perhaps seven, to a possible twelve. A child. So instead of answering questions the enquiry to France had only given them more questions needing answers. But how had she gotten to England and who were her people now?

Duprell was late. The carriage he had hired had broken down forcing him to walk the last mile to the Black Frog. He cast open the tavern door to see his contact waiting at a back table. Duprell signaled for a pint as he made his way over to the table.

"What do you have for me?"

"There is another Catholic revolt forming in the countryside. I have the leader's names—if the French are interested."

The man nodded. "Anything else?"

Duprell smiled wickedly. "This one is quite pricey."

"I'll determine that. What do you have?"

"How would you like the name of the Captain of the *Allegro*?" Duprell queried.

The man leaned forward with obvious interest. The glint in his eye was shrewd and calculating.

"Who is he?"

"How much is it worth to you?"

"Do not tempt my ire Duprell! Give me the man's identity before I regret my association with you!"

Duprell swallowed. "The Captain of the *Allegro* is none other than Lord Jamison. Garrett Jamison."

The man leaned back in satisfaction with a malevolent grin upon his lips. Then he carefully withdrew a pouch from his coat and tossed it to Duprell. "That should hold you for now, but I will remember this day when something lucrative comes along." With that he rose and left the tavern.

Duprell weighed the pouch and found it to his satisfaction. The contact had never forgotten him before when a favor was owed. It was unlikely he would forget this time.

Chapter Fifteen

The morning of the celebration dawned bright and warm as if even the weather could not bear to displease the Queen. The staff had been busily at work for days decorating the halls and dining rooms for the festivities. Minstrels and theatre players had been hired to entertain the nobles of the court. It was even rumored that the new bard Shakespeare might appear before the Queen!

Angel was beside herself with excitement. Her gown had been pressed to eliminate any wrinkles and was only waiting for her to don it. Lady Camilla had promised to send one of her own maids to help Angel dress her hair. She could hear the approach of the Birmingham girls as they came down the hallway to fetch her for breakfast with the family at their apartment. Angel couldn't help smiling. The Birminghams were a family that enjoyed life to the fullest.

As they traveled down the hallways Angel gloried in the brightly colored flowers and foliage decorating the avenues. Tapestries were hung telling stories of past glories of the English monarchy. Sweet smelling garlands hung above doorways inviting the wanderer to stop and reflect.

Breakfast was waiting when they arrived. Garrett had joined the family. Angel smiled shyly his way. When he returned her smile she became uncomfortably warm. Her heart began to race. She could feel the color rushing to her cheeks. My goodness, what would Garrett think?

Garrett was pleased by the noticeable pleasure she took in his company. His smile broadened when the color began to rise in her cheeks and he gave her a rakish wink, which caused her cheeks to inflame even more. Angel began to turn away in embarrassment but Garrett stepped forward offering his arm to escort her to the table. There was no way for Angel to refuse and save face. Besides, she really didn't want to refuse. Even through his coat she could feel the heat of his body. Why did this make her feel so cherished? Any gentleman would have done the same. Only Garrett could cause her heart to flutter and bring the most disturbing images to her mind.

The days they had spent together at court had shown Angel the pleasures of being able to trust a man and how to enjoy his company. She found herself less likely to panic at the turning of a corner as if Garrett had dispelled the monsters from her past, wiping the slate clean and allowing her to trust again. The Birminghams had shown her the way a family should interact together. She had thrived in the ability to have friends her own age. While Angel did not broadcast her deepest thoughts, as the girls did to her, she revealed it in the ability to keep their secrets and to add her thoughts to their dreams—and her dreams? More and more often they centered on Garrett Jamison.

The talk around the table was light and friendly this morning. No one, it seemed, wished to darken the festive mood that flowed throughout the castle this day. Talk turned to the evening festivities. Escorts for the girls had been arranged. One dare not leave young Ladies unattended in the mull of the evening. Too many rakes would be about that might cast a shadow upon a Lady's reputation. Lady Patience made it clear to her girls what was expected of them and who they would be with. Angel silently giggled at the girls' woebegone faces when they found that Lady Dockett would be available to them, should they have a need to flitter about out of their parents' eye. (She was a dour old widow who took her responsibilities perhaps too seriously.) Angel knew it was unkind to laugh at the girls' expense but the looks they were giving their parents were priceless.

"Angel, I'll be coming for you shortly after eight," Garrett interjected, "and I have arranged for Miles and Tanner to be by your side if I become unavailable." It was Angel's turn to look surprised. Why she hadn't thought about escorts for herself! The

Chapter Fifteen

Birmingham girls' giggles slipped out as Angel took in this news. However, Angel was a good sport about the whole procedure. Besides she liked her escorts.

"Josh," his mother interjected, "the girls have yet to have a chance to go down into town. We would most appreciate it if you could escort them this morning." The girls became very silent hoping their brother would agree. Josh groaned but resigned himself to the chore, nodding to his mother. "Perhaps Garrett and Angel will accompany you as you'll need another escort for these three."

"A fine idea Lady Birmingham," answered Garrett. "I'll have Tanner and Miles join us. That should suffice for a reputable escort for four fine young Ladies. Shall we say ten? We will meet here at your apartments for the girls."

The hour was established. Everyone made their way to their rooms until then. Josh pulled Garrett to one side once they had moved down the hall.

"God, man are you daft? Escorting that bunch to town? Do you know what you are in for?"

Garrett laughed good-naturedly. "Josh, my man, you are totally befuddled by your sisters. Lord, what are you going to do when you have a family?"

Both Angel and Garrett laughed at the astonished look on Josh's face. Plainly he had never thought of that.

"Well since you seem to enjoy them so, I'll just have to be sure to have you around when I need to get them out of my hair!"

Everyone laughed and continued making their way toward Angel's room. There the men left her promising to return for her before going on for the Birmingham girls.

Garrett was as good as his word arriving at her door smartly at ten. They circled to pick up Josh before heading to his parents' quarters. The girls were ready to go and after final instructions from Lady Patience they headed off. Josh had requested a carriage to take them to Piccadilly not wanting to be responsible for walking four Ladies through town. Miles and Tanner were meeting them there, as they had been on the Captain's business in town

Captured Pearl

earlier. They were to meet up at a jeweler's booth near the market. Garrett wanted to surprise Angel by purchasing her some adornments for her gown. He had already purchased the jewels to go with her gown but every lady should have some item purchased by her escort before a festival—or so his mother had always said.

Miles and Tanner were waiting at the appointed booth. The girls immediately began to fuss over Tanner's new gold hoop in his ear. Finally Miles broke in, "Well, Ladies, you know a sailor must have a spot of gold to pay his passage to the afterlife. It is about time Tanner took his calling seriously." Tanner looked decidedly uncomfortable with all the attention focused on him.

"I think you look quite handsome Mr. Tanner," responded Angel. "I'm sure all the Ladies at court will have their eyes on you tonight."

"Does that mean if I wear my gold hoop your eyes will be upon me all night, Angel?" questioned Garrett.

Angel was feeling especially fine this day so with a toss of her head her reply was, "Perhaps, you should wear it tonight and see Lord Jamison!"

"I believe I just heard a challenge, Captain," stated Tanner glad to have the topic turned to someone else.

"Never let a challenge from a Lady go unanswered!" stated Garrett.

"Let us examine the jeweler's offerings and see if we can purchase some gifts for the Ladies," Josh replied. The girls agreed with this course of action.

There was a fine selection of choices at the booth from pewter rings and brooches to enameled pins and points. Josh pointedly steered his sisters to enameled points and fans as they already had their gems for the night's activities. Angel tried to look unimpressed, as she hadn't any coin of her own. Garrett had been more that generous already. There was nothing here she needed—but Garrett had other ideas. His eye was captured by a baroque pearl pin of a dolphin. The symbolism of the good luck charm of the sailor was not lost on the Captain. Even though he did not consider himself a superstitious man there was no need to

Chapter Fifteen

take any chances. He motioned to the vendor settling on the coin needed. When the man saw that Garrett had an interest in the dolphin symbol he directed Garrett's attention to a finger ring and hair pins that all carried the dolphin motif.

"Angel, come take a look at these, please." Angel made her way over to his side. "Do you like these?"

"They are very lovely, Garrett. Isn't the dolphin good luck on the sea?"

"Yes, he is Angel. How did you know that?"

"Peters mentioned it."

"Would you like them?"

"Garrett, you can't buy me those!"

"Of course, I can, Angel. Every Lady needs to be adorned for her first festivity. My mother made that point over and over to the Jamison men. It would be my pleasure to gift them to you." With that Garrett paid the coin and the craftsman placed them neatly in a velvet bag for transport. Then Garrett secured them in his pocket until they reached Angel's rooms. Angel had noticed that Miles had been eyeing the dolphin items, also—obviously wanting to purchase them for his Lady Camilla. She tucked the thought to the back of her mind for further consideration at a later time.

Josh had settled for his sisters' purchases and had been prepared to travel down the street when his eye was caught by a tiny stylized dragonfly pin. He readily purchased this for his mother seeing the exact shade of her blue eyes in the graceful enameling of its tiny wings.

The group made their way along the street browsing at the booths as they went. At one, Angel saw a mermaid figure made to slide on a sailor's hoop. Cautiously she brought it to Garrett's attention shyly remarking that it would look quite smart upon Tanner's new hoop. Garrett, caught up in the fun, agreed. He paid the coin and then called Tanner over after depositing the small figure in Angel's hand.

"The Lady and I have something for you Tanner. It seems you have secured your place." Tanner seemed puzzled until Angel

Captured Pearl

gently dropped the mermaid into his hand.

"Captain . . . ," Tanner seemed lost for words then replied, "seems I'm permanently wed to the sea now Captain."

While she had Garrett's attention Angel tugged him down where she whispered in his ear. He solemnly considered her request then nodded. "Wait until we have a private moment with him Angel."

The next stall carried knives for any use a man might wish. There were single-edged blades for eating or hunting. Angel saw one with a beautiful stag for its grip. Garrett saw her interest and explained to her that any blade over four inches was considered a weapon. Therefore, unless you carried that particular blade where everyone could see it you would be breaking the law on concealed weapons. When she asked how it could be proper for him to wear his sword since it was obviously over four inches Garrett laughed explaining to her that men of title were allowed to wear their swords anywhere they might go. The obvious difference was that his sword was a double-edged blade. When she asked what that meant the men just shook their heads leading the Ladies on to another stall.

Jolene exclaimed in delight at the next stall where the vendor displayed a small selection of Venetian glass beads. They were all the latest fashion at court and still very costly. The strand Jolene was eyeing had beads of gold alternating with blue glass beads. Josh gently dissuaded her from this costly item reminding her that this was a gift a husband would give his wife, not a brother to his sister. She gave a last longing look at the beads and then headed off to the Glover's stall where her sisters were engaged in trying on the man's wares. Angel followed Jolene leaving Garrett to bring up the rear. He quickly finished his business with the man rejoining his group before he was missed.

Finally, Miles suggested they take a rest as his old bones were beginning to weary. The others agreed making their way to a tea shop that catered to the higher class citizens of the realm. After they were refreshed Josh located their carriage and they made their way back to the court.

Chapter Fifteen

Lady Camilla had sent her maid to help Angel dress. She could hardly believe that this gorgeous creation was hers. Garrett had been right when he had picked the fabric for the gown. Mrs. Lewis had turned the rosy-pink satin cloth into a stunning work of art. The large hooks and eyes lining the front of the gown were edged by tiny seed pearls and garnet chips, which ultimately created a raindrop pattern that sparkled. The undergown was the exact same hue as the tiny glittering garnets that accented the pink satin and this could be seen through the slashed sleeves and the front skirt where it parted to show off the lovely linen kirtle. The hem of the gown was also edged with the continuous pattern of seed pearl and garnet raindrops. Garrett had forgotten nothing. The girdle of the gown was silver chain with attached plaques of garnets and pearls carrying the theme of the gown throughout.

Her hair was swept up into a falling cascade that was confined with a silver mesh snood. The dolphin hairpins were placed strategically so that her hair glittered under the mutest light. Angel had the pin that matched fastened to the front of her bodice where it held the fine chain carcanet in place.

A knock on the door proved to be Miles carrying a velvet box and a jeweler's bag. Inside the first was a filigree carcanet neck band that was set with garnets and pearls. The fine workmanship drew a man's attention to her long neck. Inside the jeweler's bag lay a small strand of clear glass beads and silver balls to fasten to her girdle and a ring of silver for her to wear. Her dressing was complete.

Before Miles returned to his Captain Angel drew him to one side, "Miles, I'd like you to have this," she said presenting him with one of the dolphin hairpins.

"No, my Lady. The Captain purchased those for you. It wouldn't be right."

"I've already talked to your Captain. We both know whom you wanted them for. Please take this small token of our regard and gift it where you may."

Miles could see there was no dissuading the Lady and so without further adieu he accepted her gift with a quick nod of his head.

Captured Pearl

"The Captain will be here presently to escort you to the festivities Lady. And, if you don't mind my saying, you look quite lovely tonight."

Angel tried to wait patiently for Garrett but her nervous energy would not be contained. She nervously paced her room wondering if Garrett would find her as lovely as Miles had. Then a sharp rap at her door announced Garrett. Angel flew to open the door and was stopped in her tracks by the sight of him. The man was beautiful! His shirt of pristine white was covered in blackwork so delicate and extensive that it stole her breath. Fixed between the needlework were garnets to add color to the background. The sleeveless doublet of black brocade had a contrasting panel of ice blue the exact shade of Garrett's eyes. Instead of the hose and shoes that most men would be wearing the Captain had exercised his military connections by wearing slops with his boots, which were mid-thigh in length with flared cuffs. A dress hilt rapier completed the look. The frog it was suspended from this night was not the plain leather he usually wore but of fine black leather studded with sapphires. My, he looked grand. But the finishing touch that took her heart away was the gold hoop in his ear with a sapphire, his family stone, swinging jauntily from its center. He took her breath away!

Garrett took one look at Angel and swore that he'd run through the man that dared to touch her! The incredible Lady at the door, mystery and all, was his!

Angel stopped to close her door and Garrett wondered again how anything could be so beautiful. He knew the Ladies would be jealous and the men would have to shut their mouths to keep from drooling all over themselves. He would be sure to tell Miles and Tanner to keep a close watch on his Lady this night!

Many of the guests had already arrived when Garrett and Angel entered the great hall. Angel could see that everyone was dressed in their finest. There were many different styles of gowns from the ornate Elizabethan with the high starched collar, to French flowing gowns, to many like her own. Most had picked

Chapter Fifteen

dark vibrant colors and she wondered if she was dressed appropriately.

Lord and Lady Stapleton approached and Garrett introduced them to Angel. They were an elderly couple of considerable wealth whose Estate bordered that of the Jamison's. They had known the Jamison family for years and had been distressed to hear of the death of the Jamison parents. Lord Stapleton had graciously offered his advice and help to Garrett while he was learning to run the Estate—gaining the needed experience to handle it alone while under the protective eye of a family friend.

Lord Stapleton had entered into the Hereford cattle venture with Garrett and had helped to bring the animals to the area. Both Estates had plenty of meadows and fine grass for feeding the herds they hoped to raise. Garrett would always be grateful to them.

"Lord and Lady Stapleton, may I present Angel?"

"Why aren't you quite the lovely young Lady. Garrett wherever did you find such a treasure?" Lady Stapleton questioned.

Another lie was needed and Garrett was prepared. "This is Lady Angelina," he offered stretching her name to make it sound a little more aristocratic. Her father was an acquaintance who was recently killed in battle. He graciously made me her guardian before he died and the Queen has agreed."

"Have you heard from Shane?" asked Lady Stapleton.

"My brother should be here somewhere. He is never one to miss a festival and I had word that he was in London."

A brother! Garrett had a brother? Why this was fascinating news! Angel wondered if Shane looked like his brother.

"We must meet up again later Garrett and please bring your Angelina to the Estate any time. We are so pleased to meet you," Lady Stapleton smiled.

"That goes for me, too, young Lady," added Lord Stapleton. They thought what a lovely young woman she was. And so Angelina was introduced to everyone—or almost everyone.

Garrett continued to lead her around the great hall introducing her to acquaintances and people he knew. Miles and Tanner were not far behind. When Garrett became separated from his charge, and a few bawdy young Lords approached to size up the newest game in town, they were met by a gnarly old seaman and a tall handsome sailor who clearly made it plain that going through them to get to Angelina would not be in their best interest. Miles and Tanner continued to see to her safety as they made their way around the floor.

Angel found that she felt quite safe in their company. Who else had such handsome escorts? Miles looked very distinguished dressed completely in black. His salt and pepper hair set off the few adornments that he wore, all in pewter. Like the Captain, both men had opted for the boots of their trade, making it clear to any that approached that these men were battle wise and ready for the next call to arms. Tanner had many of the Ladies glancing his way. Although not as tall as Garrett, he stood above many of the Lords in attendance. His sun-kissed brown hair, worn too long for a gentleman, only added to the rakish pirate look. He wore tanned leather slops, jerkin, and boots but his shirt was a stunning red. The saucy mermaid swinging from his ear loop added to the devil-may-care attitude he portrayed. Neither man wore a sword but the knives stuck in their belts for all to see looked menacing just the same.

Angel was deep in thought when a hand touched her shoulder from behind spinning her around to face the second handsomest man she had ever seen. His eyes were the bluest deep-sea blue and he had a rich, deep voice.

"You simply must give me your name Lady, for you are an angel sent from heaven."

Even with the teasing tone of his voice Angel began to feel some of the old fear begin to crawl up her spine. Why didn't Miles leap to her rescue? Tanner quickly stepped to her side putting himself between the Lord in question and the Lady he was protecting.

"Unhand the Lady, Sir." His tone was soft but his hand was on the hilt of his knife and anyone looking at his eyes knew that this man meant business.

"Hold lad, no need for that. Lord Jamison didn't mean any harm. This is the Captain's brother, Shane," bespoke Miles lightly.

Chapter Fifteen

"Miles it's good to see you—and who is this lovely maiden?"

"Angelina is your brother's ward. The Queen has given him guardianship of the Lady. So, you had best watch your step."

"Why then we are almost family and you must call me Shane." With this comment Tanner slid his hilt back into its sheath and stepped back to give the Captain's brother room to move. Shane looked at the young sailor recognizing a kindred spirit and said, "No harm done, man. I'm glad to know the Lady is safe when in your care." Tanner acknowledged the Lord's praise and decided he liked the man as well.

Shane was three years younger than Garrett with eyes the lightest shade of blue. With his light complexion and contagious smile he was a ladies' man. He never left the manor without being immaculately dressed and tonight was no exception. He was dressed in the latest Elizabethan style with the ruff collar and bright colors of blue and silver. Unlike his brother he wore the nether hose that were fully puffed, and hose of the same color. Upon his feet were the latest fashion of soft leather shoes. A gold hoop with a blue sapphire adorned his ear with sapphires in his sword belt and adornments. On many other men the bejewelment would have been too much but Shane carried it off effortlessly. He was always a gentleman and very polished. Knowing from an early age that he would not inherit the family lands he had turned his attentions to other pursuits. He was a man of learning, yet with his good looks and easy wit the Ladies were fascinated with him, and he was considered quite a rake. He was charismatic and had charmed his way into many a bedroom.

Shane had just left his latest love, Sharon Russell. She had been his lover for the past two years and had been pressuring him to make her an honest woman. Shane was restless and far from ready to take a wife. He should never have let it go on for so long giving her hope of something more permanent. Garrett had warned him, but he hadn't listened. Still, there were many parties and Ladies he had yet to meet including the one right in front of him.

"Where is my older brother, that he has left you in the company of these disreputable sailors?" he joked to Angel.

"He is here somewhere. We became separated some time ago." Miles had recognized the men Garrett had been talking to, and he excused himself from their company to locate the Captain. Angel would be safe with the two younger men, and for all of Shane's rakishness he would never allow any harm to come to one in the care of the Jamison family.

Shane proceeded to entertain Angel with stories of the Lords and Ladies in attendance while Tanner brought up the rear glaring at anyone that approached whom he deemed unacceptable. Miles returned before long with Garrett alongside. The two brothers were obviously glad to see each other. They had hardly begun to enthrall each other with their latest activities when dinner was announced. Garrett and Angel proceeded in to take their place at the main table as was expected of one of the Queen's favorites. Shane joined his friends at a trestle table to one side. Being of the common class, Miles and Tanner left the room once everyone was settled to partake of their meal in the common room. They would return to resume their duties after the meal was finished.

Duprell had arrived at the appointed time with the stunning Cara on his arm. His audience with the Queen had been scheduled before the main meal. When he was allowed in her Majesty's presence he made his formal greeting then presented the black velvet box to her.

"A small token of my fidelity to Your Highness. I hope that it pleases you."

Elizabeth carefully opened the box. The widening of her eyes was the only sign that she was impressed by the fabulous creation of Mr. Shingler.

"What favor do you expect from us for this fine and unusual gift?"

"My Queen, for many years my family has been in disfavor because of my father's selfish acts. I only wish for Your Majesty to consider the fact that perhaps it is time for the Duprells to be looked upon with something other than disfavor."

Chapter Fifteen

Clearly Elizabeth did not relish the action that Duprell was searching for. She closed the box with a snap. Then opened it to look upon it once more. "We shall consider your request. But we promise nothing. Is that understood?"

"Quite, your Majesty." The audience was over. Duprell could only hope and continue to scheme. He picked up Cara and they were escorted by a livery servant to the hall where the dining would take place as soon as the Queen arrived.

Duprell and Cara made a stunning pair in their red and black clothing. Duprell, while not the handsome man that the Jamison men were, had the dark and swarthy appearance that many women had found appealing. Cara had men turning their heads as she passed. Their table had Lords and Ladies of similar family standing, although, none had brought their paramour to the dinner. The Ladies ignored Cara even though she was careful to present her best manners. Like knew like and the nobility could sniff out a pretender at thirty paces.

The Queen arrived with all the pomp and ceremony that was expected of a ruler. Everyone rose until she had been seated, then the Lords and Ladies that were favored to dine at her table seated themselves. It was at this point that Duprell became aware that Jamison was present at the top table. The extraordinarily beautiful Lady at his side looked familiar but at the moment he could not get a good enough look to determine who it was.

The meal started with the usual choices of soup and fruits, then progressed on to peacock stuffed with apples and mushrooms with a light cherry sauce. There were an assortment of meats from tame fowl to wild boar and deer. The fruits were varied and the wine flowed freely. Garrett drank sparingly and advised Angel to do the same. The Queen frowned upon drunkenness in her court. He suggested dishes to her allowing which were his favorites and which might not be to her liking. Angel was careful to take his advice to heart. She found that while she had been quite ravenous before they had been seated, being this close to the Queen and under so much scrutiny her appetite had vanished.

It was Cara who finally made the connection between the

Captured Pearl

young Lady sitting beside Garrett and the missing Cassandra. Her eyes had continuously traveled the distance to watch the Lady at his side. How she wished she was at that position of honor. Finally the Lady in question had turned to speak to the Lord next to her allowing Cara a better view. She was sure it was the missing Cassandra!

"My Lord, I believe that the Lady with Lord Jamison is your missing niece!" Cara whispered to Duprell. His eyes turned to watch the Lady until she had again turned his way and he could get a good look. Duprell almost choked on his roast boar. He would end this farce as soon as the dinner was ended. She would be coming home with him before Lucas found out she had been gone.

After the Queen had signaled that dinner was over Duprell pulled Cara to her feet and made his way over to Jamison. Cassandra was standing next to him looking more beautiful than any woman he had ever seen. She looked directly into his eyes and acted like she didn't see him! Surely she had seen him coming. He grabbed Cara's arm and pulled her along.

"That little bitch acts like I am not even here. I will straighten her out immediately!" He walked toward Angel and Garrett but Garrett saw Duprell first and took Angel's hand leading her in the other direction straight to Shane.

"Jamison, I don't believe that I have met your beautiful friend."

Garrett did not want trouble here at court. Bess would have both their heads if there were a brawl in her presence. He nodded his head coolly and replied, "This is my ward, Angelica."

Duprell was taken aback by Cassandra's cool composure. What game was she playing? And how had Jamison come to believe that he was the girl's guardian. Hell, he thought, he'd go along with it for now just to see how far she would go. Cara was about to say something, but Duprell squeezed her arm forcibly and she took the hint remaining silent.

As Garrett again turned to leave the music started to play and Duprell seeing his chance took it.

Chapter Fifteen

"Perhaps the Lady would care to dance with me." Duprell did not make it a question but a demand. Angel was afraid of this man. She wasn't sure why, but the man made shivers run up her spine. Her fingers tightened against Garrett's arm. He read the alarm and fear in her eyes as well as her grip. There was no way he would *ever* let Duprell near any woman let alone one that he cared about—ever again.

"The Lady does not wish your company, Duprell. Nor do I." With that Garrett led her away and back into the protective circle of her escorts and his brother.

"Cassandra do not turn away from me!" Duprell felt the rage rising up from the pit of his stomach. Cara stood back to watch.

Angel turned back to the disgusting man. "You know me?"

Duprell looked at her for a long time. "You really don't know who I am?"

Angel shook her head. Duprell almost believed her. Mayhap she had lost her memory. That might work to his advantage. If she really didn't remember he could have her married to Lucas as soon as the bans could be posted. This was too good to be true. He almost laughed at his good luck.

"Your name is Cassandra Gourdue. You are my niece by marriage and you disappeared several weeks ago. Where were you all this time?" he demanded.

Garrett took control of the situation steering Angel toward Shane and then positioned himself between them.

"The Lady is under my protection Duprell by order of the Queen. She has been in my care since I found her wandering mindlessly on the road in the middle of the night. I find it very fortuitous that you claim to know the Lady, yet no one was notified on her absence or that she was missing. You'll have to do better than that Duprell."

While Garrett had attempted to keep his voice down the attention they had garnered had gotten the attention of the Queen. The guards came forward to escort the involved parties to the Queen to present their case.

"Explain yourselves!" Elizabeth demanded.

Captured Pearl

Garrett waited, knowing that Duprell would interrupt, thus allowing the man to make his mistakes first.

Duprell had ever been anxious to present his side first—thus being able to slur the other party involved.

Elizabeth was not a fool and Garrett had learned over the years in her court that it was better to wait and then present his case, helping him to know his enemy before he started.

"This Lady is my niece! My sister's daughter from France. Her real name is Cassandra Gourdue. Her parents died years ago in France and she has been in my care since then—and I want her back!"

The Queen solemnly looked Duprell up and down—not liking him any better now than she had in the past.

"Why have we not heard or seen this Lady before, Duprell?"

Duprell stuttered before answering, "She is not of the nobility, Your Majesty." (Another family scandal.) "My wife's sister, Gabrielle, ran off with a merchant Frenchman when traveling with her parents. She was disowned by her father and we had not heard from her until Cassandra needed a guardian after her parents' deaths."

"We find this story full of lies and imaginings, Duprell. One has only to look at the Lady to know that you terrify her. Lord Jamison has shown great care and responsibility in his handling of the Lady in question. Until we have more information we declare that she stay in the care of her legal guardian, whom was appointed by the crown! Lord Birmingham come forth!"

Josh strode forward and knelt before his Queen. "How may I serve Your Majesty?"

"Lord and Lady Stapleton come forth!" The named couple made their way forward to report to the Crown.

"Your Estate lies not far from the Duprell Estate. Have you any knowledge of this Lady?"

Both replied that, no, they did not.

"Lord Jamison, had you any knowledge of this Lady before God sent her to your care?"

"No, Your Majesty. I had never laid eyes upon her before."

Chapter Fifteen

"Can any substantiate your claim?"

"My man, Miles, was with me when we ran into her."

"Bring him forth!" Miles was escorted to the Queen, giving the same account that Elizabeth had heard from Garrett on his earlier meeting with the Queen.

"The Crown is satisfied at this time, to leave the Lady in question, Cassandra Gourdue, in the custody of Lord Jamison."

Duprell fumed, but there was nothing he could do at this time. He would scheme and now that he knew where Cassandra was he would have her back under his control before long! The parties involved returned to the floor to resume their part in the festivities under the Queen's watchful eye.

There was no way Garrett was leaving Angel, or was it Cassandra, alone the rest of this night! Was she really Duprell's niece and if so was she working for that scallywag? He wanted to trust her but Duprell and he had long been at odds. If Angel were part of his household the man would be using her for his own ends. Was she cooperating with him or had she lived in a house of terror all these years? His heart wasn't ready to condemn her just yet.

Social niceties demanded they resume activities and Garrett swept Cassandra into a dance after dismissing Miles to look for his ladylove. Unfortunately, Duprell had the same idea and this was a dance that called for changing partners. Not willing to invoke the Queen's ire Garrett gritted his teeth and danced on. Cara and Duprell swung around to exchange partners with Garrett and Angel.

Cara loved the feel of Garrett's hand taking her arm to begin the next wheel of the dance.

"How are you?"

"Just fine Cara."

"Garrett, I have missed you so."

"So you say. I see you lost no time in finding yourself another man." He did not take his eyes off Angel and Duprell.

"I really need you Garrett. Look at me please. I have always loved you, and I still do."

"You are sleeping with that maggot," said Garrett as he watched Angel.

Cara hung her head. "I needed someone to look out for me. When you left me, I had no one else to turn to, Garrett," Cara whispered sadly.

Garrett did not feel sorry for her. "If you hadn't thought to play your games with me there would have been no reason for you to look for someone to protect you, Cara. Even then you need not have turned to Duprell. You knew there was bad blood between us."

"Garrett, please give me another chance," Cara was pleading now. Garrett found it unbecoming in the woman. Even if she hadn't been with Duprell there was no way he would take her back now. However he wouldn't tell her that.

"Cara, it's over. It has been for a long time. I don't bother myself with used goods. You should know that by now." Garrett knew he was being cruel but it was the only thing conniving wenches like Cara understood.

Angel fought to maintain her calm. Her skin crawled at the man's touch. His breath wafted hotly across her neck and she felt as if she had experienced this before. Duprell was watching her. What was he looking for? Could his story really be true? Had she lived with this repulsive man since she was a child? Angel didn't want to believe it but she was too horrified of the man for this to be their first meeting. Had Garrett been right when he had accused her of being a spy? What would she do to escape a man such as Duprell? The answer came to her unwillingly. Anything! Almost anything!

"You really don't remember me?" Duprell asked after giving Cassandra a long look. Angel shook her head. If she had really lost her memory then it was too good to be true. He could continue on with his scheme and convince the Queen that it was in her best interest, being of common stock, to marry the widower, Lucas. Duprell noticed her darting glances towards Garrett.

"He is not for you, girl. Jamison is of the nobility and the Queen would never allow her favorite to wed with a girl of com-

Chapter Fifteen

mon stock. Besides I have already picked a groom for you. Mayhap we can explain to him what has happened to you. If you're lucky he will still have you."

Angel's blood ran cold. A groom? Picked by this awful man? No! She frantically looked about the room wondering who it might be. Garrett caught her eye. The look he gave her said, "Trust me." There was no alternative. Garrett was her lifeline in the rolling sea of her life.

Just when Angel thought she'd be sick if she had to endure this man's presence any longer, Garrett swept in depositing Cara by Duprell's side and gathering Angel into his arms.

"I believe that will be enough. Angel, you look quite pale. Let me escort you out into the fresh air. There seems to be a flavor not to your liking here. A final warning Duprell. Until the Queen rules otherwise I will protect Angel with everything at my disposal. I believe you understand my meaning."

With that Garrett steered Angel toward the balcony. Duprell made to follow only to find his way blocked by a tall imposing looking sailor with a deadly glint in his eye.

"Out of my way!" Duprell barked.

"I don't believe so, Lord. I watch the Captain's back and others watch mine. Be very careful how you proceed, Lord, the Queen's eye is upon you." With that parting shot Tanner trailed along behind Angel and the Captain.

The cool breeze was a pleasant change from the stifling air that clung about Duprell. Garrett's presence calmed Angel's trembling heart and allowed her to breathe in the night air. She was afraid. Afraid to tell Garrett what she believed. But she knew it would be worse to hide her feelings away.

"Garrett, I know him," her soft voice whispered.

"Know who? Duprell? What do you know!" Garrett's hand tightened on her arm but she did not draw his attention to the pain he was causing her.

"Yes, Duprell. I mean, I think I do. I feel I do. I am terrified of that man and if I didn't know him why would I be so afraid of him? I feel as if there is a terrible nightmare in my life that has him at the center. What if you were right? What if I was willing to do anything to escape that man? Garrett I'm so afraid!"

The terror in her eyes was easily read by even the most inept man. The girl had been abused somewhere in her past, probably by Duprell. If so could a man blame her for trying to escape? She was unable to fight a battle as a man and if she were trapped in such a hell what might she do? His heart made excuses for her and Garrett realized he might be in danger of making a wrong decision. Would it really hurt to believe in her until Josh had more information — and surely there was someone at the Duprell Estate that could be bought to give them the truth. For once in his life Garrett's heart won out. He gathered Angel into his arms giving her comfort and strength. For now they would be each other's reason for believing. Neither knew what the future would bring but hope always lives in the hearts of lovers.

Chapter Sixteen

Cara painfully turned over on the bed cursing Duprell and his sadistic sexual appetite. For all his scheming, the rare black pearl had not foretold his destiny and he had taken his anger out on her. She was accustomed to most of his strange and rough sexual pleasures but this time he had gone too far! He had hit her! Cara was sure she would have a black eye, and if her nose wasn't broken it would surprise her. Already the bruises were surfacing on her breasts. Duprell had used her hard, pummeling her far into the night. When he had not been able to satisfy his sexual nature in this manner he had turned her to her stomach to sodomize her. God, even the thought of it made her cringe! Never, never would she allow him to use her in this manner again! Cara had always fought to hold on to Duprell until she had enough coin to leave. Now she was afraid that he would not allow her to leave.

Cara thought of the many times she had caught Duprell watching Cassandra in a sexual manner. She had flown into a rage, railing at the girl and then snubbing Duprell in retaliation. Now she wished Cassandra were here to relive his pleasure giving her respite from the pain Duprell had begun to inflict.

She would talk to her mother again giving Margaret no alternative but to join her in discovering Duprell's secrets. Cara would take them to Garrett and he would protect her in return. Once she was in his house she would make him take her back. Cara looked around the room mentally deciding what she could get away with taking with her when she left. Duprell had given her the house in London. It was huge and expensive but lacked the warmth of the Jamison Estate. Cara knew she was losing it just as she was losing her hold over Duprell.

Yes, once she had Duprell's secrets Garrett would have to

take her back. She would be the Lady of the Jamison Estate. Garrett would be hers or no one would have him!

At that moment the object of Cara's fantasy stood before his sovereign. He had been called to her audience chamber immediately upon his rising from his bed. "What now?" Garrett thought. Seldom was Elizabeth this early a riser, and even rarer would she call for someone this early in the day.

The Queen entered. Garrett bent a knee to the Queen waiting for her permission to rise.

"Lord Jamison come forth." Garrett made his way to the throne where he halted to await Bess's pleasure.

"We are troubled by the claim that Lord Duprell has made against the Lady. We have often found the family to be unscrupulous and centered on their own wants instead of the needs of the kingdom. Therefore, I am dismissing you from my court to make your way back to your Estate at your leisure. If you are not here perhaps Duprell will be less formidable in his desire to capture the Lady in your care." Bess's eyes twinkled with this last statement and Garrett read her meaning well. A leisurely cruise back to his home could be stretched into weeks instead of days.

"As always, I am yours to command my Queen. I shall make way as soon as the Lady can be made ready."

"Lord Jamison."

"Your Majesty?"

"I am charging you with the Lady's safety. There are many ways to keep a Lady out of another man's grip. Do search your mind for all possibilities."

"As you wish Your Majesty." Garrett bent a knee again to the Queen before turning to leave her presence. He quickly made his way to Angel's rooms where he barely bothered to stop to announce himself before entering her chambers.

"Garrett, what are you doing here?" Angel quickly drew her dressing gown closed. "For heaven's sake you can't just walk into a Lady's bedroom!"

"Angel, you need to dress quickly and pack a few things. We must leave immediately."

Chapter Sixteen

One look at Garrett's eyes told Angel that this was no time to argue. Those blue eyes were like forged steel in their intensity—and cold.

"I can be ready in half of an hour. Will that suffice?"

"That will be fine. Bar the door when I leave and don't open it for anyone but Miles, Tanner, or myself. Do you understand?"

"Yes, Garrett. But what's going on?"

"The Queen has bid us to leave with all possible haste. She believes Duprell will try some trick to have you turned over to him. If we are not here that can't happen. Haste Angel."

Garrett turned smartly on his heel proceeding to the door. He'd need to get the men on the ship and have the *Lady* ready to sail within the hour. Fortunately, he always saw to restocking his ship the moment he landed. The men would be close. They were used to a sudden call to leave.

Miles was most likely with the Lady Camilla, as Garrett had seen them leave discreetly in the same direction last night. If he could find her maid, she would know where the two lovers were ensconced. Damn! When he needed Miles to be approachable the man was off courting. Not that he truly begrudged Miles his Lady, but the timing was certainly inconvenient. Mayhap Tanner could shed some light on the man's whereabouts. Tanner, he knew, was in the kitchen breaking his fast. He had been at Angel's door when Garrett had arrived in the hallway this morning. "A good man, steady and reliable, if a trifle young," Garrett thought. He had handled himself well the night before, raising himself in Garrett's standing with his levelheadedness and his stoic refusal to partake in the wine that had been abundant. The man had sense.

Tanner was indeed in the kitchens. Quietly Garrett went over to his side, "We must make way within the hour. Do you know how to locate Miles?"

Tanner nodded, "Leave it to me Captain. I'll shake him from his bed. Do you wish me to take word to the ship?"

"If you can have Miles on his way within a quarter hour send him. If we have a fight coming I want you at my side."

"Aye, aye Captain," Tanner rose taking his slice of bread as

Captured Pearl

he quietly and quickly left the room bent on his mission. Garrett returned to his rooms and quickly packed his things. He never traveled to court with much more than a trunk but he certainly couldn't be seen leaving with it on his shoulder. There was a soft rap at his door. Garrett loosed the rapier at his side before calling out admittance.

To his surprise it was Lady Camilla. There was a soft glow about the Lady as she spoke, "Miles has already left Lord Jamison. Tanner watches your Lady. If I may interject, I believe that you should all come to my apartments before leaving. The garden outside my chamber leads to a portal that will gain you entrance directly onto the avenue leading to the docks. I have a wagon waiting to take your things as soon as you are ready. It is highly unlikely anyone would be looking for you there."

"I understand why my man is captivated by you Lady. You have a sharp wit and a coolness of head."

Camilla blushed at his compliment giving Garrett a glance of a tiny silver dolphin hairpin in her braided cornet. "If you will follow me, Sir, we should really be on our way."

"Will this cause trouble for you Lady Camilla?"

Twinkling eyes laughed back at him. "Who do you think arranged all this, my Lord? This Lady has never had any use for that family."

Duprell could have kicked himself if his leg was long enough! The marriage contract with Lucas would gain him back the custody of Cassandra. Lucas could attest to her identity, and the Queen could not object to the marriage as Cassandra was considered common stock, thus it was the final judgment of her Lord who she would be betrothed to. He quickly called for his carriage to make his way to court. Before leaving he sent word to Lucas to meet him at the London house. By God, he'd have that bitch back tonight! Once and for all he would have the wealth he deserved. He would have Cassandra back, and like the captured black pearl, she would be the pearl that put his family financially on the road to success. Yes, pearls had always been good fortune for him. His

Chapter Sixteen

most recently captured pearls would have him the envy of the court. The family scandal would be forgotten and men would open a path as he strode forward to become a contending force in Elizabeth's court!

Chapter Seventeen

The *Lady* quickly set sail heading for the open sea. Garrett piloted her out with a skill few could match. With her lines built for speed and silence they would be uncatchable once they cleared the port. Garrett pondered Bess's last words as he manned the wheel. The shouts of his crew were soothing; the breeze swept the vestiges of court nonsense from his mind. What was it exactly that Bess had said? "Keep the Lady safe . . . out of another man's grip . . . search for all the possibilities."

"Good Lord! Was Bess saying what he thought she was saying? Search all the possibilities to keep the Lady out of another's grip? Did she actually mean for him to seduce Angel? Bess would demand that he marry her if he did. He didn't want to marry, did he? The thought of Angel gracing his house without fear of her leaving was pleasant—more than pleasant. His foolish heart was refusing to listen to his mind. Could she really be trusted with his secrets? What if she was a Duprell? He'd never let a Duprell into his house! But his heart said, "She isn't a Duprell. Related by marriage. Duprell's wife's sister's girl."

Garrett recalled the visits to the Estate made by Duprell's mother, both before and after she had married the Lord. His mother, Catherine, as well as Priscilla's family had tried to dissuade her from marrying the scoundrel, but she was in love and he was a charmer.

The visits had stopped for a while after Donovan was born. Catherine had worried sending invitation after invitation to the Duprell Estate until Priscilla had resumed her visits. As a boy, Garrett had not been much interested in the conversation of the Ladies. Now he wondered about the topic. Catherine and Priscilla had always taken themselves off to the garden on favorable days.

Captured Pearl

In inclement weather his mother's solarium had been their refuge. He did remember that those visits were the only times the door was closed to the rest of the family. Now he thought it rather strange that his mother would do such a thing. What had been going on in there?

Angel had brought more mystery and excitement into his life than a mere woman should ever be allowed. Why he was the Queen's man! But Elizabeth obviously was not opposed to the idea. Why the thought, "seduce the girl" kept running through his head—the idea was not unpleasant. If he was truthful with himself the idea had been shoving its way forward since the first time he had held her in his arms on the road. Would she resist? He certainly wasn't known for being a lady's man, but then again, he was certainly no flop when it came to the arts of the bedroom.

The thought of Angel naked in his arms began to churn about in his mind. With a stern admonishment to himself Garrett forced his mind back to the task at hand. There would be time for that later.

Miles stepped in periodically to check on Angel throughout the long day of sailing. Garrett came down at mid-day to share her meal and then took her on deck for some air.

But the cabin was small and the books did not hold her interest. Thoughts of Duprell kept creeping into her mind like a snake slithering its way through tall grass. There was some connection. She could feel it. What would happen to her if Duprell was right? Would she have to go with him? The thought ran shivers of dread down her spine. The morbid thoughts continued only to be interrupted by a knock on the door. At her call Miles stepped in followed by two of the other crew members.

"Begging your pardon, Lady. The Captain thought you might enjoy a hot bath." Miles' two companions set a large tub in the center of the room and then proceeded to fill it with water. Before leaving Miles handed her a bar of scented soap. "From the Captain."

Chapter Seventeen

The thought of the hot water was already dispelling the ugly thoughts from her head. Garrett had been so kind at court and now here. As she sank into the steaming tub Angel closed her eyes relaxing into its warmth.

Garrett opened the door to his cabin silently watching the vision before him. Her long blonde hair hung over the side of the tub brushing the floor with its golden carpet of silk. Her face was flushed from the heat in a becoming shade of rosy pink—reminding him of the splendid gown she had been so stunning in at court. The water dipped tantalizingly to allow him an occasional view of her pert breast and its rosy nipple. He wished they had met under different circumstances. He would have fallen in love with her and they could have courted properly. How different life might have been to have her love and respect. Garrett shut the door softly then turned the lock. There would be no interruptions tonight.

He crossed the room silently to take the bar of scented soap from her hand. Angel's dreamy eyes registered the fact that he was there. She had no words to stop his actions. With gentle hands Garrett began to wash her body. The creamy soap glided across her back leaving tiny shivers of delight behind.

He finished, moving on to her silken limbs. Her arms delighted him; her dainty elegant fingers would thrill him when they caressed his form. He moved to the front of the tub to extract one silken leg running the bar of soap up and down its length. Her toes were perfect. Dainty feet were attached to long legs that Garrett imagined clinging to him. The thought brought heat to his male member with a rush of blood. Would she let him continue? Silently he slid the bar upward across her ribcage to the base of her throat and then down to her exciting collarbone. Garrett found the desire to nibble upon it irresistible and he bent to follow the thought in his mind. At first soft butterfly kisses made their way the length of her collarbone. Gradually they turned to soft nibbles interspersed with sharp tiny bites of love. Angel's breath escaped in a soft sigh of delight, encouraging Garrett to continue his quest on to other delights. The soap traveled lower skimming her breasts. When no protest issued, his tongue followed lapping the water from their creamy surface. His large hand cupped her breast raising to receive homage from his mouth. The tip began to pucker instantly pleading for more. Garrett complied servicing each in turn until a soft moan of passion escaped her lips.

Daringly he slipped his hand beneath the surface of the water to stoke her womanly petals with whispery touches. A flush rose encompassing her breasts and traveling up to her throat, which drew his talented mouth back to lightly suckle at the point of her pulse, while his long fingers parted the lips of her mound to seek entrance inside. She was tight and hot. Garrett found himself hardening to a painful fullness. Soon he thought. First, she must experience her first pleasure at a man's hands. Her taking would be so much more enjoyable when she was soft and hot for him.

Gently, but with increasing rapidity his fingers stroked her woman's flesh. Light forays into her heat soon had her tossing her head and spreading her legs for his touch. He sought deeper entrance plunging harder with his hand until he felt the barrier of her maidenhead. That he would leave for later. The rapid flutters and pressure soon had her honeyed cream coating his fingers. Garrett increased the rhythm and at the same time moved to draw one pert breast into his hot mouth drawing strongly on its rose tip. He felt her muscles tighten around his fingers before a soft cry escaped her lips followed by a shudder of pleasure. Gently he withdrew to gather her in his arms carrying her to his bed.

With soft stokes of the sheet the pleasure was rekindled while he dried her delectable skin. He returned to her breasts suckling strongly until her hands came up pushing at his shirt. He followed her silent request discarding his shirt, tossing it on the floor. Then he covered her with his body allowing her to feel the weight of an aroused man upon her frame.

"Garrett" she moaned softly. He did not allow her time to think. He assaulted her senses with his experienced hands and lips pushing her ever closer toward her peak. Before long Angel was tossing on his bed and pulling at his clothes. Garrett quickly removed them returning to her side covering her with his heat and hard frame. Angel's eyes opened wide at the feel of his engorged

Chapter Seventeen

member pushing against her soft belly. Garrett would have no turning back now. His mouth assaulted hers with demanding kisses followed by quick darting forays of his tongue. Soon her mouth was grasping for his. His tongue showed hers the rhythm that was soon followed by their bodies. Male hands caressed her leaving no sense untouched. Soon her delightful hands were stroking his back, shyly moving down to grasp his firm buttocks. The time had come to make her his. Strong male knees pressed instantly against her thighs demanding that she open. Angel was senseless with pleasure. Thought was impossible. Her body followed where his led. The male part of him was huge and hard. She could feel it rubbing against her woman's opening. The cream for her previous encounter eased his way when with light but demanding thrusts he began to make his way inside her body. It felt wonderful!

Garrett clenched his teeth as he made entrance into Angel's fiery heat. God, the woman was hot. Her muscles clenched against his invasion. Then relaxed and softened allowing him to penetrate further into her softness. She was incredibly tight, fitting him like a new glove. He continued to push forward dropping his mouth to lick at her breast. Her small hands clenched against his buttocks driving him onward to his goal. Her maidenhead blocked his entrance. Garrett kissed her wildly licking and nibbling upon her shoulders and neck. When he lightly bit her breast and she rose to meet him a long hard thrust had him through her barrier. Her soft gasp was the only sign of pain. Momentarily, he lay still giving her time to accustom herself to his invasion into her body. When she relaxed against him he continued on his quest, driving into her, sending her higher.

Angel began to pant. Her hot breath feeding his fire. Garrett grasped her knees pulling them up to encircle his waist. He pulled her close and began thrusting with a steady tempo. Soft nibbles at her ear drove her crazy and Angel began to moan. The tempo increased the thrusts became harder and deeper. She thought she would go mad. Her body was reaching for something.

"Garrett, Garrett!"

"I know love, let go I'll catch you," he said as with renewed vigor he pumped into her. Angel raked her nails across his buttocks tensing before the final pleasure. It came with a rush sending her over the edge into ecstacy.

With Angel's pleasure achieved Garrett turned to his own. He gripped her hips pulling her into his mighty thrusts. With her last shivers of pleasure and one last squeeze of her woman's core he stiffened releasing his seed in mighty spurts into her body. Gently he collapsed on her body breathing heavily. Soon he rolled to one side taking her with him. She felt so good, so right, that he refused to leave her body. Gently he raised one of her legs to ride on top of his allowing her more comfort. Angel made a halfhearted attempt to pull free but Garrett tightened his hold on her, licked her neck and said, "Leave it." Angel did not have the strength to resist.

Garrett watched her drift off. His body was hardening, ready to service her again. She would be his. By the time the morning dawned their hearts and their bodies would never be the same. Angel would never forget the first time she'd ever felt a man, this man, inside her. His seed had been the first seed. No man would ever erase his imprint.

Her heat was seducing him. Even in sleep her body wanted his. Gently at first and then with more vigor Garrett began to ride her again. Slowly she awoke to find his head at her breast once more and his male member driving into her woman's sheath.

"No, Garrett. Please stop."

"Don't say no, Angel. Your body wants mine as badly as mine does yours. I can feel your love juice flowing already." His deep thrust enforced his words.

"Stop it," she said angrily. "This isn't right. Just because you had me once doesn't mean you may have me whenever you wish!"

He took her face between his hands and said huskily, "Darling, I can do anything I wish whether you want me to or not. Who's to stop me?"

"Garrett, please stop." Her hands began to push at him, turning Garrett's passion into anger.

"Why should I? You came to my bed willingly enough. I cer-

Chapter Seventeen

tainly didn't force you, Angel. Why don't you just relax and enjoy the ride I'll give you."

Angel began to cry. What had happened to the caring man that had loved her so gently? Couldn't he see that she was confused? She wanted Garrett but what would the future hold for them now?

Garrett saw himself as if from another's eyes riding Angel to his satisfaction. What was wrong with him? He had never been an inconsiderate lover before. Duprell's image burst into his mind followed by Bess's words, "Out of another man's grip". Yes, he would use any means possible to keep Angel even if it meant riding her against her will. He had seduced her once he could do it again. And if she went to Duprell with his seed growing in her belly the Queen would surely return Angel to the man that had an heir growing within her. Those thoughts ran through his mind even as he gentled his thrusts and turned to arousing the lady again.

Chapter Eighteen

Angel came to hate the nights. Garrett relentlessly broke down all her defenses to bring her to new heights of ecstasy. She knew it was wrong and waited for fate to intervene, setting the two lovers at odds.

She watched Garrett as he captained his ship, learning bits and pieces of his character from the handling of his men. His was a harsh and strict discipline, but always fair. The days stretched out into weeks and Angel gloried in the closeness the two shared until the moon cast her light. Garrett would not listen to her pleas or concerns, breaking down her barriers each night till she sobbed her passion in his arms. But morning brought, once again, the feeling of dread as if a cloud lingered over their heads. After three weeks at sea Garrett turned the *Lady* toward home. By his reasoning Josh should have more information by now. If a message was waiting the time was now to return to receive the news. If Duprell had continued his game, well he would rather face his enemy in a fight he could master.

Duprell had not been idle while the *Lady* had carried her Captain across the seas. The marriage contract and Lucas had arrived at court to establish his claim on Cassandra. The Queen was disinclined to hold the marriage contract in credence, knowing from past experience that both families were not of spotless reputation. But finally, she sent word to the Jamison Estate for Garrett to return with the Lady in question.

Duprell raged at the delay making it known to the Queen that he doubted her sincerity. Elizabeth gave him an insolent glare reminding him that any marriage hinged on her acceptance of the two parties. Even if Angel was nobility, twice removed, Lucas was

Captured Pearl

a Lord of the realm and subject to the Queen's approval.

Josh had heard from his sources with little favorable information. The documentation of Angel's birth had been procured in France establishing her father's family and her mother's name. Things did not look well for Garrett keeping his Lady. The lineage was as Duprell had given, but Josh found other interesting facts in his informant's message. Yes, Angel's mother, Felicity, had been Duprell's sister by marriage, however Angel's father, while not of the French nobility was held in high regard by the crown of that country. He had been a prominent scholar at the University, and had spent time at the French court instructing the future heir to the throne. His mysterious and untimely death had aroused suspicion. Her dead father had been found clutching the rare Greek history in a death grip. All parties concerned had connected Monsieur Gourdue's death to the attempted theft of the old book, as he had been translating it for the Dowager Queen, who had quite an interest in ancient Greek history. It was said that to this day, the ancient tomb was stained with the blood of its defender.

When Felicity (Angel's Mother) had disappeared at almost the same time, his associates at the University and court cried foul play. To this date nothing had been proven, but there were subtle references to a Monsieur Jaqual, one of the underground leaders of thieving and intrigue.

Mayhap with further searching a connection could be found that would keep Angel out of Duprell's hands. Meanwhile, Garrett would have to use his best ingenuity to thwart Duprell.

The *Lady* sailed into her home harbor on a rainy September morning. The gray clouds reflected Angel's mood. She felt out of sorts with everyone aboard the vessel. Garrett escorted her to shore, giving last minute instructions to the crew. Sable was waiting to carry them home. Rudy had seen the ship coming from the hilltop outside the stables and saddled the stallion sending him down the trail. Sable knew the way from previous trips down the path. His Master always had a treat for him, insuring that the horse

Chapter Eighteen

waited until the ship came in. Garrett was pleased that he had taken the time to train Sable for the assignment. Riding to the Estate was much more to his liking than the long walk would have been. He mounted and then lifted Angel to ride before him on the stallion. Sable seemed to know that he carried precious cargo and his normally high-spirited gait was suited to the Lady that occupied a place upon his back.

Mame was waiting when Garrett and Angel arrived at the Estate. Miles had taken his leave to return to his modest home, which was not far from the big house. He and Jim Peters both lived fairly close to Garrett so that they would be available when orders came to once again carry out the Queen's business. Mame came bustling out to Angel, her arms outstretched in welcome.

"Oh! My beloved Angel. I thought something terrible had happened to you." She enveloped her in a hug, which Angel returned.

Garrett interrupted, "What about me?"

Mame released Angel. "Come here you wayward sailor. Where did you hide my lovely Angel?"

"The Queen has shown an interest in Angel, Mame, and we may have a lead on her family. Is there any correspondence from Josh Birmingham?"

"No sir, but there is a missive from the Court that arrived just yesterday."

Angel could tell by the look on Garrett's face that he was not pleased with this news. Mame looked at them both sensing the tension that her news had imparted. Whatever was going on here?

Garrett apprised Mame of his role as Angel's guardian, as established by the Queen.

"Oh my," said Mame delighted. "There is a Lady of the house again. I have to get the house in order. Both of you go on now so I can do my work. Cook would be pleased to fix you both some hot broth and bread."

As she babbled on Garrett and Cassandra turned toward the stairs and he said, "Hold on Mame. We would both like a hot bath and I will need to see my correspondence. Angel do you want something to eat?"

Angel declined the meal but agreed with the idea of a bath. "I would like to rest after I bathe."

"Please Mame, would you help Angel?"

"Of course," Mame answered a little indignantly.

"Please Mame," said Angel, "I would really love a bath and I will tell you the whole story."

Mame's eyes lit up and she smiled at Angel as they climbed the stairs. "Yes, child, let me get you out of those clothes, they smell of the sea." The women giggled and disappeared into Angel's dressing room.

Garrett had a chance to sit back and ponder the course of things to come. He smiled thinking of Angel and how perfect she was. He was sure Duprell had something to do with Angel's loss of memory. The brief flashes of her life had continued on the voyage. Each one bringing terror to her eyes. Garrett had held her gently and loved the nightmares away. At these times she had been almost desperate for his touch, as if he could wipe away anything bad in her life. Each episode had left her more certain that somehow she was attached to Duprell. Garrett knew that part of her fear came from the uncertainty of his feelings for her. Would he be able to get past the knowledge that she might have been involved with Duprell even if it hadn't been on a sexual level. His heart cried yes! He was finding it more difficult to believe that she would voluntarily be involved in Duprell's schemes, but what did he really know about her? His mother, Catherine, would have adored her, and his father would have chided him for having doubts, especially if she was his love.

Perhaps it was time for him to venture into the attic and search out the journals written by his mother that he knew were stored there. After his parents' death he'd had them taken to the attic along with other mementoes, which brought painful memories. There had been a trunk full of his mother's writings. Would they shed any light on the background of his mystery Lady?

The thought gnawed at his mind until he turned from the Queen's correspondence to track down the worrisome journals.

Chapter Eighteen

Entering the attic Garrett quickly located the trunk. Resolutely he threw open the lid determined to see this task through to completion. The journals were all dated, neatly following the path of his family's lives. Soon he was engrossed in them.

> *March 10, 1560*
> *Garrett is overjoyed with the birth of his brother, whom we have christened Shane. What a protective and caring big brother he is! My dearest love is overjoyed with the birth of another son after my unsuccessful second pregnancy. My heart weeps with joy at the sight of my wondrous family. Pray God that he shall allow us all a joyful, full life.*

Garrett paused reflecting on the stated miscarriage unfolded in the journal writings and he wondered how a woman survived such a tragedy. Truly, God had blessed women with a loving and giving heart for them to continue on in the face of such sorrow.

> *September 17, 1561*
> *My dearest love's father passed into God's grace today after a full and long life. We shall miss Father James deeply. The King sent his regrets by way of his minister, Lord Drake. Daniel was touched by the King's kind message.*

> *December 7, 1561*
> *Priscilla has finally consented to resume her visits! I am overjoyed to see her again! Truly, I have missed our talks. She arrived with Donovan, her son,*

Captured Pearl

a nice young boy. He and Garrett get along quite handsomely. Although, Priscilla seems overly subdued—almost sad.

February 2, 1562

After sending the boys off with Mame to play, I secreted Priscilla off to the solarium. Tearfully, she admitted what a mistake she made in marrying Duprell. The man has squandered nearly half of the family's fortune since their wedding! She fears for her inheritance and Donovan's future, but according to English law her husband controls the fortune of the family. It is useless to remind her of her folly and I can only hope that our visits can continue to bolster her spirits.

Thank God, my Daniel has always saw to my having coin of my own! If anything should happen to him the account in London bears my name so the boys and I would not suffer under another's ministrations.

July 17, 1562

Priscilla was quite distraught. She discovered the wastrel at the gaming halls again. This time in the company of some Frenchman, McNay? He had convinced Duprell to cast a disastrous bet on some fisticuffs match, thus losing an absurd amount of coin on the venture.

She is beside herself for the man has lost them the family business! How will they survive?

Chapter Eighteen

November 1, 1563

It's an unusually early and cold winter. I traveled to the Duprell Estate after having no response from Priscilla. Most of the staff has been dismissed and the only fire burning was in that bastard's study!

I shall have James take over fuel and food stuffs for Priscilla and Donovan. It is obvious there is nothing in the house for them to survive on.

December 22, 1563

I have discussed with my dearest Daniel the dire straits of Priscilla and her son. We have agreed to have necessities arrive at their door.

No child deserves to hunger due to a wastrel father! Christmas season shall arrive for Donovan and Priscilla!

My poor friend has miscarried. She can only be thankful there is not another mouth to feed.

April 7, 1564

The boys are growing rapidly and readily accept Donovan into their world.

The worry on Priscilla's face breaks my heart! She has become a recluse in that marked house! My heart breaks for the woman she used to be.

Donovan, too, has changed. The happy boy has become sullen – almost cruel sometimes, but my bravest Garrett takes him under his wing showing him the way of a gentleman. Shane accepts the boy because his brother

Captured Pearl

does, and Garrett already seems ever watchful.

I am so proud of my boys! Every day I thank God for my Daniel.

August 28, 1568
Priscilla came to visit today. She was quite joyful, exclaiming over the letter about her sister Felicity's marriage and pregnancy.

Her sister's husband's family has welcomed her with open arms and they reside at the family vineyard in France.

She speaks of joining her sister, but I don't believe she has the fortitude to follow through.

June 10, 1569
Priscilla came alone today. Donovan was taken by his father on some outing.

She talks of her sister's child and the wonderful life they have in France.

The misfortunes of life! Priscilla's choice has turned out to be disastrous, while Felicity, who has also married for love, has great fortune.

Garrett laid the journal down, saddened by his mother's writings. What compassion his mother had. But he found himself drawn back to the journals. Randomly he chose another volume, letting it fall open of its own accord.

May 14, 1570
My dearest Daniel has procured a place for

Chapter Eighteen

Garrett at Eaton. I shall miss him terribly! But, I put on a brave face for his sake. Garrett is overjoyed to be going off to school.

Shane is caught up in the exuberance of his brother and exclaims "Me, too~me, too!"

Garrett will depart this fall when the new term begins.

June 27, 1570

Priscilla has stopped visiting. I believe she is overcome by the embarrassment of her situation.

There was talk at the Stapleton's party that Duprell was engaged in disreputable forays to reestablish his finances.

September 4, 1570

Garrett writes of school. He learns quickly and is enjoying himself.

To my surprise, Donovan has also been entered in the fall term. I cringe to think how Duprell has managed to obtain the funds for his son's education.

Rumors are rampant in society of his alleged gambling losses.

Priscilla was taking tea at Bower's yesterday. We had traveled to London to attend the Queen's celebration. I invited her to join me as I waited for Daniel. Some altercation between my dearest husband and Duprell had the whole block in an

Captured Pearl

uproar! Daniel refuses to discuss it with me.

October 30, 1570

We traveled to Plymouth for the All Saint's Mass. Priscilla was attending. She was escorted by a rough-looking hireling. Daniel could see her distress and to my heart's joy he invited her to worship in our family pew.

Afterward we visited. She has heard from her sister Felicity, who is quite happy in her life. Felicity has a small son, Jean Paul.

Priscilla expressed her thanks that Garrett seems to have taken Donovan under his wing again. She is quite worried that his father's cruel behavior is influencing Donovan and she was quite happy to see him off to school and away from Duprell's influence. Let us hope it is not too late.

January 6, 1571

Shane shows a great ability for languages and learning. His tutor recommends that we consider applying to the Paris University when he is of age! Of course, Shane is overjoyed at the prospect.

Daniel laughs at my sorrow, winking wickedly at me. The man is incorrigible! No wonder I love him so!

Chapter Eighteen

February 9, 1572

The cruel trick Donovan has played on Garrett has forever driven a rift in their friendship. The gall of that boy to steal Garrett's report and change the marks!

More and more Donovan exhibits the behavior of his father.

May 5, 1572

Daniel and Shane departed for Paris.

Mr. Stephan, the tutor, has arranged for an audience with the Professors. If all goes well Shane will be admitted to study upon turning 15.

October 7, 1572

Daniel has seen to Donovan's expulsion from Eaton. Garrett roared about the house demanding vengeance on behalf of the girl he had become enamored with. I was afraid something would happen involving Donovan. I fear for Garrett, he has become so bitter toward both Donovan and his father. I must persuade Daniel to do something for the poor girl, if only for Garrett's peace of mind. My innocent, trusting boy has been lost forever.

Garrett continued to page through the journals. In one volume his mother had described the Duprell Estate in detail. The entry bespoke of Donovan Duprell's marriage to Anne. Garrett's mother had attended for the friendship of past years with Priscilla. The entry hinted of a strained conversation and early departure

Captured Pearl

from the party.

The last entry was dated just three weeks before his parents' deaths.

> *June 12, 1576*
>
> *Daniel is so proud of the boys! Shane excels at the University, bringing praise from his professors, and Garrett has already become a seasoned Captain of the family trading fleet.*
>
> *Both of my boys have grown into fine men that any mother could be proud of!*

Reverently, he placed the journals back into the trunk. One question had been answered. Cassandra was who Duprell claimed her to be.

Knowing this he resolved to hold the knowledge secreted within his heart for he would not give Cassandra up! The Queen herself had given him the Lady, and his heart was determined to keep her!

As Angel languished in the hot bath she came to a decision. She would confront Duprell. It was the only way to end this once and for all. She would demand that he tell her who she was. Garrett would be furious but even he must see that if Duprell held the answers they must confront him. Mame entered seeing that Angel was content and turned to leave.

"Please Mame, stay." Angel gestured to the chair. "What can you tell me about the Duprell family? I understand their Estate is quite close to this one."

"That's not my place Miss. The Master should impart that knowledge if he deems it necessary."

"Mame, Duprell made a claim to the Queen that I am his niece by marriage. Garrett won't answer my questions. What if Duprell is right? What if the Queen rescinds Garrett's guardianship and I have to go with Duprell? Shouldn't I know what I have

Chapter Eighteen

to deal with, what I am going to do?"

Mame could not argue with Angel's reasoning. The Master should have informed her. Men! They always seemed to think that by keeping Ladies uninformed they were protecting them. Well, most Ladies Mame had encountered had a mind to think. Forewarned was forearmed!

"It's a sad and ugly tale Miss. The families used to be on very friendly terms before Duprell's mother married that wastrel Frenchman Duprell. The Lord's mother, Catherine, and Duprell's mother, Priscilla, were great friends throughout their youth. The young Misses visited each other often traveling back and forth between the Estates. Then their family took a trip to France where Priscilla fell in love with a young French Lord. The family tried to discourage the romance, even Lady Jamison tried, but Priscilla would have no other. After countless forays by that Duprell boy the family finally agreed, afraid that the young Miss would run off if they did not allow the marriage. Nothing good came after! The old Lord died a few years later leaving that Duprell in charge of the Estate. He quickly ran the place down, gambling everything away. For a time the Lady Priscilla stopped visiting. Lady Catherine pursued the friendship. It wasn't until Lady Priscilla was carrying that she began to call once more. You could clearly see that she was unhappy. Lady Catherine tried to help but there wasn't much to be done except to remain a friend. Donavan and Garrett became friends maintaining the friendship into their college days. Then something happened at the school that set the two families at odds. The Master and Lord Duprell carry on the feud to this day.

"Duprell has a reputation of being mean and cruel. Unusually so, Angel. If you have any intentions of confronting him, please don't. He has destroyed several young Misses with his cruelty and deprivation. Stay away from the man! He will destroy you and take the Lord with you!"

Angel could see that Mame was truly frightened just talking about the man. This only reinforced her feelings of terror where he was concerned. It also enforced her desire to find out what the man knew about her.

Captured Pearl

"I'll be careful Mame. Hopefully the Queen will find the truth. I really don't want to ever see the man again, but if he holds the key to my memories I'll have to take that chance."

Mame shook her head, making a mental note to talk to the Lord about this conversation. He would know how to protect the Miss.

Garrett finished his bath then dressed for the day ahead. The missive from the Queen was first on his list. Making his way to the study he heard Angel and Mame's quiet murmurings through Angel's door. Mame had taken to Angel like a cat to cream. Angel returned the affections. Every Lady needed a confidant. Mame was a wise choice. She would impart wisdom to the girl, yet warn him of any actions not in Angel's best interests. Once the study door was closed Garrett took up the heavily embossed letter from the Queen. The seal of state was still intact. Carefully he opened the letter moving to stand by the window before reading the script.

> Lord Jamison,
>
> The crown finds that we must recall you to the court to confront the issues concerning the Lady known as Angel or Cassandra. Lord Duprell has produced evidence that must be confronted. His claim to be the Lady's uncle seems to have some standing and he has in his possession a marriage contract for the Lady to wed Lord Lucas Gabel.
>
> With Favor,
> Her Majesty Queen Elizabeth

Christ! Now Duprell had done it. Gabel wasn't much better a man than Duprell. Garrett knew Duprell too well to know that if he actually was Angel's uncle he wasn't wedding her for her best interests. There must be something he could do. Surely, Bess would have the answers to these questions before she would turn Angel over to

Chapter Eighteen

Duprell, and hopefully, Josh had gained some insight that would help. Garrett's skin crawled at the thought of turning Angel over to the two demented men. There had to be another answer.

Garrett remembered a time when Gabel had been a fairly decent man. Then he had become ill with a fever that the doctors could not identify.

The illness had caused him to add to his incredible girth turning his large frame into a ponderous bulk. His face became misshapen and heavy. The weight of his jowls drug at his thick, lower lip allowing his lower teeth to show at times. His stomach protruded so far that even the latest fashion of wearing rolls upon the belly to add to one's girth seemed slimming. He had special smocks and gowns made to replace his jackets allowing him to move about in comfort. He had become so large and unattractive that even the Lords and Ladies went out of their way to avoid him, adding to his self-loathing and cruel nature. With all of his wealth, he could not buy his health, but he still had the urges of other men. When the women he pursued rejected him, he became bitter and consumed by self-pity.

Gabel had always had a taste for the finer things in life, and the coin to procure them. It was obvious to Garrett that an agreement had been struck by the two, allowing both Duprell and Gabel to obtain what they wished. And Cassandra was the instrument of their desires. She was being sold to the highest bidder.

A demented man such as Gabel would revel in bedecking his arm with such a beautiful treasure as Cassandra. He would also destroy her, of this Garrett was certain. His cruel and unusual appetites would crush the light and beauty of her soul.

Unconsciously Garrett fingered the hilt of his sword, relishing the thought of seeing both Duprell and Gabel skewered upon his blade. There was no way he was going to allow their agreement to be consummated!

There was no reason to rush right back to court. Garrett would give his men several days with their families before setting sail again. Bess would understand and the delay would allow Josh more time. Garrett needed time, also. He felt that he was mounting an attack against a foe that had all the pieces to the puzzle. Something he did not have. For the first time in his life he was going into a battle unprepared and with little information. There would be no support at his back this time.

He and Angel would have to face this threat alone. Garrett had never made ready to sail with such a feeling of disaster riding on his shoulders.

Chapter Nineteen

When Garrett and Angel arrived at Court they were immediately ushered to the audience chambers of the Queen. Elizabeth motioned them forward and then got down to the business at hand. Garrett viewed the marriage contract between Duprell and Lucas Gabel. Everything was in order as far as the legal aspects of the contract were concerned; whether the Lady in question was actually Cassandra was yet to be seen.

"We must allow the parties to converse with the Lady and see if they can make identification. I fear the prospects do not look to be in your favor at this time Lord Jamison."

Garrett could see there would be no way to avoid the edict of the Queen. Therefore he made one request.

"Your Majesty, due to the reputation of the Lords involved I would request that an escort be assigned to the Lady for her safety's sake."

The Queen agreed, appointing one of her personal guards to the task and then she sent for Duprell and Gabel. The two men arrived looking quite smug. Garrett was immediately on guard. They obviously had a plan. Elizabeth explained the rules that would be in effect for the interview. Duprell would be allowed some time with Angel alone with the escort, of course, and then Gabel would be allowed to join them. Elizabeth would assign another guard at that point in time. Duprell had a scowl on his face by the time the Queen had finished. His displeasure with the rules of communication was evident, which relieved Garrett to some small degree.

"You may talk with the Lady in the adjoining room." Angel's escort followed the two out the door.

Something was vaguely familiar about this man. Angel

could not pinpoint what it was, but she became frightened with the thought of being alone with him. She looked nervously toward the Queen's guard taking some small comfort from his presence. Angel felt an intense desire to turn and race back to Garrett's side. Her skin was cold and clammy but she willed herself onward.

Duprell had been busy. The letter he had sent to Lucas had brought the man to Court days before Garrett had returned with Cassandra. They had finalized the agreement for the marriage adding its written testament to the evidence to regain Cassandra. Duprell could not afford to have Lucas back out of the contract.

When Cassandra had come to live with her aunt and uncle, Lucas had fallen in love with her beauty before he had even spoken to her. To him she was the loveliest child he had ever seen. He had patiently waited until she had grown into a woman, scheming and dreaming of her by his side. But she had no interest in him. He had told Duprell to name his price—he wanted Cassandra.

Lucas had always enjoyed the best that could be gotten from the English countryside. His parents had seen to his acquired tastes for beauty and culture, even while the warmth of human affection had been withheld. At an early age he had sought contact outside his family home. His family's station and wealth had always guaranteed its delivery.

Duprell had jumped at the opportunity. Lucas was an extremely rich man and a marriage to Cassandra could prove very lucrative for Duprell. When Duprell had proposed to make a match for her, Cassandra had flatly refused.

Cassandra had become familiar with the man during his business ventures with her uncle. She had known that he watched her, following her with his pig-like eyes, and he made her uncomfortable.

At first Duprell had tried to cajole Cassandra. When that hadn't worked he had threatened her, but Cassandra had stood firm in her refusal.

When Cassandra's parents had died, she had been too young to live alone or to manage the inheritance her father had set aside

Chapter Nineteen

for her. Her Aunt Anne had loved her sister and invited Cassandra to live with her and her husband. Anne wanted to arrange a good match for Cassandra, someone of equal, or better status, who would care for her dead sister's child. There were several good families, but none as wealthy as Lucas. Duprell argued with Cassandra and his wife but neither would budge. When Anne had died in childbirth, Cassandra was left alone without an ally. She had to fight Duprell alone.

Duprell and Lucas had gone over their stories carefully so as to present a united front to the Queen. Lucas would be persuasive when cajoling Cassandra. With his careful courting of her the Queen would be able to see the man was intent on the marriage. They had agreed to present the marriage as if Cassandra had agreed to the match. Duprell would come off as the caring Uncle looking out for his orphan niece's best interests.

Cara had been carefully coached as to her part and Duprell had used force to strengthen her resolve to get the story right. When she appeared before the Queen, Duprell was confident she would have the facts straight. Cara was to appear later before the Queen to validate her knowledge of Cassandra's identity. Fortunately, this fell right into her plans. If the Queen awarded Cassandra to Lucas, her way was clear to Garrett.

He was unaware that Cara was scheming, but her best efforts had turned up little to use against him. To add to her frustration, Margaret had been dragging her heels about helping her, afraid to lose the one constant in her life. She had been thrilled to see her daughter in the resplendent clothes Duprell had made for Cara for the night at Court. Margaret was sure that no man would spend that kind of coin on a woman it he did not care for her.

Finally after one particular night of abuse Cara had sought out her mother showing her the bruises and marks that Duprell had left upon her fair skin. Cara had ranted at her mother, "He raped me, Mother. Look at what he's done to me! I'll be lucky if he hasn't ruined my face. I'll never get another man if Duprell ruins my face! Garrett will never take me back! Do something!

Captured Pearl

Margaret loved her child and so—reluctantly, she had agreed to Cara's plan. Together they would flush out Duprell's secrets earning themselves a life of ease at last—even while, to outward appearances, they seemed to play Duprell's game. Margaret was privy to the people Duprell had coming and going from the Estate. With her shopping trips as the housekeeper she could arrange to follow some of the visitors, or Duprell, on the pretense of needing things for the household.

As they entered the room Duprell took Angel's arm steering her out to the balcony. In a deceptively pleasant voice he said, "Good morning, Niece. I am so glad to see you well. You had me quite worried with your disappearance. My men looked everywhere but could find no trace of you. I was convinced that you had been kidnapped."

Angel was taken off guard. "Kidnapped? Why would someone kidnap me?"

"I am quite a wealthy man," Duprell lied smoothly. "Over the years, as with most men of means, I have made enemies. I was quite certain that one had snatched you from the safety of my house to command some kind of payment from me. I was quite relieved to find that the Queen herself had arranged for your safety." Actually Duprell wanted to strangle her but he had too much riding on the marriage of this chit. He was almost mad with fear because all of his plans hinged on Cassandra not remembering her past. His plans would definitely sour if she was able to retell the tale of the night she had disappeared. Now that he had the Queen's attention he must tread carefully to keep in her good graces. He must control his anger hoping to turn her to his side.

"Is it true that you have no memory of your past?"

"That is so."

"Let me tell you of your family. Perhaps something will ring true. You had a bad fever the night of your disappearance, which we thought allowed some despot to subdue you without sound. In fact, earlier that evening you had been calling for your dead parents."

Chapter Nineteen

Angel concentrated hard on his words but no picture of her parents surfaced. She could not remember their faces.

"Why was I on the road that night?"

"I really can not say. If some scoundrel actually tried to kidnap you perhaps you managed to get free of the culprit. Or perhaps, in your weakened state; you imagined something that scared you causing you to flee. But let's talk about your future. Cassandra, you were approached by Lucas Gabel to become his wife. I really think that you should consider his proposal."

"But sir, I don't even know the man, how could I possibly marry him?"

"You shall meet him shortly. The Queen has recognized the marriage contract as valid. When we prove that you are actually Cassandra Gourdue you will be set for life. The man is quite rich—even more so than I. While I will admit that he is not as handsome as Lord Jamison is, he can take care of you."

Cassandra felt the familiarity of this man. Something deep inside her soul told her that the man was her uncle as much as she wanted to deny that fact. She knew the Queen was going to have no choice but to hand her over to Duprell.

"Uncle, do I have any brothers or sisters?" She did not want to talk about the marriage proposal.

"Yes," said Duprell. "You had an older brother, Jean-Paul. He died in one of the Spanish raids along the coast."

"How old was he?" She was saddened that she could not remember him.

"Jean-Paul was twenty-four. He died last year in the fall. He was a brave man." For once Duprell was telling the truth. Cassandra's brother had been a wonderful and courageous man. He had been gone for about five months when the Spanish ambushed his ship. Jean-Paul and most of the crew had been killed in the ensuing battle. Duprell had been vastly relieved when he had heard the news from one of his informants. The brother had been a constant pain. The man was as determined to look out for his sister as his wife, Anne, had been. He had always been thwarting Duprell's plans to gain riches from the beauty of Cassandra.

Captured Pearl

Finally, when the man had been killed Duprell had been able to bring fruit to his ill-laid plans.

Duprell turned to another avenue of persuasion. "Cassandra, you owe me," he said almost sadly. "I have taken care of you all these years—and how else will you survive? Your care has cost me a great deal over the years. You can't count on Lord Jamison to keep you forever. The man will be marrying you off soon enough to recoup his investment. You have no money of your own and you have no husband to provide for you. Lucas can be that man. He will provide a wonderful life for you. Just give it a few months. Soon you'll have him granting your heart's desire. And there is something to be said for marrying an older man. They are much more skilled at pleasing a woman."

Angel thought of Garrett's tender loving and knew that there was no one more skilled at bringing her to ecstasy's door.

Duprell watched the emotions flitter across her face. At one time Cassandra had a considerable inheritance from her father. He had been bestowed with much wealth and favor by the French court, but Duprell had greedily gone through the monies set side for her future when he had taken over the care and guidance of her finances. He continued to cajole Angel. Tears began to fall and she heard only the tone of his voice but not the words he spoke. He sounded consoling and caring but she knew that he lied.

Duprell motioned for the servant dawdling near the door directing him to have Lord Gabel brought to the balcony. Angel watched the doorway hesitantly, not sure what to expect. Nothing could have prepared her for the man that entered. His ponderous bulk has only accentuated by his yellow-toothed smile. The slight dribble of spittle that gathered at one corner of his bulbous lips caused her insides to cringe. Angel swallowed rapidly trying to ease her stomach. His jowls hung close to his short squat neck making his head look larger than it actually was. The fact that he was rich did him little good as far as winning the Ladies. Of course, he slept with whores, as no Lady of quality would have him. That fact had not stopped Lucas from desiring to have quality in his life. From fine wine and paintings, to blooded horses—

Chapter Nineteen

all that was missing was a fine Lady of breeding to grace his home. His lack of a Mother had contributed to his revolting idea of passion and since his bout with the fever roughness and cruelty were the only things that seemed to arouse him. To him, Cassandra was another fine piece of art to add to his collection. She might never love or care for him, but he would see that she learned to respect him.

"Good day, my Lady," Lucas broadened his sickening smile. He held his paw of a hand to receive her small delicate hand. Cassandra tried to think of a reason to refuse him. But in the end she hesitantly offered hers to the man she was supposedly contracted to.

"It is rewarding to see that you are in good health and that no harm befell you from your adventure," Lucas rambled making conversation. Though Cassandra tried to hide it, he could tell that he revolted her. This thought made it all the more pleasing to comprehend that soon she would be his. "Come, sit beside me."

"I would rather stand, thank you."

"Cassandra," Duprell admonished, "Lucas will soon be your husband. Follow the man's direction."

Cassandra moved closer but continued to stand. Lucas reached out and touched her blonde hair. He could hardly contain his excitement. "I've missed you my love."

Cassandra pulled back as if stung. Even though she could not remember him this man frightened her. There was something sinister about the way he looked at her. He kept licking his heavy lips as if she were a treat he waited to devour. Surely, the Queen would not deliver her into the hands of so vile a pair! Did Garrett care enough about her to thwart the Queen to keep her safe? She could hardly count on that knowing already that Garrett was a favorite here at Court. There must be some other way to stay out of their clutches.

The conversation ebbed around her but Angel heard little of it. This sad scene reminded her of the time she had seen a doe at bay with the hounds snapping all around her.

Papa would never have left her to these men's devices.

Captured Pearl

Perhaps Papa's family would take her in! A countryside scene sprang to mind. The French flowers blooming, the people gay and light-hearted. A beautiful, blonde woman bending over the girl child, while a dark-haired man scattered flower petals about them both. This was her father and mother! A man came up to take her father away calling him brother. Mama was laughing, waving as they departed.

Another scene flittered in of an elder man sliding a pretty ring upon her finger and remarking, "This shall always bring you home." What had happened to her family ring?

"Where is my family ring?" Cassandra asked of Duprell.

"Why I have no idea what you are speaking of, Cassandra." Duprell remarked giving her a closer look. That piece of her memory did not need to be turning up now!

"I had it when I came to your house as a young girl. What did you do with it?" she demanded. Cassandra was sure the ring of memory could lead her out of this morbid situation.

"You must have dreamed such a thing for you came to my house with little of value," replied Duprell.

Cassandra let the matter drop but made a mental note to talk to Garrett and Josh about the ring. Josh loved to hunt down a puzzle and here was one more piece for him to fit into the larger picture. Then she made a very bold move motioning over the Queen's guard and asking, "Would you be so kind, Sir, as to escort me back to the hall? I find that I am quite weary of this company and could use some refreshment."

The guard nodded knowing quite well that this Lady did not bestow favor on these two men. He had felt genuine pity for the young Lady when he realized that soon she was to be in Duprell's hands. The man was known throughout the court for having no scruples. Duprell made to protest but the action of the guard laying his hand upon his sword quickly dissuaded Duprell from following through. His time would come!

Back inside Elizabeth noticed the strain upon Cassandra's face and motioned Lady Camilla forward to take Cassandra in hand.

Chapter Nineteen

"Your Majesty, if I might have a few minutes to refresh myself I would then request an opportunity to discuss this matter with Lord Jamison and Lord Birmingham?"

"We shall reconvene here in our audience hall within the hour with the parties requested. We shall be present as well as our representatives."

Lady Camilla led Cassandra a short distance down the hall where refreshments were laid in a comfortable sitting room.

"Camilla, could you find me paper and pen and then see that Miles gets this to Lord Birmingham?"

"Of course, child, but what are you doing?"

"I remembered this ring when I was talking to Lord Duprell. I believe it was a family ring that was given to me before I came to live with my uncle. If the ring can be found, or traced to the giver, perhaps some of the mystery will be resolved."

Quickly, Angel sketched the ring on a paper along with a description of the color and stone, to be handed over to Miles for delivery. Angel, or Cassandra, as she was beginning to thinking of herself, could only hope for the best. The Ladies took tea, resting a bit before they were retrieved for the continuing audience with the Queen.

Cassandra broke the silence after the Queen had bade them all be seated. Carefully she looked about her at the faces of the people there. Garrett, Josh, two of the Queen's counselors, and the Queen.

"Your Majesty, as much as I wish this were not the truth, I believe that I am Cassandra Gourdue. I do not remember Lord Duprell or the man that he says is my betrothed, however, I feel that I know him. When he speaks to me I find myself crying 'truth' or 'lie' as if I have information to base these thoughts on. I have remembered fleeting thoughts that seem to come more rapidly when I listen to Duprell voice his wishes.

"I also know that I am terribly afraid of both of those men. Please, your Highness, do not turn me over to them until more information can be garnered regarding my past."

Captured Pearl

The Queen was not without sympathy for the young Lady and her plea, but Lord Jamison was needed in other service. Quietly she weighed the odds finding that she could not hold out to Duprell's claim without endangering other more pressing matters. Surely the man was not bold enough to cause the Lady harm knowing that the Crown's eyes were upon him!

"Bring Duprell and Gabel to our attendance," the Queen commanded.

"We are sorry Lady, but we find at this time there is no other recourse but to return you to the man you know as Uncle. However, the crown will be placing restrictions upon the man and his dealings in your behalf until a time when all parties have full knowledge of the incidence behind your loss of memory."

Cassandra had thought as much, and from the look in Garrett's eyes, he had been expecting this as well. He was grim-lipped and all glinty eyes when Duprell and Gabel returned. Those two looked as if they had just drank the Queen's fresh cream, and this did not go unnoticed by Elizabeth.

"For now the Crown finds in favor of your claim Duprell. However, we find that all concerns are not satisfied. Therefore, we make the following conditions upon relinquishing claim of Lady Cassandra into your care. First, there shall be *no marriage to Lord Gabel* without the express approval of the court. Second, we shall expect to hear that the Lady is being properly escorted about to the neighboring Estates. No Lady should be so unknown that her near neighbors do not know of her existence! Third, we shall expect all parties back at the court for the October ball, where upon, this matter will be discussed further. Are there any questions?"

The parties involved wanted to rant or rave and disagree but the opposing sides wisely held their tongues not wanting to do a disservice to their cause. Cassandra was given a few moments to make her good-byes to the men who had cherished and protected her since her discovery on the road.

Josh tried to uplift her spirits but it was Garrett's parting words that gave her hope, "Remember, Angel, I protect my own!"

Chapter Twenty

Duprell wasted no time in escorting Cassandra from the Court to the house he had given to Cara. A soon as he could arrange it he would have her back at the Estate and back under his control. Queen's permission, or not, the wedding plans would proceed. If Gabel could pay off a clergy to marry them who was the Queen to gainsay the fact after the marriage was consummated. Providing that Jamison had left her intact. Duprell handed Cassandra over to Margaret admonishing the woman to keep an eye on her while he was gone.

Cara sauntered her way into the study where Cassandra was attempting to put things in perspective. "So," she said nastily, "you're back. Did Garrett toss you away, too? That didn't take long. You must have been quite a disappointment in his bed."

"Who are you?" asked Cassandra surprised by the anger in the other woman's voice.

"Don't play stupid with me," Cara stormed. "You can stop playing your little game. We all know what an accomplished liar you are."

"I have no idea what you are talking about, but someone should have taught you some manners when you were a child!" Cassandra retorted.

Margaret shot Cassandra a hateful look. Cassandra was taken back. Why would these women be so hateful?

"Come, I will show you your room. You'd best rest before the Master gets back. I dare say he will be wanting you rested and willing when he returns." Margaret led the way up the stairs. Cassandra followed her up gazing at the oriental rugs and the incredible woodwork. The house was tastefully decorated. At the end of the hall Margaret opened the door motioning her inside.

Captured Pearl

"This is a lovely home," Cassandra offered hoping to bring some degree of warmth to the woman.

"My daughter's house. As long as she pleases Duprell." The last was said with a bitterness that could only be ingrained after years of disappointment.

Alone, Cassandra looked about the room. Her trunk would be arriving later with all the beautiful things that Garrett had purchased for her. Until then the closets stood empty. As empty as her heart at this moment.

Dinner time had long since passed before Margaret arrived to escort Cassandra to the dining room. She had begun to think that these people weren't going to feed her, not realizing that Duprell preferred a late evening meal. She entered to find Duprell seated at one end of the table with Cara at the other. That awful Gabel was seated there as well. The only seat left vacant was across from Gabel.

"Good evening, my dear."

"Good evening, Sir." Must she suffer this great oaf's presence again this day?

Duprell smiled evilly. "Lucas has been kind enough to accept my invitation to dine with us while we are in London. You two will grow to know one another much better. When the wedding finally proceeds you will no longer be strangers, eh?"

The meal was a nightmare of obscene looks from Lucas and dagger eyes from Cara. How she made it through Cassandra would never remember. But after dinner when Duprell gave his permission for Lucas to walk her in the garden Cassandra felt the bottom drop out of her world. Something in the air told of malicious schemes forming on the night breeze.

Lucas greedily sought her hand holding it in a vice-like grip to prevent its escape. He held her too close to be proper and when she protested he grinned drawing her closer to his side.

"Really Sir, this is quite improper! Loose your hold on me!"

He ignored her protests trying to draw her farther from the lights of the house. Cassandra guessed his intent when his corpu-

Chapter Twenty

lent moist lips planted themselves on her neck. Before Cassandra could think to fight her ankle turned on a stone that sent her sprawling on her knees taking them both unaware. She was the first to recover, gathering up her skirts to flee to the house sprinting up the stairs to lock the door of her room.

"Mother, you have to help me!" Cara whined later in the kitchen. Margaret looked at her daughter. She knew that look. Cara was up to something and she knew that she would do whatever Cara desired for she loved her daughter.

"What have you planned now?" Margaret worried about Cara for she would do anything and sacrifice anything to get what she desired in life. Cara thought only of herself caring little who, or what, she destroyed along the way.

"I want Cassandra kidnapped!"

"What! Why would you do that? Duprell is giving her to Gabel. Soon she will be gone and you alone will be the Lady of the house."

"I don't care about Duprell! Soon he will throw me out. You know I speak the truth. He is losing his interest in me. I want Garrett! He is in love with Cassandra. Any fool can see that! When she is out of the picture I will give Garrett the information we gather on Duprell and he will take me back. I persuaded him once, I can do it again! But I have to get rid of Cassandra first!"

"But how can I help?" asked Margaret.

"You will get Cassandra tonight and smuggle her out of the house. Find a ship that is sailing this night and make sure she is on it!"

"And how do you propose that I convince her to go with me? The girl knows we hate her."

"Mother," said Cara, "you will do it. Find a way! Get Barnabas to help you. He will do anything I ask."

"What ship?"

"There is a ship anchored in Sinclair Harbor that I believe is leaving tonight. I heard some men at Court talking about it leaving at dawn. We can get Cassandra on it and be rid of her! After

Captured Pearl

they are at sea, we will have her dumped overboard and be done with it."

Cara knew her mother was hesitant. "Mother, you don't want me to end up like you and work my fingers to the bone in some other man's house the rest of my life do you? I will not live like that! Think Mother. I can have Garrett if Cassandra is gone. The Jamison Estate and its coin will be ours! Please help me!" Cara started to cry knowing this would seal the fate of Cassandra. She knew her mother's weak points and a crying daughter was at the top of the list.

Cara was right. Margaret could not stand to see her cry. After the dismal failure at a scheme gone wrong with the newly-imported Jamison cattle her man had been jailed where he had died of the pox. At the time she hadn't known of Duprell's bribery to her man to ruin the Jamison's new cattle venture. Margaret had been forced to take any position available to support herself and Cara. Life had not been easy and she would not deny her daughter anything that was in her power to give. She would not see her daughter in such pain. Cara was right; Duprell would never make her happy. She had seen for herself that Duprell was losing interest.

"No killing. I won't have it, do you hear!"

"All right," pouted Cara.

"You talk to Barnabas. If he will help I will try."

Cara agreed knowing that Barnabas had sought her favor for many months. He'd do anything she asked hoping to gain her favor. "Have Cassandra at the harbor before sunlight. I will see to the rest."

Cassandra awoke with a start. Someone was tapping her on the shoulder. Margaret put a hand to her mouth signaling silence. "Hush, Cassandra, I am here to help you."

"But why?" Cassandra asked drowsily trying to bring some reasoning to her weary brain.

"I have to be rude in front of the others so they will not be suspicious. I heard him talking about your marriage to that man! He means to defy the Queen, bringing her wrath upon us all. No

Chapter Twenty

one should be forced to mate with that monster! We must get going early, while everyone is still asleep or we will miss our chance."

Cassandra had no reason to doubt her and thanked the woman for taking such a risk for her. Quietly Cassandra arose, dressing quickly in the dark. "Where are you taking me?"

Margaret explained in a whispered hush that she knew of a ship headed to France, the country of Cassandra's birth. Cassandra was delighted with the destination, although, she wondered how she would go about locating her family in the country of her birth. Margaret packed a small bag informing Cassandra that she would have to pack lightly as she was stealing aboard ship. Besides it was a pity to waste such fine gowns. They would bring a pretty penny in the streets of London.

"I have some money put away."

"Oh, no Margaret. I can't take your money!"

"Of course you can. How else will you survive?" If Cara married Garrett she would not need the coin anyway. They would be set for life, and then she would never have to worry about where the next meal was coming from again.

Intently they listened and waited. When all was quiet Margaret signaled for Cassandra to follow her out of the room and down the rear staircase to where Barnabas was waiting for them. Barnabas was not particularly bright, which allowed Cara to manipulate him to her own ends. He had followed her with yearning eyes since Cara had moved into Duprell's home. Cara had promised that if he could fulfill her instructions he would have a chance with her. She had promised and Barnabas had not the intelligence to see that he had not a chance. He was waiting anxiously when the two women descended the stairway.

"This is Barnabas," Margaret said pointedly. "He will take you to the ship. God go with you," then she silently melted into the darkness of the house. Margaret watched as the two made their way out the rear door. She could almost feel sorry for Cassandra, but her own child must come first. Cara's future was at stake as well as her own.

Captured Pearl

Garrett had received his sailing orders from the Queen. Howard was setting one last ambush for the Spanish Armada before the winds changed and the weather worsened. The ships had been quickly readied to sail that morning. The crew was already aboard—awaiting their Captain. The sun had not risen when he readied himself for the mission at hand. Elizabeth wanted to meet with him one last time before he set sail—reasons unknown. He thought of Angel, Cassandra, and wondered how she was faring with Duprell. Her last words haunted him . . . "was life so terrible that I would do anything to escape?" He might never know.

Miles would not be sailing along this time. Garrett had sent him back to the Estate to watch over things there until his return. Both he and Miles had agreed that Tanner was capable of the job of watching his back as shown by his actions during the celebration. Miles admitted that a younger man would more likely keep the Captain in one piece that an old codger past his prime.

Garrett had made an ass of himself last night, drinking far more than he usually did. The thought of Cassandra had been uppermost in his mind and he had not been able to push it away. Thank God, it had only been his men and Josh to see him unable to make his way to his apartment under his own steam. His head was pounding and he felt as if someone had beaten him with a club. Usually he had more sense. He'd best make his way to Bess or he'd be late for the departure of the ships sailing to intercept the Spanish.

Barnabas and Cassandra arrived at the dock while the sun was still rising in the east. There were two sailing vessels anchored at the dock he had chosen. He had forgotten the name of the one Cara had wanted the young Miss to board. Lord, he wished he could remember! Well, he thought, it really shouldn't matter as long as she was gone. Cara would love him now and be happy in his arms—she had promised she would.

"Which ship is it Barnabas?" asked Cassandra.

Chapter Twenty

He thought for a moment and then pointed to the first ship in his sight. "This one." They crouched down behind some crates scanning the area for any sign of activity. When no one seemed to be about, they hurried to a small boat, hoping the few dockworkers that were arriving would not notice them. Barnabas helped her aboard then picked up the oars rowing them out to the vessel.

"Hurry now, Miss. Climb up the ropes before you are noticed. Hide yourself behind some crates. Once the ship sets sail you can pay your passage to the Captain as he will not be able to set you off." It was evident by the many barrels and crates on the deck that this was not a passenger vessel and Cassandra heeded his warning. She thanked Barnabas and wished him a safe journey home.

Quietly, Cassandra ran across the deck and hid behind an assortment of heavy looking barrels. Voices! Coming her way! Quickly she squatted down lower, drawing the dark cloak she wore about her, hoping to be unnoticed. The men passed by unaware of her presence. That was too close she thought. There was a door by the steps and at her first chance Cassandra scooted towards it. Finding it unlocked she stealthily cracked it open and crawled inside. It was very dark and hard to see. She ran her hands along the walls feeling her way down the steps until her trembling hand made contact with a doorknob. Quickly she stepped inside. More voices coming her way! Cassandra plastered herself against the wall behind the door hoping they would pass by as the first had. But the door began to open! Spying a large desk she slithered behind it on hands and knees. Two men came in. They were dark and sinister looking. She backed herself closer to the wall as one struck a match to light the room. All she could see were the spotless boots on the feet of the men and the swords hanging dangerously low on male hips.

One voice sounding vaguely familiar through her pounding heart and the blood rushing to her ears the voice said, "Keep a close eye out for spies and boarders. Nothing must go amiss this day!"

My God! What had she fallen into?

Chapter Twenty-One

The voices were low and hard to recognize at first but when the third man joined them the "Welcome aboard," was definitely Garrett's voice!

"Glad to have you on this one Peters, Miles has become a landlubber. I'm going to rely on you and Tanner on this mission for the Queen. It won't be an easy one by any means."

"Why Captain," Tanner commented, "easy would just bore us unto death. We be seafaring men who like adventure and a little danger thrown in!" The three men laughed as they began to discuss the route they were to pursue.

Cassandra knelt, frozen to the floor. She knew these men! They had been her salvation in times of trouble. She should let herself be known but her legs refused to function at her mind's call. What was she going to do? Would Garrett keep her on board or put her off when he found out she had overheard the facts of his mission? She couldn't afford to be left on the dock in London. Duprell would find her and make her go back to that house.

But if she delayed, Garrett might even believe that she *was* the spy he had originally thought when he found her hiding in the dark in his cabin! What to do?

The ship heaved to the left as they turned out of the port—setting full sail into the East. Too late! Duprell would not be a worry now, as they were at sea. If she stayed hidden a while longer there was no way she could be set back on land without endangering whatever they were doing for the Queen.

Cassandra would take her chances with Garrett but she would have to get out of this cabin. Garrett might believe her story if she was found on deck. After the men had departed Cassandra carefully made her way up to the aft deck. She peered over the side looking overboard. The ship sat so high out of the water that it was daunting, and it moved so fast skimming over the sea! Just as she took another look over the railing the *Lady* shifted her course once again causing Cassandra to loose her balance tumbling overboard into the sea. Jim Peters turned his head just in time to see her fall over the railing. Garrett heard the splash just as Jim hollered, "Man overboard!"

They ran to the railing to see the wake from the ship pulling the struggling Cassandra under for the second time. Garrett dove into the brink swimming toward the floundering Cassandra and grabbing her under the arms.

A woman! What ever was a woman doing on board his ship? She flailed about causing him to almost lose his grasp upon her.

"Good God, woman, cease your struggling before you drown us both!" Garrett admonished the female in his arms. He quickly snagged the lifeline tossed to him by the crew before the ship was out of reach. The crew heaved, pulling the two closer to the ship with each passing second while Tanner and a few others trimmed the sails cutting back on the speed of the tidy vessel. Soon both Garrett and the dripping Lady in his arms were standing on the deck.

"Be still," he curtly ordered and to his surprise the woman ceased her struggles standing forlornly on the deck. He tipped her face up to gaze into the startling green eyes of Cassandra. What the hell was she doing here? She began to cough up water and so Garrett, none too gently, lowered her to the deck. What was going on? She was supposed to be in Duprell's custody back in London. Had she run off, or had Duprell sent her on some mission of his own?

"Cassandra, what are you doing here? Why aren't you at Duprell's house?" the words came out harsh and cold.

"Stop shaking me Garrett! You're hurting me!" Actually he wasn't—but the words served their purpose in halting the bone-rattling shake he was imparting to her body. "Could we go below? I don't think you want the crew privy to our conversation," Cassandra replied. Garrett glanced around to see that many of the

Chapter Twenty-One

crew had indeed gathered to partake in the viewing of the drama being carried out on the deck. Garrett nodded and escorted her toward his cabin.

"Your bride miss you that much Captain?" queried one of the men. Garrett forced a shaky smile remembering that to most of his crew they were masquerading as newlyweds for her safety, as a soft laugh circulated through the men. Her wet clothing clung to her body and Garrett was sure that it was causing a stir among his men. He put his arm around Cassandra as they passed through the throng and the men cleared the way for the Captain. Until he figured out what she was up to they were definitely better off below. Once inside the cabin Garrett strode to the chest fishing out a blanket to gather about her shoulders. She was already shivering. The sea was not warm on this fall day. They'd be lucky if neither one of them came down with the croup.

"Give me one good reason why I should keep you on my ship." Garrett spoke softly but Cassandra acknowledged the veiled threat. The man was on a mission for the Queen and she had no place on this vessel.

Cassandra swallowed the lump in her throat beginning, "Margaret helped me to escape from the house. Duprell was going ahead with the marriage plans to Gabel. Margaret heard some of the men talking. Gabel was going to rape me so that Duprell could give the Queen cause to approve of the marriage. Garrett that man is awful! I'm so glad that Margaret felt sorry for me!"

Tears were beginning to run down her face. Garrett wondered which man she was talking about. It would be just like Duprell to concoct such a scheme, as Garrett knew from past experience. He might have believed many things that Cassandra could have said, but this one was the one sure to capture his heart bringing out all his protective instincts. The scene of a young girl battered and broken at the hunting lodge flashed through his mind. Yes, this he could believe.

However, Margaret helping Cassandra was an entirely different matter. That woman did nothing that did not further her own gains—or that of her daughter. What was Margaret doing

Captured Pearl

throwing Cassandra back into his arms? He was sure the Mother was aware of Cara's designs upon his person.

Garrett shook his head. "Margaret would never help you because she felt sorry for you Cassandra. The woman doesn't have a decent bone in her body. There must be some other reason why she helped you to board my ship."

"But Garrett, Margaret didn't bring me to your ship; some man called Barnabas brought me for Margaret. He didn't seem very bright although he was quite helpful."

"Really Cassandra you must learn to get the players right. Margaret is Cara's mother. Cara has had designs on me long before you entered the fray. Why ever would she help you? Margaret has worked for Duprell for years, ever since I had her husband arrested for poisoning my cattle. She has no high regard for me, or mine. Are you sure that there wasn't some favor that she wanted from you to repay the favor she did in helping you to escape?"

Tears now ran freely down her face as Cassandra realized that she had been betrayed. Turning her back to him she realized that Margaret must have known that Garrett would be suspicious of her when he found out that Margaret had been her salvation. She had been betrayed. She should have known that someone that had given her such a hateful look could not have truly wanted to help her. Would Cara plan such a scheme just to have Garrett's attentions again? Her heart told her, yes, even if her memories could not.

Then she remembered how confused Barnabas had seemed when it had come to boarding the ship. He must have put her on the wrong ship for surely Cara would not have knowingly placed her in Garrett's care! But would Garrett believe her? Before she could tell him he interrupted.

"You had best get out of those wet things before you catch your death," Garrett interjected into her thoughts. "We'll discuss this further at a later time. I have a ship to pilot and no time for this now. Stay in the cabin out of the way and out of sight Cassandra. I am warning you. If you get in my way I just might be

Chapter Twenty-One

tempted to throw you back over the side and be done with this whole bloody mess!"

"Here, put these on." He threw her one of his shirts and a blanket. "I'll send down some tea and something hot for you."

Cassandra was exhausted even though the day was quite young. Her mind spun with all that had happened. She felt lost and alone. When she picked up Garrett's shirt she breathed in the fresh scent that always clung to him. With a ragged sigh she began stripping off her wet things leaving them in a puddle on the floor. The shirt was dry and a comforting reminder of all the times Garrett had comforted her. She was back on his ship wearing his things. The man infuriated and fascinated her at the same time. If Garrett truly was an agent for the Queen that would explain his suspicious nature toward her, and his unwillingness to trust her. She lay down on the bunk turning all that she knew around and around in her head until the emotional whirlwind of her thoughts finally put her to sleep.

She didn't hear Garrett come in. It was late in the evening when he turned over the watch to Peters to take his turn at rest. There could be no laziness on this mission if they were to be successful and undetected by the Spanish. He gazed at Cassandra's sleeping form, the heat in his body began to rise and suddenly the weariness of the day was replaced by the anticipation of holding her luscious body in his arms. He longed to breathe her scent and taste the perfume of her skin. He slid into the bunk gathering her soft warm body to his own.

Cassandra turned to him in her sleep searching out his warmth and he closed his arms about her burrowing his face into her golden hair. He pulled her further into his arms. What was this hold she had over him? She made him feel complete, whole, and fiercely protective. There was no way he would allow another man to touch her. Lucas would have her over his dead body! That deviant did not deserve such an angel as his Cassandra! Tomorrow he would have to sort out what to do with her but for tonight he would enjoy her soft, warm skin and the dreamy look in her eyes when he brought her to completeness.

Captured Pearl

Soft warm kisses found their way to the nape of her neck. He hugged her closer to his body turning her slightly so that the palm of his hand could caress her perfect breast. Slowly he passed his palm over the rosy nipple until its pert peak begged for his attention. His lips left the delicious appetizer of her neck to continue his banquet at her breast.

Cassandra awoke slowly. It was so warm and so . . . her eyes snapped open to find her dreams from sleep confirmed. Garrett's dark hair stood out starkly against the pale skin of her breast. The tips of its dark strands tantalized her nerve endings sending flutters of warm passion through her entire body.

Cassandra watched as his warm tongue swirled about her breast coming to rest upon the peak. Breathlessly, she waited. As she watched, anticipating his next move, her body tightened. Finally with great care he lightly tongued the tip. The sensation was extraordinary! Cassandra squirmed in his arms seeking a harder pressure from his mouth, but Garrett held her motionless as he tortured her with his passion. When her body was humming, begging helplessly for his, he raised his mouth, "Let me love you, my beloved. Let me love you."

Cassandra slipped her arms free to run her fingers across his broad chest massaging his pectorals with firm strokes. Then she daringly slipped lower wondering if she could arouse the same passion in him. Her exploring hands traveled lower combing through the crisp hair nestling his manhood. She opened her limbs shyly helping to guide him home into her warm wetness. Garrett groaned deliciously as he slid into her and Cassandra arched her back encouraging a deeper penetration, to which he gallantly replied. With care and a tenderness that left her gasping he rode her to heights previously unknown. They climbed the crest together clinging to each other as they tumbled down the valley of desire to lay gasping in each other's arms. He bent toward her kissing her deeply on the lips. She tasted delicious. Cassandra throwing all caution to the winds turned to snuggle into his warmth. Something that felt this right could not be wrong and if she was returned to her uncle at least she had this taste of paradise to last her through

Chapter Twenty-One

the ages. Wrapped in each other's arms they fell into the sleep of sated lovers.

When Garrett awoke later that evening to the tapping on his cabin door he arose and dressed quickly, leaving Cassandra sleeping peacefully. He had to admit he had never seen a woman as beautiful and giving as his angel.

They had been at sea for several days and Garrett was spending most of his time on the deck. He rarely came to the cabin. Lying next to Cassandra was too tempting. She had given him everything she had and continued to love him with a woman's giving nature to her mate. She was too distracting, turning his mind from the mission he was on. Garrett was afraid she would tempt him to distraction allowing for mistakes to be made that might cost them all their lives.

Peters finally remarked that Cassandra was looking pale and unrested causing Garrett to bring her up on the deck. Jim was right. She was pale and needed exercise. He escorted her about the deck regaling her with tales of the sea and pointing out what he thought she might find interesting on the ship. She could see how proud he was of his ship. Then he took her to the wheel showing her how to hold and pilot the speeding *Lady*. Cassandra decided she loved the sea. The spray against her face was invigorating and the taste of the salt on her tongue made her mouth water reminding her of the fresh, tangy taste of Garrett's skin.

On a night when they were closing in on their destination, a storm brewed in their path causing Garrett concern. The *Lady* had weathered many a storm in the past but never with Cassandra on board.

"Don't come up for any reason Cassandra. I can not focus on piloting us clear if I must be concerned for your safety."

Waiting for the storm to hit, Cassandra had time to try imaging how a storm at sea might be different from one on land. Suddenly, the ship rolled from left to right and Cassandra found herself thrown against the table. She steadied herself reaching for the bunk but was flung to the floor. Anything that wasn't bolted down was thrown about the cabin and she felt like a broken doll. The wind was a deafening howl as if the fates themselves were screaming in defiance. Rain began to seep in about the porthole making tiny channels of water on the wall of the cabin. Soon there was a puddle under the porthole. Cassandra began to fret about the possibility of the cabin flooding, then chided herself for doubting Garrett. But with each passing moment the storm worsened throwing her more violently against the wall the bunk rested against. She had never experienced anything like this before. Again, the ship tossed her around even more violently.

    She knew she was better off in the cabin than on deck, but all she could think of was to get out of the cramped, closed-in space of the four walls of the cabin. Her fear began to rise to an escalated level until she was almost mindless with thoughts of drowning in the cabin alone. What if the ship sank? She would never make it off the ship from the cabin. Her skin became clammy with her fear making rational thought impossible. Cassandra drug herself to the door. With strength she didn't realize she had she threw it open dragging herself up the stairway by the railing, inching herself to the top. Cold water stung her face causing her to gasp and swallow bitter seawater. She sputtered, coughing, and continued on her way to the deck. The storm was even more threatening on deck. The ominous black skies were riddled with brilliant bursts of green and yellow lightening. Even in the darkness the blackness of the rolling clouds could be distinguished from the ever-darkening sea. An ominous shadow was racing toward her! Then she felt herself jerked backwards off her feet by the devil's own swirling wave of water. Her arms failing Cassandra screamed realizing that only God would hear her above the rage of the storm. She hit something and then there was darkness and she was floating towards the sea with no gold on her person to pay her passage to the afterlife.

Chapter Twenty-Two

Garrett screamed her name as he watched the windswept wave gather Cassandra in its clutches when she stumbled—but the wind threw back his words. He could barely hold himself upright and if Jim and he were to keep the ship afloat on the raging sea he could not afford to lose his concentration. But when it appeared that Cassandra would be swept overboard Garrett miraculously made it to her side to clutch her still form to his. He and the crew were used to the violence the sea could throw at them. They had been through bad storms before and they knew that they would survive this one, too. Her form was too still and Garrett could do nothing but hold fast to the rail waiting for the storm to abate before trying to ascertain her injuries.

When he finally let go of the railing she was still unconscious. He gathered her up in his arms carrying her down to his cabin. Kicking the door open he made his way to the bunk where he laid her upon it gently. He found the lantern, lighting it by feel, to peer worriedly at Cassandra's pale face. She was bleeding. Garrett took a wet cloth and gently washed her wound. She must have hit her head hard enough to knock herself out during the storm. Fortunately, it wasn't deep. She just couldn't follow his directions!

He started to remove her wet clothing. The shirt she wore was his, and wet, it was transparent, hugging her body and leaving nothing to the imagination. He stopped to admire her curves realizing that even wet and unconscious she was the most breathtaking thing he had ever see. Garrett marveled at her delicious curves as he wrapped her in a blanket. He called to Jim to bring her some warm broth hoping to awaken her with its warmth. When the broth arrived he gently lifted her head trying to get her to take some of the soup, but he was unsuccessful. She remained unaware of her surroundings.

Finally, she began to shiver and toss about on the bed. The shivering became more violent and Cassandra began to mutter in her sleep. Garrett was worried. She alternated between sweating from the fever and shaking from the chills. He had lost his parents to a fever; he couldn't lose her, too. For the first time in his life Garrett was sacred unto death. God help him, he realized he loved her!

He sat by her side as the hours swept by alternating between wiping her down with a cool cloth when the fever raged burning her up or holding her close lending her his body's warmth when she shivered from the cold.

In her delirium she moaned, "I love someone else." Garrett's heart twisted wondering if he might be her love! Then she cried out, "No, I won't marry him! I hate him. He's an animal!"

She must be dreaming of Duprell and Lucas, "I love Garrett Jamison!"

She loved him—his heart raced at her declaration!

Garrett found his head and his heart at war with each other. Should he trust her and follow his heart? Or should he hold her at arm's length until Josh could find the answers he needed to confirm that she was as innocent as he hoped and wanted to believe? But he realized it was too late for that. Tonight he would hold her soft tortured body cradling her in a circle of warmth and safety. She turned to him as her temperature began to return to normal, snuggling deeper into his embrace.

The next morning Cassandra thought she dreamed of Garrett's embrace and turned to find his warmth. There was no one there. The indent on the pillow told of someone resting next to her through the night. Mayhap he had slept near her, made love to her? She would have remembered, wouldn't she? Her head hurt awfully. Cassandra raised her arm and touched her forehead. She felt a bandage. Then she recalled the night of the storm and her foolish attempt to make it to the deck. She felt stiff and sore but otherwise unhurt. Jim entered with a tray remarking on the fact

Chapter Twenty-Two

that they were glad to see her awake and perky. Cassandra gave him a weak smile wondering what he knew that she did not. The Captain was on the deck, she was informed, seeing to the seaworthiness of the *Lady*. A mighty storm had battered the vessel but all hands were unharmed and safe. Cassandra thanked him for the meal and the information before he left to attend to his duties.

Garrett wondered what he was to do with the Lady in his cabin. Soon his crew would be involved in the battle with the Spanish. Last night he had been smitten by her helplessness and beauty but today his logic and battle hardened senses were in command. As much as he wanted to follow his heart he could not afford to become involved with the Lady while he served the Queen. He was deep in thought when Jim informed him that the Miss had taken breakfast and tea. Good. She must be feeling better. Therefore, he could turn his attention to the task at hand.

That afternoon Garrett appeared in the doorway of the cabin. "Hello" he said in a casual voice. "How do you feel?"

She noticed the difference in his tone right away. He had changed in the past days. Something was different.

"I am better, thank you." Cassandra looked at Garrett hoping to see a sign that somewhere he had some feelings for her but Garrett covered his feelings well. He was battle ready and the Queen's man. Feelings could not hold a place in his heart at this time.

He walked over to where she was sitting and cursed himself for his weakness. He wanted her again whether it cost him and his men their lives. It was a huge chance, one that he could not allow himself to take. Resolutely he turned his back on her walking to his desk.

"We'll be engaging in a sea battle within the day Cassandra. You must stay below and to ensure that you do I'll be locking the cabin door this time. Above deck is no place for a woman when the cannon are firing and men are enraged with the lust of battle."

Cassandra agreed with him but wondered if the walls would close in on her again. Would Garrett and his men be safe? What if something happened?

Captured Pearl

Garrett left her to convene with Peters and Tanner. The Spanish had been sighted off the coast of St. Peter Port in the English Channel and the Queen's men were hot to exterminate the last vestiges of the Armada, once and for all. There were not many ships left after the battle of Calais. Garrett and his fellow Captains were sailing in to re-establish the dominance of the English at sea. Little did they know the war would continue for another sixteen years before the Spanish finally admitted their defeat at English hands. They would lay off the finger of Cherbourg, France, until night had fallen. Then they would sail in under the cover of darkness to demolish the Armada. These must be the last stragglers from the Calais battle trying to make their way home, for there were only ten ships in the formation.

The sixteen English vessels should have an easy time darting in amongst them to finish off the Spanish invaders. The *Lady* would speed in to start the fray, as she always did, for there was no vessel that could match her speed and maneuverability. The Spanish would be caught unaware.

Later, Garrett would admit that their first and most damaging mistake was in underestimating their opponents. True the Spanish had not been expecting them, but desperate men are dangerous men and Garrett admonished himself for not having his head in the game this time around. As the attack began and the English bore down upon the Spanish fleet one of her galleons let go a round of cannon fire that hit the *Lady* broadside. Cassandra felt the impact in the cabin. The ship shuddered and then began to list to one side. She screamed fearing that they would sink.

Above deck Garrett frantically bellowed orders to the crew who worked feverously to keep the *Lady* afloat. It was Peters who adjusted the sails to steer them clear of the next battery of cannon fire while Garrett prayed and coaxed his ship to right herself sailing out of harm's way. Another battery from the galleon missed the *Lady,* hitting a companion ship spewing wood and debris in all directions. Garrett felt something hit his shoulder knocking him to his knees. He staggered back to his feet as Tanner raced to the wheel to assist his Captain. A sticky wetness could be felt making

Chapter Twenty-Two

its way inside his shirt and moving down his side. Gritting his teeth he maintained his grip on the wheel. Only after persuasion from Tanner did he relinquish the wheel realizing he hadn't the strength to sail her out of troubled waters.

The rest of the English stayed in the fray recognizing that Jamison was finished for the day. Tanner shouted orders at the Captain's men directing them to loose the sails, freeing the ship from the Spanish encounter and Peters ran to the deck to guide Garrett to a safer post. Both men knew the Captain would not leave the deck until his ship and crew were out of immediate danger. Tanner made the open sea of the Channel in fine time and the winds were in their favor. The closest friendly port for the *Lady* was her home port of Plymouth. Diligently, the crew set to the task of making their way home in one piece. After both Tanner and Peters had assured Garrett that they would manage without him he allowed himself to be taken below to the cabin. Garrett fished the key out of his pocket giving it to Peters to open the door.

Cassandra gasped as she observed the bright red blood staining Garrett's shirt. He was still on his feet but he had a grayish pallor to his skin. Peters was supporting his weight now that they had left the deck.

"My God! What happened?"

"Don't know, Miss. Have to get his shirt off to see. This might not be pretty. Are you sure you want to stay?" Cassandra nodded determinedly, pouring water into the basin and ripping one of Garrett's shirts into strips for Jim. Carefully, Jim helped the Captain remove the bloodied garment revealing a wound in his right shoulder that was still seeping blood at much too rapid a rate to allow for easy breathing by any of the parties involved. Jim motioned for a cloth, to which Cassandra responded. As gently as possible the area was cleaned but Cassandra heard the gasp from Garrett's lips.

"Move out of the way, Jim. I'll do that."

"Are you sure, Miss? Ever done this before?"

"Of course not! But I'm sure I will be more gentle than you." Garrett managed a weak chuckle. What a fierce kitten she was turning out to be. After managing to remove the crusted blood a puncture wound of some size was revealed. Cassandra could not see anything protruding from the hole.

Jim shook his head. "This is going to be ugly, Captain. There is no exit hole. We'll have to go fishing." Garrett nodded bracing himself for the task to come.

"What do you mean?" Cassandra asked worriedly.

"Best let me take over Miss. I'm going to have to go digging in the Captain's arm to find what made that hole. Can't sew him up until we fish out the foreign material inside."

Cassandra grew pale before responding, "No, I'll do it. Tell me how."

Jim attempted to lighten the mood giving the Captain something else to think about. "Just dive right in with those dainty little fingers of yours, Miss. When you find something that don't belong just pull it out."

Cassandra took a deep breath steadying her nerves as Jim poured the Captain a large draught of the brandy from the desk. Garrett downed it with one gulp, and Jim refilled the glass again. Garrett nodded his readiness and Cassandra began her foray into the bloody mess of Garrett's shoulder. She felt his body shudder as she forced her fingers into the hole but he remained silent.

Garrett concentrated on the succulent pink tongue clenched between pearly white teeth. Sweat began to bead on her brow and he watched in fascination as one tiny droplet began to make its way down the bridge of her nose and then careened off to slide to the puckered lip. He longed to catch the droplet with his own tongue and the fascination he was enthralled in kept the task at hand at bay until with a startled gasp Cassandra uttered, "I have it!"

Teeth clenched and fingers straining she refused to give in to the stubborn object lodged in his shoulder. Determinedly, she kept her precarious grip pulling steadily until the tip of a blood-covered sliver of wood began to appear from the wound. Jim quickly grasped behind her fingers with a tongs adding his steady pull to her own and shortly they managed to withdraw a six-inch piece of

Chapter Twenty-Two

sliver oak from the Captain's shoulder. Cassandra tossed the bloodied intruder aside as Jim doused the wound with brandy.

Liquid fire raced through Garrett's upper body causing him to rise out of his chair with a bellowed, "Hell fire!" He sank back into the chair allowing the two to dress the wound. Jim poured him another shot of the liquor while Cassandra finished her task.

"We're making for home, Captain. I'll see to the safety of the ship. You rest. Before you know we'll be back safe at home."

Before leaving Jim explained to Cassandra what to watch for and to call if there was need. She assured him that she could tend to the Captain for she realized that the ship was also in danger of scuttling before they made their way safely to port.

When they limped into port near the Estate four days later it was with a sigh of relief from all aboard. The *Lady* had brought them safely home one more time even though she was badly in need of heavy repairs. The Captain remained without fever, although he had no use of his shoulder at this time. Jim explained to the crew that the Captain was still not out of danger for the limb was swelling even though the poisonous red lines of death had not appeared. The Queen would need to know of developments immediately and someone would need to ride to London at once. Again, Tanner proved his mettle by volunteering to take the news. A quick trip was essential. Garrett handed Tanner his family crest and had Jim fetch him the pouch of gold coin from the desk drawer in his cabin.

Sable was waiting at the dock, as usual, to carry his rider home but this day he would carry someone new to a different destination. The stallion was the fastest and strongest in the Jamison stable and once bidden by his master to carry another he took to the task of traveling overland at the ground covering gait he was known for. With any luck the two would make London before the week was out. With the Jamison crest on his finger and the mount of the Captain between his knees none would doubt the authenticity of Tanner's news.

Mason Hurley and Robert Danley were sent to the Estate to bring back a wagon to carry the Captain to the house and to warn

Captured Pearl

Mame of the unforetold events. The housekeeper was well versed in treating wounds and they hoped she could bring the Captain back to himself. Cassandra waited with the rest of the crew tending to Garrett and watching diligently for any sign of the household staff.

Mame was riding on the wagon seat carrying her basket of herbal remedies. Carefully the crew loaded Garrett aboard. Then Cassandra climbed in next to Mame. Several of the men made their way along with the wagon to the Estate while the rest scattered to their homes. Jim would send word round if there was any change.

Chapter Twenty-Three

Duprell was plotting. He was furious when he found out Cara had arranged for Cassandra to evade his clutches again. He had raged and stormed about the house in London until he had finally terrorized Barnabas to the point that the man had admitted that he had done it for Cara. When Duprell had confronted Cara she had denied everything at first until Duprell had threatened to eliminate Margaret. Then she had told him everything. Tearfully she had pleaded with him not to hurt her that she loved him and only him. But Duprell wasn't flattered, or falling for that lie. He had ordered everyone back to the country Estate before Lucas could find out what had happened—again!

But not before he had dealt with the whore's punishment! He had searched her out. Then he had beaten her until his knuckles were bloodied. He had viciously raped her until Cara had lost consciousness. His men had deposited the bloodied girl on her mother's threshold and then ordered her to pack for the country. Cara never shed a tear.

She hated Duprell with every fiber of her being. After they had made the journey back to the Estate and she was well enough to move about, Cara had taken up with one of the laborers at the Jamison Estate to obtain information on Garrett in exchange for her favors. When she found that Garrett was back and that Cassandra was with him her fury knew no bounds. She would kill that idiot Barnabas herself! Could nothing in her life go as planned?

Duprell was through with her. She was unwelcome in his house so she had been living in the cottage that was her mother's on the Estate. Now that Garrett was back things should have been easy but Cassandra was back again like a bad penny.

Captured Pearl

Cara's scheming mind soon came up with a plan. Finding out that Garrett had been injured in the last voyage turned out to be her leverage with Duprell. She went to him explaining her plan to get Cassandra back into his clutches.

"I'm sure the little twit loves Jamison. The men say she hasn't left his side since they returned. If you send her a message saying that you have information about who leaked the information about the mission against the Spanish I'm sure she'll come flying to find out.

Duprell considered. He couldn't afford to lose Lucas's money and land. Cara might be right. This might bring Cassandra back into his clutches.

"And what do you want for carrying out this scheme?"

Cara considered. She was never going to have anything if she didn't start stockpiling now. Carefully, she considered how badly Duprell wanted Cassandra.

"I want the house in London deeded in my name, Duprell"

Duprell considered carefully. If he worked his cards right he could still get Cassandra without paying Cara for her efforts. "Very well. After Cassandra is back in the house I will have something for you."

Cara's ire rose. She knew that he would not go through with the payment after he had Cassandra in his power.

"No. I want the deed to the house first, before I bring Cassandra to you."

Duprell fumed but he knew Cara would not give in and there were still ways around her legally.

"All right. Make your plans and I will see to the house."

Tanner reached London dusty, weary, and sore of posterior. His time at sea did not stand him in high regard for horsemanship, although, in his younger days he had ridden with the best. Sable had stood his Master in high regard traveling the distance much faster than Tanner had originally thought. To be sure, the horse was in much higher spirits than his rider when they approached the gates of the court.

Chapter Twenty-Three

"Ho man, you look fair done in!" the court guard joked as Tanner dismounted to present the credentials Garrett had prepared for him.

"Just about," Tanner replied, "I've come from Plymouth in four days."

"That's quite a ride. Queen's business?"

"Yes, Sir." Tanner thrust the papers of admission forward and flashed the Jamison family crest under the guard's nose. The guard quickly called over another of his brethren to escort Tanner to the Queen, assuring him that his mount would be properly taken care of in the meanwhile.

They entered the castle proper at which the guard sent a young page dashing off to inform the Queen's advisors of his arrival. As he strode through the halls Tanner attempted to brush some of the dust from the journey off his breeches and boots. He deliberately ran his fingers through his hair to try to look more presentable before meeting with royalty. When he reached the alcove outside of the audience room he found a page waiting with basin and towel so that he might freshen up before proceeding. He was thankful for the respite. The cool water felt wonderful, sharpening his wits and soothing his windburned face.

He didn't wait long before finding himself striding into the audience chamber of the Queen where she waited with several of her advisors. Tanner bent his knee gracefully performing the deep bow of respect due to a Ruler of men.

"Rise and state your business."

"Your Majesty, I bring news from Lord Jamison. The attack on the Spanish off St. Peter Port was foiled and the *Green-Eyed Lady* was badly damaged—as was her Captain." There was whispering among the men present until a stern look from the Queen silenced them.

"Continue."

"Captain Jamison fears there is an informant loose within the ranks of the Captains for we had every advantage against the Spanish. They were waiting, Madam, and they were ready. Captain Jamison also wished for me to impart news of the Lady

Captured Pearl

Cassandra."

Tanner waited knowing that the Captain had not wanted this information to become the rumor of the court.

"We are waiting, Sir." Tanner removed the Jamison crest from his finger presenting it to the Queen, and as Garrett had predicted the advisors were dismissed. When they were alone, but for the guard, he continued with his story relating how Cassandra had been found on the ship and all that had transpired.

"The Captain is recovering at the Estate at this time Your Majesty and awaits your instructions. Lady Cassandra is also in residence. I would willingly return with your missive should you honor me to carry your message."

"We shall have to think on this matter, Mr. Tanner. We shall have your response in the morning. Meanwhile we shall see that you have the hospitality of our Court. Your Captain puts much faith in you, Sir."

"He is a man worthy of serving, Your Highness."

"Yes he is." With that parting comment he was dismissed from her presence.

As Tanner strode out of the room Elizabeth found herself wondering what Garrett knew about his man. There was breeding in his background or she wasn't the Queen of England!

The morning summons from the Queen arrived after Tanner had broken his fast. The servant assigned to see to his needs had done an admirable job of restoring his attire to a semblance of respectability. Tanner was mindful to tip the man from the coin furnished by the Captain, knowing that extras were few and far between for one of service.

He resolutely strode from the apartments following the liveried servant that led him to the Queen. Elizabeth was resplendent in her robes of State. Tanner was mindful to accord her proper respect, again knowing his manner reflected directly on the Captain. He was aware of the Queen's keen scrutiny—wondering what gave rise to her curiosity.

"Rise, Mr. Tanner. We have responded to Lord Jamison's worries and are grateful for his service to the Crown. Deliver this

Chapter Twenty-Three

letter into his hands. We believe you to be a trustworthy man in his service and so we shall impart our decision unto you. We are highly displeased that Lord Duprell should scheme behind our back to pursue this marriage before the Crown has settled upon a course of action. Therefore, we are calling the parties concerned back into our presence to settle this matter in a manner agreeable to us. Warn Lord Jamison to hold fast to the Lady until then. We shall make it known to Duprell that the Lady is expected to be presented unto us in a week's time."

"I am honored to convey your message, Your Majesty, and shall make all haste back to the Estate."

"Lord Jamison's week begins five days hence, Mr. Tanner, thus, giving you time to return to your Captain at a somewhat more leisurely pace than you demonstrated in your journey to London."

"I am most grateful for the additional time, Your Majesty." The Queen smiled at him before adding, "As, we are sure, is your mount and your posterior."

Tanner was taken aback by the Queen's humor—not knowing whether to be aghast or amused, but the twinkle in her eye assured him of the right response.

"You are quite right in that regard, Your Majesty," he responded with a smile and a courtly bow.

Elizabeth held him to her side by not signaling his dismissal, causing Tanner to wonder what else there might be she was waiting for. His question was answered when her Master of the Horse was received into the court.

"We are most impressed by your timely arrival with Lord Jamison's news. So we wish to reward you for your service to the Crown, Mr. Tanner. My Master of the Horse has readied one of the mares from my stable to help speed your way back to your Captain's side. Jewel should make a nice cross with your Captain's Sable. Good fortune, Sir."

Tanner was momentarily speechless. To be gifted by the Queen with such a mount was rare; even rarer for one without title or family. But his teaching as a lad had held him in good stead.

Captured Pearl

"You honor me, Your Majesty. My Captain's service was more than reward enough. Be sure, that should the need arise, I shall answer your call as if it were my Captain's."

"Be careful what you promise, Sir. You might find yourself dancing in our Court with all the Ladies eyeing up your jaunty mermaid that resides upon your person. Amongst other things!" The Queen chuckled as Tanner blushed—not at all becoming to a man that had fought and mastered the sea. But Elizabeth was taken with Jamison's new man and she did not take offense at his speechlessness. The Master of the Horse handed him the documents putting Jewel under his ownership, and he was dismissed to marvel at the happenings of Elizabeth's court all the way back to the Jamison Estate.

At the stable Sable and Jewel had been readied for the return trip to Plymouth. Tanner was astonished at the fine mare that was now his. Of course, he knew the Queen would not own a miserly horse, but his mare was fine and obviously bred for speed and endurance just as Sable was. Where the stallion was rich black-brown, the mare was a bright, blood-red bay with a single stocking running up her off front leg. Her chocolate brown eyes were friendly and wise. Tanner immediately lost his heart to the horse. Jewel nuzzled him gently, to which he rewarded her with a light pat. Time was flying. There would be hours to admire her later. Sable seemed to agree with his perusal nudging the mare affectionately.

"Keep to yourself, old man—that girl is mine," Tanner joked before mounting the stallion; and leading the mare alongside the three made their way out of London and soon set a ground covering pace back the way Tanner and Sable had come. But this trip was much lighter of heart and the promise of the future was much brighter than the overcast days of the past.

Back at the Estate Mame's administrations to Garrett's wound had been timely and knowledgeable. The swelling began to dissipate within a few days to everyone's relief. Mame insisted Garrett take things easily for he had lost much blood from the

Chapter Twenty-Three

wound and she admonished him daily, "The blood poison can still set in if you are not careful. Do you desire to be a one-armed Captain?"

He fretted at the inactivity worrying about inconsequential things such as the cattle, which Miles had in hand; and Cassandra's health, which was fine. Today, he was in a fine mettle growling at anyone who had the courage to come close. Cassandra left the house and wondered down to the stable to gaze at Garrett's fine stable of horses. There, she met Rudy, the stable boy who looked after the Jamison mounts. He was young and naïve, but willing to work and he did have a way with the animals. He shyly offered comments to Cassandra about the mounts until they were farther down the aisle where he secretly slipped a note into her hand before leaving the stable. Hesitantly she opened the folded paper.

If you want to discover who betrayed Garrett to the Spanish come to the Duprell Estate tomorrow morning.

Cassandra was astounded! Garrett had suspected she knew from snatches of conversation she heard aboard the ship. But that Duprell might actually know! She had to discover the truth! She located Rudy drafting him to help her with a mount in the morning. Then she returned to the house—never once stopping to consider the source!

Cassandra awoke early the next morning dressing quickly to make her rendezvous. Facing Duprell was not something she looked forward to—she did not want to go. But Garrett was not able to defend himself and besides Cassandra had other questions that needed answers. She slipped down to the stable where Rudy had saddled a mare that was not too big for her to handle. She had directions from Mame, garnered last night when she asked about the neighbors and their locations. It was only a few miles so she should be back before anyone knew she was missing.

Something was vaguely familiar, but she could not pinpoint exactly what it was. For some reason she became afraid and unsure about seeing her uncle. As she pulled up to the large house she wanted to turn and run back to the Jamison Estate. Her skin was cold and clammy but she willed herself to go on. Cassandra regretted not telling Garrett where she was going, even though she knew he would have forbidden it.

Before her feet hit the ground several of Duprell's crew had surrounded her. One man was almost toothless. When he smiled his mouth was just a black endless hole, and his eyes—the way they looked at her made her cringe.

One of the men said loudly, "Well, what have we here? You decide to come back, Missy?"

"Duprell will be very anxious to see you," commented another.

"Do you know me?" asked Cassandra, hoping for some bit of information that might spark a memory.

The men roared with laughter. "Lady, we would love to know you—really know you!" and they laughed as they circled about her. The circle started to close in on her and the leering men made an ominous picture that was ingrained in her memories. This had happened before! The foul odors, the unwashed bodies, made her want to gag.

"That's enough, men."

They immediately backed off leaving her room to breathe. It was Duprell himself who came down off the front steps to dissipate the crowd.

"Good morning, Niece," he said in a deceptively pleasant voice that did not invoke reassurance in Cassandra. His voice might be welcoming, but his eyes were calculating and cold.

When she had disappeared for the second time he had almost been mad with the thought that his plans would fall to pieces. He could hardly contain himself when Cara's plan had actually worked! His ticket to wealth had come home and was standing on his front lawn. He would use more care this time and have his men watch her around the clock to guarantee that she didn't escape from him again!

"My dearest Niece, where have you been? We were quite worried about you," Duprell walked forward to put his arm around

Chapter Twenty-Three

her, escorting her into the house. Once inside she would not evade his clutches. He almost laughed to himself. He had missed his calling! He should have been an actor.

"Please have a seat, I will send for tea."

"Thank you. Your note said you could tell me who had set up Garrett and his crew with the Spanish?"

"Did it?"

"Of course it did! That's why I've come."

"I have great plans for you, Niece, plans that will be finalized. Lucas will not be patient forever."

"But the Queen said the marriage was to wait until she decided what to do!" Cassandra was becoming frightened by the intense emotions flickering across Duprell's face. His voice was cold and even but her instincts told her she was in great difficulty.

"There are always ways to hasten a decision. If Lucas has already had you, honor would demand that he give you his name." Duprell sneered as an evil smile lit up his face. Cassandra realized she had made a grave error in going there alone. Duprell would never allow her to leave!

"But Uncle, I can't marry him. I love someone else."

"Jamison? Well, my dearest niece I will never allow Jamison to thwart any of my plans! Margaret, show Cassandra to her room. Oh, and dear, just in case you feel like leaving, some of my men have been assigned to watch you. They will not be as understanding as I." His malicious laughter followed Cassandra out of the room and up the stairs.

Tanner's return caused quite a stir at the Jamison Estate. To have found favor with the Queen was a great boon and the mare was an even stronger indicator of her favor. Garrett hoped her decree for them to return to court would be in his favor. But when Cassandra could not be found he began to worry for her safety. A search of the grounds revealed that one of the mares was missing so at first the household thought she had gone for a ride. When morning teatime had passed with no sign of her, Garrett had Tanner organize the men for a search. Just as they were readying to leave one of Duprell's men rode up the lane leading the missing mare.

"Where's Cassandra?" Garrett spoke menacingly.

The man smiled a toothless grin. "Captain, Duprell thanks you for the use of the mare, but the Lady won't be needing it now that she is back in his care."

Garrett wanted to fly for the man's throat!

Tanner quietly came to his side and in a low tone uttered two words, "The letter."

Garrett understood at once the reasoning behind Tanner's comment and used his knowledge to send a sting back to Duprell.

"Very well, tell Duprell I await the Queen's decision and shall see him in court within the week with the Lady at his side. May the better man win. Of course, we all know who that is!" The Jamison crew laughed heartily, the sound chasing Duprell's crony far down the lane.

Duprell had no sooner begun to gloat about having Cassandra back in his clutches than the Queen's messenger galloped in delivering the missive from the Queen. The implied threat was easily discerned and Duprell could see all of his well-laid plans falling into pieces, again. The rage he felt was awful! His arm swept the contents of his desk top to the floor. Hearing the crashing of glass and the storming in the study, Margaret crept to peer inside. The scene she witnessed was terrorizing. The man looked as if a demon from hell had possessed him with his face black with rage and his eyes bulging nearly out of their sockets. Just as quickly Margaret crept out of the house to hide herself away from the mad scene being played out in the study.

Chapter Twenty-Four

Garrett fussed and worried as he readied himself to return to Elizabeth's court. The shoulder wound was healing, but not as fast as he had hoped. Mame would be sending along her herbal potion and the poultice recipe for his continuous application while he was gone. Confound it! He needed all his strength, for Garrett was sure that in the not too distant future a physical fight between himself and Duprell was brewing. There was no way that he would allow Duprell to keep Cassandra! The question of how Duprell had gotten hold of her again continued to haunt him, as well as the nightmares Cassandra had endured pointing ever more exclusively at Duprell as their apex.

The knock at his door interrupted his thoughts bringing him back to the time at hand. Mame entered carrying a small bag that was bound to be his medicine.

"I've packed a trunk for Lady Cassandra, Sir. I hope that she is all right." Mame's worried look was much more desperate than Garrett thought the situation called for.

"Mame what is wrong? You know Duprell won't harm her. The Queen would have his head."

"I know, Sir, but . . ." Mame trailed off.

"Mame out with it!"

"I believe that the Lady is with child, Sir!" she blurted out abruptly. Garrett stopped motionless in his tracks. Wasn't this what he had wanted? A reason to keep Cassandra at his side? For the Queen would surely not allow Duprell's marriage contract to go through now, would she? He drew a deep breath before consoling Mame.

"Be sure Mame that I shall return with the Lady and I will keep her safe." Mame nodded with a tearful smile before leaving him alone to finish his packing for the trip.

The *Lady* was still being repaired from the last encounter with the Spanish and so Garrett had been faced with the choice of taking one of his lesser trade ships from the family business or going overland to London. Mame had put her leaden foot of guilt down upon the choice of riding, and Garrett truly detested submitting to the choice of going by carriage. The *Falcon*, though smaller and not as heavy cannoned as the *Lady*, was a tight ship that bore the Jamison colors proudly. Peters had notified him she had put to port shortly before they had returned and the day before she had finished unloading her cargo from Africa. Garrett had sent word to her Captain to have her ready to sail today for the trip to London. Garrett had sent word to several of his own crew to meet at the dock. There was no way he was traveling to London without fighting men at his back for if worse came to worse he would take Cassandra himself. Miles was going along as well as Peters and Tanner. Duprell would not find him unprepared!

The *Falcon* sailed into London two days later and Garrett had to admit that while he was partial to his own ship and crew the *Falcon's* was not second rate. Her Captain was knowledgeable and the crew was top notch. Garrett thanked the Captain for the ride on the vessel bidding them to be available for the return trip to the Estate. He watched covertly as the Captain gave out coin to each man for the off shore time and then came upon the deck himself to add his own reward for a job well done. The crew was appreciative letting Garrett know there were no finer colors to sail under than the Jamison colors. The Captain stood by as the trunks were off loaded.

"Lord Jamison be aware that should you have need the *Falcon* and her crew are at your back. We may not be of the quality of the Queen's Navy but each man in your service realizes that if not for you, he and his family would not have as fair a living as they do. Should you need to call you will not find us lacking."

Garrett accepted the comment with good grace, giving the Captain his hand and for the first time he really understood his father's long-standing words, *"Treat a man fairly and then add*

Chapter Twenty-Four

some and you will be surprised at the ties that will be forged in your name." He found himself thinking that his father would be proud of the path the Jamison name had taken and the feeling buoyed his step as he departed.

Miles had gone on ahead with some of the crew to ready things at Court and, as usual, to position men about London. A battle was brewing and he would be ready. Tanner had commissioned a coach for the ride to Court and Garrett grimaced as he lifted himself into the interior. Tanner followed, wisely keeping his thoughts to himself when the Captain cursed the uselessness of his shoulder.

"Miles will have found out if Duprell and Cassandra have arrived yet and where they are housed. Try to remain unseen as much as possible, Tanner, but stay near my Lady. I'm putting her welfare in your hands."

"Aye, Captain. I'll be a mouse in the closet with the teeth of a rat." Garrett laughed at Tanner's comparison wondering not for the first time where the man came from and what he had been before coming aboard ship. He was trustworthy and bright and would have done well at the Court. He reminded Garrett of Josh Birmingham with his quick wit and predisposed nature for ferreting out hidden secrets. Some day he was going to have to find out.

Garrett had not been in his apartments long when the Queen sent a summons requesting his presence. Garrett smiled as he read the missive wondering why it was called a request when he knew damn well that it was a command. Such was life at Court. The Queen called and men scurried to obey. The audience room was a private one and her physician and her guard attended Elizabeth. Bother! He knew what was coming. Nothing for it but that Bess would have him examined for herself. Garrett was inclined to throw out whatever the court physician gave him and stick with Mame's remedies as they had pulled him through so far!

"Lord Jamison, we are relieved to see your person after the word delivered by your man, Tanner."

"As you can see your Majesty I will survive to fight again"—and soon, he thought to himself.

Captured Pearl

"Nevertheless we would have you examined by our physician."

Just as he expected. Garrett began removing his shirt to find his hands swept away by the physician. Greedy man! Garrett gave him a scowl that would have backed up many another man but the physician was used to dealing with Elizabeth and so was undaunted by a mere Lord of the realm.

"The wound is closing nicely, Your Majesty. Healing is slow but he shall retain the use of the limb if he is careful to heed the words of the person who has dealt with this. A knowledgeable healer you have Lord Jamison."

"I'll pass on your compliments, Sir."

Elizabeth dismissed the physician beckoning Garrett to be seated by her side.

"We are informed that the Lady Cassandra did not accompany you to our court."

"She is back with Duprell, Your Majesty. I'm not sure how. Her mount was returned to us the day Tanner returned and we were informed that Duprell had her at his Estate. I thought it best to not confront the man but to leave it to your discretion."

Bess nodded wisely. "Do you feel that the Lady is safe?"

"She had better be!" Garrett exclaimed vehemently. Bess caught the emotion behind the statement. Garrett took a deep breath before continuing for he knew of Bess's temper.

"Your Majesty, there has been a change in the Lady's situation, I believe." Bess motioned for him to continue.

"I believe that Cassandra may be carrying my child." Garrett waited for her wrath to fall but a tiny self-appreciative smirk curled her lips.

"Well, Lord Jamison it seems that there will be a wedding shortly after all. Duprell will be most putout!" And her laughter filled the small room. Garrett was stunned by the humor Bess saw in the situation. When she had herself under control again her parting comment brought laughter to his lips.

"That shall teach that weasel to thwart the power of the crown!"

Chapter Twenty-Four

"Has Duprell arrived yet, Your Majesty?"

"Not yet, Lord Jamison. Our spies tell us that he chose to come overland and will be in London tomorrow. Be patient Jamison. Your time will soon be at hand. And what of your ship?"

"The *Lady* will require many weeks of repair, Your Majesty. We were fortunate to make it back to port I believe, but the *Lady* has always taken care of her crew. I came in on the *Falcon*." Garrett was sure Bess already knew that but she was after conversation now.

"Lord Birmingham has taken himself off to France following some clue about the Lady's past. It seems that he is discovering many twists and turns in the path of her life."

Garrett wasn't sure if he should take this as good news or not.

"What do you know about your man Tanner?" The question came out of the blue and Garrett was unprepared to answer.

"Not much. He signed on the last time I was looking for seaworthy men. He had good recommendations from a Captain with the Blackstone Company. He is quick and smart and doesn't miss much."

Elizabeth nodded seeming deep in thought. "The man interests us."

"I can't imagine you gifting one of your horses to someone who doesn't."

She smiled. "The Ladies of the court will find him interesting, also, we believe."

"He's taking Miles' place aboard ship. Am I soon to lose him to your service?"

"We don't think so Lord Jamison. One Birmingham at court is enough!"

Garrett laughed, "Those were my thoughts exactly, Your Majesty."

She waved her hand dismissing him from her presence. "Be off with you. You keep us from our duties with your gallant manners and quick conversation."

Garrett bowed then strode from the room feeling better

Captured Pearl

about the situation at hand and knowing Bess was behind him.

Cassandra was relieved to reach London. Duprell had been ugly and short tempered the entire trip to London. And the men that had traveled with them were loathsome! Cassandra feared for her safety the entire trip and as much as she hated Duprell's presence the only safety lay in staying near him. His gaze made her uncomfortable. Daily the look was more intense, more malevolent. The sight of the court gates made her breathe a sigh of relief. Although, she might not be safe for long.

Guards were waiting to escort her to her rooms. Cassandra appreciated the fact that she had the same rooms as her last trip to Court for they were familiar and closer to where Garrett was lodged. A maid was already there to help her off with her cloak and offering tea and refreshments. There was no word from either Garrett or the Queen. The tea seemed to sooth both her nerves and her stomach. Lately she hadn't much appetite and contributed it to the tense situation in the Duprell house. Her trunk from the Jamison Estate was already unpacked and her things laid on the dresser while her clothes were hung in the dressing room.

The afternoon passed slowly. Cassandra began to wonder if the Queen had any intention of settling this matter in a timely fashion. Then a page arrived to deliver a note bidding her to attend an audience with the Queen that evening. What to wear? She suddenly felt cold and flipping through the dresses she spied the green and blue velvet dress that carried the Jamison colors. Well, why not? Her choice would be clearly shown by the colors she wore. After all, how much worse could things get if she was returned to Duprell and forced to marry Lucas Gabel?

She was escorted to the receiving hall by one of the Queen's own guards. Passing by an alcove just off her rooms she noticed a slight movement out of the corner of her eye. Turning to look again she recognized Tanner and knew that Garrett had sent him to watch over her. Her heart was lightened by the thought.

The Queen was seated on the throne of England with her ministers in attendance. A conflict decision between two Lords of

Chapter Twenty-Four

the realm was an event. Garrett stood to the Queen's right seemingly at ease. While Duprell was off to the left with one of his men behind him. His look was frosty.

Cassandra was escorted to the Queen were she curtsied waiting for the Queen to speak.

"Lady Cassandra, we would have you remain here next to us." Cassandra nodded and moved to the appointed place. Tanner slipped through the receiving doors to stand off to the side that Garrett had taken for his own. It seemed they all waited for someone or something. The question was answered when Lucas Gabel entered with an attending servant in tow. The man bowed before crossing to stand next to Duprell. The two smiled at each other looking Cassandra over as if she were on the sale block. Her heart went cold. She glanced Garrett's way but there was no sign of encouragement from him.

"Don't give up," she thought to Garrett. "Don't leave me alone." One of the ministers handed the Queen several papers. She scanned through them quickly then addressed the room.

"We have considered the opposing claims of the parties involved. The marriage contract between Lords Duprell and Gabel is of legal consequence." Lucas smiled. "However, the Protestant church and her clergy have always felt the final say at the altar belongs to the bride to be. Cassandra Gourdue what say ye to this binding?"

Cassandra looked the Queen straight in the eye and clearly spoke, "No, I do not favor this marriage."

"Your reasons?"

"Your majesty, I do not find the man to my liking."

"You understand that Lord Gabel could provide you with a secure life for as long as you live? And that your uncle may well know what is better for you than you may?"

"I will not marry the man, Your Majesty. I do not love him."

"Love does not always have a place in the union of families."

"That may be true Your Majesty, but my uncle has told me that I have no dowry to bring to a man so I will marry for love."

"That may not be your choice, Lady."

Captured Pearl

Cassandra hung her head. Would Garrett not speak for her?

"Is there any other in this room that may give cause that this contract not be honored?"

Garrett stepped forward, His long legs striding toward the Queen's throne with determination.

"I have reason, Your Majesty."

"Proceed Lord Jamison."

"I am afraid Your Majesty that I have broken my oath to safeguard the Lady and have compromised her virtue."

"Lord Jamison you greatly disappoint us!" But the eyes of the Queen were twinkling in humor not flashing with anger.

Lucas spoke up. "Your Majesty I am willing to overlook this one indiscretion as the Lady is young and I am sure that Lord Jamison caught her unaware."

Garrett turned to Lucas cocking his head jauntily. "Sorry to disappoint you Gabel, but it wasn't just once. I have had her on many occasions."

Cassandra thought she would die of mortification! To have the whole Court aware that Garrett had loved her was more than she was willing to endure. A quick look from the Queen held her in place. Was that compassion she saw in her face?

"Then it seems that the Crown shall be privy to a wedding, although, it shall not be the groom that was originally intended. Minister Farley see to it that the proper papers are in order and find the Crown's clergy. He shall expedite the needed paperwork and perform the ceremony!"

The audience chamber was a buzz with the news while Duprell made as if to approach the Crown.

"Lord Duprell, the Crown would warn you to tread warily. We have never held your family in great regard. We find that we would not be unduly disturbed to find you residing in the Tower of London!"

Duprell was furious and Gabel was not well pleased. Garrett would be sure to watch his back for he knew the two men were not above committing murder to get what they wanted from life.

The Queen turned to the Court addressing its occupants,

Chapter Twenty-Four

"The Crown shall ensure the Lady's safety. Guards shall be assigned to her corridor. Lord Duprell we find your manners lacking in this situation and so we forbid you to have contact with the Lady! Once she has become Lady Jamison this shall be her husband's realm. Lord Jamison do you wish to add further security for your piece of mind?"

"Your Majesty, I am sure the Crown is well able to fulfill this task. However, I would ask that my man Tanner be allowed to keep watch for the Lady's piece of mind as she knows him as one of mine and he has safe guarded her upon other occasions."

"Very well, Lord Jamison. We shall also assign our Lady Camilla to ward the Lady's honor, for she will not be daunted by a man such as yourself."

Garrett bowed deeply and then escorted Cassandra from the room with Tanner and the Queen's guard falling in behind. Duprell and Lucas exited shortly thereafter but they made their way out of the castle to discuss their next move at a spot where the Queen did not have eyes and ears watching and listening.

Garrett made light conversation on the way back to Cassandra's rooms. "I am pleased to see that this was the gown that you chose to wear today. Thank you, Cassandra for your favor."

"You're welcome Garrett. We can't marry! We hardly know each other!"

"Actually, Angel we know each other quite well." Cassandra blushed furiously. "The Queen has mandated the wedding. There will be no turning back now Cassandra. You may be able to refuse a man but not the sovereign Queen of England."

"Do you know when the ceremony will be Garrett?"

"I would assume you have about a week to adjust to the idea Cassandra. Things can move very quickly when the Queen puts the force of her will behind something. If you will let me know what gown you chose to wear for the ceremony I will see to finding you a proper adornment to compliment it."

"That isn't necessary Garrett. We aren't marrying for love."

"But Angel, I am marrying to love you continuously, over

and over, wherever I can have you!" Cassandra's mouth dropped open when he whispered those words into her ear. My God, the man had no propriety! The cock jaunt of Tanner's head and the jingling of his mermaid told Cassandra that the man was finding it almost impossible not to laugh with mirth at his Captain's words. He winked at her and suddenly Cassandra wasn't mortified but willing to tease as well.

"Well, my Lord there's a likely looking alcove that seems to suit Tanner's needs near my room."

At first Garrett didn't comprehend the meaning and then it was his turn to be mortified. The little witch! A least he had lowered his voice! Her eyes were twinkling instead of being full of self doubt and fear. It suddenly struck him that this might be her first try at teasing anyone — let alone a man. He smiled down upon her, cupping her fingers gently in reassurance. Her smile brightened so brilliantly that he was sure that it outshone the sun.

The following week was a flurry of activity for Cassandra and sheer hell for Garrett. The Queen and her staff took their safeguarding of Cassandra very seriously leaving them no time alone, or for a private conversation. Garrett was frustrated and his bad humor was soon visited upon his men. Tanner finally suggested that he visit one of the men's clubs and take some of his bad humor out on someone else. Garrett was astounded.

Dally with a whore when he was soon to wed? The sheer obscenity of the idea appalled him. Had he been that unjust in his words to two of the men he trusted above all others? Tanner's frozen line of a mouth said, "Yes."

"Good God man, I am truly sorry. I feel like a mouse cornered by the cat with nowhere to turn."

"Too bad you don't have the teeth of a rat," Tanner replied sending Garrett into a sudden fit of laughter.

"Come along," Garrett said, "let us proceed down to Piccadilly and I'll pick up something for my Lady. Tell Miles to come along. We all need to get free of this place for a while."

The three friends made their way through the streets of

Chapter Twenty-Four

London stopping to look at the baubles that might catch a Lady's eye. Miles was obviously shopping for Camilla, but when Tanner purchased a small pin enameled to look like a butterfly, Garrett raised his eyebrows in surprise. Tanner had a sweetheart? Tanner saw Garrett's surprise and shrugged his shoulders stating, "Just in case, Captain."

Garrett was at a loss as to what to purchase for Cassandra. What did a man buy for his wife to be? She did not seem to set high regard in the jewels that most females set such store by. Then tucked into a nook in one of the stalls he saw several volumes of sonnets by the new bard Shakespeare. He knew that she could read. Perhaps this would be more to her liking to while away the hours in her rooms.

The fresh air and change of scenery put a new light on his situation for if he was honest with himself the thought of Cassandra in someone else's arms drove him to madness. And if they never found out about her past? Well he could live with that. Sometimes not knowing was a godsend in itself.

Chapter Twenty-Five

A week to the day, as Garrett had predicted, the wedding was held in the Queen's own chapel. Garrett waited anxiously at the altar with the clergy hoping that Cassandra would appreciate the ring he had the jeweler make for her. His mother had always favored the sapphires that were the blue of the evening sky and so his father had given her a ring banded with the blue stones. However, Garrett could not see the band on Cassandra's finger and Shane also favored the stones. Hopefully, some day, his brother would marry and Garrett would give him their mother's band for his wife. Cassandra had never expressed any favoritism in the jewels he had given her but he personally had a weakness for emeralds. The green of her eyes were a perfect match for the stones he had purchased for her band. Shingler had performed a piece of magic by setting the stones in a twisted band of gold giving the illusion that nothing held the stones in place.

He fidgeted, wondering if Cassandra would find fault with his choice of black for this occasion. The slashed sleeves of his doublet were set off by the pristine white shirt worn underneath. The heavy blackwork on the sleeves and neck attested to the wealth of his coin to procure such an extravagance—but would she think black too sober for what should be a joyful occasion?

Then his attention was drawn to the side door being opened by the Queen's guard to allow Cassandra to enter as the minstrels played softly in the background.

She had chosen the emerald green velvet Mrs. Lewis had made on her first wardrobe visit because she knew the color was one of his favorites, and Garrett couldn't have been happier. The fitted sleeves drew his eye to her slender fingers, reminding him of the delights to come this night. The bodice revealed just enough

Captured Pearl

of her collar bone to be enticing and the chain of links that encircled her waist complimented the gold appliqué threadwork of tiny hummingbirds that wove their way down the front of the skirt drawing attention to the creamy underskirt revealed in the front.

Her golden hair was entwined with pearls and green glass beads, which set off the dress and brought out the green of her eyes. She carried a nosegay of white and yellow roses and baby's breath with trailing bits of English Ivy.

The emerald wedding band would be stunning with the gown and he knew just which of his mother's gold chains would finish off the look.

When Cassandra reached his side Garrett took her hand in his. The ceremony was over sooner than he had expected. The wedding band was slipped onto her finger and he was directed to kiss the bride. One hand cupped her chin to raise her face to his. Then his lips met hers partaking of her sweetness. The kiss soon turned possessive until a jab from Miles brought him back to the present. He ended it swiftly turning her to face the small gathering.

A small reception had been planned to follow the ceremony. Elizabeth had extended her hospitality until the next day moving them into a larger chamber with several rooms. The fire had been lit by the time they retired and a bottle of wine with fruit and sweet breads was waiting on the table. Garrett had felt a sense of relief when Duprell had left shortly after the ceremony, but he expected trouble to follow. He gratefully uncorked the bottle of wine and filled two glasses offering one to Cassandra. She shook her head to refuse but Garrett prompted her to accept. "Cassandra the wine will sooth your nerves and help you relax. Please take it."

"Maybe we could sleep in different rooms?"

"I think not! What happened to the little tease that eyed up the alcove in her hall?"

She blushed prettily taking a small sip of the wine. "I think she flew away."

"There is plenty of time for loving, wife. We have time for you to relax and settle in before the madness of loving you over-

Chapter Twenty-Five

whelms me."

Cassandra giggled at the face he made and the light banter continued easing the mood. Before she quite realized how it had happened Garrett had maneuvered her to the large bed.

His fingers skimmed over the large hooks and eyes that had not only decorated the front of her gown but also held the edges together. The green velvet parted to reveal a creamy chemise that barely concealed her breasts. Garrett's touch was reverent as he caressed the globes and he watched with satisfaction as her eyes darkened with passion. He lowered his mouth watching her tense in anticipation before his lips settled on the tip of one to possessively suckle through the translucent material.

The pressure was satisfying and the slipping of the material across her tender flesh drove Cassandra to the edge of madness. Briefly she wondered how she had been so lucky as to have a man for her own who was such a skilled artisan in the bedroom. His passage down her body was slow and teasing. Kisses and soft bites followed the unveiling of her body to his gaze and Cassandra felt as cherished as if it were the first time they had lain together. He blew lightly upon her belly causing her to sharply inhale before rolling his tongue across her flesh.

The lovely gown was discarded at the foot of the bed as his voyage took him to the hidden folds of her womanhood. Tonight," he thought, "she wouldn't be just a girl who had known the intimacy of love, she would become a well-loved woman." He parted her limbs to puff small breaths of warm air against her tender flesh, drawing closer to her hidden treasures with each breath.

When his moist warm mouth descended upon her secret folds Cassandra melted into the bed. He fed on her as if she were a fine wine that must be savored to its fullest. The feelings were intense and powerful. Her hands gripped his shoulders to hold herself to the earth.

When he nuzzled against her folds then slipped his tongue inside her Cassandra was shocked by the intensity of the feeling and was too overwhelmed to move. Soft mewling sounds escaped from her throat. Garrett brought her to the edge of the precipice,

Captured Pearl

and then withdrew to leave her feeling achy and empty. Before she could protest his large staff slid through her folds to replace his mouth. Grabbing her thighs, he opened her more fully to his penetration filling her with his length and hardness. By inches he withdrew giving her the full benefit of his expertise. Leaving just the head of his staff within her Garrett paused to look into her eyes before sliding back in just as slowly.

Cassandra thought she would die. The frightened, undemanding girl transformed into a scratching demanding she cat. She gripped Garrett's hips demanding a faster, harder pace to which he was happy to reply. Together they climbed the stairway of passion to tumble down its slopes into oblivion.

Chapter Twenty-Six

Duprell and Lucas finally settled on an out-of-the-way tavern that Lucas had frequented upon occasion. The staff there catered to gentlemen of unique tastes. Duprell eyed up the scantly-clad girl serving them, promising himself to have a taste later.

"I still want her," Lucas broke the silence. "But you'll have to eliminate Jamison for I won't have a man alive that can say he has tasted what is mine!"

"Well enough. I'll even do the task for a nominal fee as I shall enjoy eliminating him from this world."

"We'll have to adjust your payment, Duprell, for obviously the Lady is no longer a maiden and that was part of the agreement."

Duprell silently cursed the man. "If you had taken care of things in the garden this would not be necessary. You could have made Jamison's claim!"

"Granted, we've both made errors! Now what are we going to do about it?" Lucas reminded Duprell of a fat, slouchy-looking badger. Their looks were deceiving for they were fast-moving and dangerous.

"Leave Cassandra to me. I'll have her back at the Estate before long and this time she will not be leaving."

Lucas eyed him up suspiciously. "How do you propose to do that?"

"I have a contact at the Jamison Estate. That's all you need to know."

"What about the wedding? You won't find a clergy in England that will disavow a wedding commanded by the Queen." Lucas licked his lips as the wench refilled their drinks. He had noticed Duprell eyeing her up, also. Perhaps he could persuade

Captured Pearl

him to join a threesome?

"I have that covered."

"How?"

"If you must know, I have Papal connections. Rome will recognize the wedding as a true union from there it will be up to you."

"All right. But I won't wait forever, Duprell."

"You won't have to. Expect your bride before the winter season, Gabel."

The men finished their drinks together as a sign of their agreement. Soon they were on to other pursuits.

Cassandra awoke, stretching her sleek body. When she had dressed for the day she went in search of Garrett, but he was not in their rooms. Tanner informed her that he had gone with Miles to ready the *Falcon* for the return trip to the Estate. He would remain to see to her safety. If she desired he would see that she had a breakfast tray. Cassandra shook her head. The thought of eating did not sit well with her. Funny, she had thought that leaving Duprell's presence would have cured her nerves. Mayhap, it was all the excitement from the previous day. Her trunk was already packed from the move to these quarters so there was not much to occupy her mind. Cassandra fetched the collection of sonnets Garrett had presented her with a few days before. Sometimes the man could be endearing.

Garrett had located the Captain of the *Falcon* informing him of his wish to leave London yet that day. The Captain replied that he would be ready by mid-day. Stocking of the ship would be finished shortly and the last man of the crew would have returned by late morning. Garrett nodded his agreement and headed back to court.

"I've yet to find out how Duprell got a hold of Cassandra again, Miles. We'll have to be more vigilant now."

"Aye Captain, but if you'll take my advice you'll wait till you have the Lady back at the Estate before riling her up. Back among familiar people and things she may feel less jumpy."

"You're probably right, Miles."

Chapter Twenty-Six

They arrived back at the Estate several days later during a late afternoon rainstorm. Cassandra had been pale and refusing the hot meals Cook had prepared for them aboard ship. Between the delicate disposition of his new wife and the aching of his wound caused by the cold rain it had been a miserable return trip. Garrett tried to be civil to the crew and Captain but finally retreated to the cabin. One look at Cassandra's miserable condition had forced him to hold his tongue. A cross word from anyone might have sent her into tears.

Once she had brought up the subject of the Birmingham family wondering why they had not attended the wedding, as they were the only friends she had. Garrett had gently informed her that the entire family had sailed for France. Josh and Lord Phillip were tracking down pieces of her past and the Ladies had gone along for the excursion. She seemed accepting of the information, but Garrett noticed that her mood became more despondent after their conversation. Women! Perhaps Mame could figure her out.

The carriage was waiting at the dock, another blow to Garrett's bad temper. He still had the devil's own time griping anything with his hand and the shoulder ached from the cold weather. Perhaps if his mood had been better or he had stopped to think things through Garrett would have used more finesse when he broached the subject, but factors had united to forestall the happiness they had just begun to experience.

"How did Duprell get hold of you that day, Cassandra? Were his men waiting for you when you went riding?"

She looked at him guiltily before replying, "No, Garrett. I went to see him."

"You what?!" he bellowed startling the horses drawing the carriage. That should have been his first clue that he was out of control but he barreled on unsuspecting.

"Garrett, please stop yelling. Duprell sent word that he knew whom the informant was who told the Spanish that you would be at St. Peter Point. You were hurt so badly and I knew that you couldn't go. I know that I should have told you but I just wanted to help," she pleaded with him.

Captured Pearl

"My Dear, you don't know the meaning of the word help. Whatever could have possessed your woman's mind to think that you were a match for Duprell. Such stupidity I have never before seen!"

Cassandra began to cry in earnest from his outburst, sobbing as if the world had come to an end. Soon the sobs led to her unsteady stomach wishing to empty its contents and Garrett found himself with a smelly watery mess all down the front of his boots.

"Good God!" he snorted in disgust. This was one reason he was sure that men did not rush into marriage!

"From now on I will be watching every move that you make," he said in an icy voice. "Don't underestimate me Cassandra. If you so much as go near Duprell again I will wring your sweet little neck! Is that understood?"

Between sobs he caught her nodding yes as she frantically tried to regain some kind of control. After deliberate consideration he resolutely handed over his own handkerchief for her use vowing to never use that one again as she wiped her mouth and then sucked in a loud breath.

Cassandra's blood ran cold. She knew he was beyond listening to anything she had to say. She had made a terrible mistake. They rode the rest of the way without a word. Garrett's face was stone. The carriage stopped and he awkwardly descended then turned to offer his hand.

"Ever the gentleman," Cassandra thought despondently. "Well fie on him! She didn't need his help!" And she nearly fell on her face in her effort to avoid the hand he had extended to help her down. Caught in her skirts there was no choice now but to accept, or fall on her face in the lane. She took his hand wishing she had the nerve to wipe the triumphant smile off his face. But prudence was the thought for the day and she bit her tongue as she descended.

"Wisely done, wife."

God help her she could not help herself and she stuck out her tongue at him. He was caught off guard by the childish display of temper and then he roared with laughter, which only made

Chapter Twenty-Six

her feel worse.

Mame was waiting at the door and at the first opportunity Cassandra dropped his hand to hurry to Mame's side where she began to sob again. Garrett looked on disgustedly. Did she never plan to stop? Mame gave a look of disapproval to her Lord before hustling Cassandra inside and up to the Master's chambers.

"Mame I've done something so stupid," she uttered between sobs.

Mame took her to her bosom. "Go ahead and cry child. Let the bad times be washed away." When she could finally stop the tears she explained to Mame what had transpired.

"You've had a hard time of it child, no doubt of that. Things will be better now that you are home."

"Will they Mame? He gets so mad and he yells at me. Then he is such a gentleman. How do I know which one will appear next?"

"He will get over it child. A sure sign that a man cares is his fury at silly little mistakes. It took me years to learn that one from my man. He will learn that you are telling the truth. Then he'll learn to trust you, just give it time."

But Mame was wrong, Garrett did not get over it and he treated her as if she were invisible. With his disposition on edge from the aching in his shoulder, and being preoccupied with thwarting any new foray by Duprell, Garrett plowed on bad temperedly until even his men gave him a wide berth. The happiness that might have been his began to dissipate without his knowledge, driving a wedge between Cassandra and himself.

Cassandra's heart ached for the love that had barely begun to grow between the two of them for now it seemed that she had destroyed it for all time. She'd had no idea that her actions could be so damaging. This one stupid act seemed to have erased any feelings he ever had for her.

Shortly after their return he moved to the other end of the hallway giving his men strict orders that his wife was not to be out by herself, and that under no circumstances was she to leave the property.

Captured Pearl

He didn't bother to inform the staff, or Cassandra, that he had received information that Duprell was on the move and plotting to regain control of Cassandra once again.

Several times, with persuasion from Mame, she tried to approach Garrett and reason with him but he made it plain that he wanted her to stay away from him. Cassandra began to realize that she was a prisoner in what should have been her own house.

Weeks passed and Cassandra became so despondent that Mame started to worry about her. She, too, tried talking to Garrett to no avail. Mame had an intuitive trust in the girl and she had a good eye for people, but Garrett told Mame to mind her own business. She didn't pursue it any more but she worried. She could only hope that having a friend in her would be enough for Cassandra.

It was Tanner that finally broke through the cloud that overshadowed Garrett's life. He had come in for Peters to give the Captain a report on the repairs to the *Lady* to find Cassandra sitting on the front steps shadowed by two of Garrett's tougher men. Tanner was appalled by the change in the Lady. Her pale skin spoke volumes for the unhappiness she felt and the hell she was living in. It radiated from the air around her leaving one near feeling the weight with which it fell upon her shoulders. He wished her a good morning and delayed his report to the Captain trying to draw some conversation from the Lady that had teased him in Piccadilly and gifted him with his mermaid. There was no response. By the time he reached the study Tanner was ready to take his Captain to task, even if it cost him his position.

He broached the subject with the same finesse that he had accomplished every task set before him.

"Captain, has Lady Cassandra been ill?"

"Not to my knowledge." Garrett continued to study Miles' reports. Tanner, a man rarely ruled by temper, was fast reaching his fire point. There was no use being subtle—the Captain needed a knock about his head.

"Well, she looks like she's been beaten and starved to death, Sir!" Garrett raised cold eyes to his newest friend.

Chapter Twenty-Six

"You'd best remember your place before you don't have one, man."

"Then mayhap I'll have my release paper for I'll not be employed by a man that kills a woman by inches! I thought you a better man than this Captain. If you were marrying her just to torment her, you might have left the job to Gabel. At least he would have accomplished if more swiftly!"

"Why you bastard!"

"Yes I am, and I am familiar with how a Lord of the realm may kill a woman without actually touching her! I never knew you to be so cruel to your men, perhaps you prefer to torment women for they have no way to fight back!"

With his first words Garrett was almost across the desk to knock Tanner to the floor but as the man continued he began to see not only the larger picture with Cassandra but with Tanner, as well. The disgust that was evident in his man's eyes shamed him, as had his words. If the elder Lord Jamison had still lived he'd have called Garrett out. The torment he had been living with began to dissolve and as it did Tanner spoke again.

"Why do you hate her, Sir?"

"God, man, I don't hate her! But I am tormented by the wondering if the babe is mine and if she is, too."

"Captain, if the Lady didn't love you she would not care that you paid her no attention. And would you blame an innocent babe for something that his mother surely was not able to prevent?"

"You sound like my father Tanner, and as if you speak from experience, I thank you for the words. It seems I have some apologizing to do."

"Then I leave you to right your wrong, Sir."

"Tanner, what memories are in your heart that allow you such insight and outspokenness before a Lord? Not that I mind, for it was sorely needed."

Tanner gave his Captain an emotionless stare before replying. "A woman is most usually condemned for a bastard child, even when there was no way for her to refuse. If a woman is forced, or seduced, should the child suffer for the adult's actions?

Captured Pearl

Many Lords of the realm are not as fair as you tend to be, Sir."

"First-hand knowledge, Tanner?"

"Let's just say I have been on the receiving end of both the advantages and the cruelties a Lord can bring into play and not be called to task for as he comes from blooded stock."

Garrett looked anew at his second in command, his friend, with new respect. Hadn't his father always said that a man's past built his future? Obviously Tanner was a man of great fortitude and courage, a man to sail the sea with, a man to call friend.

When Garrett went to find her, she was no longer on the front steps. Cassandra had retired to her room where she had started to weep uncontrollably. She could cry for hours and then she would be dizzy and despondent again. Eating had no appeal, for everything that she tried made her run to her dressing room to relieve herself of her stomach's contents. She looked pale and ghostly. When Garrett looked in on her he was shocked at how much her health had deteriorated. He began to worry about her health and that of the babe. Mentally he kicked himself; Mame had tried to warn him without success. If she lost the babe now he had only himself to blame.

"Cassandra I'm truly sorry."

"For what Garrett?" she answered tiredly.

"I've been an ass and have taken my foul mood and doubts out upon you. I am afraid that it took someone else to point that out to me."

"It doesn't matter."

My God, Tanner was right; he had been killing her by inches.

"Yes it does, Sweetheart, for my doubts and fears would not matter if I didn't care for you. Please, Cassandra, give me another chance. Please don't leave me."

Gently he took her into his arms holding her gently and stroking her hair.

"Go away, you will only break my heart again." Suddenly she felt ill again and struggled to make her way to the dressing room. Garrett released her when he realized where she was going.

Chapter Twenty-Six

When she returned there was hot tea and biscuits waiting for her.

"Any better, Sweetheart?"

She wanted to cry. Had he actually forgiven her? "Some I think." Mame appeared in the doorway and with Garrett's approval entered the room.

"I think we'd better have Doctor Thorpe take a look at you, Honey," Garrett stated.

Cassandra looked at Mame to see worry lining her brow. "Why? What's wrong with me?"

Mame answered her question. "Lady, we think you are with child."

Cassandra's face lost all color. It had been a while since her monthly but she had never thought that a babe was the reason. So, that was why he was talking to her! Well he could go to hell! She would get well for her child but Garrett would not have a place in her heart again!

She bolted upright, "I don't need your help or anybody's help. I will be fine. I can take care of myself and the babe, thank you very much!"

She surprised both Garrett and Mame with the outburst but Garrett figured that anything was better than the despondent view of the world she had previously adopted. Mame shook her head when he made to close the distance between them and instead followed Mame out of the master bedroom. Outside the bedroom Mame explained that it was not unusual for expecting mothers to act erratically, especially when their husbands had been acting like jackasses. Mame wanted to knock some sense into the man but settled for a stern talking to instead. He must treat Cassandra with care and start all over again to court the Lady assuring her of her place in his life and home. Couldn't he see that Cassandra was nothing more than a beautiful child who had lost her memory? She was suffering from more than just the loss of her memories, she thought she had lost her love. Why were men such a self-centered species?

Mame shooed Garrett off to finish his own business before turning back to Cassandra's door. She knocked and after a short

Captured Pearl

pause, "It's me, Honey. May I come in?"

In a small voice Cassandra responded, "Please do."

The room had darkened as the afternoon had expired and Mame lit several candles to cheer the room. Cassandra was lying on the bed and Mame walked over and sat on the edge reaching out to Cassandra and stroking her long hair.

"He cares for you, you know."

Cassandra began to sob again. "No he doesn't. He despises me and he thinks I am working for Duprell. I'm not Mame, I'm not! He won't believe me and I've grown tired of trying to convince him otherwise."

"He knows that, Dear, even if he won't admit it, just as I know it, also. He is worried Cassandra. Not only about Duprell but other matters, too. Cassandra, every woman in his life that he ever cared about died, was driven mad, or betrayed him. He is afraid to trust again. His heart has been broken so many times, just like yours."

"Do you really think he cares Mame?"

"Of course he does child or he would not go to such lengths to make you as miserable as he is himself. When I told him that I thought you were with child his whole face lit up and he sat straight up in his chair."

"But that's just it Mame," replied Cassandra sadly. "He only cares about the child not me. That's why he was so caring now. I thought he had come to believe in me and trust me after all. I don't wish to spend the rest of my life with a man who does not love me. I am so miserable—what am I going to do?"

Wisely, Mame did not reveal that Garrett had suspected her condition before going to London. The poor child did not need to think that the man had married her just because she carried his child. Mame knew better, but Garrett could be a hard man to read. He controlled his feelings, too well sometimes, and did not speak to others of things that really mattered.

"You're going to do nothing but think about feeling better. Why don't you get some rest and things will look better in the morning." She left Cassandra to cry herself to sleep again.

Chapter Twenty-Six

The next morning found Cassandra feeling somewhat better. She searched out Mame to find her in the kitchen with Cook. Cook had fixed an old family recipe of warm milk, bread, and honey for her to try. As unappetizing as it looked the concoction set well on her stomach. Chamomile tea followed. She felt better than she had in days.

"I think I'll take a walk in the garden Mame. I am going to have to take better care of myself if I'm to have a child."

It was a beautiful garden even with Garrett's men watching her like hawks. There were large, shady, English oaks scattered about with colorful flowers of every kind boasting their fall colors. Everything smelled wonderful and fresh. She imagined getting lost in the gardens to wander forever in its paradise. Fanciful thinking but delightful just the same. The birds chirped as she inhaled the aroma of the scented flowers. Garrett's men had left or had hidden themselves away out of her sight. Either way she didn't care.

Cassandra returned to her room later that morning to find a perfect stem of lavender resting on her pillow. Garrett she assumed. She wouldn't be won over that easily. A shiny round stone lay next to the washstand and in spite of herself she smiled. His attempts at courtship reminded her of a small boy's treasures. Everywhere she turned that day some small token lay waiting for her eye and she found her heart lightening. The pink ribbon, a hawk's tail feather, even the small green frog in her water glass brought a smile to her face. As she readied for bed Cassandra began to wonder what items she might find the next day for she was sure that his boyish assault had only begun.

The next morning an intricate folded paper bird lay outside her door. My goodness, the man had hidden talents! The chair that Mame seated her in for her breakfast was covered in flower petals of every hue. When she left the house to take air in the garden Tanner was waiting in the entry to escort her about the grounds. He was sensitive to her mood leaving her to wander in silence. His eyes steadily followed her progress but his familiar face and unthreatening presence were a gift that went right to her heart.

"Mr. Tanner, come walk with me, please."

"Yes, my Lady." He offered his arm as they continued about the garden lane.

"Tell me, Mr. Tanner, do you enjoy serving the Captain?"

"Mostly, my Lady."

"What do you mean by that comment, Sir?"

"I don't suffer employment by jackasses so I was gladdened to see that the fairies had seen fit to change him back to his human form."

Cassandra had to laugh at his comment for he said it with such a straight and solemn face that she could not help but know that he had been heartily disgusted by his Captain's actions.

"So, Mr. Tanner, do you think the fairies will come to fly off with him again?"

"I'm sprinkling him with salt every chance I get to ward them off."

Again Cassandra laughed especially when he showed her a pocket filled with Cook's fine house salt. She could just see Garrett shaking the salt out of his hair and then wondering where it had come from.

Two days later at the dinner table she found a velvet bag that, when opened, was found to contain salt along with a note:

> **The jackass would like to dine with you this evening. The fairy banisher will relay your message.**

Tanner relayed her assent to dinner warning Garrett that he would be getting liberally sprinkled as the day continued. He had to laugh for who could find fault with the man's admonishments when they were gifted with such a wiley sense of humor?

But when Cassandra entered for dinner that evening Garrett was not alone. Shane had returned from his foray in France and had landed that evening. His presence was a welcome diversion. He told stories of Paris and soon had Cassandra laughing. The sound filled the house and Garrett's heart and he wondered, "How

Chapter Twenty-Six

long had it been since he'd heard her laugh?" He couldn't help but notice how relaxed Cassandra seemed with his brother.

Miles came in after the meal to report on the fall calving. The new Herefords were surpassing their expectations and soon the three men were involved in a complicated discussion of farming. Shane soon turned the conversation to the wedding telling Garrett that a friend of his at court had let him in on the news. Shane then gave Garrett a talking to for not inviting his only brother.

"But brother mine I never know whose bed you're in from one night to the next so how would I know where to find you?"

Cassandra enjoyed the easy relationship between the three, sitting back and listening with enjoyment. Then the room hazed and the table was rectangular instead of oval and there were five men instead of three. Her papa she recognized, but the others were strangers to her mind's eye. Two of the men were older with white hair and they talked excitedly about something. The other two where her papa's age, although, the one man she didn't like. It was a child's dislike, intense and unrelenting. She was watching from the alcove for she was supposed to be abed. The evil man had seen her and she had rushed back to her bed.

"Cassandra, Cassandra, are you well?" Garrett's words shook her from the past.

"Yes, just a memory."

Garrett leaned forward eagerly. "What did you remember?"

"A meeting at the house. My papa and four other men. One man I didn't like."

"Anything else?"

"No." She raised her eye to see the men watching her intently. "What?"

Shane spoke stilling her heart with his words, "You called someone the *diable*. It means the devil Cassandra."

"Cassandra, picture the memory," Garrett demanded. "See every detail. What did you feel?"

Even with their unsettling relationship Cassandra trusted Garrett in this. She forced herself to look at every detail about the scene.

"I don't know the men. I don't think I did as a child. Two were older with white hair, two were younger. The one man I hated. I didn't really feel afraid, I hated him for my papa. I didn't hear what they said."

Garrett firmly entrenched the scene in his mind to relay to Josh upon his return, and then watched his brother entertain his wife. Shane was telling the most outrageous story of Paris, where he had been studying, and interjecting French words every now and again. Some Cassandra seemed to understand some she did not.

"You've become very learned in the French language brother."

"I've had reason to." And he proceeded to tell Garrett of a French girl named Thea Turbefield. She was a dance teacher for several of the aristocrats of the French court and Shane was enthralled. He wanted Garrett to meet her. This was earthshaking news, for Shane had never taken any Lady seriously enough to want his brother to be introduced. Shane informed them that Thea was residing in the town while he had come to visit at the Estate and he was anxious to get back to the Lady. Things being what they were in the country at the time Garrett suggested that Shane bring her to the Estate to stay. There were plenty of rooms at the house and Cassandra interjected that she would enjoy the company. Things were settled and in the morning Shane would arrive back with his new Lady.

Garrett was pleasantly surprised the next day when Shane arrived. Most of his previous women had been fortune seekers trying to set their claws into the Jamison fortune. But this Lady, for it was obvious that she was, was something quite different. Thea was a petite, pretty girl with large, blue eyes and sleek chestnut hair. She was pretty but not stunning, as Shane's previous women had been. Her manner was warm and earthy. Thea was considerably younger than Garrett had supposed for a woman that had to make her way in the world. She readily informed Garrett that her Papa had been the youngest of eight brothers of a minor French Lord with no hope of ever receiving any of the family's modest fortune. He had married a merchant's daughter. Both families had

Chapter Twenty-Six

been pleased with the match for the Turbefield name had lent stature to the merchant's reputation while the girl had brought an income to the Lord's son. Together the two had been very happy, but then the sickness had come to the village where they resided. Both her parents had been taken, as well as most of the townspeople. Her father's family had known of her great interest in the dance and had secured her a place at Court as a dance teacher. She was well versed and Garrett could see that the two younger people loved each other very much. He was impressed with his brother's choice and teased him about finally settling for one woman.

Shane responded in kind. "Yes, since my sister-in-law would not run away with me at the Queen's ball I had to search the world over to find a woman that could tame my wild ways."

They laughed. Garrett had the feeling that what Shane said was very close to the truth. He could tell that if Shane had been the rider on the road that night their positions might have been reversed. But Shane was deeply in love with this lovely French girl—there was no doubt of that.

Thea and Cassandra soon became friends. Nearly the same age, as far as anyone could tell, they spent the days together and Garrett smiled to see Cassandra bloom with the newfound confidence her friend installed.

To cement her lightheartedness daily gifts continued to arrive. Soon Shane joined in leaving tidbits for Thea. The two girls laughed and giggled at the men's foolishness, But, the day a wicker basket with a pink bow arrived sporting a soft, gray kitten with Cassandra's name attached was the turning point for the couple's happiness.

Cassandra was teary eyed, cuddling the feline protectively against her neck. The kitten purred contentedly until Garrett arrived. Then when Garrett attempted to caress the kitten, the tiny spitball sank his sharp kitten teeth into Garrett's hand.

Cassandra was mortified! But Garrett laughed, stating that his feisty kitten had a fierce lion of her own! And so, "Lion" became Cassandra's newest protector.

Captured Pearl

Shane was often with the Ladies, leaving Garrett to feel secure in the knowledge that Duprell would have difficulties spiriting his Lady off the Estate. Shane had been apprised of the circumstances so he was sure to keep a sharp look out. His brother might seem the dandy and a ladies' man, but he was as skilled in the sword as any man that Garrett had encountered. Tanner still spent many days on the look out for trouble, but now Garrett felt more at ease when he was called back by Peters to help with the repairs of the *Lady*.

They received word from Josh that the Birmingham family was returning near the end of the month and the Ladies of the family were most insistent to meet with Cassandra. Might a meeting be arranged in the town of Plymouth before the family finally sailed home to Portsmouth? Cassandra was ecstatic with the news. She realized how much she had missed the young Birminghams, and Josh's sealed note to Garrett spoke of revealed secrets that must be shared. Their ship would dock at Weymouth on 21 October. If a meeting could be arranged, might Garrett send a rider with a missive to watch for the *Seagull?* All the parties involved agreed that a meeting would be most fortuitous. Garrett arranged for a rider to leave on 15 October, giving him plenty of time for the trip. The rider should wait until the end of the month to be sure he had not missed the ship. If the *Gull* did not arrive by then he was to return home.

The day of 22 October found Garrett's rider galloping up the lane to report that the Birmingham ship had docked three days prior, and the family was even now making their way by ship to Plymouth. Garrett sent word to the staff to ready itself for the invasion of the Birmingham family for one night before deciding if they would then extend their visit to the Jamison Estate, or sail for home.

Rudy rang the bell that very evening to announce the arrival of a ship approaching the Jamison dock. The carriages were prepared and ready before he resumed his exercising of the Jamison mounts. But today he would travel a different path.

Cassandra was beside herself with the joy of seeing her

Chapter Twenty-Six

friends and she ran down the steps barely waiting for the carriages to stop to welcome them to the Jamison Estate. Josh and his father stepped out of the first carriage carrying an impressive looking document. The girls almost tumbled from the second carriage in their eagerness to see Cassandra. Introductions of Thea to the Birminghams were made on the way into the receiving room where Mame and Cook had laid out refreshments for everyone. When a proper amount of time had passed the gentlemen retired to Garrett's study and firmly pulled the doors shut. The girls hardly noticed but Lady Patience watched the move by the men and also noticed Tanner and several other men stationed about the Estate.

Inside the study Garrett waited impatiently for Josh to begin. It was Lord Phillip who broke the silence. "You have garnered yourself quite a catch there Garrett."

Josh silently held out the impressive looking document to Garrett. As he received it the seal caught his eye. He raised his eyes in surprise to Josh who merely nodded. The seal of the Court of France decorated the bottom of the document. Garrett skimmed through the writing then returned to the beginning hardly able to believe what he was reading:

> On this day of eleventh September the crown of France advises the English Lord Jamison of the history and lineage of the girl child, Cassandra Gourdue.
>
> Be it known the Lady's father, Jean-Luke Gourdue, while of merchant stock, was a great favorite and scholar of this court. Upon many occasions the so named Monsieur Gourdue had advised this court in matters of national importance. His knowledge of the histories of past empires had garnered him a highly decorated position at the University of Paris. With his English wife he had conceived a girl child, which was named Cassandra. Often did the child visit the court with her father, and we found the child to be both

Captured Pearl

engaging and beautiful. Upon the mysterious death of her parents the child disappeared to her father's family's distress. The Gourdue family has long been looked upon as one of the premier wine producing families of Europe. When Monsieur Gourdue was murdered a costly tomb of ancient Greek writings also disappeared. This crown has been concerned for the child since her disappearance and she can be recognized by the unique ring given to her by the Court of France. The Dowager Queen gifted a gold twisted band with a solitary small blue diamond to her on her eighth birthday.

If the Lady you are seeking to discover is the child in question this Crown would appreciate knowing that she is in capable and friendly hands.

His Majesty
King Henry IV of France

Garrett viewed the two Birmingham men in shock. His Cassandra was favored by the French Court? Her father attended the King of France? Good Lord! Who would have thought? No wonder she had the manners of the Court! And the ring? She had often dreamed of it and had described it to both himself and Josh on numerous occasions. What had Duprell done with it, for she remembered having it at his home.

Bess would have a field day with this information! Either it would endear Cassandra to her forever or land them both in dire straits with the Queen. And she would have to know before Garrett could respond to the King of France, after all, he was the Queen's man. And now it seemed Cassandra was a King's woman. What a tangled web had been woven to bring their lives together. Would the fragile thread of their lives survive the political intrigue that was sure to evolve from the favor of two Crowns in two different countries that at the best of times had not been easy friends?

Chapter Twenty-Seven

The next morning the Ladies readied themselves for a shopping trip into Plymouth. Garrett and Josh, after careful consideration, had decided to agree with their request that this day be just for the Ladies. Of course, several of Garrett's men would accompany them, for no gentleman would send his Lady out unescorted.

The men decided Mame should accompany the Ladies and the Birminghams, rather than one of the younger maids. One wise head among the group of young Ladies was a must. Shane and Garrett had planned to travel with them to town, but an envoy for a new trading company was arriving to negotiate trade contracts that week. One of the men employed at the Estate, a John by name, would escort the group as well as Geoffrey, Johnson, Robert, and Hurley.

John was receiving a few extra coins from a man named Duprell, not known by Garrett, and all he was asked to do was report the whereabouts of the Lady Cassandra to a man he met in town every few days. If the Lady left the Estate, a written message delivered through Rudy in the stables, would reach Duprell within hours. Neither man could see the harm; John was too worried for his family and Rudy too young and naïve to realize the trouble that they would visit upon their Mistress.

They left early, for the Ladies had much shopping to do, as Josh had been informed by his sisters. He grumbled under his breath at the thought of the bills that would be forthcoming from the town merchants. Hopefully, his mother and Mame could keep them under control. Garrett had instructed Cassandra that the merchants in town would add to his account whatever she wanted and then before they departed he pressed a modest amount of coin into her palm.

Captured Pearl

"Mad money, my father always called it. Something a Lady might purchase without having to answer to her husband for its purchase." Cassandra was pleased by his consideration and gave him a rare smile.

The ride to town was uneventful but delightful. Beth rode with Cassandra, Thea, and Mame while the other Birminghams rode in the second carriage. The drivers were instructed to take the carriages around to the Wayside Inn, where the Ladies would meet them when they had tired of town.

John and Geoffrey dropped back to give the Ladies space to proceed with their shopping and conversation.

After a few hours of drifting among the shops and stalls Cassandra began to feel fatigued. Mame noticed almost immediately and pointed out a small tea shop tucked back in an out-of-the-way corner of the street. They coaxed the Birminghams and Thea to continue their shopping and to return for them at their leisure.

Cassandra had not thought of Duprell all week. With Garrett's renewed interest and playful courting the worries of the past had melted back to a distant corner of her mind.

"What are you smiling about?" asked Mame.

"I was just thinking," she replied to Mame, "how nice it would be if you and Sampson would marry some day."

"Why, I won't marry that cocky, English boob!" Mame blurted out referring to Garrett's manservant and butler. "He thinks he knows everything!"

"Mame the man is enamored with you!"

"And you, Miss, are blind!"

Cassandra laughed, "Why Mame, what was it you told me? A man only wants you as miserable as he is, when he cares for you so much that he is miserable. I can see it in his eyes each time he looks at you."

"That old butler only wants someone to argue with."

"Do you like him?"

"Do I what?!"

"Do you like him?"

Chapter Twenty-Seven

"Why, he's been around for years!" Mame replied with a startled look upon her face.

"Mame living alone is a horrible thing. Especially in a houseful of people. I should know. Do you think that if you didn't like each other it would be so easy to annoy each other?"

Mame looked at Cassandra like she had lost her mind and gently shook her gray head.

"I'm too old to hook up with anyone, especially with that old codger."

"Of course, that's why you fuss over him every chance you get."

"That's just my nature," Mame shrugged her shoulders as if she didn't care, but deep down Mame did feel something for Sampson. In fact, upon occasion she had noticed Sampson looking at her that certain way.

They continued chatting as they waited for their tea and scones to be delivered to their table. Then to Cassandra's dismay Duprell entered with a lovely young woman.

"Don't look now," Cassandra tried to control her voice, "Duprell is being seated directly across from us."

Mame whipped her head around and then looked for the Jamison man to find him surveying the situation from the opposite corner. It wasn't Geoffrey but the man that worked on the Estate, John. Mame settled back into her seat remarking, "Do you want to leave?"

"No, we'll stay. I cannot run away every time I see him." Mame knew Cassandra was right but she wished that Garrett were here to take control of the situation.

Duprell had spotted Cassandra by this time and he was filled with a sudden elation. His tip had been right on the money. The little bitch was here in town and alone except for the old hag who ran Jamison's house. He nodded to the man from Jamison's Estate, who quietly slipped out the back to inform Duprell's men to be ready. Before the Ladies could notice that he was gone, John was back in his corner. Yes, things were finally going to work out for him. He would retaliate against Jamison where it would hurt the most.

Duprell's companion talked non-stop. She was a feisty, red-headed girl who was resistant to her father's control. She and Duprell had met at a party recently where her father had, in no uncertain terms, warned her off the man. As far as she was concerned that was the perfect reason to carry on a liaison with Duprell. Not that she would marry him, for he wasn't what she wanted, in that respect, but hopefully this would show her father that she wasn't to be trifled with. Duprell had played along for he had tired of Cara and her grasping ways. The little red head was pretty and if past experience had taught him anything it was that a disobedient girl would turn out to be a good scramble under the covers. One that didn't follow the dictates of society could not expect any better than to be treated as a strumpet once she had been used and discarded by a man such as he. Served the little bitch right.

Duprell leaned over the table catching a glimpse of his companion's creamy-white breasts before stating, "Excuse me, dear, but I see an old acquaintance of mine. I must go over for a moment." The red headed pouted, but she smiled when Duprell promised that he would not be long.

Cassandra saw Duprell headed her way and tensed at the table. He walked to Cassandra making an exaggerated bow when he reached the table. He nodded to Mame who stuck up her nose at him.

"Well my dear niece how have things been for you? I have missed your presence in my house."

"I haven't missed you at all Uncle," said Cassandra in a short bitey tone. She was anxious in his presence and worried what Garrett would say. Then she stiffened her back thinking fiercely to herself, "I won't let him intimidate me!"

"You must come and visit soon, my dear."

"There is no reason for me to visit you," replied Cassandra.

"But, of course, there is. You owe me," Duprell replied in a low menacing tone. He gathered in his ire not wanting to make the two suspicious. "You stayed with me for quite a while when your

Chapter Twenty-Seven

parents died and all that time you lived on my generosity. In return you unjustly left me just when I had arranged a good marriage for you. Seems you arranged your own marriage quite nicely to a wealthy man." Duprell watched with satisfaction, as Cassandra grew pale at his words. Good! Let her think on that for a while. Then she returned his words leaving him cold.

"Just how much did you get for my ring, Uncle? I'm sure you remember it. The one with the blue diamond setting? That should have more than paid for what miserly care you gave me." Cassandra wasn't quite sure where that had come from. But she knew, without a doubt, that she had *not* given the ring up voluntarily. Even as a young child she had been aware of its value and importance.

In her mind was a crystal clear memory of an important woman of stature and regality who was the giver of the gift.

Her father bowing low gracefully before a throne, and her first royal curtsy. Her father's awed thanks and a quick pat upon her cheek by the bestower of the ring.

Her father had gathered her small hand in his before leading her out of the richly decorated room to join her waiting mama.

She heard Mame mutter under her breath, "Good for you, Honey."

"I've heard quite enough from you, Uncle, and I am sure your companion is missing your presence, although I don't know why. As we have nothing more to discuss, perhaps you should leave."

"You and I have plenty to discuss, Cassandra. Perhaps another time and place?"

"I don't think so."

"I will be seeing you again, Cassandra. Now if you two Ladies will excuse me?" He turned to return to his table.

"Good for you, Miss. That man needs to be put in his place."

Cassandra forced a smile not wanting Mame to know how badly shaken she was by her uncle's words. She was glad that Garrett's presence was visible in the man waiting by the door.

Duprell returned to his Lady friend and Cassandra saw him

Captured Pearl

bend down to the woman and whisper something in her ear. The woman smiled brightly and extended her hand to Duprell. Together they strode out of the tea shop and down the street. Cassandra watched in relief as they left.

"I wish Garrett didn't have to know about this Mame."

"Well someone had better tell him! If not you or I, surely John will report it. Best to put out the fire before the flames can be fanned I always say."

"You're right, of course. I worry what he'll do Mame. If he re-injures his shoulder he might lose the use of it. Then what would he do?"

"If he loses it in defense of his Lady I'm sure he will count it as a cost well paid. Don't worry so much, Dear. He is a full-grown man and can take care of himself."

They had been sitting and talking for quite some time when Cassandra asked to be excused to the Ladies convenience. The proprietor pointed to the back citing that it was just to the left of the door. Telling Mame that she would return shortly Cassandra made her way outside. Finding it just where the man had said. She finished her business, then exited to make her way back inside, only to find her way blocked by several men.

"Come along quietly Miss. I don't want to have to hurt you and you don't want me to," spoke Simon, one of Duprell's men. Cassandra looked at the gathering of dirty, leering men and decided to take her chances. She opened her mouth to scream. Simon shook his head right before his fist met with her jaw rendering the Lady unconscious.

"Nice piece of work there man," stated one of the other men as Simon caught Cassandra in his arms.

"Shut up and get to the horses. Meet me outside of town. Griswald, ride to the Estate and bring Margaret to the appointed place. Move!" Quickly he gathered the Lady in his arms moving slowly down the alleyways to rendezvous with his horse. Simon knew Duprell had thought of releasing him from his service for he was too well kept, too well mannered, and too handsome to fit in with the rest of his men. But on the inside he was just as cold as

Chapter Twenty-Seven

winter in the highlands of Scotland. He did his job with as little fuss as necessary. He had realized as a young man that manners and good looks could often talk a man out of a bad spot. Now, as he made his way, anyone would have thought him a gallant lover carrying his love home. The horse was waiting along with one of the men to help him settle the Lady in front of his saddle. Gathering up the reins the two made their way out of town using the less traveled routes and then galloped for their appointed meeting place.

Mame began to worry when Cassandra didn't return in what she thought was a timely manner. Finally, she made her way outside to find no sign of her Lady and the convenience empty.

Hurrying back inside she alerted John to the disappearance of their Mistress. He went out back to look around but did not return, either. Frantically Mame cast about looking for a familiar face. Down the street the laughter of the Birmingham girls could be heard. Dashing out with her skirts gathered in her hands Mame called for their attention.

"Geoffrey, the Lady Cassandra is missing. Hurry, Hurry." Geoffrey calmed Mame enough to comprehend that she had disappeared from the tea shop. When Mame also replied that John was missing and that Duprell had been in town—it was easy to put all the incidents together. He admonished the Ladies to stay together as he set off for the Inn to enlist Johnson's aid.

Lady Birmingham quickly flagged down one of the street boys asking who had the fastest mount in town.

"Jim Tipper, Lady."

"Can you deliver a message to Mr. Tipper?"

"Yes, Lady."

"You tell Mr. Tipper that if he will deliver a message for me I will pay him three silver pieces on this end and there will be more at the end of his ride. Can you do that?"

The lad's eyes opened wide at the thought of three silver coins and even wider when one was pressed into his hand to speed his delivery of the message. "Yes Lady!" and off he sped.

It wasn't long before a flashy mare was speeding toward

Captured Pearl

them. Lady Birmingham urgently relayed the message he was to deliver and the three coins. The young miller was off like a flash—heading to the Jamison Estate. By horse and cross-country Garrett should be in possession of the news before the hour was out. There was nothing the Ladies could do but wait.

Lady Birmingham admonished them to make their way to the tea shop on the off chance that Cassandra would return but no one thought for a moment that they would be so fortunate. Mame blamed herself and Patience gently chided her for being so foolish.

"Mame you could not have known and if anyone is to blame it should be the man assigned to protect her. Where did he get off to anyway?"

Garrett was looking out the study window when he saw the madly dashing horseman clear his hedgerow headed at break-neck speed for his front steps.

"By God I'll have that young buck's neck! He's going to kill someone!"

He was standing in the drive when a spray of pebbles littered his boots as the horse sat on its haunches sliding to a stop. Before he could utter a word the rider frantically began to speak.

"Lord Jamison, I must find Lord Jamison!"

"Steady there man, I'm Lord Jamison."

"Sir your Lady's been taken, at the tea shop. Lady Birmingham sent me . . . an hour ago . . . no sign!"

Garrett paled as he tried to make sense of the man's ramblings. "Slow down man, here sit down. Sampson bring the man a drink."

The fellow took a breath and started again.

"The Lady Birmingham sent me to tell you that Lady Cassandra has been taken from the tea shop near Market Street. Duprell was in town. Come right away. The men can not locate her in the town and John has disappeared."

"How long ago, man?"

"I left at the noon bell," Garrett checked his timepiece as the

Chapter Twenty-Seven

rider began to walk his steaming mount. Twenty minutes. Duprell had a start of twenty minutes right now!

"Fine riding man. Please wait while I ready my men." Soon Garrett returned with five silver coins for the young rider. "Thank you for your fast delivery of the message, and please feel free to rest here as long as you wish."

Tanner and Miles had been conferencing with the Captain and at Garrett's bellow rushed to see what was up. Garrett explained the situation. Tanner rushed to the stables to ready horses while Miles ran to ring the bell calling the crew back to the house.

Striding back into the house Garrett returned with sword buckled in place and his pistol thrust through his belt. In his hand he carried another sword. Tanner came leading Sable and his mare Jewel.

"Know how to use one of these?" Garrett asked as he tossed the man the sword.

"Well enough," Tanner replied. His eyes held a steely glint and his mouth was hardened in resolve.

"Not your fault Tanner. I never expected him to try in town. My fault, I underestimated Duprell again."

"Doesn't matter. I'll kill him."

"You'll have to wait behind me," Garrett spoke with feeling. "Let's find her first." Tanner nodded. Miles came running around the corner of the house with two other men.

"I'm riding for town, Miles. I doubt that she is there but we have to start somewhere. You head to Duprell's. Gather the men and meet us near the large oak just outside of Duprell's Estate."

"Aye, Captain." The old sailor looked mean and nasty as he watched his Captain and friend ride off and he promised himself that if the Captain didn't finish off Duprell he would teach the man the meaning of pain.

Chapter Twenty-Eight

Cassandra awoke to find herself held in place by steely arms. She struggled briefly until the man admonished, "I'd prefer not to hit you again." She sat still looking about her realizing that they must be riding north for she could not see the sea or hear the crashing of the waves. Other men began to join them until there were twelve or so riding along. Presently the riders slowed, coming to a halt before an old stone church that was falling into disrepair. They dismounted and with a firm grip on her arm Simon drew her inside. Toward the back, almost hidden by the altar, were stone steps leading downward. This was where Simon pushed her—forcing her down into the darkness. Cassandra carefully felt her way down. As she turned a corner a light appeared. Simon was behind her and she could feel his breath on her neck.

"Keep going, Madam." She gathered her skirts so as not to trip as she moved toward the light. Several men were gathered about a large room. Two men were wearing the garb of Catholic priests and one dandy was dressed as if he were attending a royal conference. They were speaking in what Cassandra assumed was Spanish. They quieted as they turned to face the intruders.

Cassandra began to shiver, not so much from the cold as from the looks upon the men's faces. Clearly, they were up to no good. Their cold, ferocious eyes traveled slowly over her person, leaving her shaking again, but this time on the inside.

But, she gathered her courage and her newfound passion for her life with Garrett about her in a protective cloak, swearing not to give them the satisfaction of seeing her fear. She had lived in fear long enough.

"I believe that Duprell spoke of the Lady. You are to keep her safe until his arrival."

Captured Pearl

One of the priests spoke up, "Yes, of course, Señor. We have a place arranged where the Lady will stay out of trouble. This way please."

Simon's hand in the small of her back forced her forward. The priest led the way to what was revealed to be a small alcove in the rock fitted with a door and lock. Cassandra began to struggle as she was forced toward the darkened room.

"Now, Lady, this will get you nowhere. Please go inside. Father, bring her a light and some water."

The Father returned with a lantern and a beaker of water. Cassandra could see there was a chair in the middle of the room, but nothing else. She turned pleading eyes to Simon, "Please, Sir, do not do this."

"Inside Lady." Cassandra could tell there would be no swaying the man and after taking a deep breath she forced shaking legs to move forward. Behind her she heard the turning of the key in the lock.

Darkness tried to close in upon her, and Cassandra struggled to stay calm. She brought to mind her vision of Garrett upon the deck of *The Lady* standing tall, proud, and true. Over and over his men remarked on their Captain's loyalty and steadfastness to his crew and friends. Garrett would *never* rest until he found her. Cassandra's heart knew this for the truth. Now her heart must convince her mind.

Resolutely, she brought forth all the small caring moments she had shared with Garrett—the trip to Piccadilly, his care at court, the small green frog in her water glass. A slight smile graced her lips and she gathered the calm and peace close to her heart.

Carefully, she settled upon the chair, determined to present a calm demeanor to whomever should enter through the door. For some reason Cassandra knew this was her best defense—that these men dined on another's fear.

Duprell arrived later that evening to confer with the delegate from the Spanish court and the priests. He had been right to believe that the Catholic priests would not recognize a marriage

Chapter Twenty-Eight

by a Protestant clergy. The marriage to them was null and void. They would be happy to save the Lady's soul by marrying her to a Catholic man in a Catholic ceremony. The envoy would help with spiriting the couple out of the country until such time as the Lady could be brought around—in exchange for a small favor. Duprell must capture Lord Jamison whereupon he would be taken to the Spanish Court in chains and where the Spanish jail masters would convince him to divulge all of England's secrets. Duprell couldn't have been more pleased. He would win in the end.

He made his way to Cassandra's cell throwing the bolt free and opening the door. She was on her feet when the door opened. Duprell sneered with glee at his niece huddling in the dark, dimly-lit cell.

"I told you we would continue our discussion. You shall marry Lucas and then you shall travel to Spain where he shall instruct you in your wifely duties until you are so well versed that you will not care if you return to England. And your lover? Well I am sure the Spanish jailers shall eventually persuade him to talk. I wouldn't hold out many hopes for him as there may not be much of him left when they're finished."

Cassandra stared at him in horror. How could one man be so evil and intent only on his own glory? Had Duprell already captured Garrett? Would Garrett be able to rescue her in time to forestall this unwanted marriage to a man almost as deviant as her uncle? And what would happen to her unborn child?

Perhaps Duprell would relent when he discovered that she carried Garrett's child, for surely Lucas would not want her now.

"Uncle there is something I think you should know."

"What is it?"

"I am carrying Garrett's child."

The silence was deafening. Duprell's whole body became rigid. His hands clenched and he turned his back to her. Duprell's anger was black and heavy. The bitch had gotten herself with child! What to do, for Lucas would balk at this newest development he was sure. The child would have to be disposed of quickly. Perhaps Margaret would know of some remedy for Cara had never ripened in all the years they had been together. His mind boiled, running new scenarios for the success of his plans. Yes! He had it.

"Uncle did you hear me?" Her heart sank as her hopes began to disappear.

"Excuse me Cassandra," he said turning to face her. "You are quite right. This does change things." Duprell considered his options. He could leave Cassandra here for the night returning to collect her in the morning. That would give him time to set up the taking of Jamison. Margaret could be ready at the hunting lodge with the things to eliminate the child. Yes it could work.

"I am afraid that you shall have to savor the hospitality of the Fathers this night niece as I have business to attend to." With that he quickly closed the door, sliding home the bolt and ignoring Cassandra's protests. Making his way back to the Spanish envoy and the Catholic priests Duprell bid the Fathers to hold the girl until he came for her tomorrow. The wedding would have to wait a few days, he lied, as the groom had been called to Court. To the envoy, Duprell warned him to be ready for Jamison within the next few days. Then he left taking Simon with him.

They rode to the hunting lodge to find Margaret and Cara waiting. Griswald was already explaining before Duprell dismounted.

"The daughter insisted on coming Captain. There was no way to leave her behind without causing a ruckus and before I left the watch notified me of riders approaching the Estate. Must have been Jamison and his men."

Instead of the wrath Griswald expected Duprell emitted an evil laugh. Yes, everything was falling his way. Jamison would know by now that Cassandra was not at the Duprell Estate and he would be gathering his men to search the countryside. Jamison's men would have to split up making it easier for Jamison to be taken. Duprell rubbed his hands together in glee.

"Simon, go back to the Estate and gather up Judah. The two of you watch for Jamison in the search and take him. He must be alive and able to talk other than that I don't care how you get him.

Chapter Twenty-Eight

When you have him send word here but take him to the church. The envoy shall be waiting." He was very glad he had kept Simon on for the man was so opposite of his usual crew that Jamison would not suspect Simon until it was too late. Judah could add bulk and muscle to the job.

Not for the first time Duprell wondered how he had managed to acquire the services of so obviously a well-trained and careful man. Duprell eyed up the man as he left for the Estate. He wondered if Simon had been sent by his contact, Monay, to keep watch on Duprell himself.

Simon grimaced as he rode along the path. There wasn't much he wouldn't do for the right amount of coin. Killing and mayhem had always been his way of life, but usually his large fee could guarantee him more upstanding surroundings. Duprell was crude and incredibly easy to read—not at all the usual sort Simon associated with, but his employer was quite free with his coin, making even this assignment lucrative.

Inside the hunting lodge Duprell sought out Margaret and Cara.

"Margaret!" he hollered.

"Yes, Sir."

"Cassandra has gotten herself with child. Can you get rid of the brat?"

"Sir, I have had many occasions to help women avoid an unwanted child." She offered without hesitation.

"How?"

"An old healer woman taught me. I have been very successful."

"Can you do it without anyone knowing?"

"Yes, Sir. I have done it many times in the past for Ladies who had lifted their skirts a time too many. I will do it for you, Sir." Her eyes were shining with excitement.

"Good. I'll have Cassandra here tomorrow morning. Do it immediately for Lucas will not wait forever. If you pull this off I will see that you are rewarded."

Margaret wanted Duprell's trust. She hated him for how he

had discarded Cara but she hated Cassandra more. After all, she was the one who had destroyed Cara's hopes of ever being Lady Jamison. When Cassandra was finally out of the picture perhaps Cara would get another chance for happiness.

At this moment she had Duprell's respect. They were equal partners in an evil game. She wondered just how much she could get out of Duprell for this service.

As if reading her mind he offered, "When this is over, Margaret, I will see to it that you live in comfort for the rest of your life."

"And what about Cara?"

"She will be taken care of also, Margaret." The housekeeper was delighted.

Before the sun had risen the next morning Duprell was back at the church to collect his niece. He was taking no chances and bound her hands as he led her horse on the way to the hunting lodge. The ride didn't take long and Cassandra wondered what waited in store for her now.

Margaret was there to help her inside fussing over her condition.

"Men they have no sense at all. To do such a horrible thing to you when you are with child." Cassandra needed a friend and Margaret seemed so sincere that she fell into the trap of trusting the woman, again.

"I will make you some tea. It will relax you and be good for the child."

The cup was sipped until it was gone and Cassandra found herself relaxing.

"Come, Lady, I will take you to your room where you can rest. I will come back later to check on you."

She listened outside the door. She knew the potion was already taking effect. In a few hours Cassandra would be screaming in pain and the process would begin. The child would pass out of her body leaving Duprell with a woman that Lucas would want. She couldn't wait to tell Cara what was happening. Her daughter

Chapter Twenty-Eight

would be so pleased.

Later that afternoon everyone returned to blood curdling screams coming from the back room. Margaret stayed close to the room waiting for what she knew would happen. Duprell made as if to barge into the room but Margaret warned him off.

"No sir, don't go in, please. Let me handle this. Send Barnabus to get the doctor. Hurry we don't want her to bleed to death."

Duprell complied with Margaret's instructions. Then returned to the great room to pour himself a drink, and wait.

Within the hour Dr. Stokes arrived. His appearance, when Duprell summoned him, was always timely for he had learned over the years that he would be rewarded well. Duprell paid handsomely for his services and his silence. Margaret was waiting in Cassandra's room holding her down on the bed. She was hemorrhaging badly.

Cassandra knew that something terrible was happening. "God," she moaned between contractions, "what is happening? My baby. Please keep my baby safe." She sobbed as she curled up in pain. Margaret held onto her. "You will be fine Miss, don't worry."

But Cassandra wasn't so sure. The pain was agonizing. Had it not been for the baby she would have wished for death. The doctor examined her and he knew without a doubt that the woman was in the process of losing her child. He felt sorry for this girl—she had always seemed so kind on his previous trips, and this was one of the worst miscarriages he had seen in his many years of practice. He felt hopeless watching her in so much pain, but there wasn't much he could do for her. He wouldn't think of the possibilities that had caused such a terrible accident. For he knew that most accidents associated with Duprell were well planned in advance.

When he and Margaret came downstairs Duprell was waiting.

"How is my niece?" Duprell was concerned for the girl for her screams of pain had been awful to hear. The girl could not be allowed to die. That just wouldn't do at all.

Captured Pearl

"Lord Duprell there is nothing I can do to save the baby. But the mother is strong. She will survive to bear other children. I would suggest at the earliest possible convenience you see that she is moved to more comfortable surroundings such as your Estate." Then the doctor bid them farewell.

Margaret and Duprell exchanged knowing glances—they had accomplished what they set out to do. They were very pleased with themselves.

"Margaret how soon can we move her? It wouldn't do for Lucas to be visiting her here at the lodge."

"A couple of days, Lord. The horseback ride will not set well with her so you will have to take it slowly."

"What is the earliest possible date that can be set for the wedding?"

"A week, Sir. I am not sure if she will be fully recovered within that time but she will probably look healthy by then."

"Well enough. I shall meet with Lucas and inform the priests to have things ready."

Garrett and his men had turned up nothing at the Duprell Estate. The few men that were in residence did not offer any resistance to their search making Garrett suspicious of the events. He thought it strange that both Margaret and Cara were also missing but his uppermost thoughts right now were on finding Cassandra. Perhaps Duprell had not returned with her yet. Where would he hide her?

Garrett separated his men into groups assigning as leaders Miles, Peters, and Tanner. They would scatter, searching the countryside for any trace of Duprell and Garrett's Lady. He was not returning home without her!

Garrett's group set off due north of the Duprell Estate while the other groups set off, each in a different direction. After several hours of riding they reached a particularly dense patch of trees. Before they had ridden far into the thick undergrowth several men poured out from their hiding places. Before Garrett had time to draw his sword two of the three men with him had fallen to the

Chapter Twenty-Eight

swordplay of the attackers. One man pulled out a pistol firing in his man's direction and Garrett was alone to face his attackers. His sword drawn, he wheeled Sable in a tight circle trying to keep the men in his sight. One broke clear of the others and with a mannerly tone commented, "Why don't you concede to us Lord Jamison? There is no way that you shall escape. I am sure that your Lady would prefer to see you in one piece at least one more time."

It was knowing they had Cassandra that convinced him to throw down his sword in disgust. The leader came forward to bind his hands before the group moved off to the north. One man wheeled off riding in a more westerly direction and Garrett wondered where he was going. He was saddened at the waste of his men but had more pressing matters to think about at the moment. Where were they taking him and where was Cassandra? That they did not seem bothered by his perusal of their faces did not bode well for the ending of this ride.

"Where is Cassandra?" he growled.

"All in due time, Sir. There are others of more importance that you should be worrying about."

What was the man talking about? Duprell gave little importance even to his own men and this man was so unlike Duprell's other hirelings that his words actually made Garrett nervous.

"Where are we going?"

"All in due time." Simon was closed mouthed but Judah was not.

"Duprell has a real surprise for your Lordship. And your Lady will be knowing Mr. Lucas most intimately before long." The man cackled in mirth and Garrett saw red. He drove his spurs into the stallion's sides sending him crashing into Judah's lighter mount. The man tumbled to the ground as his horse struggled to rise. But Garrett wasn't finished as with voice and leg he incited the stallion into a rage aimed at the man. Simon quickly jerked Garrett out of the saddle brandishing his reins in Sable's face sending the stallion into a gallop toward home. Garrett was rising from the ground when he was hit from behind by what felt like a ton of rock.

Captured Pearl

With his hands tied behind him Garrett was no match for the massive man who had decided to beat him unto death. Judah snatched Garrett's hair pounding his head into the rough ground before turning him over to begin pummeling his face. Garrett heard the leader speak, "Not his face! He must be able to speak!" Judah rose pulling Garrett with him delivering blow after blow into his rib cage, until the breath he tried to snatch between blows became painful and hot. Almost as soon as it started the leader called a halt to Judah's abuse snapping the men into action with a cold, "That's enough, let us go."

Garrett was thrown over the neck of the nearest horse gasping as newfound pain laced up his sides. A firm hand on his back held him in place as the group continued their journey to parts unknown. A red haze began to accumulate before his eyes with each continuing jar to his ribs. Garrett gritted his teeth. He would not pass out! He must gather what information he could if he was to escape this new danger. Handicapped as he was escape was going to be difficult, even more so, if he was unaware of the path they had taken.

After what seemed like forever he was unceremoniously dumped to the ground. The leader, they called him Simon, grasped him beneath the arms hauling him to his feet. He was half carried and half pushed toward a dilapidated church. The place looked deserted and badly in need of repair and Garrett wondered why here, until he realized that this must have been one of the country Catholic churches that had been burned to the ground in the religious revolution. They made their way to the back then down some stairs and soon Garrett found himself in a subterranean cave beneath the church.

There, two priests and some dressed up dandy were gathered about a table. The men looked up when he entered. The dandy smiling with evil intent.

"Ah, Señor Jamison. I am so glad you have decided to join us. Your friend Duprell said it would be so but you have been like a ghost across the water evading us each time we have tried to snare you."

Chapter Twenty-Eight

"Who the hell are you?" Garrett asked with pained breath.

"Ah, of course, we have not been properly introduced. I am Señor Gabray de Luis Montique investigator for the King of Spain. My sovereign is most anxious to have a conversation with you about your Queen's intent."

"You'll get nothing from me," Garrett growled.

"Señor Duprell said as much but I think you underestimate the lengths to which I am willing to go to have your cooperation. My King has been most anxious to extend you his hospitality. Yet, each time his invitation is extended you manage to avoid his request. Who would have thought your ship would evade us at St. Peter Point when you were so badly damaged.

"We have long sought your identity. So you can imagine our delight when Señor Duprell provided us with your identity and then offered to arrange your presence here."

Garrett kept silent waiting for the pompous ass to finish his remarks. The man was trying to incite him and he would not be so foolish, again.

"Perhaps if Señor Duprell can not convince you to tell me what I wish to know, my friend at the castle in Madrid will be more persuasive. Please lock him up gentleman. You need not be gentle."

Garrett was shoved along the hallway to a small cell that was dark and enclosed. The door slammed behind him leaving him in complete darkness with only his thoughts for company.

Left alone in the darkness time was difficult to gauge. He supposed that it was morning when the cell door opened to reveal Duprell with the two men that Garrett recognized from their previous encounter. The man, Judah, had a smile upon his face that did not bode well for the safety of Garrett's person.

"Bring him out," Duprell commanded. Garrett did not resist the tugging hands that gripped his still bound arms. Best to save his strength for the moments to come. He was on his own for now and he could only hope that somehow his men might discover where he had been taken. He would never allow them to force his exit from the country for Garrett knew if he reached Spain there

Captured Pearl

would be no coming back.

Down the corridor they traveled to find the Spanish envoy awaiting them in a brightly-lit room that contained a table and a chair. An iron ring was suspended from one wall and it was to this that Garrett was taken. Quickly his hands where unbound and wrenched overhead to be fastened to the ring in the wall. It went against Garrett's nature to be docile to his captor and when Judah bent to tie his feet Garrett put his weight behind the force of his kick to the man's jaw. Judah fell back but came up bellowing like a mad bull swinging at Garrett. Duprell restrained the man with a word. Then Simon moved in to help and soon he was tied hand and foot.

"I'll give you one chance to tell my contact what he wishes to know and then I shall release Judah to play. What will it be Jamison?"

Garrett leashed his temper hoping to gain time and information.

"Perhaps if I knew what you were looking for I could be more forthcoming."

"Come now, Jamison, sadly for you we all know that you are a favorite with the Queen and are privy to her plans. I thought this had been explained to you. I see you are going to be difficult."

"What have you done with Cassandra, Duprell?"

Judah was the one who replied as he stuck his foul face up to Garrett's.

"I didn't get a chance to enjoy the Lady last time around but my master has promised me another chance with her if she refuses Lucas' persuasions. I'll admit I hadn't thought she would fight me so hard after those first few slaps. I still got the scar from her braining me with that flower vase. I truly liked that look of terror she showed me before she got away. Me and the boys chased her through the trees till we lost her. That witch ran through brush a rabbit would avoid. Still can't believe she got away. I'm really going to enjoy the taste of her this time around."

"You won't get away with this Duprell. Cassandra has the Queen's favor. The Queen will send her forces to discover her

Chapter Twenty-Eight

whereabouts."

"Oh I don't think so Jamison, for as soon as the priest has performed the ceremony the newlyweds will be off to Spain where Elizabeth has no power." Garrett's heart pumped with fear for his Lady for if Duprell succeeded there was no way that she could be found with the hostilities between the two countries.

"Last chance, Jamison, although perhaps seeing the Lady in the embrace of Lord Gabel would persuade you to talk."

"You swine!" Garrett roared struggling in his bounds. "I'll see you speared on my sword before we're done!"

"I don't believe so—you seem to be all tied up at the moment." Judah laughed and even Simon smiled at his employer's remark.

"Go to hell, Duprell."

"Perhaps, but I believe that you shall reside there first. Simon you know what to do. Be sure that Judah doesn't kill him for the Spanish are so looking forward to his visit. Sorry I can't stay longer Jamison but I have a wedding to plan."

Duprell turned on his heel leaving the room and Garrett in one last bold move remarked, "Well, Gentlemen, I don't believe we've been properly introduced. Lord Garrett Jamison, Queen's man and Captain of the *Green-Eyed Lady* at your service. You are?"

Simon smiled shaking his head. "I give you credit, Sir, you have courage. Judah, you may proceed."

Judah moved in, a wicked smile on his face and fists at the ready. He enjoyed inflicting pain and always had. To see the fear on another's face brought him great pleasure and this man had made him look foolish in front of others. The pleasure would be more gratifying than ever before.

Left alone in the darkness Garrett took shallow breaths to minimize the pain that was radiating from his ribs. Judah had been responsible for Cassandra's loss of memory! The man was a braggart—spilling vital information as he loosed his blows on Garrett's person.

He had found great pleasure in tormenting Garrett with the

details of his attempted rape of Cassandra. Duprell had been furious with her for turning down Lucas' proposal again, and had sent Judah to Cassandra's room to beat her into submission. When he had attempted to hold her down on the bed with his large body she awoke with a fury. Scratching and biting at the intruder attempting to hurt her, the feisty maiden had brained the man with a crystal flower vase, rendering him out cold. Then she had escaped out the balcony and down the trellis to run terrified through the woods. Duprell had sent his men to locate her to no avail, as no one seemed to know how she had escaped her fate. And now, his love was being held against her will by the very tyrant who had terrorized her. Thinking of her in the clutches of Duprell and Lucas could drive him to madness.

Garrett forced himself to breathe slowly and push the image from his mind. He was of no help to either of them unless he could get free. He could not count on his men to free them. Plans began to form in his mind and the brilliant strategist that had confounded the Spanish at sea emerged once again to foil King Phillips' plans. He would be ready when they returned.

Garrett's men had returned to the Estate when it became to dark to search. When Garrett and his men had not arrived at the rendezvous they had backtracked to find the dead men where they had fallen. They had fanned out searching for prints and making little progress when Tanner came upon Sable. No help there for the horse bore no sign of the rider. Miles had sent out the call to all men loyal to the Jamison family and Josh had sent the *Gull* to London to inform the Queen.

Tanner left to parts unknown working on his own search. Josh did not dissuade him for the man was an enigma and often had his own methods that provided results.

Josh tried to reassure the Ladies that matters would turn out for the best, but Mame was beside herself. Over and over she blamed herself for the loss of Cassandra and the ensuing mess.

Sampson finally coaxed her off into a corner of the kitchen where he served her tea and toast and roughly patted

Chapter Twenty-Eight

her wringing hands.

"Now there Mame, you know the Lord has often been in worse situations than this, and surely Cassandra's guardian angel will look after her until the Lord can locate her. Have faith, woman!"

Mame wearily leaned into the butler, relishing his knobby shoulder as the tears began to fall again. The Master had endured so much in his life, surely God would not be so cruel to such a good man. Sampson patted her shoulders offering solace from his presence and together they comforted each other through the night.

The door creaked open to reveal Duprell and the Spanish envoy. Garrett hung limply eyes closed waiting.

"Come, come, Jamison that won't work," Duprell slashed him across the face startling Garrett into wakefulness. "You must try to be more cooperative. Cassandra has certainly come around since I managed to eliminate your brat."

The comment had the desired effect. Garrett could not stop the roar that charged up from the pit of his stomach. "What have you done to my child?!"

"As I said, I have managed to eliminate the obstacle. There was no way that Lucas would accept another man's child. Your wife has certainly been cooperative ever since. Why she is most docile. I am sure Lucas will be most appreciative." Duprell was enjoying this. He could see the pain on Garrett's face. The love and anguish for his woman showed clearly in the news of the murdered child. Duprell was well on his way to destroying everything that Garrett loved. This was delicious!

"You see," Duprell said continuing on, "my housekeeper prepared a special tea to help soothe our poor little Cassandra. She was so upset with her unexpected visit.

"As I was saying it seems the tea caused her to lose the brat." He delighted in seeing the blood drain from Garrett's face.

The force of Duprell's words hit Garrett directly in his heart. "NO!" he roared thrashing against the ropes binding him.

Bleeding wrists and bruised ankles were as nothing as he struggled to escape his bonds. Wet with sweat, Cassandra was all he could think of and their unborn child torn from her body.

Duprell looked at his nails turning his hands over as if inspecting them. "I'm afraid I haven't time to chat further for I have a wedding to attend the day after tomorrow. What would Lucas do without his best man and who would walk the bride down the aisle? Perhaps we will settle this matter after the ceremony. Our ship shall be sailing directly after the ceremony Lord Jamison. I have prepared a special room in the hold for your convenience. Until then."

Chapter Twenty-Nine

Once Duprell had Garrett imprisoned he moved Cassandra back to the family Estate with all possible speed. She was compliant and withdrawn since the loss of her child. Duprell had set Margaret and Cara to the task of bringing her to some semblance for normalcy before the wedding. Cara had been informed by Duprell that her very livelihood rested on how fast she could bring Cassandra to a resemblance of health by Saturday when the wedding ceremony would be take place.

Cara hated her task. She tried tormenting Cassandra with made up tales of how, since her disappearance, Garrett had taken Cara back. She vividly described imagined lovemaking in his bed. At one point she had even told Cassandra that she, Cara, carried Garrett's child. There was no response from her victim. Cassandra never reacted but the pain in her face was evident. Cara reveled in each small dig that hit home.

Slowly Cassandra was improving. She had washed this morning and dressed on her own. Margaret had come to see that she was scrubbed and clean during which time the women spouted vile and ugly names at Cassandra. Together Margaret and Cara tormented her both physically and emotionally, calling her a slut and a child killer. They inflicted bruises upon her person, being careful to inflict their damage where it would not be seen by Duprell. Cassandra did not have the energy, or the will, to fight back until . . .

Thursday before the wedding Cara and Margaret shoved and cursed and berated her as they tired to get her dressed for a visit from Lucas.

"Too bad my mother only poisoned you enough to kill your brat. She should have killed you, too."

Captured Pearl

Cassandra, dazed, felt the blood rush to her face. She lifted her hand slapping Cara violently. She had no idea where the will and the power had come from. It was just suddenly there. Cara screamed pulling her hand away from her bloody mouth.

"If you or your mother ever lay another hand on me I will kill you both," Cassandra spoke her eyes flashing dangerously. Cara and her mother backed away in fear. They had never seen Duprell's niece exude such a force. The fire in her eyes oozed malevolence to the two women who had cost her her child. They turned and left as one, fearing the wrath behind them.

Duprell had arranged for a seamstress to come by the estate to take measurements of Cassandra for a gown for the wedding. The seamstress was distressed with the short time she had to come up with a suitable gown, but Duprell assured her he'd pay handsomely, and, again, he stressed this must be an exquisite creation—not just any common wedding gown. In the back of her mind the seamstress was picturing a gown she had hanging in her work room. It had been made several months ago for a lovely young woman who had died suddenly before her wedding. She could alter it for this poor girl and no one would be the wiser. After all, this shady character deserved whatever tricks the woman needed to do and she could double her fee on this occasion!

Cassandra could have cared less if she wore a rag. There was no reason now to fight. The child was gone. The one presence that might have held her and Garrett together was gone. Her heart was dead and cold. What happened to her now was of little importance.

Against the wishes of the priests Duprell commanded that the wedding would take place at his family home. Few would attend because of the Catholic ceremony but he could defend the Estate much easier than a rundown church in the woods. Besides, he was not keen on having Cassandra in the same structure as Jamison. Her belief that he was dead added to her compliance with his wishes.

Cassandra descended the stairway that evening to attend the mockery that Duprell was calling dinner. Lucas was present to

Chapter Twenty-Nine

survey his art piece and to conclude that she was still fit to marry. Cassandra ignored both men, off in her own world, as they chatted and planned the forthcoming events. She had drifted over to the bookshelves skimming the titles when she heard Garrett's name. Evidently Duprell and Lucas had forgotten her presence.

"Is Jamison taken care of?"

"You need not worry that he will interrupt your life again."

"That did not answer my question, Duprell. Is he taken care of?"

"The Spanish envoy will be taking him to Spain in chains tomorrow. Between the attention of my men and the jailers of Madrid there will not be enough left of him to stuff into a thimble. Satisfied?"

"Quite."

Garrett alive! Duprell had hinted at his death by his men! She should have known that the man could not tell the truth to save his soul! But what to do? Cassandra continued to strain to hear the conversation eventually learning that he was being held in the woods north of the Estate. She must help Garrett! But how? She was too closely guarded to be able to escape. There wasn't much time. Who could she trust to take a message? There was no one . . . or was there?

Cara was still hoping for a life with Garrett by the way she talked and tormented Cassandra. Could her desire for Garrett's love tempt her to thwart Duprell to ensure Garrett's rescue? It was worth a try. The only problem would be finding a moment alone with the witch.

The evening wore on and Cassandra struggled to maintain her appearance of disinterested compliance. Finally, when she thought the men would never call an end to the night, Lucas rose to leave.

"So pleasant to see you, my dear," he commented as his wet lips brushed her cheek. "I am so looking forward to Saturday when we will be able to converse at length."

His words sounded innocent enough but Cassandra recognized the learious glint in his eye and the sweat upon his brow for the passion that it was. She murmured something stupid as he withdrew to mount his carriage for the ride home.

"I am tired Uncle I would like to retire."

Duprell eyed his niece noticing the flush on her cheeks and hoped that she was not coming down with a fever now that everything was so close to falling into place.

"Of course, you will need to be well rested for the wedding."

Cassandra nodded as she forced her feet to drag—rather than rushing out to locate Cara.

In her room she waited for the appearance of one of the women and luck was with her tonight as Cara appeared to act as her maid.

Cassandra flew to the door when she entered closing it firmly behind Cara and standing on guard in front of it. Cara backed away thinking that Cassandra had finally lost her mind and was intent on killing her rival.

"Cara listen to me. Duprell has Garrett imprisoned somewhere in the woods north of the Estate. He is sending him back to Spain with the Spanish envoy. If you truly love him you must let his men know."

Cara eyed her with suspicion.

"Cara if they get him to Spain he will never return alive. Do you hear me?"

"Why would you want me to help Garrett?"

"I love him." Once stated the emotion traveled throughout Cassandra's senses. She loved him! Why had she not seen it before this when they would finally be lost to each other? "I love him. I would rather see him with you than dying in a Spanish prison."

Cara eyed Cassandra and then replied, "I will think on this."

"Don't take too long they are boarding him tomorrow night."

Cara left hurrying to the kitchen her heart a flutter. One last chance. One last chance to have Garrett!

"Mother you need to get some money from Duprell."

"Cara what do you think you need now?" uttered her mother with disapproval.

Chapter Twenty-Nine

"We can't be seen in these rags at the wedding. If I have to attend that bitch I might as well have something decent to wear!"

"I'll see what I can do, but I'm not promising anything!" Would the girl never be satisfied?

The next morning Margaret told Duprell that she and Cara needed money for clothing for the wedding. After all, he wouldn't want them looking like beggars in front of his guests.

Duprell would have loved to knock her about but right now he needed the two to help with Cassandra. Margaret had been too high and mighty lately making demands of him he didn't wish to fulfill. After the wedding he would make sure they were not a problem, again.

"Very well," he said to Margaret as he counted out sufficient coin for the needed purchases. "I'll have one of the men drive you to town this morning."

Margaret nodded her assent—nearly dropping the coin. Never in her life had she seen so much at one time.

"Thank you, Sir!" She grabbed the coins with both hands holding it close to her bosom as if he might rip them out of her hands.

Her gratitude was sickening. He couldn't wait to put a stop to her groveling. This would be the last coin she ever received from him! He thought of the wedding and gave a satisfied sigh.

When the women reached town, Cara shooed her mother off to the dressmaker's and then sashayed down the street.

"Where are you going?" cried Margaret.

"I'm going to the jewelers."

"My God, Cara will you squander every coin?"

"I'm just going to look Mother. Besides I can wear the gown I had made for the celebration at London. Margaret shook her head knowing that her words had fallen on deaf ears.

Cara made a show of looking at the market wares and idly fingered the jeweler's stock all the while watching for one of Garrett's men. But someone was also watching her.

Tanner had come to town seeking out the elders of Plymouth searching their brains for any mention of a hidden retreat in the woods that might be used to hold the Captain. There had been hints of an old church once used by the Catholics but its location remained hidden. His eyes followed Cara, knowing that she kept Duprell's bed warm and wondering how he could get her alone to question her.

Cara finally caught him watching her and felt a thrill run up her spine. Someone new! Someone new, and handsome, and strong! Perhaps a dalliance was in order first. It had been so long since a young, strong, virile male had been between her legs. Her breath caught when he made his way over.

Tanner saw the lust in her eyes and used it to his advantage. Sweet words were whispered in her ear before he left, and soon Cara meandered her way to the appointed dalliance. From there things did not go as she had planned. The gentle hands stroking her throat turned hard and cruel. His chocolate brown eyes became daggers of steel and his lover's embrace caused her to cry out in pain.

"Shut your mouth. Where is Duprell keeping Captain Jamison?" The veiled threat was evident in the rough shake he delivered.

He was one of Garrett's men. Well, this just got better and better! "I've come with a message for you," she whispered breathlessly.

"I'm listening," Tanner's voice was cool.

Cara eyed him up deciding to trust that he was what he said.

"Duprell is holding Garrett somewhere north of the Estate. I don't know where."

"Tell me something I didn't know."

"He has turned him over to a Spanish envoy who is taking him back to Spain. They are boarding ship this night," she uttered breathlessly.

Tanner thrust her away disgusted with the woman's lack of restraint. There wasn't much time. The local port was Plymouth but he hadn't noticed any strange ships in the harbor lately. Miles would know other locations where a ship might put in if it wanted to enter unnoticed.

Chapter Twenty-Nine

"Wait!"

"What do you want now?" His tone was cool and uninterested. Cara could see that if she held out any hope for Garrett's affections she must tread carefully with this man.

"Duprell docks his ships off the coast four miles west of the Estate. There is a small cove that looks too shallow but actually it is deep enough for a ship to dock if the Captain is knowledgeable of the sea. You will tell Garrett that I sent you?"

"Why, what do you hope to gain?"

"I will have Garrett again! Once he was mine and so he shall be mine again!"

Tanner stepped close grasping her about the arms and dragging her forward until he towered over her in close proximity. "Tell me Cara, why would the Captain, a Lord of the realm, a Queen's favorite, a man of wealth, lower himself to obtain secondhand goods when he can have any woman in the country that has not been used by every male with a cock between his legs?"

"If he thinks to save Cassandra he will be too late. By the time Lucas and Duprell are through with her she'll be as mad as Chantelle, the last one they fought over! I've seen Duprell look at her! If she makes it to the wedding before Duprell ravishes her it will be a miracle. And Lucas? Everyone knows that he drove his last wife to kill herself!"

Tanner thrust her away, and turned to leave after uttering a parting remark.

"You're such a bitch Cara, why don't you go find some dog to mount you."

Just who did he think he was? She ought to tell Duprell, but no, Garrett was her dream for the future. Cara mused upon the possibilities as she made her way back toward the dressmaker's and her mother—only to bump into Simon.

"Who's your new friend, Cara?"

This man scared her. Something about his cool, calculated response to every situation made her skin crawl. "No one you would be interested in."

"Try me."

Captured Pearl

Cara shrugged her shoulders trying to bluff through the situation.

"Someone new. He wasn't as interesting as he appeared. Let me pass, Simon."

"Seems to me Cara that I fit that description."

"Why Simon, I didn't know you were interested! Care to go smell the flowers?" Cara used what had always gotten her out of a tight spot—sex.

"I don't." Simon walked off leaving her with the feeling that mayhap she had just escaped the hangman's noose. She hurried to catch up with her mother.

Tanner raced his mare down the road toward the Jamison Estate. As soon as he was able he flew cross-country pushing Jewel to her fastest speed. He knew it was reckless but the Captain's life was on the line. Gallantly Jewel leaped the ditches and hedges separating the fields carrying her rider ever closer to his destination. He was spotted by the lookout who rang the bell calling the crew to readiness. Miles was waiting at the front steps when Tanner drew hard on the reins bringing his mount to a sliding stop.

"Duprell has him hidden but he is being transported to Spain tonight! Probably from Duprell's secret cove. Do you know it?"

"Slow down boy, of course, I know it. You don't think the Captain would allow that snake to live this close and not know where he docked do you? What's this about the Spanish?"

Tanner paused to draw a deep breath and slow his racing heart. "That bitch Cara came sniffing around. Evidently she still thinks she can steer the Captain her way by helping with his rescue. Duprell has connections to the Spanish Armada and one of its investigators is here. They have the Captain and intend to return with him to Spain for questioning. Tonight, Miles!"

"Hurley, inform the Captain of the *Falcon* to stand ready at Sabbath Point. He's not to let any ship through. Robert, send word to the fishermen of the area to see what they know of a strange ship. They are the best eyes we have for the sea. Peters get the *Lady* under sail now! I don't care if you have to push her—get her

Chapter Twenty-Nine

guns manned and ready, that ship is not leaving here with the Captain on board. The rest of you get armed. Hopefully, we can surprise them on route and spring the Captain before they get to the sea."

The crew of the *Lady* waited silently in the brush—waiting, watching. Evening had fallen and the moon was an orange globe in the sky when the steady cadence of hoofbeats was heard coming their way. There were six of them. By the slumped posture of the man in the center Miles figured that must be the Captain for he had assumed that Duprell and his men would want first chance at the Captain. As prearranged the group of rescuers waited until the mounted riders were directly in their midst. Miles signaled and the entire group of Jamison men burst forth—silent swords at the ready. Tanner led a group on horseback into the fray to surround the Captain, keeping him safe. The Spanish fought fiercely for they knew the fate of invaders on English soil. Their leader, the dandy, was surprisingly talented with his sword fending off attack after attack until only Tanner stood between him and his prize. As the moon burst through the trees Tanner could see the white teeth of the man threatening his Captain. The Spaniard raised his weapon driving his horse forward to skewer Tanner upon his blade only to find that the man had flipped his sword into his left hand thus bringing his blade under the guard of his opponent's blade to expertly slash the man across the throat. No words escaped the Spaniard's mouth as his surprised eyes registered that he had failed.

His men turned to appraise the situation and to insure there were none of the enemy left when a muttered oath broke forth from the Captain.

"By God, someone untie me! I feel like a hobbled mule!" Tanner was quick to comply.

"How do you feel, Captain?"

"I never thought you a stupid man until now Tanner. Anyone know where Cassandra is?"

Miles came forward hobbling to the side of Garrett's mount.

Captured Pearl

"At the Duprell Estate, Captain. The wedding is set for Saturday evening at the Estate chapel."

"We have one day to figure out a plan to rescue Cassandra. Any ideas?"

"What about at the chapel, Sir," Peters interjected. "They shouldn't be expecting us then."

"Smart man Peters, but somehow I'll have to get in and let Cassandra know what to expect. She mustn't give up hope."

Miles shook his head. "Captain there is no way you're going to be able to accomplish that. From the looks of you your ribs are busted."

"I'll go," Tanner volunteered. "Seems Cara has a desire to taste my wares. I could use that to my advantage."

Garrett argued but his men simply would not allow him a choice in the matter. Tanner would deliver the message and Peters would go with him. Miles was willing but the fight had taken the wind out of his sails. Garrett would be escorted home to rest until his part in the wedding rescue.

Quietly Tanner and Peters slipped out of the trees and over the wall surrounding the Duprell home. They had to find Cassandra. They silenced one of Duprell's men with a savage blow to the head before Tanner began the climb up to the balcony on the second floor with Peters keeping watch below. Lady Luck was with them for the first door Tanner chose led to Cassandra's room. Tanner looked through the glass-paned door to see Cassandra standing with her back to him. The silhouette in the mirror warned Cassandra of his presence and she hurried over to open the door.

"Whatever are you doing here Tanner? Is Garrett safe?" Then she realized that Cara had come through.

"Yes, Madam, the Captain is on his way home at this moment. He will be fine. The Captain and his men will be at the service—you will not be marrying Gabel. Watch for the Captain but you must not give the game away. Oh, by the way Madam, the Captain sends his love." Then he was gone like a shadow slither-

Chapter Twenty-Nine

ing down to the ground where another shadow joined him before they were gone.

Cassandra stood on the balcony watching the place where the men had disappeared convincing herself that it was real. Cara had lied about everything. Sweet would be her vengeance when Cara saw Garrett rescue her from Duprell's clutches on Saturday. Her thoughts turned to Margaret and her heart knew a bitter hatred. The woman had caused the death of her child. That could not go unpunished. Only a while longer. She didn't know how she was going to wait until Garrett rescued her. One more day of pretending. One more day of enduring Lucas' advances and then she would be free.

Hurley and Robert rode off toward the cove to signal the *Falcon* and the *Lady* to begin their plans to take the other vessel anchored there. The Jamison men hoped to take the vessels without firing, for the sound of the *Lady's* cannon fire could carry to the Duprell Estate. The gunners of both ships would stand ready as their crews slipped aboard the enemy vessels. The plan was to disable the ships by breaking large holes in the keels below the water line. If the plan went well, Duprell would never know that the vessels had been breeched. Miles was taking no chances that Duprell or the Spanish could bring their cannon to bear on the Jamison Estate, or ships, at a later date. If their first plan didn't work, the *Lady* and the *Falcon* would blow the enemy ships out of the water.

The rest of the men rode in silence setting a leisurely pace in order to save Garrett as much discomfort as possible. By the time they had reached the lane leading to the house Garrett was gasping for breath as a fire spread across his mid-section.

Mame and Sampson hurried out as fast as their legs could carry them.

"Where are you hurt, Sir?" questioned Sampson.

But Garrett was focused on the task of dismounting. Tanner came to catch him as his legs gave out when they touched the ground.

Captured Pearl

Garrett felt surly and useless. His Lady needed rescuing and by God, he was the one to do it. "Leave off, man. I can walk on my own two feet!" he snarled at Tanner.

Tanner just shook his head then sprinkled salt on Garrett's head. "The fairies must be back for you're acting like a jackass again, Sir. If you plan to ride with us on Saturday you'd best take what help you can get now."

"Don't you ever get tired of being correct?" Garrett mumbled.

"Become tired of correcting the Lords of the realm? Why the occasions are so few and far between I am surprised that you have noticed Captain."

Garrett forced back a laugh knowing that his sides would not stand the jarring. "If you make me laugh I am going to make you walk the plank Tanner."

"Then I am mightily glad that I know how to swim," Tanner replied as he helped the man up to his bedroom.

Mame and Sampson where already there. Mame had brought her herbal remedies and Sampson was ripping a sheet into strips to bind up his ribs. The two worked over him diligently until Garrett thought they would drive him mad. Finally, Mame was satisfied and they left. Tanner, Miles, and Peters went over the plan for Saturday with Garrett before they, too, left him to his rest.

God, he felt awful! Duprell's men had been thorough. He was bruised from his chest to his hips. Mame thought he had several broken ribs. He had wanted to bathe after being confined for several days but Mame would have none of it. Perhaps tomorrow she stated.

"Tomorrow, my ass," he thought. He would not go to Cassandra's rescue smelling like some scum fresh out of the gutter. With that thought he passed into sleep.

Lucas paced the rooms of his fine home reflecting on how the lovely Cassandra would set off the paintings and fine furnishings. He wanted everything to be perfect when his bride came home tonight. He was merciless to the help carrying on incessant-

Chapter Twenty-Nine

ly on the upkeep of the house and grounds. Joseph his valet, who had been with Lucas for years and was too old to go anywhere else, received most of the abuse.

Lucas demanded immediate responses from his staff and today no one was quick enough. His rantings became louder and louder as the morning wore on. Finally, his housekeeper, Stella, attempted to calm him down.

"Please, Sir, calm yourself. You don't want to collapse from exhaustion before the ceremony tonight. How would that look to your bride?"

Lucas forced himself under control, "You're right Stella. You will get along with your new Mistress will you not?"

"But, of course, Sir. I will help her any way I can." Stella was sincere and she had always taken very good care of Lucas. After all, she was rewarded well for her trouble and if she had to pacify and watch over the woman he married, so be it.

Lucas thought again of his lovely, young bride. He would so enjoy erasing Lord Jamison from her memories. He would carefully teach her his preferences introducing her slowly to his warped sense of love. By the time his control could no longer last she would be ready for his rough and unusual play. Lucas rubbed his hands in glee as he imagined Cassandra spread for his pleasure. Spittle began to dribble from his massive lips as he, again, began to work himself into a state of readiness.

Joseph interrupted his revelry to ask, "Sir, what will be your pleasure of attire tonight? I shall make sure that it is freshened for the ceremony."

"Have the red and gold ready. The cloth is particularly rich. Yes, I shall display my wealth for my bride tonight. Make sure that the carriage is immaculate when we depart for Duprell's Estate — and don't forget the jewels for Cassandra. Have the items from town arrived for my bride?"

"Yes, Lord. Everything is in readiness. The Lord's chambers have been freshened with fresh flowers and linens, and Cook has prepared your favorite dishes for later.

"Your trunks were sent to the ship earlier so that everything will be ready for an early departure tomorrow morning. When shall we expect your Lordship to return?"

Lucas considered. The trip to Spain would take several days. The Captain had relinquished his cabin for the Lord and his new Lady for the trip. Lucas considered if he dared take Cassandra on the deck during that first week. The thought of crude sailors spying upon his mounting of the beautiful Cassandra quickened his blood. Yes, he was sure it could be arranged! Enjoying the best life had to offer while others watched had always thrilled him.

Lucas was not so self involved as to believe Cassandra would acquiesce easily to his desires. Several months of seclusion at the villa in Spain would be necessary before returning to England. Perhaps he should plan on spending the winter in a warmer climate where his preference for unusual outdoor sports would not be cut short by England's cold winter.

The mountains where the villa was located were not predisposed to visitors. The less interference, the better. And while England had always been his home, the countryside was far too crowded to accommodate the plans he had in store for his new bride. Besides, he had always felt the woods of England watched on in disapproval throughout all of his pleasures. Yes, the open lands and treeless hills of Spain would be much more accommodating.

Cassandra was being readied for the wedding. Duprell had sent Margaret to town to pick up the lavish dress from the dressmaker in time for the Saturday ceremony. He was expecting an enormous amount of coin from Lucas after the wedding so there was no limit to the expense he was ready to dispense to have her meet the approval of her groom. She must be elegant, for after all, she was representing the Duprell family.

The gown Margaret brought back was full of pearl beading down the front. The four underskirts changed color from creamy ivory to the palest sheer white all to enhance the creamy gown that she wore. The neckline was low, immodestly so, and Cassandra fretted that she might fall out of it before Garrett could rescue her.

Chapter Twenty-Nine

Tiny glass beads hung from the waistband of the skirt alternating with seed pearls. The sleeves and cuffs were encrusted with rich lace. Cassandra felt gaudy after the classic simplicity of the gowns that Garrett had preferred for her.

Garrett! She held fast to the thought of his rescue. Why did she always trust the wrong people? Twice she had trusted Margaret, to the destruction of Garrett's trust and her child. She had trusted Duprell, to end up facing a marriage to a man that revolted her. Why could she not trust the one person that had not misled her or played her false? Even when he did not trust her, he looked out for her welfare putting her needs on a priority with his. Cassandra vowed that if she got out of this mess, there would no longer be mistrust on her side of the relationship. Her heart was afraid of being broken but Garrett had never played her false.

Duprell entered the room looking at Cassandra. She was so lovely that for a moment he considered keeping her for himself. Then monetary greed won out. He watched her face carefully but saw nothing but acceptance. There was no way that she could know that Garrett had escaped the clutches of the Spanish. He had sent every available man to look for Garrett but he had not been located. Duprell contemplated that the man might be at his residence, however, the Estate was too heavily guarded to risk a new face poking around.

He bemoaned the fact that most of his crew did not know the meaning of the word subtle. Discretion was not a word they understood. Sometimes he could not believe their stupidity. Then there was Simon. The man worried him. So unlike his other men in manner and vigilance that Duprell often wondered how he had managed to employ the man.

The men periodically reported that there was no trace of Jamison. A few more hours and the vigilance would not be needed. Duprell's men were stationed around the Estate and tiny family chapel that was nestled just off from the house. In disuse for many years, Duprell had the staff clean and refurbish it so that the chapel was presentable to the few people attending.

Appearing concerned he asked Cassandra if there was

anything that she needed. Nervously, she replied that there was nothing. He chuckled at the thought of her surprise when she would enter the marriage bed. Yes, she had reason to be nervous with Lucas as the groom.

Duprell was pleased with the lovely picture Cassandra presented. Once Lucas was satisfied and the coin and land changed hands he would personally lead his men on the hunt for Jamison. Once and for all he would rid himself of that thorn in his side.

He presented a box to Cassandra in which lay her wedding gift from Lucas. Carefully, he removed the diamond and sapphire gems, which would adorn her throat, and held them up for her viewing.

"This is from Lucas. He wants you to wear it at the wedding."

Her eyes widened and her mouth fell. The necklace was exquisite! Duprell turned Cassandra around to face the mirror and placed the gems around her throat, lingering much too long with his hand on her bared shoulder. Cassandra fought her panic attempting to retain her meek acceptance of her fate. Finally, he withdrew and she stared in the mirror in awe. As beautiful as it was the diamonds made her skin crawl. They were so cold and empty just like the eyes of her tormentors. She shivered again and reached to remove the gems.

"Cassandra I warn you this wedding will take place and you will do nothing to displease Lucas! Is that clear?"

"I'm sorry, Uncle. I know it is for my best interests. I am just nervous."

Duprell smiled, "Of course. Lucas wants you to wear this. He had it especially made for you and brought it over earlier himself. Anyone giving so magnificent a gift will care for the woman wearing it. And you can have more where that came from. You will be dripping in jewels."

Cassandra didn't think she could conceal the disgust that crawled through her veins. Carefully, she nodded her agreement feeling that she might scream if he did not leave soon.

Duprell gently placed his hands around her shoulders again

Chapter Twenty-Nine

gently squeezing her soft flesh. Cassandra could see the greed in his eyes—and the lust. She wondered if he was planning to own the necklace, or the wealth in general, that her marriage to Lucas would bring him.

"My dear we must get on with it. I shall escort you to the chapel where you will wait the last few minutes until the ceremony. Margaret will attend to you until it is time for you to approach the altar."

"I'm almost ready, Uncle."

"I will be back in time to walk you down the aisle."

"Thank you, Uncle," Cassandra responded. Duprell bent over her kissing her cheek, something he had never done before. She thought it strange. Cassandra could feel one of her headaches coming on. Probably just anxiety. Perhaps the cool air of the balcony would sooth her nerves.

"Please, God, keep him safe." She looked out over the Estate picking out the men guarding the walls and grounds. There were so many! If something happened to Garrett life would not be worth living. She could not live through the despondency of his death.

The color had returned to her face over the last few days and the shock of losing Garrett's child had become bearable. The darkness she had been living in had dissipated with the visit from Tanner and Garrett's promise that he would be there to stop the wedding. Tanner had said that Garrett sent his love. She held that thought close to her heart in the minutes that followed.

She loved Garrett and there was nothing she could do to change that and it was about time she started acting like it.

Duprell checked with his men. There was no sign of any trespassers about. "Keep looking. I don't want any surprises." Duprell thought of the night Cassandra had disappeared. Everything had gone wrong that night. He should have finished her off before she had gotten away. He had been certain his sea wolves would follow her scent and bring her back to him without delay. Instead they had lost her. Ah well, that did not matter now. She was to marry Lucas and that was the key to his power and wealth.

Duprell looked at himself in the mirror thinking that he looked extraordinarily well today. Perhaps it was time that he took a bride as well. After Jamison was finished off he would need an heir to carry on the name of Duprell. Cara had been fine to warm his bed but she would never do for a wife. Especially, since she had started sleeping with his men. More than once the conversation had stopped when he had passed by. The men had been comparing her ability in bed he was sure. To think that he, Duprell, had once been enamored with that slut! Soon he would be rid of both her and her mother. They knew too much. They had become a danger to his continued existence. He would arrange for Cara to become the prize of Judah. If she had thought that his rutting was lustful she would have a pleasantly appalling tryst with Judah.

Lucas had arrived earlier with his man, Joseph. He knew he was outrageously early but he didn't care. He wasn't sure he could count on Duprell to keep his hands off Cassandra. Best that he arrive and keep his eyes on things. He nodded to himself. In the chapel, Duprell had done an admirable job of cleaning up the place and making it fit for this evening.

He withdrew the ring from his pocket handing it to Joseph. "Put this in your pocket and don't lose it!"

"Of course, Sir. I shall guard it with my life." He kept a bland expression on his face not wishing to antagonize Lucas further. His rages this day had been awful reflecting back on all employed in his service. When a fit took him the staff was exposed to vile language and if the master managed to get his hands upon you a most terrible beating might follow. It had been this way since the fever that had rendered him so ugly. Joseph wondered if this treatment would extend to his new bride and found himself feeling sorry for the new Lady Gabel.

Garrett and his men had been hiding in a cave Garrett knew of that lay on the coast near the Duprell Estate.

Mame had berated him for leading the rescue for he was battered and bruised from his visit with Duprell and the Spanish. The

Chapter Twenty-Nine

attentions of Judah had aggravated the shoulder wound from the battle leaving him, for the time being, one-handed.

Tanner had finally taken her aside and lectured the elder housekeeper, "He loves her, you know this. Would you have him lay in bed when her life is in jeopardy? Could you respect him if he did not respect himself?"

Protest died on Mame's lips as she bound his ribs giving Garrett what support she could before the ride and fight ahead.

Garrett studied the men gathered with him: Jim Peters, Jason, Mason Hurley, Robert Danley, Tanner, Marcus, and Miles. Men he trusted with his secrets and his life. They had proven their loyalty, time and time again, and he knew he could trust them with his life, as well as Cassandra's.

The early morning had been spent tossing ideas about as to how to pull off the abduction of Cassandra with the least amount of resistance, for Duprell had an army of men positioned about the grounds. Mason had managed to make his way onto the grounds as a Catholic supporter who would stand as witness to the ceremony. Garrett did not ask how he managed to answer the questions of the priests for the man's religious preferences were not his concern as long as the man preformed his task adequately, and he had on numerous occasions. Mason had come back with a rough idea of where the players could be found and how many there would be in the small family chapel. Duprell's men were being uncharacteristically cautious and the new man, Simon, seemed to be in charge.

Mason and Robert would slip back inside and pose as guests for the ceremony. Robert, who had a gift for languages, was fluent in Spanish and would pose as one of the Spanish crew. It was highly unlikely that anyone would question them once they gained the chapel. They hoped that if Cassandra recognized them she would remain quiet and not acknowledge their presence. Before the ceremony could begin they would locate Lucas escorting him from the chapel.

The guests at the chapel were becoming restless. The wedding party was assembling with Cassandra arriving in a closed carriage attended by Margaret and Cara. Duprell followed soon after attending to details outside the building.

Cara and Margaret helped Cassandra with last minute preparations. Cara compared herself to the bride. The red and black gown from court set off her exotic beauty. She knew that all eyes would turn her way, but compared to the bride . . .

Cassandra was exquisite in the creamy silk gown. The gown was flawlessly made revealing that she was no longer a child, but a woman. She was stunning and nervous. She waited for Duprell to collect her for the walk down the aisle while praying that Garrett would arrive first.

Lucas was studying his reflection in the mirror, again. He straightened his neck cloth and smock for the fifth time. When was this wedding going to start? It was dangerous to linger too long with the priests who had been thrown out of England. He wondered if Duprell was up to something again—this was taking too damn long! A knock sent Joseph scurrying to the door.

A man asked Joseph to come along so that he might be shown where Lucas would need to stand during the ceremony. Lucas nodded his approval. The servant was driving him to distraction; he needed some time alone.

The door had no sooner closed than a stranger burst through a side door with an evil-looking sword drawn and pointed at Lucas' throat. He looked about the room and quickly proceeded to the door locking it from the inside to halt admittance from the chapel.

"Not one word or I'll slit your throat," murmured the stranger. Lucas felt the tip of the steel separate the folds of skin of his massive jowls. Though large and massive, Lucas was a coward at heart. He only dominated those less powerful, or weaker, than himself. The thought that a stranger had violated his person had his heart quaking and his bladder releasing its contents. The stranger viewed him with disgust motioning with the sword toward the opposite door. "Move! Not a sound."

Mason followed him out the door leading to the alcove where the altar boys prepared the items for the priests. No one was

Chapter Twenty-Nine

in attendance. One of Duprell's men spotted them, coming over to inquire as to their destination.

"Lord Gabel wishes to double check on the carriage for his bride. Everything must be perfect." The sword had been sheathed when the man had approached but now Lucas felt the sharp prick of a long knife in his ribs.

"Yes that is so," he replied. The man looked at them suspiciously but could find no reason to halt the groom's perusal of the carriages. Duprell had warned them that everything should proceed without complications. He would be furious if Lucas found fault with something when the wedding was so close to completion.

One man laughing chided the groom remarking, "Not trying to run out on your own wedding are you?"

"No, of course not," Lucas laughed nervously. They continued to walk past the line of carriages then when Duprell's man was entertained elsewhere, Mason hustled Lucas into the nearby woods. Mason let out a sigh of relief when he spotted Robert hurrying his way motioning for them to follow. Robert quickly showed Mason the way and hurriedly returned to the chapel to finish his assignment.

The priests that were to perform the ceremony saw a man hurrying their way motioning for their attention. In perfect Spanish he uttered, "I have never heard of such a thing Fathers, but the bride and groom wish to confess before they commit their lives to each other and God. Can this be done?"

This was a strange request but if a soul was so burdened before the ceremony the Fathers wished to ensure a peaceful union. They hurried to follow Mason to the rooms occupied by the couple only to find themselves held at sword point by two dangerous looking sailors.

"Escort the Fathers to their ship and see that the *Lady* escorts them out of the bay. Do not return Fathers, it would not be in your best interests, or God's." One more look at the dark, dangerous faces of the English persuaded the Fathers that this was not the time to resist. God had surely seen to their survival for a reason.

Captured Pearl

Minutes before the ceremony Duprell made his way to Cassandra's room. He dismissed Cara and Margaret to take their places in the chapel. Cassandra was standing at the window staring outside. He marveled at how lovely she was. Soon she would deliver to him all that he had dreamed of.

The only thing missing was Jamison, but soon he too would bend to Duprell's plans. He knew Jamison was out there somewhere but for now he would not think on that. The wedding was going on as planned, his men were stationed outside and it was impossible for Jamison to get in. After the ceremony he would send his men and Simon to capture Jamison. And they would find him!

"We are about ready to start, Cassandra."

"Very well, Uncle."

Cassandra was visibly nervous. He still had doubts that she would proceed with the ceremony. They needed to conclude the ceremony so that he could get Lucas to sign the papers for the payment. The tension was beginning to tell as he was crueler that usual to the staff and his men.

"Cassandra it is time we must go." His remark was interrupted by a knock on the door.

"Lord Duprell, they are waiting for you."

"Yes. We will be there momentarily."

Cassandra took a deep breath and another look at herself. Where was Garrett? The panic of the moment threatened to overwhelm her and she wanted to run. Where was her faith in her love? She must believe in him as she had sworn to do earlier at the house.

She walked over to Duprell accepting his arm as he opened the door.

Her heart pounded so furiously, how could Duprell not hear it? She was certain that everyone there could see her chest heaving to draw in sufficient air. She vaguely saw faces of people that she didn't know. Why were they racing so fast to the altar? Dear God, where was Garrett?

Duprell, on the other hand, could only see months and

Chapter Twenty-Nine

months of planning finally coming to fruition. He escorted her down the aisle looking every inch the proud Uncle. And why shouldn't he be proud? His captive pearl would soon deliver the treasure of a lifetime into his hands. He gloried in all the eyes upon him even if most where Catholic sympathizers that he did not know. He saw Joseph, Lucas' man servant, waiting at the altar. The priest had not yet entered which struck him as odd but then he did not profess the Catholic faith, or any other.

One of the men was sent to fetch Lucas but returned stating that the room was empty and the door had been locked. Duprell's anger rose like a demon. Damn that man — wanting to upstage him again! He would come in at any moment, pompous and arrogant, to claim his bride.

As they neared the altar the priest emerged and holding up his hands halted Duprell and Cassandra. Mason, in the priest robes began the Latin liturgy just as a large, black stallion leapt from behind the altar carrying none other than Garrett! Mason grabbed Cassandra helping her up in front of his Captain before making his way out the back to his waiting mount. Garrett spurred Sable causing the horse to rear and knocking Duprell to the ground upon his pompous ass. Garrett leaned over putting his face level with Duprell's and uttered, "What is mine I keep!" before fleeing out the door scattering the guests in all directions as they sought safety from flying hooves.

Duprell screamed commands at men but the commotion in the chapel was as nothing to the commotion outside where the carriage horses had spooked, careening into one another and causing a mess of broken wheels and lathered harness. Garrett's men had planned well and executed every detail with precision.

"Stop them or you're all dead!" screamed Duprell once again seeing all his plans vanishing like fog on the sea. He was infuriated and his men quickly rushed to do his bidding leaving the areas of the storm. Duprell marched around like a man possessed. Where was Lucas? His hopes vanished in an instant and he saw his imagined empire collapsing before his eyes — he would not get a coin without Cassandra. His eyes fell on Cara. Yes, it was more than time that the bitch paid for her traitorous ways. Simon had informed him of her tête-à-tête with Garrett's man. She was the reason that he had lost his prize and his pearl. He had needed her to attend to Cassandra but now Cassandra was gone.

"Judah," he roared. The lumberous ox made his way toward the man that was not only his Master, but also his father.

"You are one of the few that has served me well in the past days and I have a reward for you."

Judah's eyes brightened.

Duprell grabbed Cara's arm to hinder her withdrawal from the scene as he thrust her into Judah's arms.

"Take the bitch, she is yours. I don't care what you do to her as long as I never set eyes on her again!"

"No Duprell, you can't do this," Cara screamed as Judah lifted her onto his shoulder making his way toward the stable. Margaret made to intervene but Duprell grabbed the woman whispering in her ear, "Intervene and your fate shall be the same." Margaret wailed her misery but did not pursue the departing couple.

Cassandra hung on to Sable's mane with all her might. They were flying through the woods at breakneck speed. Garrett was trying to hold onto her but she had noticed when Mason had placed her up in front of Garrett that he was working with only one arm. She steadied herself trying not to jostle him for she could tell that he was hurting.

As they slowed their pace through some particularly dense trees he asked, "Are you well, Cassandra?"

"Yes, Garrett, I am fine . . . now."

Soon Garrett's men began to join them until there were nine galloping along the path. They rode back to the cave, where they had waited before rescuing Cassandra, rolling the large stone in front of the entrance to block any intruders attempting to enter. The light was blocked by the stone and only Garrett's hands on her shoulders kept her from panicking. He helped her down and turned her towards him holding her in his arms. It seemed that

Chapter Twenty-Nine

finally they had realized their love for each other.

A small light came from the cave mouth and as their eyes became accustomed to the dimly-lit interior the friendly faces of Garrett's men became apparent.

"Miles, Jim, it is so good to see you!"

"Thank the Lord you're safe, Lady," Jim took her hand in his to give it a gentle squeeze while Miles thumped his Captain on the shoulder.

She began to choke back tears as the men made her welcome and Cassandra realized for the first time that she was not alone. "Garrett I can't believe I am finally here with you."

"Believe it," said Garrett in his deep, warm voice. God, he thought, she has my heart. She had looked beautiful standing at the altar so brave and alone. He had been hard put to remember his part in the scheme of things. Garrett had been afraid to look away fearing she might be whisked away from him, again. Even now he could not take his eyes off her. She was radiant.

The group waited patiently for several hours to ensure that Duprell's men were not about before they moved. But time passed slowly, especially for Cassandra. Garrett felt her body begin to tense as the closeness of their hiding place began to weigh upon her.

"You know, Cassandra, Miles has been with me for years. Do you know how we met?" He felt her shake her head. "I was on my first voyage as Captain of the *Lady*. We had made berth in the port at Istanbul. It had been a long voyage and I was eager to taste something besides ship's fare.

"This sailor walked up telling of a tavern just up the way that served mouth-watering meals and he offered to show me the way. The black guard tried to jump me! I may have looked the part of an inexperienced youth, but I soon proved my mettle."

"I've been serving the Captain ever since he cold-cocked me!" Miles broke in. "Best decision I ever made was trying to shanghai the Captain. Lady Luck smiled upon me that day and she's been smiling ever since. The Captain gave me a chance to reverse my course. Not many would have done that, and now that the sea begins to settle in my bones, the Captain has allowed me to serve him upon land, managing his Estate."

Mason chimed in tell the story of Garrett's intervention on his behalf.

Mason had been accused of thievery after being abandoned by a Captain who had run off with his sponsor's funds. The unscrupulous Captain had involved Mason by persuading him to sign on with his crew to their next port of call. When Mason had seen the mettle of the man he served he had opted to sign on long-term with the crew of the *Lady*.

Each of Garrett's men, in turn, told the tale of his first meeting with the Captain. Tears began to fill Cassandra's eyes as the knightly virtues of her love unfolded before her eyes.

The sound of someone moving drew her attention to the rear of the cave where, dimly, she could see Tanner searching through a pack. Tanner approached with a flask of drink and a small packet for Garrett. "Mame insisted that you take this when there was a chance, Sir. Something about deadening the pain of those ribs," he remarked. There was also bread to tide them over until they might reach safety.

"Mason told Garrett the tale of Lucas losing his bladder and they all laughed until Cassandra cried. Mason and Robert had dropped Lucas several miles into the woods beyond the Duprell Estate knowing that it would take the man several hours to find his way back. And if he didn't? Well, wouldn't it be ironic that the large man bent on intimidation was lost in the woods? Eventually Duprell's men would pick him up.

It wasn't much longer before they heard a tapping on the stone at the entrance, signaling that all was clear. Marcus had returned from his sentry duty to announce that Duprell's men had moved on. It was safe to move.

The night deepened—the soft blues and grays of the evening sky were just visible as they left the cave to rendezvous with the *Falcon* for the *Lady* was still not seaworthy.

"Duprell will come after you," Jim stated the obvious.

"Yes, but the man is a coward. He will send his men first

Chapter Twenty-Nine

before he enters into the fray himself. He won't rest until I am dead."

"Garrett," whispered Cassandra, "please be careful. I love you so."

"I will love. We need to sail for London. The Queen must know of Duprell's treachery and the threat to Lady Cassandra's well being." Garrett knew that he could settle the matter himself but unless the Queen had given her stamp of approval killing another Lord of the realm, even one as depraved as Duprell, could earn him censorship from the Court and the Queen. The Jamison family had always been true to the law of England. He had taken an oath in the name of the Queen of England. He was one of a chosen few whom followed the rules of engagement for a privateer, never crossing the line to pirate or making their own rules. Now was no time to start. There was Cassandra to consider. He gathered her close into his arms.

"I was so afraid I had lost you," he whispered. They held each other close.

She remembered the smell of his skin, and the safety of being in his arms. She felt emotion returning to her body. For the first time in weeks she felt pain, excitement, sadness, hope. Cassandra felt alive.

Miles would not be sailing with them to London. Garrett wanted him at the Estate watching and guarding against Duprell's retribution. The Birminghams were still congregated at the house and Garrett had mixed feelings about allowing them to stay. If Duprell decided to seek satisfaction by harming his friends Miles would be canny enough to discover the plot. He could gather the men left behind into a large fighting force in Garrett's name.

Peters and Tanner would sail with Cassandra and himself aboard the *Falcon*. Her Captain and crew had shown their mettle in this latest altercation. He felt safe enough leaving some of the *Lady's* crew ashore. They made their way to the cove that Duprell favored, for the two ships still sat in a sentinel position there. *The Lady* would return to her home berth to complete her repairs, once Garrett and party were aboard the *Falcon*.

Captured Pearl

Once aboard the ship they raised anchor and set sail. The Captain informed Garrett that there was a message for him on the desk in the Captain's cabin. Garrett led Cassandra down to the cabin seeing that she was settled before turning to the missive. It was from Garrett's contact requesting that he stop in Hastings for urgent news. Garrett sighed in irritation. Would there never be a moment's peace in his future? Every second Cassandra became more and more important to his life. Would Bess understand if he asked for his service to be rescinded?

Then he looked at Cassandra. His wife. There were too many secrets between them—some withheld on purpose, some unintentional. If they were ever to find the key to their happiness honesty must come first. Silently he sat beside Cassandra on the bunk taking her hands into his.

"Cassandra we need to talk. There are things you don't know about me that must be brought into the light."

"Garrett there is nothing you could say that will change my love. I trust you," replied Cassandra following her heart.

"Listen well Cassandra for many of the things I will reveal are not my secrets alone. They must be kept secrets to ensure the safety of more than just myself." Garrett began to weave his tale, the history with Duprell, coming to the Queen's service, and his part in the latest sea battle, which had led Duprell to give his identity to the Spanish.

Tears had filled her eyes at the ugliness of Duprell's treachery throughout Garrett's life. No wonder he had been suspicious when he had come upon her in the road.

"Truly, Garrett, I understand. But will you understand if my memory does not return or ugly things emerge from my past?" Cassandra quizzed him.

Garrett's warm smile told her all she needed to know. But his words startled her.

"I am afraid, my love, that I know more about your past than you do. Josh was quite successful in France when he went looking for you lineage." He withdrew the letter from the King of France showing Cassandra her history.

Chapter Twenty-Nine

"It seems the only mystery now is how you came to be on the road that fateful night. If we never know, I will still thank God that you appeared in my life."

The tears began to flow as Cassandra's happiness overflowed. His soft kisses dried her tears and she began to tell him her secrets.

"Margaret killed our child."

"I know love. Duprell, that bastard, was more than eager to share the information with me when I hung in the abandoned church."

She had been dreading the time she had to tell him. That he did not blame her was a glorious revelation. For she had blamed herself over and over again.

"This is not your fault Cassandra. You had no idea that Duprell could be such an unscrupulous man. There was no way that you could have stopped Margaret from following Duprell's orders. You have gone through hell and it is my doing. If I had explained why I distrusted Duprell perhaps you would have been more on guard against him. Even so he is fixed on his own goals and would have found another way."

"Garrett I can't stand this gown another minute. Please help my out of it."

Her lover moved to help her discard the symbol of everything that might have gone wrong. His quick hands had her gown fluttering down around her waist before she had finished with his shirt. She nuzzled and caressed his chest moving slowing down his body worshiping him as she went.

Shyly she bent to the task of unlacing his breeches finally turning to Garrett for help. His lusty smile sent the blood pounding in her veins, heating her blood, causing her temperature to rise. They shared the sweet, tender union of a man and a woman deeply in love.

Then slipping into the bunk they began to rediscover each other. There was no sense of urgency as Garrett fed at her mouth, tugging on her lips, silently begging them to open for his tongue. Cassandra complied yielding to his expert administrations. This was not the passionate lovemaking of their past. This was a treasured indulgence of two lovers rediscovering each other. This time Cassandra took the lead wanting to show Garrett how very much she adored him as she pushed him on his back hesitantly.

Cassandra was amazed at the gentleness in her bold privateer. His every action was calculated to bring her exquisite pleasure, and she strove to bring the same pleasure to him. She shyly made her way down to the thatch of springy curls encircling his staff. Soft husky words of encouragement directed her untutored hands and mouth to the task of pleasuring her mate. When he could no longer maintain control Garrett gathered her into his arms, encircling her with his love. With a dedicated deliberateness his hardened staff inched its way into her softness. When he had buried himself deep within the warm velvet glove of her body he paused to look into her eyes. Cassandra was breathless with pleasure. Suddenly things were moving much too slowly. Her hips began to move suggestively urging him on. Ever ready to accommodate his love, Garrett increased the tempo of his rhythm of love until they both tumbled into the exhausted sleep of satisfied lovers.

Chapter Thirty

Judah watched Cara with a wicked pleasure. A woman of his own. Cara had begged Judah to let her go but he had only repeated the slap that had originally been used to get her attention.

"If you ever look at another man or even talk to one I will kill your mother and teach you the meaning of pain."

This wasn't pain? What more could there be? Judah had made her do things that even Cara hadn't known existed.

Cara cursed Duprell for what he had done to her and she cursed Cassandra for causing the whole mess. If she hadn't been so enamored with the tall handsome Tanner none of this would be happening. Why couldn't a man love her? Why wouldn't Garrett love her? She had lost everything for him! How would she live with this animal Duprell had given her over to? His beastial ruttings in the stable stall he used for his home were beyond imagination. There was no satisfying him, either. His lust knew no bounds now that he had Duprell's permission to use her as his own. And her mother? What had happened to Margaret?

The last time Cara had seen her Duprell was beating her mindlessly. If something happened to Margaret who would make her the teas to rid her of Judah's brats? She could think of nothing worse that having his brats. Oh God, how would she get out of this mess?

Once, she tried to escape but Judah had caught her and almost beat her to death—raping her repeatedly. Cara had shared her body with many men and was used to rough treatment but Judah was large and physical in his sexual habits, hurting her each time. Cara loathed him.

After a particularly brutal beating her mind had finally broken. When Judah had turned over, going to sleep, she had grabbed the hunting knife that always lay beside his head stabbing him repeatedly as she screamed demonically. The men had found her the next day babbling incoherently and rocking back and forth. The knife was still in her hand.

Duprell had left the Estate in search of Garrett, so the crew had locked her in one of the cells in the cellar until Duprell's return. The once beautiful girl was pale and dirty. Her long, black hair dirty and dull. The eyes that had captured so many men's attention were muted and dull. Even the lusty men of the crew were put off by her madness and left her alone.

The crew of the *Falcon* kept diligent watch for signs of pursuit from Duprell. Everyone expected the man to try some form of retribution. Garrett was loath to leave Cassandra when they docked in Hastings, afraid that she might disappear before his eyes once more. She gently caressed his face admonishing her Queen's man to go tend to her business. After all, wasn't Tanner at guard once more?

"Stop worrying love. Duprell would be foolish to try anything aboard ship with a full crew set to stop him. Go tend to your meeting and come back swiftly to my side."

Reluctantly Garrett agreed to taking Peters along. They silently exited the ship making for the tavern by the dock to find Sir Riley waiting at a back table.

"Good. You made fast time Jamison. Peters. Sit down. We have much to discuss." Riley had already ordered a meal for his companions and pints to go around. Best to look like travelers stopping in for something other than ship's fare.

Garrett filled Riley in on the latest developments, adding that they were on their way to the Queen.

"What happened to you, Jamison? Never saw you eat left handed before?"

This time Peters took the lead knowing his Captain would make light of his injuries.

"Well, perhaps the news I bring will not surprise you as much as I thought. The Spanish have placed a bounty on your

Chapter Thirty

head Garrett. If they catch you and don't immediately string you up to the mast, you will be making the acquaintance of the jailers in Madrid. Not something I'd want an acquaintance of mine looking forward to. Nasty piece of business."

"Sorry to disappoint you, Riley, this is old news. The Spanish envoy was trying to get me to ship when my men burst in on his plans."

"This will probably end your service as a privateer to the Queen. Too high a profile old man. And if the limb doesn't heal you would be a threat to the safety of your crew and yourself. The Queen already has this information. Your voyage to London will save her the trouble of calling you to her side. I can't imagine that your Lady will be disappointed. You'll probably be around to help raise your children."

A black cloud passed over Garrett's face causing Riley to inquire as to its cause.

"Does the Lady not wish children? I can't imagine that you could not persuade her."

"Duprell murdered our child. Cassandra has barely recovered."

"Sorry, old man. Sounds as if you will be needed at the hearthside for a while." The men were catching up on business when the cry. "FIRE! FIRE! On a ship!" brought them to their feet with a rush. Garrett had bad feelings about this. He feared that Duprell had struck, again.

Duprell had indeed struck. He had shadowed the *Falcon* into port bent on Garrett's destruction. If he could include Cassandra in the equation, so much the better. The men he had brought along were of Simon's choosing this time. Simon himself had taken the task of setting the brand that would ignite the ship. The *Falcon's* crew was diligent but Simon had planned well. By the time the fire was noticed all hands were needed to combat the ravenous flames devouring the wooden ship and some of the crew.

Tanner kept his vigil watching out for his Mistress. Drawn sword in one hand, long knife in the other, he barred the way down the steps to the Captain's cabin. Cassandra had poked her head out at the alarm only to have Tanner bellow to bar the door and stay inside. For once she obeyed.

Simon appeared around the corner, facing Tanner squarely. A rapier of Spanish steel in his hand. He quickly drew his long knife, also. Each man measured the other striving to discern any weakness. Cold gray eyes met the liquid fire of burnished brown. Simon had the advantage of position for Tanner would not leave the way clear to his Captain's Lady.

"You have your father's eyes" Simon commented.

"He sent you?"

Simon saluted Tanner in reply. "Seems you have improved your talents since his last try."

There was no reply from Tanner. Simon examined him closely. The young man reminded him of an Indian Tiger he has once seen. Predatory, cool, power coiled to strike. He idly wondered if this had been such a wise choice of employment. The young man might, just might, be his match.

"Seems that being the bastard son of a powerful Lord has its disadvantages. Do you miss your mother?" Simon knew that the Lord he worked for had the Lady who had borne him this bastard son removed from his life. He had hoped that the insult would force a false move on Tanner's part. He was wrong. There was no visible sign that Tanner had heard a word he said. Yes, the boy had learned well. With a sigh of resignation Simon leapt into the fray. His course was already laid. He could not fail.

Tanner met his attack with a quick defensive move still blocking the way to Cassandra's door.

"Ah, well, this was going to be tougher than he had anticipated," thought Simon. The assassin re-engaged Tanner with a speed and ferocity that pulled Tanner off the stairwell below. Simon kept up his fast and furious assault allowing Duprell the time and opportunity to descend below.

Tanner was wise to the move, but this assassin was better than the others and if he planned on surviving Cassandra was going to have to rely on her own defenses for the moment. The shadow of movement seen from the corner of his eye was gone so

Chapter Thirty

swiftly he wasn't sure it had been real. A slash of Simon's blade across his stomach caused him to suck in air leaping backward if order to thwart being gutted by the man's rapier. Resolutely he turned his full attention back upon his father's hireling. They continued to attack and repeal making their way across the deck, first one and then the other gaining advantage.

But Duprell was shadowed by a malicious spirit bent on revenge. Margaret had regained consciousness in time to hear Duprell's plans and Cara's screams. The protective mothering instinct demanded justice from the man that had destroyed her daughter. So Margaret followed Duprell when he slipped aboard his ship and she hid amongst the rigging as they shadowed the *Falcon*.

She would take her revenge on the monster who had cost her a husband's love and her daughter! If she died—so be it, but Duprell would reside in hell before the night was over!

The door shattered with the blow of an ax, swinging open to allow Duprell's entry. Cassandra backed toward the desk searching with her eyes for something, anything, to ward him off.

"Hello my dear. We meet again. I have been waiting for this moment for years."

"Why? Why would you want to hurt me?"

"Because it will destroy Jamison. And I have always wanted you. You were the pearl amidst the pebbles. Your beauty and manners have always been mine for the taking but I needed Lucas' wealth to survive so you had to be his. But Jamison has ruined that, too. Lucas went quite mad you know after his days in the forest. He can't even piss in the pot anymore without help. My men found him quite mad by morning. Babbling about the trees having eyes, and some nonsense about his dead wife's spirit. You've lost me everything! Lucas' money and land, the support of the Spanish, and the Queen's favor! You must be made to pay, dear niece. Since Jamison has destroyed my chance at wealth I may as well satisfy my carnal craving for you." He reached for her and Cassandra tried to avoid his grasp but he was too fast. He grabbed her arms in a crushing grip jerking her into his embrace.

No! Cassandra thought. She would rather die than have this animal touch her! Garrett would never accept her if Duprell succeeded. She twisted violently kicking at his legs, and when he forced his mouth to hers stabbing her with his tongue for entrance Cassandra bit down hard upon the offending appendage.

"Damn you!" The back of his hand connected with her face and if he hadn't held her up she would have fallen. He continued to punish her with fists battering her face until Cassandra began to sway fighting to remain conscious. The blackness would not be denied however and she collapsed with nary a sound.

Duprell thrust her against the desk madly pawing at her gown. Minutes later when Margaret crept in he was posed over the girl with breeches open and his staff exposed. Margaret gathered the ax that Duprell had used to open the door creeping silently forward to destroy the man that had killed her man with his intrigue, and drove her daughter mad. Her life was finished but she would take the devil with her.

She struck with a ferocity that belied her age and size sinking the blade deep into Duprell's skull. The man turned in time to see his attacker and sink his knife blade into her chest before dropping to the floor. Margaret tried to pull Duprell's blade from her chest to no avail. With her last rattling breath she commanded, "Die devil!"

Garrett burst onto the scene in time for Duprell's last words, "I have won!"

"You sick bastard this isn't a contest!" roared Garrett.

Duprell, the light fading from his eyes looked at Cassandra and laughed. "I have defiled every woman you have ever loved — all three of them." As the laughter died on his lips Duprell died leaving a lingering doubt in Garrett's mind. Had the man defiled his love? He looked at her battered and bruised face, seeing the torn dress and vowed that if Duprell had, Cassandra would never have a reason to doubt his love.

Carefully Garrett bathed his love covering her with one of his shirts before she awoke. Her haunted eyes convinced Garrett

Chapter Thirty

of the right thing to do. He would never regret the lie as long as Cassandra could be by his side.

"It's all right love. I'm here. Cassandra he didn't have you. I arrived in time to stop his attack. You will be bruised for some days but put your mind at peace. He didn't rape you."

Her tears came fast, but silently, as she thanked God for this small grace, and Garrett swore that the truth, whatever it was, had died with Duprell. He held her close giving her peace and comfort with his words and his presence.

On deck the battle had been won and the fire put out. Tanner had used a move thought impossible by Simon to sneak under Simon's guard delivering a death stroke with his blade. As the light began to die in Simon's eyes he left Tanner with a parting remark, "You're a better man than your sire."

The fire for all its fury had not accomplished its purpose for the *Falcon* was still seaworthy. Garrett sailed into London two days later making his way directly to the Queen with Cassandra by his side. As before, Tanner stood guarding his Captain's back with Peters by his side.

The Queen was most pleased by the outcome reminding everyone that she had never liked Duprell and this was a fitting end to his misdeeds. Cassandra, as his only living relative, would inherit what property there was. Lucas' Estate would revert back to the Crown. Elizabeth was saddened by Cassandra's misfortunes but the letter presented by Garrett from the French King added an excitement to the Court. Garrett was given permission to write to the King and Josh Birmingham would act as envoy for the Crown. Perhaps at a later time the Jamisons might visit, but for now the thought of home was uppermost in both Cassandra's and Garrett's minds. Before leaving, however, Bess had one more surprise.

"Lord Jamison, it has come to our attention that your head is most wanted by the Spanish. Therefore, we revoke your commission. Your talents will be called upon for other service in the future but for now we wish for you and your Lady to recuperate and bless this court with heirs as loyal as their parents."

Then to Tanner's embarrassment the Queen called him

forward. "The Crown understands that you have ties to one of our Lords. Do you wish to divulge to the crown?"

"No, Your Majesty. I do not claim the ties. I am the Captain's man."

"The Crown could eliminate these threats to your person if you would commit to the question."

"I am honored, Your Majesty, but this is such a small problem that you need not concern your royal person with its ending. I shall settle the issue shortly."

"Very well, Tanner. Be it know that the Crown would be very displeased should anything happen to you in the near future."

"I shall keep that in mind, my Queen."

They were dismissed to leave the court and return to Plymouth and all concerned agreed that all possible haste was required. Cassandra was more that ready to assume her duties as Garrett's wife, and Garrett was looking forward to spending time on the Estate that he had called home, but he had never remained there long enough to make it feel like his home. Cassandra had changed all that—she was his home.

Epilogue

Several months after Cassandra and Garrett had safely arrived home Shane brought Thea back to visit, asking for Garrett's permission to announce their engagement. Garrett shook Shane's hand jubilantly agreeing that he had found the perfect woman, himself, and hoped Shane would be as happy as he was.

Cassandra wanted to plan for the wedding as soon as possible, for, after all, Shane would be an Uncle soon. The sooner they married the sooner Cassandra and Garrett's child would have an Aunt.

Shane had laughed, admonishing Cassandra to take the matter up with Thea. Even though Thea was not close to her father's family, she still wished for a representative at her wedding. To Garrett's horror, Shane was considering his love's request to marry her in her homeland of France.

Cassandra laughed at the predicament, sure that she could convince Thea to stay in England. With that thought in mind she whisked Thea off to the solarium to discuss wedding plans.

Garrett steered Shane into his study, where he informed his younger brother that it was time for him to assume his responsibilities in the family business. After all, soon Shane would have a family to support.

Garrett had been delighted to learn that Cassandra was carrying another child. This time he would be home to love and cherish both of them.

Miles was returning to London with a request from Garrett to be excluded from the Queen's present service as now he had a family and two Estates to oversee. Miles was pleased to deliver the missive for he had promised someone in London that he would return.

Captured Pearl

As Garrett surveyed his brother, he knew exactly how to keep him in England and to solve the problem of managing two Estates. If Shane would consent to run the Duprell Estate, Thea would realize that England was her family's future and perhaps with a manager in residence the problems that kept plaguing the Duprell Estate could be solved. For some reason Garrett felt, that even from the grave, Duprell was pulling the strings of the mischief maker there.

Tanner settled in as Garrett's first mate aboard the *Lady*, which was now a part of the fleet of Jamison ships carrying goods for trade. His land time would be spent riding between the Birmingham and Jamison estates. Seemed as though he was taken with the oldest Birmingham daughter, Beth.

Twice since the night on board *The Gull* Tanner had met with altercations along the road and in the tavern. After the last event he had informed Garrett that he had personal business and he had ridden off, only reappearing several weeks later. Garrett had called in favors, but it was the Queen's missive that had enlightened him of Tanner's background.

> To Our Loyal Subject, Lord Jamison,
>
> It has come to our knowledge that the altercations affronting your man, Tanner, originate with one Lord Byrne.
>
> Many years ago the Lord became enamored with a Lady of good standing but no protector, and thus the Lord presumed to have his way with the said Lady. When a child was produced from the unblessed union, matters worsened for the Lady. In fear for her child she made a bargain with the Lord's wife for the safety of the child.
>
> The boy was apprenticed to an acquaintance of said Lady Byrne, aboard ship where he was treated fairly and showed great talent for the craft. Said Captain, a younger son of one of the realm's powerful Lords, was quite taken with the boy, Tanner,

Epilogue

and saw to his education in a lordly manner.

It has come to our attention that Tanner has recently made a visit upon Lord Byrne, the elder, and his eldest son. The Crown has also made it known to said Lords of its displeasure of said altercation upon Tanner's person. The Crown promises you that your well being and that of your man is assured.

When the Lady Jamison feels well enough to travel, the Crown would be most pleased to grant you a visitation.

With favor,
Queen Elizabeth of England

Garrett still smiled when he thought of the missive. Yes, indeed, Tanner was headed for court service. But not too soon.

Cara had been found wandering the countryside quite mad and had finally thrown herself from one of the cliffs into the sea. Cassandra and Garrett could not find it in their hearts to feel sympathy for her plight.

Garrett pondered the vision that haunted Cassandra the previous night. Shane, with all his cavorting about the table, had tumbled a wine glass to the wooden floor shattering the fine lead crystal into a thousand shards of glass. Cassandra had gone white as the memory of another time and place with shattered glass and red blood, instead of red wine, covered the floor.

The description she gave had turned Garrett thoughtful. The scene was one he and Josh had often discussed since the Birminghams returned from France. The ghastly murder of both her father and mother in front of a small child's eyes had been truly a nightmare—an event he wasn't sure she needed, or wanted, to remember.

Perhaps later, after the child was born, would be the time to broach this subject—or he might just leave it to the French relatives to explain. Being surrounded by her newly-found family might lessen the blow of the past terror in her life.

Captured Pearl

And, if Cassandra wished to pursue the search for her memory Garrett would take her to France. Her father's family had written expressing an interest in meeting her. Perhaps after the child was able to travel they might tour France, giving his love her past—if not through her memories—then through her family's love and remembrances.

Lying in bed Garrett remembered the night he almost killed Cassandra with his horse. God, she had been through a lot. They rarely spoke of the past focusing instead on their bright future and the family they were expecting. He turned looking at the green-eyed lady snuggled next to his side. His life had taken a strange twist that night and as much as he hated Duprell, in the end it was his cruelty that had given Garrett paradise. He would forever thank God for that dark night on the road and the fates that had saved Cassandra and brought the two of them together.

Meet the Author, Rachel Gies

Although this is Rachel Gies' first romance novel, she has been writing for years. Her first book, *One Size Fits Most,* was published in 2001. Previously, Rachel had written a column for the St. Charles (Illinois) *Press-Republican* for several years. The column offered amusing commentary on the funny side of ordinary life situations.

Of course, *Captured Pearl* is only the beginning of a story, and Rachel is looking forward to continuing the story of Garrett and Cassandra in many sequels.

Other offerings are also in the works including a children's book and a mystery.

Amsterdam, Holland, was home to Rachel until 1960. Reading mystery and romantic novels helped Rachel master the English language when she first arrived in the U.S. As Rachel quickly became acclimated to the American culture her special writing talent took root. However, marriage and her family took first priority for several years. Now she finally has time to cultivate her writing, many publications will follow.

Rachel's imagination and special writing style will take you on an exciting read through the pages of *Captured Pearl*.

About the
Captured Pearl
CD, and Denny Farrell

Denny Farrell, award winning radio broadcaster, began in radio more than 30 years ago. Denny also worked as a television weather man and TV talk show host with various NBC affiliates. Denny was a program director for a major 50KW, radio station in Chicago. Denny's voice may be familiar in other venues. From commercial recordings for such companies as Motorola, Jewel Food Stores, Dominick's, and Walgreens, to name just a few.

Denny has worked with many famous stars over the years, including Bing Crosby and his brother Bob. Denny emceed for Bob Crosby's Dixieland Band, as well as for Frank Sinatra, Tony Bennett, Artie Shaw, and many others.

Denny was recently inducted into the Big Band Hall of Fame, in West Palm Beach, Florida, as one of only three announcers to ever have been inducted. He was also honored with the National Ballroom & Entertainment Association's "2001 Award of Excellence" for his radio show.

Today, Denny produces and records all his own radio shows from his studio. Denny's radio show can be heard at: www.DennyFarrell.com